ALPHA KING

ALPHA SERIES, BOOK 1

RK MUNIN

Warning: Author is dyslexic as hell.

The editing and beta reading team: Mary Alegre, Gary Anderson, Martha Collins, and Lauren Meghoo

Profession editing: Amanda Brown Edits, LLC

Cover Illustration: @Ami_nsfw (Twitter)

Want some free books or links to social media accounts? Check out my website:
www.RK-Munin.com

About the Alpha Series World

Plenty of laws govern how paranormal creatures and humans can interact, but not too many regulate the interactions between paranormals themselves. That means an alpha of a wolf shifter pack can abuse his members or kidnap and exploit an innocent mage or other types of shifter. In a world where the government isn't interested in the problems of magical creatures, they must rely on themselves or form communities and stay safe.

If that fails, they may be forced to look for an alpha strong enough to help. But help can be hard to find, and it's never free.

Content Warning

This book is a bit darker than I normally write.
This novel includes:
- references to and evidence of sexual assault
- Several scenes involving torture
- Scenes containing violence and fighting
- PTSD/recovery

DEDICATION

To the Kinky Quilters: you ladies are just fabulous! Shopping, sewing, and afternoon cocktails. What's not to love?

Emma watches her alpha and one of his martinets drag the semiconscious woman through the kitchen, wincing when the stranger's shin smacks hard against a table leg. The woman makes a low sound of pain, and then she's gone, taken through the door down to the basement. The poor thing is tiny compared to the wolf shifters carrying her. They don't need to drag her. Even one of them could easily lift her, but they don't. It's typical of the cruelty that Alpha Michaels encourages in his martinets.

Emma remembers when the pack martinets did the job they were originally meant to do—protect and help the pack. All the former kind and caring martinets have been replaced by these nasty violent goons.

Taking a quick sniff as they pass, Emma smells heavy magic coming from the woman. She may not be a shifter, but she's something powerful. It's astonishing that Michaels and the others could capture her. They must have laid a trap. That's the only explanation. Shifters might not be at the very bottom of the magical community as far as power goes, but they're not far from it. More reliant on their physical prowess than magic, shifters tend to steer clear of other powerful magical creatures.

Except for Michaels, who's captured something very powerful and brought her into the ramshackle house Emma shares with her brother Jason. This can't possibly bode well for either of them.

"What the hell's going on?" she hisses to her brother as several more martinets file past her and down the stairs. "Why is Alpha Michaels bringing this person here?"

"Shhh!" Jason looks anxiously at the open door to the basement and then back at her. "I don't know what's going on. I was just pulling up when they got here."

Taking another deep breath, Emma tries to catch the last of the woman's lingering scent. "I can't tell what she is."

Jason opens his mouth to reply when the sound of flesh hitting flesh makes both of them jerk and stare at the door. At first, she thinks they're beating the small woman, but as she listens the sound becomes more nuanced.

"Are they…" She can't finish her question. It's just too horrible to say out loud. She knows her face probably mirrors Jason's shock and horror.

"I don't know who she is, but she's powerful," Jason whispers quickly, both of them staring at the empty doorway. "She reeks of magic."

"News flash; I can smell that too," Emma retorts, making her brother snarl with annoyance.

"News flash," Jason growls back at her. "I think Alpha Michaels is hoping to get control of her." His distress hits her through their sibling bond, making her ashamed of taking her stress out on her brother.

"Sorry," she mumbles. "I just don't like this."

"Me neither." His tone is softer as he pulls her into a quick hug. They're silent for a moment but then Jason's earlier words register.

"Control her? But how? Our pack doesn't have any witches or druids to cast a spell, and none of the other packs will let us even talk to theirs."

Jason tries to keep his expression blank, but he's never had a poker face so his disgust shows. Appalled, she realizes what he means.

"No," she shakes her head with disgust. Pulling away from the hug, Jason nods grimly.

"I think he's trying to see if he's a mate match with her or can force a mating. He's got that charm he bought a couple of years ago. If she's a match at all for him, the charm will bind her to him."

Shuddering at the thought, Emma grabs one of Jason's hands in her own. "We have to stop him. He's going to make a slave out of her."

Violently pulling his hand out of her grasp, Jason focuses hard eyes on her. "Shut up, Emma. What do you think we could possibly do? This isn't a pack. It's a prison. Alpha Michaels is just adding another inmate. We can't help her, so just be quiet. Or do you want to get punished again?" It's obvious that Jason's words aren't only for her, but for himself as well. He doesn't like to see anyone hurt any more than she does. His next words confirm that he's warning both of them. "Do you want Mom and Dad to get hurt? Because he'll do it! He'll do horrible things to them if we step out of line."

The familiar helpless feeling invades her, but after years of Alpha Michaels' abuse, she doesn't cry. Crossing her arms over her chest, she hunches her shoulders and works on maintaining her signature calm. The punishment last year, when she tried to keep a fellow packmate from being hurt by a martinet, is still fresh in her mind. She tried to go to the authorities, but neither the state nor the local government was interested in getting involved with an inner-pack dispute. Generally, unless humans are involved, the authorities couldn't care less about what happens to nonhumans.

The packmate died, and after Alpha Michaels found out what she did, Emma barely survived her punishment.

The sound of flesh on flesh stops, and they hear low voices, then the heavy tread of Alpha Michaels coming up the stairs. They both stand silently as he appears in the kitchen, sweaty, with disheveled clothes, and a small drop of blood on his chin. His canines are exposed, and there's a hint of blood on his lip. During a mating, shifters will bite each other, but as far as Emma knows it won't work on anything but other shifters. Heck, mating with a shifter of another species is often problematic, requiring the aid of charms or spells. Alpha Michaels just bit the woman for probably no reason. And raped her. And now he's going to invite all of his martinets to do the same thing.

But he has a reason, even if his actions don't work. He enjoys all the pain he causes others.

"She's not a fucking match for me," he growls out. His anger pricks along her skin, making her inner wolf urge her to flee. "My men are seeing if she might match one of them, but if that doesn't happen, I'll be sending others here from the pack. We're going to keep her down there until we find a match. Your job is to make sure she's cared for. If she dies, both of you die."

With those words he stomps out, thrusting the heavy kitchen table out of his way instead of going around it. The bulky piece of furniture hits the kitchen counter, cracking the Formica and breaking a leg off the table.

A howl sounds from the basement and then a flurry of movement. Something hits a wall followed by the distinct sounds of fighting. Finally, Robert, one of the alpha's goons, comes up the stairs. His face is bruised and bloody, but he's grinning.

"That bitch is a wild ride," he tells them as he goes to their fridge and starts rifling through it. "Too bad we didn't match. I could've had fun keeping her in line. Don't you have any beer?"

Robert, just like the rest of the goons, is cruel. He probably started hurting the woman and had to be dragged off to keep him from killing her. Even if the woman survives the attentions of Alpha Michaels and his martinets, she's going to be seriously injured. Making a mental list of all the things she's going to need, Emma pushes down the part of her that demands she run. The woman downstairs is going to need her help. Besides, even if she ran, it would take Alpha Michaels very little time to hunt her down. Just like all other wolf packs, Michaels has alpha bonds with her and all her packmates. He can't track her through the bond, but he can make her life very painful until she returns.

"We couldn't afford any this week," Jason explains when Emma can't get herself to respond to the dangerous martinet. "Alpha Michaels made Emma quit her job, so our finances have been tight."

"Get some beer in here," Robert orders as he slams the fridge shut. "I know we're going to have second helpings of that bitch downstairs until we find her a match. I like beer after sex, so stock the fucking fridge." Without even looking at either of them again, he leaves, almost breaking the kitchen door in the process.

Emma and Jason exchange looks. Nothing about this situation can possibly turn out well for either of them, and it's going to be especially bad for the woman downstairs.

As the last martinet leaves, he carelessly cuffs Emma and tells her to see to their "guest." He cackles at that, thinking himself quite witty. Emma and Jason both try to smile as if amused by his humor. Thankfully, he isn't interested in them and leaves after complaining about the lack of food in the house.

The side of her head throbs from the martinet's blow, but she's gotten very good at ignoring pain and discomfort over the years. She already has her supplies gathered in the kitchen, and she picks them up along with a bowl of warm water. Looking over her shoulder at Jason who's right behind her, she frowns slightly.

"You need to stay here," she tells him firmly. At first, Jason looks perplexed. He might be big, even for a wolf shifter, but he's a gentle soul. His violence only comes out in the defense of others, which is why Alpha Michaels never tried to make him a martinet. Still, he's big and after what's been done to this woman, Emma doesn't want to cause her any more distress if possible. "No extra males down there for now," Emma says.

Nodding with understanding, Jason backs away. "Yeah, you're right." He flops back in one of the unbroken chairs. His body is tense and his expression pained. "I'll be right here if you need me."

"Thanks, Jason," Emma murmurs and makes her way down into the basement.

Unsure what to expect, Emma walks softly into the dank room. She's never actually gone down into the basement before. When she and Jason moved into the pack-owned house, Alpha Michaels forbade them from going down there, so of course, they didn't. Now she sees why.

In the very middle of the room is a chair bolted to the floor right next to a convenient drain. The stark light coming from the single bare bulb dangling from the ceiling makes the empty chair even more ominous. When she gets closer, she can see claw marks on the arms of the chair and scoring the concrete in front of it. It is obvious shifters were bound to that thing and then tortured. That must be why Alpha Michaels occasionally sends her and Jason to stay with their parents across town and why, when they get home, they smell the remnants of a strange shifter and blood.

Turning away, she sees a bare mattress against one of the walls. Sprawled out on it is the same woman who was dragged in earlier, naked and chained by one ankle to the wall. Her eyes are closed, and she's still, but she's breathing and alive. Multiple bite marks mar her neck, most of them trickling blood. Mating bites don't need to be so deep or be so vicious, but why would the martinets bother to be nice when they could cause hurt?

The woman's hands are secured behind her back by a thick zip tie, the flesh under it swollen and bloody. Her body is covered in welts and bruises, and she can see their semen on her thighs. The sight of the poor thing makes Emma suck in a breath and start to shake in sympathetic pain.

Unexpectedly, the woman opens her eyes and Emma takes an involuntary step back. The captive's eyes are a brilliant violet, glowing with rage.

"Mage," Emma whispers, and the woman gives her a humorless smile.

"Shifter." Her voice is rough but calm, even mocking. What amazes Emma is that there's not a single tear on the woman's face. Her eyes are red from damage, not crying. This woman is filled with rage, not fear or sadness. Those startling violet eyes regard Emma for a few moments and then narrow. "I don't suppose you're here to let me loose."

Shaking her head, Emma makes her way to the mattress and drops to her knees on the concrete floor next to the mage. "I can't do that. But I can try to make you more comfortable."

"By all means," the woman says coolly. "Clean me up before the next round starts."

Tears she didn't think she could shed any longer threaten to leak from Emma's eyes. "I'm so sorry," she whispers. Now she understands why Alpha Michaels is so insistent on finding a match among his shifters. If they have control of this mage it will increase the power of the pack exponentially. Most packs have at least a few witches or druids, but mages are in a league all their own. They're so powerful they never need the protection of a pack, and if Alpha Michaels controls one, he can start claiming territory with impunity. In theory, he could become the most powerful alpha on the West Coast.

"It won't work," the woman states as she shuts her eyes with a small, tired sigh—the only sign of weakness from her so far. "I can't be bound by a shifter, even if they are a match for me. It doesn't work that way for mages. They can be bound to me but not the other way around."

Emma moves to lay a gentle hand on the woman's shoulder, but then she thinks better of it and lets her hand drop back into her lap. Violet eyes open and regard her with composed interest. "Don't tell anyone that mages don't mate," she whispers urgently, hoping Jason can't hear them. "If he finds that out, he'll just kill you."

"I'd hate for that to happen before I'm able to personally thank all the shifters who've made me feel so welcome," she announces with false gaiety as she shuts her eyes again. Emma isn't sure how to take this woman. If their roles were reversed, Emma would be a weeping, screaming mess, begging and pleading until her voice was hoarse. At least, that's what happened when Alpha Michaels "interviewed" her as a potential mate when he first took over the pack three years ago. Who is this woman who possesses such poise in the face of so much brutality?

"If you ever get to thank them," Emma murmurs, her voice thick from remembered pain. "Make it hurt a little extra for me."

The mage smiles but doesn't open her eyes. "Certainly. It would be my pleasure."

"Thanks. My name's Emma. Will you tell me yours?"

Opening her eyes, she pins Emma with her violet gaze. "Avery."

"I'm going to clean you up and treat the wounds. Do I have permission to touch you, Avery?"

A genuine smile forms on Avery's mouth. "For that, Emma, I won't make you suffer before I kill you. You have my permission to touch. If you can get the stink of those men off me, I'd be grateful."

"I will," Emma promises and tries to ignore the mage's threats of death as she reaches into the bowl of warm water for the soft wash cloth and starts cleaning Avery. She goes slowly, being especially careful around the bite wounds on her neck and shoulders as well as the lacerations on one leg. As she works, she watches the bruise on the woman's abdomen noticeably spreading in the hour she spends cleaning. It worries Emma, so she lays a hand on the woman's abdomen and seeks the injury with her gift. It only takes a moment before she hisses in concern and withdraws her hand. This woman's in so much pain she shouldn't be functioning. On top of all the obvious injuries, Avery's suffering from some internal bleeding that's rapidly getting worse.

Avery shifts a little when Emma draws her hand back. "Are you a healer?"

Feeling self-conscious, Emma opens the large toolbox she commandeered from Jason's shop for her medical supplies. "Not a very good one. Except for finding out what's wrong, there's not much I can do with my gift." Deciding to be her usual blunt self, she meets the woman's eyes. "You're bleeding internally, and you're not healing."

"I was afraid of that," Avery says without surprise. She doesn't even look afraid or anxious. If someone had just told Emma she was dying, chained by her ankle in a cellar and at the mercy of a savage alpha, she'd at least be a little scared.

What's wrong with this woman? Anyone who reeks of magic like this should be at least stopping the injuries from getting worse, not dying of internal bleeding. "I thought—"

"You thought I would have shifter-like self-healing abilities?" Avery asks, cutting Emma off. "Normally, my self-healing is even better than shifters. Only vampires heal faster than mages. But this damn charm is suppressing my power."

"Charm?"

"The chain around my ankle," Avery explains. "When it comes off, everyone dies nice painful deaths." Those last words are said with a wistfulness Emma usually hears when people talk about buying something they covet, not brutal execution. Then again, Emma can't blame her.

Glancing at the heavy chain securing the mage to the wall, she leans in close to sniff at it. The smell of acrid magic fills her nose, making her cough and rear back.

Experimentally, Emma puts a few fingers on it. Not only is the charm powerful, but it's old magic. It must have cost Alpha Michaels an insane amount of money.

Looking back at Avery's face, Emma's struck again by the woman's calm confidence. Anyone else would be terrified, but Avery only looks put out and annoyed.

The incongruity of the mage's reaction makes Emma realize that this is a woman so powerful it doesn't occur to her to be afraid. Perhaps she should make sure Avery knows that not all the shifters here are the bad guys.

"Please don't hurt my brother, Jason," Emma begs. "He didn't hurt you, and if he could, I'm sure he'd free you."

Blinking at the sudden plea from Emma, Avery regards her with mild amusement. "Interesting that you beg for your brother's life before your own," Avery comments. She tries to move and hisses in pain. Quickly, Emma reaches down to assist the woman in rolling over. She tries to be gentle, but very few places on Avery's body aren't wounded to some degree or another.

"Free me, and I won't hurt either of you," Avery offers once she's settled again.

"I can't," Emma whispers, casting another fearful look at the basement stairs. "Alpha Michaels would kill us and my parents." The thought of her sweet parents at the alpha's mercy is enough to make terror rip through Emma. He wouldn't just kill them; he'd make sure they suffered for a long time first. "He takes pleasure in causing pain. You of all people should understand that. I can't leave others behind to face his wrath."

"You have a soft heart," Avery murmurs, her expression calculating.

"You're going to die," Emma blurts out. "When the next martinet comes down here, you need to tell him that you'll die if they don't take the charm off."

Shifting again, Avery sighs and then coughs and groans. "You and I both know they won't take it off. It's too dangerous."

"I'll beg. He might—"

Cutting her off with an icy glare, Avery pins her with unwavering eyes. "How bad is the bleeding?"

"Bad." Emma puts her hand back on the mage's abdomen to feel the injury again. She's shocked at how much worse it's gotten in just a short time. The pain must be excruciating. How is this woman talking instead of screaming?

"Correction, it's terrible. The charm isn't suppressing all of your healing abilities, but it's quelling it enough that you're quickly getting worse. Unless I can get a powerful healer to help you or the charm comes off, you've only got a couple of days at best."

Taking short, shallow breaths, the mage nods and shuts her eyes again. "I can feel it. I knew my addiction would be the death of me. I just didn't think it would be like this."

Emma wants to ask what the mage is talking about but keeps focused on the problem at hand. "I don't want you to die."

"Then take the damn charm off. I'll save you, your brother, and your parents." Avery eyes her thoughtfully. "I'm a mage. Current circumstances aside, I'm one of the most powerful creatures there is. I can protect as many as you request." The mage pauses for a moment to breathe, her expression pinched from pain. "I'll adopt your whole damn pack if I need to. Except for those men I need to kill. Those wolves get to feel what it's like to piss off a mage."

This woman is offering to be the pack's savior, and Emma feels a moment of intense hope until her eyes fall back on the charmed chain.

"Brought low by a charm," Emma mutters, eyeing the restraint that's not only keeping Avery's physical form in check, but also her magic.

"Brought low by my own foolish choices," Avery corrects her. "Those choices made me vulnerable." The woman's face goes hard. "Trust me, that'll never happen again."

She can at least try to take off the charm. If she can't free the mage, no one needs to know she tried. Leaning over, she grips the iron cuff around the woman's ankle in both hands and exerts her strength. Just like all shifters, Emma's immensely strong, but the spelled chain doesn't give at all. The magic in the charm is just that powerful. Slumping back, Emma hunches into herself.

"I think it needs to be broken by magic."

Pale, eyes closed, and panting now from pain, Avery makes a sound of annoyance. "Of course it does, foolish wolf. I could have told you that." Emma places a hand on Avery. The woman's body is rapidly weakening. So much for her having days to live. There's not much time to get Avery free.

"I don't know anyone who has the kind of magic that can get this off," Emma explains urgently. "Tell me what to do!" If Avery dies, not only do she and Jason die, but so does the hope for freeing her pack.

"Keep me safe. Get Kade." Avery's voice is fading.

"Kade?" Hoping for more information, Emma leans forward, but Avery's gone still. Emma's healing gift tells her that Avery has suppressed her body's functions. Her heart is beating at an extremely low rate, and her breathing is so slow as to be nearly undetectable. Emma's heard of this ability in vampires and a few other magical creatures, but this is the first time she's witnessed it.

"Emma?" Jason's voice from the top of the stairs makes her start. Turning and looking up, she sees Jason crouched on the top step, gazing down at her. Then his eyes land on the mage, and he stiffens. His pupils dilate and he crawls down the steps on all fours, sniffing as if he's in his wolf form.

"Mine," he growls out and pushes Emma away from the unconscious mage, forcefully but not violently. Surprised by her brother's odd behavior, Emma scoots away from the mage while Jason softly growls, staying crouched between her and the

wounded woman.

Once Emma's several yards away from Avery, Jason bends over the unconscious mage and reverently lowers his face to her mauled neck. When he licks the wounds, Emma realizes what's going on.

It turns out Alpha Michaels is correct. There *is* a mate match for Avery among his pack, but it's not one of his martinets. It's Jason, one of the least aggressive pack members. Although the draw of the mate match might make him willing to take on anyone trying to hurt Avery, he has no combat or fighting experience.

Even if Jason fights off the martinets, Alpha Michaels can simply use the alpha bond to put Jason on his knees.

Michaels wants the mage controlled by the pack, something Jason just isn't capable of doing. The alpha's solution will be to kill Jason and find another mate match in the pack. Or kill the mage. And probably kill Emma for good measure.

Crap.

The first thing she needs to do is get them out of there. Leaving Jason to guard and care for his new mate, Emma runs up the stairs and furiously packs some bags. In a large duffle, she throws in clothes for herself and Jason as well as a few things that might fit the mage's smaller body. Then she grabs a smaller bag and fills it with anything valuable they own—a few pieces of jewelry, Jason's laptop, and a few collector's items she might be able to pawn for a little cash. Because everyone in the pack pays such high tithes to Alpha Michaels, no one has much money, but the two of them have been able to save a little in secret. She grabs that and hopes it's enough to tide them over until she can figure out who Kade is and how to contact him.

Running outside with the bags, she dumps them in the trunk of their old Toyota. Then she dashes back inside for some camping equipment, an idea forming in her head. Soon the trunk is full of sleeping bags, food, and other necessities. Slamming the trunk closed, she hurries back down to the basement.

Holding the mage gently in his lap, Jason is cradling her to his chest and murmuring soft words as he rocks her. He's ripped the zip tie off her wrists and pulled the non-charmed end of the chain out of the wall.

Looking up, Jason growls at her, making Emma stop in her tracks and laugh. The laugh is half-hysterical, but it seems to calm her brother down. "And you were lamenting you'd never find a mate," she mutters to her brother.

Intelligence bleeds into his eyes at her words, replacing the threatening wolf from moments before. "Em, I'm sorry. I don't know why I did that. I just…"

"She's your mate, and she's hurt, and we're in a fucked-up situation," Emma says with a wave of her hand. "I understand the aggression, but you need to tone it down around me if you can."

Moving slowly, she walks to the mattress and sinks to her knees next to Jason and Avery. Keeping her movements nonthreatening, she hands over a thick soft blanket. With a grunt, Jason accepts the blanket and wraps his mate up tightly. Once only her head is peeking out from under the blanket, Jason grabs her and cradles her gently against his chest. The little mage looks even smaller compared to the massive shifter holding her, and Emma is struck by the contrast. The tiny mage probably only stands about five-foot-five compared to Emma's six-foot or Jason's six-foot-eight. But in the magic community, size doesn't necessarily mean anything. This mage, though petite, wields an intense amount of power if her smell is anything to go by.

Besides, Jason might be huge, but all of his touches are tender and soft as he cares for the unconscious woman.

Ideally, Emma wonders if Avery will even accept Jason as a mate. She wouldn't need to mate him back, just let Jason bite her. And touch her. Shifter mates need a lot of touch from each other. If she rejects him, Jason will be inconsolable. Shifters don't do well when rejected by their mates. It's common for wolves to go feral if their mate dies or rejects them.

Shaking her head at her idiocy, she pushes that thought aside. Worrying about Avery rejecting Jason is something for the future. She needs to deal with the here and now. One crisis at a time. First, they need to get out of pack territory. Then they need to find a charm to block the alpha bond before Michaels realizes they're gone.

Even though Jason turned her into a mage burrito with the blanket, Avery doesn't react. Emma wants to press her fingers to the mage's neck to check for a pulse, but she doesn't dare touch the woman. With Avery so wounded, Jason's not entirely in control of his wolf. He could hurt her out of instinct without even realizing it. He might be talking now, but she needs to tread carefully until Avery's up and moving again.

"I've got the car loaded up," Emma starts to explain but stops when Jason gives her a startled and confused look.

"Car?"

"Jason, we need to run," she states bluntly. "We can't be here when a martinet shows up or Michaels gets back."

Understanding dawns on Jason's face, and he looks frantic. "Our parents! What's he going to do to our parents?"

"We'll call them from the road and tell them to run too," she tells him. "But none of us are going to survive this if we don't get moving now."

Nodding, his expression one of fearful resolution, Jason stands up, easily holding the small mage to his chest. The chain dangling out from the other end of the blanket clacks on the floor. After they get somewhere safe, that will be the next goal. If they can get that chain charm off, Emma's sure Avery can raze her old pack without breaking a sweat. The thought of no longer being under the control of Michaels or his goons makes Emma feel giddy. It's not something she's ever allowed herself to contemplate until this moment.

Avery could be their key to freedom.

Or get them killed. Right now it could go either way.

Pushing those thoughts away, Emma urges Jason out the door and into the backseat of their ancient car. Once he's settled in with Avery securely ensconced on his lap, Emma starts driving. The moment she's on the road she calls her mom and puts the phone on speaker so Jason can be part of the conversation.

"Hi, honey, I was—"

"Jason found his mate, and it's a mage Alpha Michaels was torturing in hopes to match her to one of his martinets. We've stolen her, and we're running." She hears a snort from the backseat and meets Jason's eyes in the rear-view mirror.

"Way to be diplomatic and break it to them gently," he comments, and she lifts her eyebrows at him.

"Sorry for trying to be succinct and save our parents' lives by getting them as much information as quickly as I can," Emma snaps.

"You didn't have—"

"Children!" Her mother's reprimand makes them both fall silent. They might be twenty-nine years old, but June is the matriarch of the family. "Congratulation, Jason. I want to meet her someday if we aren't all murdered by Alpha Michaels in the next week."

And that's where Emma gets the irreverence that's gotten her in trouble numerous times in her life.

"That was funny, Mom," Emma says with a snort as Jason makes a grumpy sound in the backseat.

"Suck up," he bites out.

"Dickhead," she snaps back at him.

"Emma! Jason!" June's tone is beyond exasperated. "Can you two stop long enough to focus on not getting killed!"

"Sorry, Mom," they say together.

They can hear their father chuckle in the background. "Imminent doom and they're still fighting. But then again, they came out of the womb that way, so you shouldn't be surprised, June."

"They get it from my side, Mateo," June tells her husband with obvious pride. "My line is full of scrappers." That makes all of them laugh, but they sober quickly when June starts speaking again. "Don't worry about us, kids. We'll pack and leave. Just tell me you three have a plan. You can't stay on the run indefinitely."

"If he's mated a mage, why the hell are they running? Just have her blast Michaels into little itty-bitty wolf bits," Mateo says, his voice full of bloodthirsty glee.

"I wish," Emma mutters as Jason answers Mateo's question.

"She's hurt, Dad," Jason calls out. "There's some kind of charm on her ankle that's keeping her from healing."

"She's unconscious right now," Emma adds. "But she told me to get hold of someone named Kade. I'm hoping he's another mage. Does that name mean anything to you guys?"

"I'm afraid not," her mother replies. "And your father is shaking his head." June's voice muffles for a second as she talks to Mateo. "Start packing up because there's going to be an angry alpha at our door soon and I don't want to be here when he arrives."

Her voice comes through the phone clearly again. "You two get somewhere safe and figure out who this Kade is. He might be the only thing standing between the three of you and death. We'll head north and disappear in Seattle. I suggest you guys head to Sacramento. Dense cities are going to be the best place to hide. It'll be harder for Michaels to use his alpha bond if you're surrounded by a lot of people."

"I was thinking about heading to Uncle Leo's old house," Emma explains.

"That's a good place to hole up. Feed the kitchen sprites if they're still there." Only June would think of kitchen sprites at a time like this.

"I will, Mom," she promises and hangs up.

"Uncle Leo's place?" Jason asks from the backseat. "Technically, I think he's our Grand-Uncle because he was Dad's Uncle or something like that."

"Whatever. It's free, furnished, and there's no record of that place in our pack. Uncle Leo was part of Dad's pack. You know, before Dad moved north to mate Mom. Dad should've sold it back to the pack when Uncle Leo died, but he forgot. And no one ever asked him to, so it's been sitting empty for the last year. It's just northeast of San Francisco, nice and close to a lot of humans and nonhumans, so it should help us hide."

"Good idea. What made you think of it?"

Emma doesn't answer Jason's question right away, and when she finally meets his eyes in the rearview mirror, she guiltily looks away.

"You've been thinking about running from the pack before all this happened," he concludes grimly.

Wincing, she gives a little shrug. He doesn't know about what Alpha Michaels did to her, but after that horrible night, she was determined to have an escape plan if he ever thought to do it again. "I wouldn't have left without you."

"Yeah, it's fine." His tone tells her he feels betrayed but doesn't want to talk about it. "Where is this house anyway?"

"Leo's place is in Martinez, a little town just northeast of San Francisco. I'm going to be driving most of the night so you should try to sleep."

"Sure," he says, settling down and nuzzling his face into the mage's hair. He takes several deep breaths, as if pulling her scent into his lungs is going to make everything better. Knowing how mating bonds work, it probably will for the moment. The scent of a mate grounds a shifter, makes them calm and centered. A good alpha does the same thing to the entire pack with the alpha bond. Once again Emma longs for Alpha Julia. Under her leadership the pack was stable, kind, and prosperous. The moment Michaels took over with his band of miscreants, everyone suffered.

The question now is: Can they rescue Avery so she can rescue them back?

The drive to Uncle Leo's house is made mostly in silence. By the time they get there, Emma's exhausted, and Jason doesn't look much better. She knows he's suffering because he can't cement the mating bond, but there's nothing any of them can do. Jason wants Avery's consent before performing a mating bite, which she can't do while unconscious. It might not do anything, but Avery could be wrong and they could be bound.

The flip side to that is that if he created the bond while she's hurt, he could help lend her strength for healing.

"Wait here. I'll get the house open for us."

Jason just grunts at her order, his eyes closed and his arms locked around Avery. He's probably pushing as much power into her as he can, but without the bond, it would only be a trickle.

The house is a big, run-down Victorian. Breaking in through the back door is easy, and Emma finds the inside fully furnished, but everything's covered in a thick layer of dust. Although the electricity isn't on, she's prepared for that. Going out to the car, she grabs the camping equipment she stowed and lights a few of the lanterns.

The place is stuffy, so she opens every window and picks a room with an attached bathroom for Jason and Avery. Shaking out the bedcovers, she finds them clean if a little musty. Once the room is ready, she goes back out and leads Jason in. Carrying Avery with ease, he lays her on the bed gently and pulls the covers over her.

"Watch her for me," he demands, and disappears into the bathroom. She's not sure why she needs to watch Avery for the few minutes he's using the facilities, but mates are overprotective and anxious about each other, so the request isn't surprising.

He's only wearing his boxers when he emerges from the bathroom, and Emma nods in approval. More skin-to-skin contact will help him push healing power into Avery.

"I'm going to get us food and supplies," she explains as he crawls into the bed and carefully snuggles around Avery's petite form.

"We need to get that charm off," he mutters to her, his eyes already closing.

"We will. But first, we need to eat, and I need to get some sleep. Tomorrow I'll figure out who Kade is and get him to help us."

Already half asleep, Jason mumbles a goodbye as Emma leaves the room and closes the door behind her.

Looking up the nearest grocery store on her phone, she finds one still open and rushes in to grab essentials. The middle-aged woman at the checkout eyes her speculatively. "Are you one of those shifters? I only ask because you're so tall. I've heard they're big." Emma doesn't want to engage with this woman, even if her open face shows genuine curiosity instead of suspicion and prejudice. Why couldn't this store have self-checkout?

Resigned, Emma nods. "I'm just traveling through. Heading to my new pack in San Diego," she lies easily. Paying with cash, she ignores the stares from several other shoppers. Uncle Leo was the last shifter to live in the area, and he kept mostly to himself. He hired a series of humans to do his shopping and other errands for him, so he never needed to leave the house. Many years ago, when the new alpha moved the pack closer to national forest land, Leo requested to say in Martinez. At that point he was old enough that the understanding alpha let him stay and live out his life in familiar surroundings. That was over ten years ago, and no pack member has moved into the territory since.

The fact that no other wolves are here will help the three of them hide from other shifters, but it also means they will stick out like a sore thumb to the humans. Hopefully, she'll be able to find Kade soon because Alpha Michaels is well-versed in using technology, and she's not confident she can keep her image off social media for very long. Even if she finds a witch to break their alpha bond with Michaels or a charm to hide them from him, it would only take one picture of her with a location tag to have him arriving in Martinez with his best trackers.

Leaving the store quickly, she hurries back to the house. She brought a cooler and fills it with ice to stow the perishables she bought. Then she puts together a few sandwiches, eating one and piling two more on a plate to leave on the nightstand for Jason to eat when he wakes up.

Nosing around in the other rooms, she finds another furnished bedroom and collapses on the bed. Dust fills her nose, making her sneeze several times. Despite that discomfort, she's asleep within seconds.

She's sitting in her favorite spot watching the waves crash against the cliff below her. There's a chilly breeze, but she feels warm and content.

"This is a nice place," Avery murmurs as she sits down on the ground next to her. Emma looks over and smiles, relieved to see the woman whole and healthy. No wounds mar her neck. There aren't even scars. Emma knows that should be significant, but her happy brain refuses to contemplate the implications of what she's seeing.

"I come here all the time," Emma confesses. A bird flies overhead, and they watch it dip down toward the ocean, gliding elegantly.

"I feel like seagulls get a bad rap," Avery comments absently. "They're amazing birds."

"You might feel differently if one pooped on you."

Chuckling, Avery eyes her with amusement. "Has that happened to you?"

"Many times. I think one did it on purpose. It's probably a predator-prey thing. I must've walked too close to a nest and not realized."

"Pooping as a defense? Creative."

Wrinkling her nose, Emma turns her gaze to Avery. "Disgusting." When the mage's violet eyes meet hers, Emma realizes something. "This can't be."

Tilting her head with interest, the mage asks, "What can't be?"

"You can't be here. I can't be here. I haven't been to my favorite place since Alpha Michaels took over the pack. This doesn't make sense."

Even knowing she should panic right about now, Emma finds herself strangely calm and at peace. Placing her hand on the ground, she finds the wild grass damp to the touch. Lifting her face, she sniffs, filling her nose with salt air and all the smells that go along with being this close to the sea. "It feels so real."

"You know what it is," Avery assures her with confidence.

Emma gives a little sad sigh of disappointment. "I'm dreaming." Suddenly, the breeze turns to a harsher wind, and the sky darkens. "Are you really here?"

"Do you mean is this the real Avery or an Avery created by your subconscious?" At Emma's nod, Avery continues. "I'm both. I can feel you through Jason, but the bond is so tenuous I can only touch you like a shadow in the woods. This person you're talking to is part me and part what you think I'm like. I can feel Jason better, but he's so full of concern and fear that he can't hear me yet."

Emma bites her lip. "You know you're his mate?"

"I know. Tell him to bite me and get it over with. It'd be nice to be able to talk clearly through a true mate bond."

Knowing it might be Emma's own wish being expressed by dream Avery, she pushes the request aside. "I can't be sure if I'm making you tell me this because I want it or the real you is asking me. That means you'll need to tell him yourself."

Reaching down and resting her hand on a jean-clad ankle, Avery rubs the spot as if it hurts. "I was afraid you'd say that. Is the charm still on my ankle?" The breeze picks up, tossing Avery's unbound hair around. Emma's hair is getting annoying as the wind becomes fiercer, so she quickly braids it.

Almost absently, Avery keeps rubbing her ankle, making Emma curious. "We haven't managed to get it off yet. Can't you feel it?"

"I think so. I feel like I'm underwater right now. Everything is muffled and distant. The only thing that feels real is Jason. And you because of Jason. You need to get that charm off." The wind is pulling at their clothing and the birds in the sky disappear, flying far away as the wind pushes them out of that section of sky.

"That's part of a long list of things I need to do," Emma mutters, suddenly feeling a little overwhelmed by how hard it will be to keep them all safe.

"I'm sure you'll figure it out."

The wind is howling now, and Emma's having a hard time hearing Avery's soft voice. Lightning crashes down into the sea in the distance. On the heels of the bright flash of light, booming thunder rolls over them. She can see rain falling out where the lightning struck. All she can hear is the raging sea and the wind. This dream is rapidly turning dark.

Leaning close, Emma shouts. "Tell me how to find Kade."

Avery puts her lips to Emma's ear. "Who's Kade?" The expression on Avery's face is childlike. Innocent and confused.

Grabbing the small mage, Emma pulls her diminutive body into her lap to shield the tiny woman from the raging wind. "You told me to find Kade," she shouts, but the mage just looks bewildered.

"Why would I ask you to find Kade? He hates me."

The ground at the cliff edge is disintegrating, falling into the sea below. Standing up and cradling Avery to her chest, Emma tries to move back but finds nothing but a stone cliff behind her.

"Avery, tell me how to find Kade!" Emma demands, pushing her body against the stone behind her back as the ground disappears in front of her. Avery rests her head on Emma's shoulder, snuggling against her chest. A small, content smile curves her lips.

"You and your brother are perfect," she murmurs contentedly. "Both of you are inherently good. Do you know how hard that is to find? I never thought I'd get so lucky. I think I'll keep both of you. Don't worry. I won't be mean. Do you like Florida?"

"Focus, Avery!" Emma screams. Letting go of Avery with one hand, she shifts the fingers of her free hand into claws and does her best to sink them into the cliff behind her, just as the ground under her disappears. Dangling now, she holds Avery around the waist, but the other woman doesn't seem to be inclined to fight for survival, satisfied to let Emma hold on to her and the cliff. Giggling, Avery points down at the crashing waves below.

"The sea is angry," she says in a child's sing-song voice. "Angry, angry sea!"

Heavy rain falls, soaking the two of them in moments. As a shifter, Emma rarely gets cold, but the rain chills her body, making her shiver and lose feeling in her limbs. She can feel Avery's body sliding away from her.

"Damn it, Avery. Grab on to me. I'm losing my grip."

"It's a dream, Emma, yet you fight to save me. Kade would let me go. He's practical, our Kade. He'd just say, 'It's a dream, Avery. Grow wings and fly,' and then he'd toss me into the air."

"Tell me where he is, and I'll tell him to be nicer to you in your dreams," Emma demands, desperate to get Avery to tell her how to find the man who can help them. This childlike dream version of Avery smiles dreamily up at Emma.

"Kade likes cliffs too. He likes storms like this one. Maybe he's here too."

As if summoned by that thought, a large warm hand grabs the one Emma's using to hold on to the cliff face. With one pull she finds herself sprawled at the feet of a tall, powerfully built man who's looking down at her, his violet eyes full of disgust.

"You should just have grown wings," he declares, making Avery laugh and clap.

"See, I told you," she sings to Emma. "Hello, Kade!" she calls out to the new presence.

"Avery?" Violet eyes widen at her laughter and then narrow as a scowl takes over his face. Crouching down, he pulls Avery from Emma's arms and sets her aside before focusing his attention back on Emma.

For her part, Emma's much too glad to have company in this strange dream to be intimidated. She tries to smile at this newcomer, but it fails and she knows her expression is a strange grimace instead of a welcoming smile. Sitting up, she wraps her arms around her legs for warmth.

"Hi there. Are you real, or did Avery create you?" She hopes that's a reasonable question to ask in a dream.

"Who are you?" he growls out, ignoring her question in favor of his own. "And what the hell do you think you're doing?"

"I'm dreaming, I think." Her good humor vanishes in the face of his fury. "Are you really here or are you part of me?"

His hand shoots out, and his fingers close around her throat tightly enough to hold her in place without restricting the flow of air. "What do you think, little wolf?" She feels power prick along her chilled skin and suddenly she's so very tired. Closing her eyes, she leans into his grip, letting him choke her. Maybe that will wake her up because it doesn't feel like she's getting any rest in this dream.

Cursing, he pulls his hand away from her throat and then threads his fingers in her hair, pulling her head back. "Open your eyes."

Feeling childlike herself now, Emma's lips form a pout. "No. I'm done with this dream. I don't want to be here anymore. I'm cold, and Avery won't tell me how to find you. And you're being mean."

"I'm hurt," Avery volunteers, and Kade's fingers painfully tighten in Emma's hair. "And there's a charm. Stupid shifters."

"This one is a shifter," Kade roars out, dragging Emma to her feet by her hair. "Is this the one who hurt you?"

Unable to speak now with so much power pouring over her, Emma just whimpers and keeps her eyes closed. This might be a dream, but she's under no illusion she's safe. She's pretty sure this is the Kade that Avery wanted her to find. Turns out Kade is a mage and probably powerful enough to kill her from a distance, even when they're connected only by the thinnest of magic.

Then Avery's there, grabbing Emma around the waist and trying to pull her away from Kade. "Stop that. She's a nice wolf. She and her brother are caring for me. Stop it right now."

Suddenly, power builds from Avery, pouring into Emma and crashing against Kade's power. Pain explodes as the two mages fight for dominance of her.

Screaming, Emma opens her eyes. Kade's face is right there. Following her instinct as a healer, she cups his face with her hands. When he looks down, she meets his fierce violet eyes with her pleading gray ones.

"Hurts," she whispers. His face transforms from fury to confusion and then regret before he lets go. Without his hold on her hair, she drops to her knees in front of him. At the same time, the cliff under them comes apart and all three of them fall.

Wings appear in Kade's back, beating lazily to keep him aloft. Avery makes a loud chirping sound, and a giant seagull swoops down under her so the mage is riding its back. Emma just falls. The two mages watch her descent, Avery with concern and Kade with derision.

"Grow wings," Kade shouts down to her. His mocking face is the last thing she sees as she plummets to the craggy rocks below.

Waking with a scream on her lips, Emma bolts upright in bed. Sunlight is streaming in through an open window, and she can hear traffic outside. No sounds of the sea, no howling wind, and no violet-eyed angry mages.

Swinging her legs over the side of the bed, she puts her elbows on her thighs and drops her head into her hands. The dream is still vivid in her mind, and she pushes herself to remember every bit of it before it fades away. It might not have been Kade in her dream. Heck, it might not have been Avery either, but she can't afford to discount any lead right now.

Kade likes cliffs.

Avery's words echo in her mind. Could that mean he's living on a coast? Could she be lucky enough to find him here in California? Of course, she can only hope the real version of him is nicer than her dream version because she's not interested in getting choked again. Or having her hair pulled. At least not in that context!

That makes her wonder if the real Kade even looks like her dream version. The mage in her dream was handsome and as tall as Jason, with a broad, muscular build like a shifter. She half expects him to be on the small side like Avery. Mages don't need to be big, like shifters; their power is in their magic, not their size. The dream version of him was probably created by her subconscious that equates size with strength. No matter how big he turns out to be, Emma knows to be cautious.

A tug at her pack bond makes her gasp and hunch over. Frantically she tries to shield herself but only mutes the pain not completely stopping it. Alpha Michaels must know they're gone now, and he's going to try to drive them back by using the bond he has with all pack members. The longer he pulls on it, the weaker she'll become. Even shielded, he's going to draw power from her, eventually making her pass out.

If he keeps it up, he could even kill her.

Fearful for Jason, she pushes herself out of the bed and stumbles down the hall into his room. He's awake and sitting up, leaning against the headboard with Avery in his lap. His face is twisted in pain. "You too?" he asks.

Rubbing her chest, she drops down to sit on the bed. "Yeah."

"He's not going to stop. I think I might be partially shielded because of Avery. My instinct is to protect her, and I know Alpha Michaels will hurt her. Him pulling at the bond like this is painful, but the pain seems like it's in the back of my mind. Like he's trying to hurt an area of skin that's been numbed."

Feeling relieved, Emma puts a hand on a lump of covers she believes is his calf. "That's good." Seeing the empty plate on the nightstand, she smiles. "You ate. That's also good. I'm going to fix you more food, and then I'm going to take your laptop and find some Wi-Fi. Maybe see if I can figure out who Kade is or see if I can find a witch to break the charm."

"Do you think any mage might help Avery? Does it have to be this Kade guy?"

"I have no idea. I don't know anything about mages except to stay away from them. What if they're like the jinn and get power by eating each other's magic? If we invite one in, and he or she decides to make a tasty snack out of Avery, neither one of us is going to be able to stop them."

The blood drains from Jason's face, and he clutches Avery tighter to his chest. "I didn't think about that. Do you think we can trust Kade?"

"She asked for him." Emma decides not to share her dream with Jason. No point in borrowing trouble when she doesn't even know how much of the dream to trust. "I'll be right back with some more food."

Hurrying to the kitchen, she puts together a few more sandwiches and takes them up with a few bottles of water. Setting them down on the nightstand, she meets Jason's concerned gaze.

"You look like shit."

"Gee, thanks, asshole. You're such a charmer," she says dryly, and he gives her a tired smile.

"Shit, sorry. I was just wondering how long the two of us have before... before we can't handle it anymore."

"Let's not dwell." She holds out her arms. "Here, give me Avery. I'll hold her while you hit the bathroom. I'm not sure how long I'll be gone, so grab a shower too."

Transferring the petite mage to Emma, Jason gives her a thankful smile. "I'll be quick," he promises and hurries off. Emma rocks Avery as she holds her, pushing magic at her as best she can and singing softly to her. She's almost out of shifter lullabies to sing when Jason comes back into the room, eager to take Avery back and settle them both down in the bed.

"Do you think I should pick anything up while I'm out?" Emma asks before she leaves.

"No, just hurry back. I feel better when you're here. When I know I've got you to watch my back."

"I will," Emma promises.

It doesn't take her long to find a coffee shop with free Wi-Fi. She gets a few stares when she buys a cup of coffee, and then she settles down to do a little research. After forty minutes, she's no closer to finding Kade or a witch to break the charm than when she started. She can't find any records of mages anywhere. Except for a few brief articles, nothing is written about them. They must be one of the most secretive groups out there. She can't even find a picture.

Stumped, she gets up, tosses her empty coffee cup, and packs up the laptop. Back in the car, she sits for a minute and wonders what to do next. What she needs is someone who knows the magical community and will share information.

What she needs is a gnome.

Pulling out her phone, she searches for gnome-owned businesses in the area and finds one, a small bakery only a mile away. Her stomach rumbles insistently. She realizes she can kill two birds with one stone: get food and hopefully gain some important information.

"Welcome, wolf," the gnome behind the counter calls out the moment she steps inside the small bakery. "I don't see many of your kind around here. Can I recommend the fritters? You wolf shifters like apples."

The apple fritters do smell good, so she nods and holds up three fingers. She'll eat one and take two home for Jason. Two human males huddle at a small round table in the corner, but other than that, the shop is empty of customers. Leaning down on the counter and trying to make herself seem less tall and intimidating, she fixes a friendly smile on her face.

"There was a gnome who ran a little bistro where I grew up," she tells him as he bags the fitters. "Made the best venison stew."

"You wolves and your love of game meat," the gnome huffs out with a smile. "I never could get a taste for it." The gnome holds the bag out for her to take. As she reaches out to grab it, his nose twitches. Dropping the bag, he steps backward, violently coming up hard against the shelves behind him, toppling several items to the floor.

"Mage!" he hisses out. "Get out, wolf! Out, out! You stink of mage. It's all over you. Out! Don't come back!"

When the gnome dropped the bag, Emma automatically grabbed it, her shifter reflexes easily snatching it out of the air. Now she's standing, clutching the bag to her chest and her mouth forming an O of surprise as the gnome makes shooing gestures with his hands.

"Can I just ask you—" she starts when another gnome appears from the back. She's female, but aside from the lack of facial hair, she looks just like the male.

"Mage? Did I hear you say there's a mage?" she asks the first gnome.

"This wolf stinks of mage! Stinks, stinks!" the first gnome yells to the second, even though she's standing right next to him. She turns her attention to Emma and adds her voice to the first gnomes.

"Mage? Mage! Out, out! Go, go! We don't want you here!"

"I'm going. Just let me pay—"

"No pay. No stay! Out, out, out!" the female gnome screeches, making Emma wince as the high-pitched voice grates on her sensitive hearing. Without another word, she's out the door and heading to her car. Apparently, gnomes are going to be no help in her quest for information.

"Are you a wolf shifter?"

Turning, Emma sees the two humans who were talking in the corner have followed her outside. She answers warily, unsure why they followed her. "Yes."

Both men grin at her reply. They look to be in their mid-twenties and on the smallish side, even for humans. She doesn't smell any magic on them, making them nonthreatening. A human can do little to a shifter unless they have witch-bought charms or very large guns.

"What do you want?" she asks.

"I'm Hal, and this is Mark. We're graduate students from Berkley. If you'd be willing, we'd like to interview you. I'm working on my dissertation on pack stability and its effects on individual pack members' happiness. Mark's working on how different magical communities interface."

"I don't think I can help you right now," Emma hedges. Normally, she loves interacting with academics as long as they're respectful. Alpha Julia always made it clear that pack members could talk to researchers if they wanted to, so she's no stranger to students working on projects. But right now, sitting down for an interview is out of the question.

Hal looks disappointed, but Mark looks downright devastated. "I heard the gnome say he smelled mage on you. Does one of your pack members have a mate bond with a mage? That would be an incredible thing to add to my research."

Eyeing Mark with interest, Emma straightens up to her full six-foot height. "What do you know about mages?"

Not intimidated at all, Mark grins at her enthusiastically. "No one knows much about mages. They never give interviews. It's impossible to take their picture, and few of them are out there. I know three live on the West Coast: Avery Mason, Kade Allard, and Samantha Li. Although there might be—"

Jumping forward with excitement at getting a real clue, she startles both men into stepping back. "Kade Allard! That's him! What can you tell me about him?"

Wide-eyed, Mark's earlier enthusiasm diminishes slightly. He gives a little shrug and rubs his hand through his hair nervously. "He's got a mansion just outside of Monterey. I've seen pictures of it, high on a cliff, overlooking the ocean. But other than that, no one knows much. I can tell you a lot more about Samantha Li. She—"

"Thanks! You've really helped!" Emma calls out as she rushes back to her car, leaving both the men protesting. She only feels a little guilty as she speeds off, but mostly she's elated.

When she gets back to Uncle Leo's house, she finds Jason asleep, so she leaves two of the fritters for him and goes back down to the kitchen. As she eats her fritter, she researches Kade Allard on her phone. Eventually, she finds a number for him and tries it. It only rings once; then a chipper female voice answers.

"This is Kade Allard's service. May I take a message?"

"I need to talk to Kade. It's about a friend of his."

"Sure you do, honey," the voice replies with a hint of sarcasm. "Look, you can leave a message or just hang up. They're both going to get you the same basic thing."

Frustrated, Emma slumps in her chair. "Does that mean he doesn't respond to his messages?"

"I know he gets them. We have tracking software that tells us how often he accesses our database. But I don't know if he ever answers them. Considering how often I record repeat callers, he doesn't call back very many people. But hey, if you know a friend of his, maybe he'll get back to you. I'd drop names if I were you. That would probably work the best."

A thought occurs to Emma. "Um, how can I be sure this is *The Kade Allard's* answering service?"

The woman laughs. "You're a rare one! Hold on a sec." Before she can protest, horrible Muzak fills Emma's ear. Grinding her teeth, she waits for the woman to come back on the line, but instead the Muzak cuts out, and the voice from her dream talks.

"This is Kade Allard. Leave a message. Or don't."

A click sounds, and the woman's back on the line. "That's the message we play after hours. Does that tell you what you need to know?"

"That's him," Emma confirms with a little sigh of relief. She's a step closer to getting in touch with Kade. At least she is if he gets this message. "Tell him Avery Mason is with me. Tell him that she's hurt, and we need him."

"It might help if you tell me who you are and how he can contact you." The woman's voice is all business now, and Emma gets the feeling this faceless employee believes her—or at least believes she's in dire straits.

"My name's Emma Martin," she says and gives her cell number and Leo's address, just in case Kade decides to come to them.

"Can you add that we're going to head south tomorrow toward Monterey? Tell him…" Right then Alpha Michaels pulls hard on the pack bond, making Emma wince and curl into herself from pain. Gathering her breath, she wheezes out, "Tell him I don't know how much longer any of us can last."

"I've got it, Emma. You hang in there, honey. I'll put this in the system right away and mark it urgent. None of us have ever done that with his messages, so maybe he'll read it soon."

"Thank you," Emma whispers and lets the phone fall from nerveless fingers.

Slowly, she sinks to the floor, shaking from the pain as she fights to build up barriers against her powerful alpha. The pain is intense, and no matter what she does, she can't seem to block it.

He must be depleting the pack, pulling power from everyone to fuel this magic. He's using the bond to push one thought at her—return. He's filling her with urgency and pain. It's the type of push through the bond that could kill her if it goes on long enough.

Crying, she fights the urge to get in her car and drive back to the pack. Alpha Michaels is pushing so hard at the bond she can hear him in her head. *Get back here. Get back here. Get back here.*

"I can't go," she moans to the empty room.

Get back here. Get back here. Get back here.

"I can't go. I need to protect Jason." Those are her magic words. Those words keep her from giving in to her alpha no matter how bad the pain.

Get back here. Get back here. Get back here.

"I can't go. I need to protect Jason," she whispers to herself over and over again. That's the only thing that keeps her curled up on the floor as the pain builds to unbearable levels. Those words keep her from getting in the car and returning to Alpha Michaels. Those words keep her from betraying her brother.

The pain hits her even harder as she keeps repeating those words until she has no breath to say them. She can only think them. Relief comes when she blacks out.

A seagull cries out overhead, and she opens her eyes to see the familiar unblemished cliff. She's curled up on the ground, but instead of old linoleum under her cheek, dirt is pressed against her skin. The pain is still there, making her sob. She's dreaming again. It's not fair she should feel this much pain in her dream.

"You're back."

Rolling her eyes up, she finds Kade towering over her. That's all she can manage. She's unable to talk through her anguish as she hears the mage crouch down next to her; then a warm hand touches her shoulder.

"That isn't very nice," he murmurs, as if commenting on someone with poor manners. "Let's see what I can do about that." Warm magic flows into her, and suddenly the pain is gone. All the tension in her body eases, and she draws in a deep breath.

"There. Isn't that better?" She opens her eyes again to see Kade crouched next to her, smiling pleasantly down at her.

Staring up into his face, she's struck dumb by his beauty. In her first dream with him, he was handsome in a dangerous and arrogant way. But now that he's smiling, his face is transformed.

Her silence makes the smile disappear, and his expression turns mildly annoyed. Lowering himself the rest of the way to the ground, he sits cross-legged and peers at her. He puts his hands on his knees, palms up, showing her that he's not holding anything.

"Are you scared of me now, little wolf? I'm sorry I was a brute before. I thought Avery was playing one of her games." Looking up, he examines the cliff and sea. "This is your special place. Isn't it? I don't recognize it, and it isn't Avery's style, so this must be your creation."

"It's my being spot," Emma volunteers, slowly sitting up. She can talk now that's he's not looking at her with those entrancing violet eyes. "It's where I go back home to sit and be. To let my brain be quiet. Thank you for taking the pain away."

"It's the least I could do for you, considering you're sharing this lovely place with me." He turns his face to the sun, and the breeze ruffles his black hair. Just like in the last dream, he's massive. Taking a tentative sniff, she tries to catch his scent. Nothing fills her nose but the sea.

"This dreamscape is exceptional. You have quite the talent for stitching. If I don't end up needing to kill you, I might need to hire you to stitch some dreamscapes for me in the future," he comments absently. Abruptly, he turns his attention back to her, making her jump a little. "Are you curious about my smell, little wolf?"

"I'm not little," she mumbles, dropping her eyes to her lap. She watches with fascination as his hand enters her field of vision and envelopes one of hers.

"You're little compared to me," he points out, cradling her hand in his. He feels warm, like another shifter, and suddenly his scent fills her nose. Her eyes shut of their own accord as his smell takes all her focus. Magic and masculinity are the only ways she can describe his scent. Well, maybe desirable and delicious also. That thought makes her face heat.

"It appears you like the smell of me." His amused voice makes her eyes fly open. He's watching her with an expression that's both entertained and interested. "You should see if you can earn my favor, little wolf. Do you know why?"

No words form in her brain and she loses herself in his eyes, his voice rolling over her with sensual promise. When she doesn't answer, he smiles and leans closer, surrounding her with his delectable scent.

"Shifters like us for the same reason I'm able to block your alpha's pull."

She should care about what he's saying. It's important to her survival. There's something she should tell him, but she just can't seem to remember what it is. The only thing she can think about is this mage and his scent.

Giving in to impulse, she launches herself at him, knocking him down and covering his body with hers. He laughs as she puts her knees on either side of his hips and lowers her face to his, rubbing her cheek against his, basically trying to cover herself in his scent.

Strong arms go around her, drawing her flush against his body. She gives a little whimper when her head is forced to his chest, but she tilts her face up and finds she can kiss his neck.

"This is a first," he murmurs as she squirms against him. "Be still, little wolf. Let me work on something." She stops moving but gives a soft sound of protest. She doesn't want to be still. She wants to unleash her claws to better rip his clothes to get to his bare skin. Then she wants to rip her clothes off. She needs every part of her skin to touch every part of his skin.

A cold wash of magic flows over her, taking away his scent and her amorous urges. In its wake, she feels cold power pulsing under her. His arms open as she scrambles off him to crouch on all fours several yards away.

Embarrassed, she forces her gaze to meet his. "I'm very sorry, Mr. Allard."

Sitting up, he watches her, expressionless. The lack of any emotion showing on his face seems even more terrifying than his anger in her first dream. "You're a strange one, little wolf. I find I'm fascinated."

With the tantalizing scent gone, she can focus. Avery and Jason are in danger, and hopefully, this mage is the answer. "Please, we need your help."

"We?"

"My alpha is looking for us and—"

"I'm not interested in inner-pack disputes," Kade tells her, his expression bored.

"No, this isn't that. I mean, it's not entirely about that. It's about a mage named Avery." That gets his attention.

"So that was Avery who pulled me in before. It felt vaguely like her, but I wondered. Go on. What can I do for the high and mighty Avery?"

"She needs you. She's dying right now. If you could just come—"

Cutting her off again, he gets to his feet. "If a mage dies, they deserve it. We're too powerful for anything but another mage to kill, so she must have been monumentally stupid to find herself in a place of weakness. Let her die. It will purify the rest of us."

Stunned for a moment at his callous words, she gapes at him. Then anger mixes with fear, giving her a voice again. "But you don't understand. My brother is her mate. They'll both die. Please!" Scrambling to her feet, she grabs him by his lapels and shakes.

His expression turns annoyed as he pulls her hands off his coat. He holds them trapped in his bigger ones for a moment; then his expression becomes contemplative. "What will you trade me for my help, little wolf?"

His expression indicates that he doesn't expect her to offer anything of importance. He's probably just playing with her. "I'm rather rich and powerful. Can you give me anything I don't already own?"

This is no time for dithering or negotiations. "Anything. My life. I don't care."

This gets his interest. He raises an eyebrow and runs his gaze down her body. "Your life? You would let me kill you to save this mage?"

"And to save my brother."

His lips twist into a sardonic smile. "Of course, your brother as well. Wouldn't want to make it an even trade, a life for a life. But I suppose one life for two isn't all that much more. I get your life for saving theirs?"

Shock makes Emma close her eyes. She just gave up her life. She's going to die. But at least her brother will live. And if Avery lives, she might protect him from the pack. And knowing Jason, he'll talk Avery into protecting their parents as well. Under the circumstances, it's the best outcome she can hope for.

"Yes, my life for theirs," Emma agrees.

"You're not much good at bargaining. Are you?" he asks, and she gapes at him.

Worried that she's being toyed with, Emma reaches for her inner calm. Getting aggravated at this sneering mage isn't going to help any of them. "Are you going to save them or not? Avery's dying, and my alpha's probably on his way to find us right now. If you don't—"

"Quiet." He silences her with that sharp word. She shuts her mouth with an audible click and watches him warily, fighting the urge to smack him. Even healers have limits to their patience.

"Let me assess if fixing them is worth it," he continues as he lets go of one of her hands to cup her chin in a firm grip. When his power pricks painfully along her skin, she tries to draw away, but he just makes a disapproving sound and holds her still.

Power pushes inside her, and it takes a great deal of concentration to keep herself from trying to move. It feels intrusive and uncomfortable as he moves his magic through her with ease. At one point, it feels like something deep in her chest is being tugged upon, and she makes a small sound of discomfort.

"We're wasting time," she reminds him.

"You're much too impatient," he reprimands her but doesn't stop his exploring. "There's depth to you, wolf. Your kind rarely feels like this. I'm intrigued enough to care."

"Hurry," she begs.

"Just show me where you are, little wolf. I'm going to follow you home."

His power stabs into her. She opens her mouth to scream, and then there's blackness again.

Eyes fluttering open, Emma finds herself back on the kitchen floor, but this time a pair of familiar boots stand right in front of her face. Sobbing from fear, she looks up to find Alpha Michaels staring down at her, his face twisted in a cruel sneer.

"Dumb bitch, kept your cell phone. You know those can be traced. Right? Thought you could hide from us because you'd be among so many humans? You didn't even think about ditching the cell phone."

He draws back his foot and kicks her in the face. She doesn't even try to avoid the hit. There's no point. The kick catches her on the cheek and rattles her brain around in her head. Blood gathers in her mouth. She spits and feels a tooth leave her mouth along with the blood.

She can hear heavy footfalls coming into the house and then Jason snarls upstairs. He'll fight to defend Avery. And because it's just him against a dozen martinets, he won't survive the battle.

All three of them are as good as dead now.

Another kick, this time to her stomach, makes her retch. "I gave you a chance to come back," he tells her as he stalks around her. "I called to you. Damn near killed a few of the pack to draw enough power to keep calling to you and Jason. But no, you wouldn't respond. Not even a text."

Crouching down next to her head, he grabs her by the hair and forces her face up. Pain blossoms on her scalp, adding to her misery. Wrenching her head to the side, he brings his face close to her. "Do you know what the most important quality in a pack member is?"

Knowing she's dead anyway, she spits in his face, making him rear back. "Compassion," she hisses out.

Standing up, he kicks her again. She flinches away so only his heel catches her on the shoulder.

"Loyalty!" he screams at her. "You all belong to me. I own you. All of you. I'm your alpha, and your loyalty should be absolute." He emphasizes his words with several more kicks. One blow gets past her arms and lands a solid strike to her head. The world goes unfocused and she can't hear anything but the ringing in her ears for several seconds.

At least if he keeps this up, she won't be conscious long enough to feel whatever torture he wants to inflict on her before he kills her.

"What are you doing with my wolf?" a voice asks from behind Alpha Michaels.

That familiar voice fills her with hope. She tries to open her eyes but finds that one won't open and the other one will only open halfway. Lying on the floor of the kitchen, bleeding and barely able to see, she watches Alpha Michaels turn to face Kade.

Because Kade's significantly taller than her alpha and standing very close, Michaels is forced to look up to see his face. He pales as he gazes into those glowing violet eyes.

"Mage," Michaels whispers, fear edging his voice.

"I asked you a question." Kade's voice is mild, and his body relaxed, but Emma can feel his power crackling through the room. "What do you think you're doing with my wolf?"

"S-s-she's a member of my pack," Michaels stutters out. "I'm her alpha, and she left against my wishes. She must be punished."

"Ah, I see." Kade looks down at her with a frown. "I believe you're mistaken. We struck a deal, she and I. She belongs to me now."

"Sure, you can have her," the cowardly alpha proclaims, backing away from the mage. "I'll just go collect my people."

A familiar roar and a crash from upstairs pushes Emma to speak up. "My brother." Her voice isn't very strong because she's having trouble breathing, but Kade seems to hear her and nods.

"That's right, little wolf. We made that bargain. Will you live for a few more minutes while I fulfill my side of our agreement?"

Emma manages to give one small nod, but she might be lying. She's not sure. She knows she's got some serious damage to her head, and it might kill her sooner rather than later. Hopefully, she'll live long enough to be of use to the mage, so her part of their agreement is fulfilled.

"You stay there, little wolf. I'll go see to Avery and your brother." He moves to leave, and the moment his back is turned, Alpha Michaels bolts for the door, ready to abandon his men to the mage.

"Oh no, I don't think so," Kade says, facing him again. With a flick of his wrist, he grabs the alpha with powerful magic and flings him against a far wall, pinning him there with invisible hands. "I don't approve of how you've treated my latest acquisition."

"I didn't know! Have mercy! I didn't know!" Michaels screams. Despite the pain in her face, Emma smiles at the sight of her abusive alpha rendered helpless. "She's yours! If she's not enough, I have more bitches. Ones that are prettier. Younger. You can have them too. All of them. Don't hurt me!"

Real disgust fills Kade's face. "I believe you were screaming about loyalty when I arrived. Offering up your pack to me doesn't strike me as particularly loyal. This one—" Kade points down at Emma, "is willing to give everything to save another. That's loyalty. Your cowardice is so atrocious that you're not worthy to be the same species as she is."

Magic builds thick around Michaels as he screams and writhes. As the magic presses in, his form shrinks until finally he's no larger than her thumb. With another movement of his hand, the magic pulls away and a cockroach drops to the floor.

"Enjoy your new form. I'm sure a cockroach colony somewhere needs an alpha." With another motion of his hand Michaels the cockroach disappears, and the alpha bonds that connected him to the pack snap and break.

At the same time a flash of pain shoots through her chest from the broken bond, she hears howls from upstairs. A horrible emptiness hits her like she's missing a limb. Wolf shifters aren't meant to be alone without a pack. They aren't meant to live without an alpha bond. She sends a silent prayer that the rest of the pack survived the bond being severed so violently.

Noise from upstairs draws her attention. Someone is screaming. And then she hears the impact of a body against a wall.

Her brother is talking, but she can't make out the words. Then she hears a metal clank, and a flash of power slices through the house. She can't feel her brother anymore. They've had a bond since conception, but now it's gone. This is so much worse than losing her alpha bond. She didn't just lose a bond with another wolf. The connection to the soul closest to her own is gone. She's weeping by the time Kade returns to her.

"Hush now, little wolf. There's no need to cry. I'll make you feel better."

"He's gone," she grieves. Kade doesn't even ask who she's talking about. He just seems to know.

"I'm sure he'll be fine. Avery will take care of him."

That makes her pause in her grief. "He's not dead?"

Chuckling, Kade gathers her up in his arms. "No. The moment I broke the charm, Avery claimed him. After exacting a little revenge, that is. She's transported both of them somewhere. She probably broke the bond between the two of you because she instinctively saw it as a threat. I'm sure the two of them are sitting on a lovely tropical beach, secure and healing already."

"Thank you," she whispers as he stands up with her cradled in his arms. Her brother's safe. With Alpha Michaels gone, her parents are safe as well. Except for forfeiting her own life, everything seems to have worked out wonderfully.

"Now let's focus on you." His words should fill her with fear, but they don't. She's in too much pain to care what he's going to do to her. The blows to her head have made her dull-witted and accepting.

"Fuck," she moans out. "I'm ready." Death means the pain will be over. Hopefully, he doesn't need her to hurt more to fulfill their bargain. It's not just the pain that makes her ready for death. Losing both her alpha bond and her sibling bond with Jason makes her feel like her magic's draining away. She whimpers when he jostles her a little as he negotiates the stairs.

"I know you hurt, little wolf. I'll make it better. And we'll stay here until you're stable. After that, we'll discuss your deplorable tendency to cuss."

That sounds like he doesn't plan on killing her. "You're not going to sacrifice me for some kind of spell?"

"Now why would I want to sacrifice my brand-new pet." She feels his magic flare, and then power punches into her chest. It doesn't hurt, and once the impact dissipates, she feels a new alpha bond, pulsing with magic and much stronger than any she's felt before.

"There now," he murmurs. "A proper leash for my little wolf."

Exploring along the new alpha bond, she finds Kade's power is solid and more comforting than Michaels's, or even Alpha Julia's. The bond's reassuring, even if his words are concerning. Pet? That doesn't sound good, but then again, Michaels called them pack and treated everyone like slaves. She probably shouldn't read too much into a word.

Secure in the new bond, she lets herself fall into unconsciousness. The last thing she's aware of is Kade's gentle hands as he settles her on a bed.

"Rest, little wolf. I'll make sure you feel better soon."

A soft, kind voice draws Emma toward consciousness. "That's a good girl. Just a little more. Can you open your eyes for me?" The woman talking reminds her of her mother, so Emma focuses hard on getting her eyes to open. Her lids feel heavy, and it seems to take an inordinate amount of effort to get them even halfway open.

"There we are, what lovely gray eyes. And your pupils are the same size now, perfect. Can you talk, sweetie?"

"What—" Emma's startled by how scratchy her voice sounds. She tries to clear her throat, but it feels too dry. She lets her eyes close again, tired from even trying to do that much.

"Oh no, don't go back to sleep yet," the voice insists cheerfully and then speaks to someone else. "Sit her up."

Strong arms push behind her back and maneuver her into a sitting position. Her head lolls, and she tries to straighten it out, but it's a much more arduous task than it should be. Why does her head feel so heavy?

"There now, very good. Open your mouth, sweetie." Obediently, she parts her lips, and a straw is pushed into her mouth. Closing her lips around it, she sucks and is rewarded with cool, refreshing water flowing down her throat. She almost moans at how good the water tastes and feels. All too soon the straw is being drawn away.

"Not too much, honey," the voice says. "I promise you can have more later. Now I need you to open your eyes again."

Forcing her eyes open, she finds a face leaning in close to hers. An older woman with gray hair artfully braided and coiled in a bun on top of her head, smiles warmly. Emma smiles back. The longer she looks, the more she notices the woman's smile isn't entirely true. Lines of worry bracket her mouth, and her brow is furrowed.

"It's okay," Emma tells her, wanting to soothe the other woman. The woman's smile drops for a moment in confusion; then she laughs.

"Healer," the woman declares, turning to look at someone else in the room. "Always worried about others before themselves."

"Pathetic healer," Emma objects. Her mind is muddled, but she knows that much. A real healer would have the power to help her fellow packmates better instead of just cleaning wounds and slapping on bandages.

The woman's eyes narrow for a moment, as if she's considering something. Emma feels fingers touch her skin, just under her ear at the corner of her jaw. The woman makes a considering sound, and Emma feels a small fissure of magic go through her, testing and then receding.

"Hmmm, powerful healer but untapped. You're hiding yourself away."

"What do you mean?" a strong masculine voice asks, and Emma rolls her head to the side so she can see the owner of the voice. Her breath catches when her eyes land on Kade's handsome form. Memories flood back to her. Kade agreeing to help in the dream. Michaels hurting her. Jason and Avery disappearing. Kade creating an alpha bond.

Worry and fear well up in her, making her eyes burn with tears. A lump forms in her throat, making it hard to draw in air.

Warm hands frame her face and force her attention back to the kind face of the elder woman attending to her.

"Breathe, Emma," the woman commands, and she feels power gently brushing into her, encouraging her lungs to breathe past her uncooperative throat.

When she breathes in too deeply a sharp, stabbing pain in her side makes her exhale with a whoosh. She knows what the pain is. Her ribs are hurt. Next time she keeps her breathing shallow but even. That makes the healer happy.

"There now, that's good." The woman lets go of Emma's face, and then the straw is being pressed to her lips again. Emma drinks until there's nothing left.

"More please," she requests.

"Do you think you can swallow a few tablets for me? They will help with the pain. I need to do a few more things to heal you, but they'll hurt while I'm doing them."

Giving one small nod, Emma obediently opens her mouth and lets the woman place a few pills on her tongue. They taste bitter, and she's glad when the straw is back. Sucking on it fills her mouth with more cool water, washing out the unpleasant taste and slaking her thirst.

"Should she eat?" Kade's voice is concerned, and Emma feels a little flutter of pleasure. It's nice that he's worried about her.

"No, not yet. But it would help if I could draw from you," the woman tells him.

"I already told you, Bethea. You don't get to do that."

With a sound of annoyance, Bethea places her hands on Emma's arms. "Then just touch her and lend her some of your power. I can manipulate it in her instead of taking it directly from you."

"I'm paying you enough. I shouldn't have to help," Kade grumbles.

"If you want her healed by tomorrow, I'm going to need assistance," Bethea informs him, censure clear in her voice. Healing is a tricky business, and Emma knows pushing a body too hard to heal quickly can backfire and end up causing catastrophic organ failure and death.

"Please don't hurt me," Emma whispers. She's just getting her head around the idea that she's still alive. She'd rather not give up breathing just yet.

"Don't you worry about rapid healing. I'm far too skilled to kill a patient." Bethea's voice is teasing and kind, her hands warm and reassuring where they're resting on Emma's forearms. "You're safe, wolf. Kade doesn't hire just anyone."

A large hand slides behind her neck and grips gently. Kade's thumb rubs the flesh under her ear, making her eyes flutter shut with pleasure. The wolf part of her relaxes inside, overjoyed at her dominant alpha's calming touch. Kade might not be a shifter, but he knows how to calm a subordinate pack member.

His warm breath blows across her skin as he puts his mouth next to her ear. "I'm in charge, little wolf. Can you feel the alpha bond in your chest? That's me. You're mine and I take care of my own. I won't let anything happen to you."

The words are just as reassuring as the touch. While he's talking, she tests the bond and feels nothing but strength and security. Relaxing back, she pulses her submission up through the bond and feels him take a surprised inhalation. As familiar as he is with shifters, and specifically wolf shifters, he mustn't be familiar with being an alpha because he obviously didn't realize the bond goes both ways. Security and assurance from the alpha to the pack; submission and joy from the pack back to the alpha.

"Do that again," he demands. Happy to oblige her alpha, she pulses the bond again. His hand tightens minutely on her neck and makes her moan. When Alpha Julia asserted her dominance, it always felt nice, but with Kade it feels pleasurable and downright erotic.

"That's good, Kade," Bethea murmurs as warm magic floods Emma from where the woman's hands rest on her arms. "Focus on the strong alpha bond for me. That's giving me a lot to work with."

Pain stabs Emma in the chest, making her gasp and try to move away from Bethea's touch. "Be still, Emma. I know it hurts, but I need to get these ribs mending. The pain meds will kick in soon and make everything feel nice and fuzzy. Just keep breathing. Kade, push more through the bond. Help Emma deal with the pain."

His warm hand on her neck tightens and loosens a few times as Kade pushes at the alpha bond. The pain in her chest keeps going, but her attention is drawn to Kade and the delicious things he's doing. His power tingles over her skin and strokes deep inside her. Turning her face, she nuzzles him and wonders why she can't smell him. It's disappointing and something she files away to investigate later.

The pain eases, and soon she can draw in a full breath of air without her ribs protesting. The pain might be lessening, but thinking is becoming difficult. Concentrating on any one thing is impossible.

"How are you feeling, sweetie?" the healer asks.

"Floaty," she murmurs.

"I think the pain meds are working," Bethea says with a chuckle, and Emma feels the woman's hand under her chin, turning her head forward and holding it still. "Open your mouth, Emma. It's time to put that tooth back."

Obediently, Emma opens her mouth but keeps her eyes closed. Something hard is pushed in her mouth and wedged between her molars, keeping her from being able to bite down. It's uncomfortable and worrisome, but it doesn't occur to her to fight. She wants nothing more than to please her new alpha.

She's unprepared for the flash of pain on her gum, causing her to make a soft noise of protest. Even though it hurts, she doesn't move. She screws her eyes shut and accepts the pain her alpha wants her to endure.

"What do you think you're doing?" Kade growls out, and at first Emma thinks she's done something wrong and tries to draw away from him. His hand on the back of her neck tightens at the same time the healer's hand on her jaw clamps down, keeping her head firmly in place.

"You want her tooth fixed. Don't you? Well, I need to cut the gum so I can bind the broken piece to the root," Bethea explains, her voice tinged with annoyance. "I don't tell you how to be a mage, Kade. Don't question my healing."

"Just get it done," he demands, and Emma relaxes into the hands gripping her, happy to know Kade's not angry with her. Bethea's hand moves in her mouth, and she feels something pressed hard against the cut on her gum. She's proud that she stays quiet and still as the healer sets her tooth.

Finally, the hand withdraws. The uncomfortable bite guard is removed, and Emma is able to close her sore jaw. Just as she explores the replaced tooth with her tongue, the healer taps her cheek.

"Don't chew on that side of your mouth for at least a few hours," she warns, and Emma withdraws her probing tongue. Bethea's touch disappears entirely. Emma feels the bed move slightly as the woman stands up.

"The injuries to her brain are completely healed. Her ribs and the bruising to her kidneys will be healed within the hour. The tooth will take longer because it's low priority, but by this evening it should be fine," Bethea explains. Kade's still holding her neck in his strong grasp, and now that the healer doesn't need access to her mouth anymore, Emma rolls her head back toward Kade. The mage accepts this movement, letting her nuzzle his shirt-covered chest with her nose and mouth.

"Thank you, Bethea. The payment is already in your account," Kade tells her.

"Call me if she develops a fever. It's unlikely, but sometimes there's a backlash from doing this much healing so quickly. Also, it would be good if you could join her on the bed. Cuddle with her for the rest of the day. Shifters need contact, as much skin to skin as you can provide. It will be especially helpful because you're her alpha now."

Already falling back to sleep, Emma doesn't hear Kade's response. She feels him lay her back down and draw her against his body. Warmth and the feeling of safety surround her. Sighing with contentment, she burrows against him and lets sleep drag her under.

Dolphins are jumping and playing in the sea. From her spot up on the cliff, she can just see them cavorting with each other. The sight makes her smile.

"You must be doing this on purpose," Kade muses, and she turns her head to see the mage sitting next to her. "I'm not easy to pull into dreams. The first time I assumed Avery did it, but I think she used you to pull me in. The second time I assumed she was lending you some help also. But now I know she's not here to help, so this must be all you. This dreamscape is incredibly detailed. How long have you been a stitcher?"

Leaning into him, Emma gives a little content sigh. "What's a stitcher?"

"That only creates more questions," Kade mutters; then louder he explains. "A stitcher is someone who can build dreamscapes and bring others into them. Mages live far distances apart, so we rarely meet in person. Instead, we meet in the dream realm. There's a lot of demand for stitchers, and not just by mages."

"You invite other mages into your dreams?"

"Never." The word is harsh and Emma tries to draw away, but Kade wraps a long arm around her shoulders to hold her against him. "I'm not upset, little wolf, just adamant. Inviting another mage into my dreaming mind would be infinitely dangerous. We hire stitchers to build us meeting places instead. It looks like my days of hiring others to do this are over. I'm going to train you to be my own personal stitcher. You're going to be more useful than I anticipated."

"Whatever you need me to do, Alpha," Emma agrees, relaxing into his embrace.

"How very accommodating," Kade murmurs thoughtfully. "In theory, I know how wolf shifter packs work, but I find having a subservient wolf of my own is a rather eye-opening experience. I can feel you're genuinely willing to do anything I ask. This bond between us is quite revealing.

"Of course I would," Emma agrees. "You're my alpha, and you saved Jason and Avery. And now I get to live. Why would I want to disagree or refuse you anything?"

"Why indeed," Kade says, sounding amused. "I'll try very hard not to take advantage of you too much, Emma."

"Thank you, Alpha."

"Just Kade, Emma. I want you to use my name, not that title."

"Yes, Kade."

They sit like that, listening to the ocean crash below, watching the dolphins play in the distance. The scent of the ocean is heavy in her nose, tickling her with its complex smell of salt, fish, seaweed, and so much more. The ocean is full of the living and dead. Movement and tumult. It's one of her most favorite things about this spot, the complex smells that she can never fully unravel.

"You know, it's rare that a stitcher can create smell," Kade comments as a seagull wheels over their heads. She doesn't feel like getting pooped on, so she pushes the seagull out to sea.

"Smell is the best part," Emma explains as the bird dips below the cliff line.

"It's so real I can even smell the ocean," Kade tells her, and Emma almost rolls her eyes.

"Of course. It wouldn't be right if you couldn't smell it."

"That's what I'm trying to explain to you, Emma. You have a gift for this. I've never hired a stitcher who could make smells work in a stitch. This place feels so real. So perfect. Most stitchers create something much simpler. A bare room with chairs, or a field of green grass. Even that can be hard for them to maintain when more than one mage is present. But you created this cliff perfectly."

Remembering that dream, Emma winkles her nose in distaste. "That wasn't pleasant at all."

Chuckling, Kade gives her a little squeeze. "I was harsh. I'm sorry about that. I thought Avery was being flippant. I thought Avery had created everything, or that you were a hired stitcher. The place was so perfect it didn't occur to me that you were untrained and unaware of what was going on."

"So that was Avery in my dream? Not just a part of the dream that I created?"

"Yes, little wolf, that was Avery. She put herself in your dream and then pulled me in. I was annoyed, so I pushed the dream you created toward chaos. I shouldn't have been able to do that, but now that I know you're unskilled at hosting mages, I can teach you to protect your dream realm from manipulation."

"I'd like that," she affirms. "I want to be useful to you, Alp—uh, Kade."

"Just useful?" Kade asks. She's not sure what he means, and his tone makes her tense.

Warily, she pulls away from him until she can see his face. "What more do you want of me than to be useful?"

"We'll see, little wolf," he says mysteriously. "For now, just focus on healing. I need to get a great deal done tomorrow, and I need you up and moving to do it."

"I'll be ready, Kade," she promises. She can move through pain. She's done it plenty of times in the past. Even if she's not fully healed, she'll make sure her injuries don't get in the way of whatever her alpha needs from her.

"Right now, I want you to sit in front of me, between my legs, and let me wrap my arms around you. Bethea said shifters need a lot of contact. In the physical world I'm holding you, so I might as well do the same here."

Eagerly, she moves between his legs, putting her back to his wide, muscular chest. A contented sighs issues from her mouth as his arms come around her and squeeze her against him. "Thank you, Kade," she whispers.

"Don't thank me yet, little wolf," he warns her, his tone pleasant even if his words are full of foreboding. "You don't know how much I'm going to demand of you later."

This time, waking up is a painless process. Feeling better than she has in years, Emma opens her eyes and assesses herself. Breathing is easy and without discomfort. Probing her tooth with her tongue, she finds it just as solid as the rest, and her mind feels clear and coherent.

Sitting up slowly, she tests her limbs as she swings her legs off the bed. She's naked, but clothing is folded and piled on a chair next to the bed. Standing up, she staggers, a dizzy spell making her unsteady on her feet, but it passes quickly and in its wake she feels ravenous. Hastily she pulls on her clothes, eager to search out food and Kade.

The alpha bond is warm and strong, pulsing in her chest and making her smile. Even with Alpha Julia, the bond was never this strong. The strength of this bond is probably because she's in a pack of two. Without dozens of other pack members to share, the bond is immensely powerful. Not to mention this alpha bond is with a mage instead of another shifter. She wishes she could share this amazing feeling with her parents.

Walking quietly, she steps out of her room and is assaulted by the smell of blood. The scent only gets stronger as she walks down the hall. When she gets to the bedroom door where Jason and Avery were staying. She pushes it open, already half knowing what she's going to find but unprepared for how gruesome the sight is.

Inside are dead bodies and blood. Everywhere.

One body is whole, lying crumpled at the foot of the bed. It's Michaels' favorite martinet, just as sadistic and cruel as the alpha himself. A few claw marks mar the man's chest, but nothing that would have killed him. The body is strangely unhurt, but his face is a mask of torment and agony. Whatever killed him made him suffer first.

Although she resists the urge to spit on the body, it's a near thing. Looking around, she notes no mystery about what killed the rest of the wolf shifters in the room. The bodies are headless. It's easy to deduce by the splattering of blood, brain matter, and skull fragments, that the heads were exploded by someone powerful. Either Kade or Avery did this. No wonder everyone is so afraid of mages.

Flies buzz around the room and the blood is old enough to have turned brown. If things aren't cleaned up soon, the bodies will start rotting in the room, making the house uninhabitable. She's never dealt with dead bodies before. Who does one call to clean up after a massacre? Slayers Cleaning Service? Maids for Murders? Homicide's Happy Helpers?

"Smiling at all the carnage, little wolf?" Kade asks. "I like you more and more."

Her smile widens as she looks over to find Kade lounging in the doorway, just as big and handsome as in her dreams. He's wearing a suit that's a little on the wrinkled side, but he's showered and shaved. Going to him, she stops in front of him, clasps her hands together at her belly, and bows her head in respect.

"Good morning, Alpha Kade."

"Don't call me alpha," he reminds her as he closes a broad hand around the back of her neck, pressing his thumb into the hollow just over the corner of her jaw and under her ear. He draws her against him, bringing his face down and rubbing his cheek against hers. Scenting her like packmates would do as a sign of affection.

"I can feel your wolf inside. She's a cheerful little beast but hungry too." Pulling away from her, he takes her hand and leads her out of the room and down the stairs. "I've put some cheese and crackers in the kitchen. Eat that, and then we must be off."

The rest of the house is just how it was before the arrival of Michaels and his martinets. Kade pushes her to sit at the kitchen table and sets a plate of cheese and crackers in front of her. Both are tasteless, generic store brands. She didn't have the money to buy anything nicer the other day, but to her starving body they taste like ambrosia.

Shoving food in her mouth, she notices for the first time the expression of distaste on Kade's face. Forcing the bite of food down, she keeps her tone soft and respectful. "Have I done something wrong?"

Focusing his gaze back on her, he gives her a perfunctory smile that doesn't reach his eyes. "No, little wolf, you're fine. This place, however, is disgusting. You won't be returning here. And this food," he waves his hand, indicating both her plate and the rest of the kitchen. "This food is unacceptable."

"The house was my uncle's, but it belongs to my father now," she explains. "No one's lived here for almost a year."

"That explains the dust and general decay," Kade mutters. "But there's still no excuse for the amenities. It's rather intolerable." Unable to figure out what Kade means by "amenities," she gives a mental shrug and awaits instructions. Turning his violet eyes back on her, he takes in her jeans and t-shirt with a disdainful sniff. "Your wardrobe also leaves a lot to be desired. Today we'll pick up the necessities for you, spend the night in a hotel, and drive south tomorrow."

Swallowing the last of her food, she nods. "Yes, Alpha. Kade," Wincing she corrects herself. "Yes, Kade. Can I ask a question?"

"Ask," Kade orders her impatiently. "Don't request to ask a question. Just spit it out."

Noting that too much deference seems to annoy him, Emma asks her question. "How did you get here so fast?"

"Teleport," he explains succinctly. "It's one thing all mages can do."

"Can't we just teleport back to your property? Why do we need to drive?"

That question makes his lips thin in displeasure. Emma swallows hard and braces for his bad mood, but he doesn't do anything to her. He just tugs at his clothes, trying to straighten out the wrinkles.

"That question tells me that you lack even the most basic information about mages. While all of us can teleport, most of us can't move more than just ourselves. I can transport myself, my clothes and a few small items like my wallet and phone. Other than that, I can't take anything with me. Teleporting you is beyond my skill set."

"Oh, I didn't realize," Emma says, startled to find out that a mage can't do some things. Instead of finding it worrisome, she decides it's endearing. Even the most powerful of the magical creatures have limits.

"You're all finished? Very good, come along." Smiling, he leads her outside. It's a beautiful day with a bright blue cloudless sky above them. A big black SUV sits in front of them, blocking her compact car in the driveway. "I don't know how I'm going to get out," she warns him, her eyes on the SUV. It must have belonged to Michaels. "Maybe we can call a tow truck to move the SUV."

Holding up his hand, he dangles a set of keys in front of her. "I searched our guests' pockets and found these. Considering the ancient state of your vehicle, I think we'll take a nicer one instead."

"Oh, but we," she stops herself mid-sentence. The expensive shiny SUV belonged to Michaels as a pack communal property, but now, by rights of conquest, Kade owns it. Pack law is very clear on this. Even if Kade doesn't create bonds with any of the other pack members, everything the pack owned now belongs to him, including this very nice vehicle. "Do you want me to drive?"

"I do indeed." He drops the keys into her hand and makes his way to the passenger side. "I find driving makes me irritable. When I get irritated, people suffer. Probably best for everyone that you deal with this annoyance."

Wordlessly, she gets in the SUV but doesn't start it. Glancing anxiously over at Kade, his vague threat about being irritated is weighing heavily on her mind.

It takes no small amount of courage to ask the next question. "Sir, can I go get my things?"

"Your phone is broken, that laptop is ancient, and your clothing is old and atrocious. Did you pack anything of sentimental value that I might have missed? I didn't come across any heirlooms or jewelry in your bag or the room you were using. And you need to call me Kade although sir is an improvement over alpha."

Startled at his rapid assessment of her worldly possessions, Emma frowns. "No jewelry or anything like that. I don't own any. When Alpha Michaels took over, he claimed all the wealth for the pack coffers."

"Reprehensible," Kade mutters. "No matter. I'll get you all kitted out. You're in safe hands now, Emma." When she still doesn't start the vehicle, he tilts his head questioningly.

"I'm still worried about my brother," she admits, gripping the steering wheel with white knuckles, afraid Kade will react badly to her words. She's not trying to challenge his authority, but she's concerned Jason isn't safe and happy, as Kade promised.

To her relief, he doesn't get angry. He just sighs and puts his hand on the back of her neck. The pressure calms her wolf and makes her relax back into the seat.

"The best I can do is to see if we can contact Avery in the dream realm," he offers.

Sliding her eyes over to him, she keeps her head still, unwilling to do anything that might dislodge his comforting hand from the back of her neck. "Can we try tonight?"

"No, tonight you're going to practice. If you make enough progress, we can try the night after. But only if I think you have enough control. I don't want Avery to accidentally hurt you."

She wants to object and point out that she's already successfully hosted Avery in a dream, but she quiets her protest. She needs to bow to Kade's superior knowledge of mages.

Withdrawing his hand, Kade pulls a phone out of his pocket and starts tapping. Soon he looks up and starts pointing.

"Head in that direction," he tells her. Eager to please, she starts up the SUV and maneuvers the beast out of the driveway and down the street. After a few miles, she feels more confident driving the large vehicle.

"I need to contact my parents," she tells him absently, turning right at his direction.

"Why is that necessary?"

"They need to know I'm safe and that I left dead bodies in Uncle Leo's house." Kade seems to ponder her words for a moment and then comes to a decision.

"You can call them this evening, but only tell them you have a new alpha, not who he is. And don't bother them about the dead wolves. I'll send people to deal with them. At the next intersection turn left."

"Why can't I tell them about you?"

"Because I'm a mage, Emma. Telling your parents that I'm your new alpha won't reassure them."

The gnome's reaction at the bakery the day before comes back to her, and a small shiver of fear flows down her spine. "Would you hurt me?"

He doesn't answer right away, and the silence is worrisome. When he finally speaks, it makes her jump a little. "There are only two reasons I'd hurt you," he tells her. "One reason would be if it furthered a significant and important goal."

Those vague words aren't reassuring at all. "A goal such as…"

"I don't know, Emma," he says, his tone still casual. "I can't think of anything right now that I want badly enough to hurt you for it. But I can't preclude it in the future."

The alpha bond burns, making her shift uncomfortably in her seat. When she pulses submission through the bond, the burning stops. That's when she realizes that he's more unhappy about his own words than she is. Who says things like that and then gets upset? A lot is going on with this mage, a storm of thoughts and emotions she can only see the edge of.

Her healing gift nudges at her to help him, and she wants to roll her eyes. Her healing gift is so weak it's laughable. How the hell could she help a mage? Wealthy, powerful, influential mages don't need the help of pathetic shifters with feeble healing powers.

Ignoring the push from her healing gift, she focuses on the road. "And the other reason?"

"If I decided you were no longer amusing or useful to me," he states blandly. She flinches, making the SUV swerve slightly. He doesn't react to her minor loss of driving coordination, just continues to tap on his phone. "Don't mistake my generously for kindness, Emma. I find it entertaining to care for you, and I believe you will be useful as a stitcher. But if both of those change, I'm not inclined to bother keeping you around."

Swallowing hard, she concentrates on the road as she asks her next question. "Would you kill me?"

Still not looking at her, he taps on his phone for a moment before answering. "Maybe. It would depend on my mood. But I wouldn't worry about that now, little wolf. I'm much too delighted with our arrangement to even think about hurting or withdrawing the alpha bond and casting you aside." Looking up, he points to their right. "Ah, here's the mall. Pull in over there, near the Macy's. It's the best this area offers, so for now it will have to do."

Shaken by their conversation, Emma tries to drive smoothly where Kade points, pulling the SUV into an available spot and scrambling out of it. When Kade reaches for her hand, she shies away. When she realizes what she's done, she freezes in fear, waiting for a reprisal. He frowns for a moment, considering her with his intense violet eyes, and then smiles ruefully.

"I've scared you," he murmurs. "That wasn't my intention. We mages are a little too honest and rather blunt. How about I promise I won't kill you. That's an easy promise for me to make. I haven't killed a retainer yet."

"But do you always keep your promises?"

Although she wasn't trying to be funny, Kade barks out a laugh. "Yes, little wolf, I always keep my promises. Now come here."

He holds out his hand and waits for her to take it. Once his fingers close around her shaking hand, his frown is back and he tugs her to him. Wrapping his other hand around the back of her neck, he leans his tall body over and brings his face down to hers. He rests his cheek against her in the shifter wolf way. He's trying to be soothing, but her heart is still thundering in her chest.

"I'm sincerely sorry, Emma," he whispers. "Please don't fear me. I'm not capricious or vindictive. I'll lay out rules and expect you to follow them, but I understand you're fallible and will make mistakes. You already possess the trait I find most important, so I'm willing to be lenient with everything else."

"What trait?"

"Loyalty," he states simply. "Despite what your former alpha said, you're fiercely loyal, Emma. You were ready to sacrifice everything for your brother. I expect that same loyalty."

That kind of currency she understands. If there's anything wolf shifters are good at, it's allegiance.

"Yes, my alpha," she intones softly, deliberately using his title. "For you, I'll be loyal."

"Ah, there's my good wolf," he murmurs and gives her cheek one last rub with his own before pulling back. Keeping her hand in his but removing his other hand from her neck, he leads her toward the mall.

"Now, let's get you more appropriate clothing," he declares cheerfully. "I can't have you wearing jeans and t-shirts around me. It's just unacceptable." When her stomach grumbles, he laughs. "And food. Mustn't forget the food."

Staring at her reflection in the dressing room mirror, Emma wonders how she's supposed to move in this outfit. The knee-length pencil skirt doesn't allow her to take a full stride and the fitted blouse won't let her even bring her arms all the way up or forward. On top of that, both the blouse and skirt are made of nonnatural fabrics, so they're irritating her skin.

"Hello in there, how's it going?" the fake cheerful voice of Beth calls out.

The moment they entered the upscale area of Macy's, Kade insisted on talking to a manager. Soon they were ensconced in a small private area and assigned Beth to find them clothes. After a brief discussion with the mage, Beth left and returned dragging a clothing rack full of outfits.

Taking a seat and sipping the cappuccino he'd requested earlier, Kade waved Emma off to the dressing room with the order, "I want to see each outfit." Now she's standing in the first outfit and already regretting her life choices.

Maybe she should have just let Alpha Michaels kill her.

"I think I might need a size bigger," she calls out to Beth as she tugs at the skirt. Everything feels too tight. Too stifling. Shifters are meant to be able to move. Even those female shifters she knows who like tight clothing wear items that stretch and give.

"Come out here, Emma. I want to see," Kade demands. Ignoring the impossibly high heels Beth put in the room along with the outfit, Emma opens the changing room door and pads out barefoot. Her steps are short and mincing because she's afraid a full stride will rip the skirt. Three steps out from the room she stops and refuses to go any further. The closer she is to the room the sooner she can get back in there and change.

"It fits just fine, Emma," Kade assures her.

"No." Emma shakes her head violently, tugging at the neck of the blouse. "It's too tight. I can't move. I can't wear this." She can hear the edge of anxiety in her voice but can't seem to quell it.

Taking another leisurely sip from the decorative ceramic cup, his gaze sweeps over her. Feeling horrifically self-conscious, she tries to cross her arms over her chest but finds the blouse won't let her accomplish the motion. Frustrated, she rolls her shoulder and hears the distinct sound of ripping.

Embarrassed, she meets Kade's amused gaze. "I see what you mean about too tight. I forget about shifter strength."

Flushing with embarrassment, she drops her face into her hands. That action makes her blouse rip even further. She never considered buying clothing traumatizing until today!

"There's a Target in this mall. Can I just go buy some jeans and shirts there? Please." She begs, her hands still covering her mortified face.

Laughing, Kade is suddenly in front of her, putting his hand on the back of her neck and squeezing just enough to help her calm.

"How about this," he murmurs, amusement lightening his voice. "Beth can find you some nice jeans and slacks. Then she can pair them with some tops that will allow you to move. In exchange, we'll pick out a few outfits suitable for when I need to meet clients. I promise Beth will find you things you can move in."

"Certainly, Mr. Allard," Beth simpers, sliding herself up next to Kade. Emma feels a growl tick out of her throat, making Beth gasp and Kade chuckle.

"I'd step away, if I were you, Beth," Kade comments, taking another sip of his drink. "I don't think my wolf likes you so close."

"Animals," Beth sniffs as she steps away. Used to that kind of insult, Emma doesn't give it another thought. She's just glad Beth isn't touching Kade anymore.

However, Kade hears her comment and isn't amused.

"I don't think we will require your assistance any longer, Beth," Kade says, turning his violet eyes on the woman. "Go find someone else to assist us. Someone who won't upset my wolf or annoy me."

"But, Mr. Allard, I—" Beth protests and then goes pale.

Emma can't see his face, but she guesses his eyes just flashed because she can feel power prick along her skin. Stumbling back, Beth hurries away. Soon a different woman walks in, her smile open and amused.

"I'm Mrs. Cooke," she introduces herself. Emma likes the woman right away. She looks to be in her mid-forties, short, round, but well-dressed and self-assured. "I'm sorry Beth wasn't as helpful as she could have been."

Looking at Emma, she raises an eyebrow. "Or helpful at all. Wolf shifter?" Emma nods and Mrs. Cooke makes a small annoyed sound. "Those kinds of fabrics and cuts won't work at all for you. I'll be right back with better choices."

Giving Mrs. Cooke a relieved smile, Emma offers her a hand in a traditional human greeting. Mrs. Cooke's handshake is firm and short. "That would be great. Maybe some jeans and shirts too?"

"Stylish ones," Kade interjects. "And a few outfits suitable for business meetings. Include at least one cocktail dress."

"I think we can accommodate all that," Mrs. Cooke assures them. Looking at Kade, she points to a door at the far side of the room. "The tailors are here for you, Mr. Allard." She holds her hand out for his cup. "If you wouldn't mind stepping in there for your fitting, I'll go gather things for Emma to try on."

Handing her his cup, he graces her with a polite smile. "I want another one of those and see that Emma has something to drink as well." With that, he's out the door in several long strides.

His eagerness to meet the tailor makes Emma realize he didn't just want new outfits for her but also for himself. Now that she's looking, she notices his clothes aren't just rumpled. They're stained and torn in a few places. He's worn the same outfit for two days; it must be bothering him immensely.

Vain mage.

"Go ahead and get out of that outfit. I'll be right back with better choices. Oh, and what would you like to drink?"

"Regular coffee would be great. With a little cream, please," Emma requests, and hurries back into the changing room, keen to get out of the blouse and skirt.

Over the next hour, she tries on dozens of outfits, glad that Mrs. Cooke hands her clothing that fits and feels good to move in. Never once does the woman make any disparaging remarks about Emma's size. This woman is used to dealing with shifters. She even picks items that are mostly made from natural fabrics like cotton, wool, and linen so Emma's skin won't itch.

"How did you know?" Emma asks as she admires the jeans she's wearing. They might be fancier than what she's used to, but they feel perfect.

"My best friend growing up was a tiger shifter," Mrs. Cooke explains. "She mated another tiger and moved to India, but we still email and talk on the phone. Every few years one of us will travel to visit the other one. But she taught me a lot about what it's like to be a shifter. Now I'm the one they usually send to deal with shifter customers." She makes a face. "I get all kinds of commendations because they all think shifters are difficult or troublesome."

"We aren't," Emma starts but stops when Mrs. Cooke makes a soothing motion.

"Oh, I know," she says quickly. "You guys just don't handle certain things well. So really, it's a win-win. I get to help, and you guys get to be comfortable and don't have to put up with snide comments."

"Then why did we end up with Beth first?"

"Mr. Allard," Mrs. Cooke explains succinctly. "Our manager is an idiot. He sends her in when we need to get a man to buy things. There's a little charm on the doors that alerts us when a shifter comes in, and when it didn't go off for Mr. Allard, it was assumed he was human."

Snorting out a laugh, Emma cocks an eyebrow at Mrs. Cooke. "How could anyone think he's human? Those eyes are a dead giveaway. Even if you don't know what mage eyes look like, that color should clue you in that he isn't human."

"Did I mention my manager is an idiot?" Mrs. Cooke reminds her with a grin. "Back to business. How did that dress fit?"

"Perfect," Emma admits. "But I can't wear those shoes."

Frowning, Mrs. Cooke examines the shoes. "Too much heel?"

Nodding, Emma sighs. "I've only ever worn hiking boots or tennis shoes. Or I go barefoot. I don't know how to walk in slip-on shoes, especially with those heels." Making a considering sound, Mrs. Cooke stares at Emma's feet for a minute.

"I have an idea," she says finally and hurries away. When she comes back, a young man is trailing behind her carrying a stack of boxes.

"Boots!" Mrs. Cooke exclaims happily. "Let's get you into some nice boots—tall ones for the business casual outfits and ankle-high for the jeans," she says as she shoves a box at Emma. "This way you only have to wear slip-on shoes with the fancier outfits, and I'll make sure they have very low heels."

By the time Kade returns, wearing a perfectly pressed and tailored brand-new suit, Emma's wearing one of the outfits Mrs. Cooke put together for her.

The knee-length skirt flares out so she can take a full stride and the soft cotton blouse doesn't bind or irritate her. The jacket that matches the skirt is soft, lightweight and breathable so she doesn't feel like it's going to make her sweat. The knee-high boots have almost no heel and are so comfortable she could probably run in them if she needed to. Emma's never worn such nice clothes or felt so fancy. She adores them but worries Kade won't like them because they're nothing like what Beth originally chose.

Rubbing her damp palms on the skirt, she looks to Kade for approval.

Tilting his head, he takes in her appearance. "You look perfect, Emma," he announces finally, making her breath whoosh out in relief. That makes him smile. "Were you worried, little wolf?"

"Mrs. Cooke said everything fit right, but I don't know much about clothes or fashion," Emma admits.

"Shifters often don't," Kade murmurs. "Never fear. I'll make sure you're always appropriately outfitted." Turning his attention to Mrs. Cooke, he pulls out his wallet and hands her a black credit card. Mrs. Cooke's eyes widen as she takes the card, telling Emma there's something special and elite about that credit card.

"She'll wear that out. Settle our bill and have everything boxed up and people ready to carry to our vehicle," Kade instructs. "Also, where is a good place to eat? Someplace close. My wolf is starving, and I find myself rather hungry as well."

Glancing down at the card and then back up at Kade, Mrs. Cooke gives him a wry grin. "For you, it would need to be The French Laundry. There's a six-month waiting list, but I have a feeling they'll let you right in."

"Excellent," Kade says dismissively as he pulls out his phone and starts tapping on it. Mrs. Cooke disappears to carry out his instructions. Emma waits as Kade uses his phone. He steps away as he talks to someone in low tones. Looking satisfied, he hangs up and turns back to her.

"We have a table for two in an hour," he informs her as he looks her up and down. "Did Mrs. Cooke treat you well?"

"She understands us," Emma agrees. "Shifters, I mean. Could you compliment her to the manager?"

"I'm sure she's going to make a good bit of money from commission, but I'll do that too if it will make you happy." Kade draws closer to her. Not sure what his expression means, she takes in a few sniffs. Scent tells so much about a person, including their emotions, and Kade's lack of any smell is bothersome.

"Is it magic?" she asks, trying to keep the frustration out of her voice. "Is that why I can't smell you? I know mages have a scent. Avery smelled so strongly of magic when I first met her it burned my nose. A gnome could even smell her on me. But you don't smell at all except in that one dream. Why?"

"I'm blocking you from smelling me," he admits and puts his hand on the back of her neck, quieting her agitation. "You reacted so strongly to my smell in the dream realm that I didn't want to risk it here in the real world."

She blurts out the real reason his lack of smell is bothering her. "But what if you're my mate?"

He's silent for a moment, and she risks a glance up. His face is impassive, but he hasn't withdrawn his hand from her. "Mages don't have mates," he states flatly. "If you mate with me, it will be one-sided. Always. I can be your alpha, but not your mate. Mages can't love. Would you want that?"

Disappointment flares through her. "No," she agrees. "I wouldn't want a mate who doesn't want me back."

Kade's expression turns seductive. "I didn't say I don't want you."

"But—"

"I said I can't be your mate. Don't shifters enjoy sex for fun? Sex outside of being with your one true mate?"

Emma doesn't look away or blush. Wolf shifters can't get pregnant outside of a mating bond, and they don't carry disease. Those two things mean they are a rather lustful group. There's no stigma attached to casual sex among wolf shifters and before Michaels, she had her fair share of partners. But after mating, everything changes. Mates only want each other, and the bond between them can be intense for the first few years. Even alphas know to give newly mated pairs plenty of space.

But the idea that Kade isn't her mate never occurred to her. His scent was so intoxicating in that dream, she didn't question the impulse to create a mating bond with him. Now she faces the stark reality of having a mate that isn't a wolf and can't bond back. And what's worse, he's not bothered at all by his inability or unwillingness to mate.

But sex is still on the table. She's not sure how she feels about that.

"Of course, shifters have sex for fun," she answers, trying to keep her voice from sounding grumpy.

"Then I'll keep my scent masked so you don't need to be burdened with a one-sided mating. And perhaps in the future, you'll decide to enjoy intimacy with me," he tells her. "Don't worry. I'm not interested in an unwilling partner. You can come to me if you ever wish. Otherwise, I'll be your alpha and employer only."

"Thank you?" Emma's not sure how to take that little speech. The alpha bond is warm in her chest, but his words are cold and formal.

"It's important you don't think this is more than it is," he states bluntly. "I'm a mage. We don't take mates. We don't fall in love. Pining after such things will only make you miserable."

Those words are like a splash of cold water. She schools her face to remain neutral, but Kade can feel her emotions through the bond. One of his eyebrows wings up, and the corners of his mouth turn down.

"And now I've hurt your feelings," he mutters with impatience. He stares at her for a few moments, and she drops her gaze politely. He makes a displeased sound, so she looks up to meet his eyes again. Right, he isn't a wolf. Signs of submission like dropping her gaze aren't pleasing to him.

"Better," he comments as he pulses warmth through the bond, making the stiffness in her shoulders ease. "I'm not trying to hurt you; I just want to make everything clear between us. No false hope, no assumptions."

"Everything is crystal clear," she assures him. She's just going to set all of this aside. Later she'll think about it. Later she'll debate having sex with the gorgeous mage and potentially risking her heart. For right now, she's going to concentrate on being a good submissive wolf to her new alpha. That's a much easier assignment.

Mrs. Cooke comes bustling back in with his card and a small bag. "Here's the other item you requested," she says, handing it to him.

"Ah, perfect." He reaches into the bag and pulls out a jewelry box. Opening it up, he withdraws a necklace and drops the box back into the bag.

He holds the necklace in his palm for a moment and closes his eyes. Emma can feel power coming off him in a short sharp wave, and then he opens his eyes and smiles at her.

"Turn your back, and lift your hair off your neck," he orders. When she does, he drapes the piece of jewelry around her neck and secures it. It's a choker-style necklace, so she can't see it, but the weight of it is heavy and she can feel power pulsing out of it.

Pressure on her shoulders has her turning to see a deeply satisfied expression. "Never take that off. Do you understand me, Emma?"

"Yes, Alpha," she responds, the title an automatic response to the order.

With a sigh, he gives her a gentle smile. "I guess I deserved that. The necklace is for your protection. It makes sure no one can sever the alpha bond between us. And it'll make it easier for me to find you if we get separated."

She runs her fingers over the piece of jewelry. "Thank you, Kade."

"I also tuned it to you, so it will help you focus when you're stitching. Later we'll make you several more so you can have some variety, but for now, never remove this one."

The protective aspect of the necklace hits her submissive wolf hard, making her want to burrow against him and lick at his mouth. He must have felt the need in her through their bond because his smile widens. He grabs the back of her neck and pulls her in close. Although there's no scent for her to rub all over herself, she still revels in the warm, solid feel of him.

"Your wolf is happy. Isn't she?"

"Very." Then her stomach growls loudly enough to make Mrs. Cooke chuckle.

He lets go of her neck and takes half a step back. Taking her hand, he twines his fingers with hers.

"Well, now that you look the part, let's go get you some food."

"Look what part?" Emma asks, feeling a little thrown by the quick withdrawal of his warm body from hers. She tightens her grip, wanting more but willing to settle for this.

"You look like you belong to a mage now," he elaborates. "We are an elitist group." He's downright cheerful as he tells her this, obviously unconcerned at how pompous he sounds. "We still need to deal with your hair, but that can wait until we're back home. I know just the place to take you."

His words make her self-conscious. Reaching up, she feels the loose bun she twined her hair into, holding it in place with an old pencil.

"If I may," Mrs. Cooke says, stepping forward. "Give me just a minute and I can get rid of that pencil."

With a nod, Kade lets Mrs. Cooke approach but doesn't let go of Emma's hand. Out of the pocket of her suit jacket, Mrs. Cooke pulls a small brush.

"Lean over a little," she requests. Soon she's brushing and tugging at Emma's hair. When she's finished, an ornate stick holds half of it up in a similar bun as before, but now the rest of her hair cascades down her shoulder and back.

"Artful disarray. It's in style right now," Mrs. Cooke assures her.

"I can see why," Kade murmurs. "It looks like she just got up from being tumbled."

Blushing, Emma decides she's had enough. "Food," she growls out.

"As my wolf wishes," Kade says gallantly with a knowing grin and leads her away.

Just like the clothing and the food, the hotel he directs her to looks expensive and haughty. To their credit, none of the staff blink an eye when she gets out of the car. Maybe it's the new clothes, but more likely it's the commanding presence of Kade as he effortlessly directs the staff to see to their needs.

In short order, they're ensconced in a luxurious suite with an amazing view. It doesn't escape her notice that the large room has only one bed. It looks to be king-size, but still, only one. She's not against having sex with her new alpha, but a girl likes to be asked first.

"Take off as many clothes as you're comfortable with and get on the bed," he instructs the moment they're alone in the room.

Staring at him, she tries for the same raised eyebrow look he's given her. "That's not very romantic."

Giving her a puzzled frown, he tilts his head. She dips her head to indicate the bed.

"One bed?"

He regards the bed and then makes an impatient sound. "Your room is next door. I wouldn't be so presumptuous," he tells her, nodding toward a connecting door.

She glances over and feels mildly disappointed. She wouldn't ever want to be forced to have sex, but taking it entirely off the table isn't what she wants either, damn it! She's still eyeing the door when he speaks again.

"Now if we're done with the sophomoric humor, I'd like to focus on something of value. You need to practice stitching," he explains. "And we can't do that awake. You can keep all your clothes on and lie on the floor if you wish."

Understanding his intentions, she takes a seat on the bed and pulls off her boots followed by the suit jacket. Feeling more comfortable, she lies back on the bed and then gives a little surprised gasp when he settles down next to her.

"I'm going to drop you into a dream state. In the future you'll learn how to do that yourself. For now, I'll do it for you." He stretches out on his side and puts his arm around her waist to pull her flush against him. She gives a little squeak of protest, which he hushes as he makes himself comfortable.

Ordering her body to relax, she tries not to think about how nice he feels pressed against her. Taking a deep breath in through her nose, she just barely keeps from growling when she only smells the clean sheets on the bed. As far as smell goes, he might as well not be in the room with her.

The lack of smell doesn't seem to calm her libido, though. She's still very aware of his large masculine body taking up a great deal of space on the bed. Wolf shifters, like bear shifters, are large in their human forms, so the fact that he's a proper fit for her only makes her wolf want him more, even if he doesn't smell.

"Close your eyes," he orders, making her focus on the task at hand. Once she shuts her eyes, his arm leaves her middle and his fingers touch her forehead. After a moment of blackness, the world changes.

Suddenly, she's on her cliff again.

Taking a deep breath, she sighs out a joyful sound. She's gotten to spend more time in her favorite place in the dream world over the last few days than she has in the real world in the last three years combined.

A large body takes shape next to her. "Why am I not surprised at the setting?" Kade comments.

"It's the best place," she responds unapologetically.

"Do you ever dream of other places?" he asks casually as butterflies flutter around them.

"Only when I have nightmares," she admits.

"Well, we need to work on that. I have a feeling you wouldn't want to invite strangers to this special place. And honestly, it doesn't sit well with me either. I need you to think of a place you've been and can remember very well. It would help if you liked it, but feeling neutral about it is fine as well. Don't use anything too personal, like the home you grew up in. Those kinds of places can be used against you much too easily."

Running through places in her head, she dismisses most of them until she remembers the botanical gardens. She and her mother would visit them every year until Alpha Michaels took over the pack. She has nothing but pleasant memories of the place but nothing with heavy emotion.

"I think I have a place," she answers.

"Good. Now close your eyes and picture the place. Build it step by step in your mind. Start with what the ground under you should look like. The final thing I want you to do is to picture yourself there. Understand?"

"Sure." She's already closed her eyes and concentrates on building her favorite spot at the gardens in her head. The stone paths under her, the wooden benches, the fragrant bushes, and the pond with koi fish flashing around the water lilies.

"You astound me, little wolf," Kade murmurs, and she opens her eyes to find they're now sitting on a bench in the Japanese area of the botanical garden. Pulling in a deep breath, he looks at her with wonder. "I can smell the flowers."

He's smiling with approval until he sees what she's wearing. His expression turns appalled, and he slowly shakes his head in disapproval. "What are you wearing?"

Looking down, she finds she's dressed in a pair of old jeans and a faded t-shirt. She plucks at the familiar shirt and frowns. Of course, she knows the reason for his dismay, but this opportunity is too good to pass up. Raising her eyes to his, she gives a small shrug and a half smile.

"Clothing," she answers impertinently. "Would overalls be better?"

One corner of his mouth tilts up, and his eyes flash with amusement but only briefly. His face resumes a condemning expression, and he tugs at the sleeve of her shirt.

"It's unacceptable. That's what it is. And you know it, little wolf. You need to change your attire. Picture what you were wearing earlier today. That's more appropriate. Remember, I'll be meeting fellow mages and clients. You need to look professional."

With a sigh, Emma closes her eyes and pictures the outfit he requests. When she opens her eyes, she's wearing the suit. "Better," he says with approval.

"Snob," she mutters.

"Probably," he agrees, and she flushes, realizing he heard her insult. It's never good form to insult your alpha.

He must feel her inner criticism through the pack bond because he pulses reassurance to her. "Be calm, little wolf. I'm not a child to be upset at such minor offenses." She breathes a little easier with those words.

"Thank you, Al—Kade." Although she catches herself just in time, he smiles knowingly.

"Now, let's work on the next step—dealing with a stranger in your realm." He closes his eyes, mumbles a few things to himself, and then opens them up again. "I've issued an invitation. He should be here shortly."

Before Emma can ask who's coming, a young man wearing a business suit strolls into the garden. He's about as tall as Emma, but much broader, and doesn't have the violet eyes of a mage. Emma takes a sniff but can't smell anything coming off the man. No smell along with no obvious physical indicators means she can't figure out what type of magic creature he is.

He's smiling and looking around with interest. He seems harmless enough, but Emma knows better than to judge by appearance alone. If only he had a scent, she could figure out if she should be wary or not. The dreams she always created were full of smells, but now that she's stitching, it appears guests need to create their smell or nothing is there. To a wolf shifter, there's nothing so annoying as lacking the ability to scent things.

Stifling a growl of frustration, she plasters on a welcoming smile and waits for the man to reach them.

"This is truly amazing, Kade," he comments as he strolls up to them, stopping once he's reached the bench that faces theirs. His smile widens when he sees Emma. "And it only gets better. Hello, beautiful. My name's Daniel."

"Mine," Kade tells him in a congenial tone. He wraps an arm around Emma's shoulders and draws her against him. "You're here to help her train, not flirt. Leave my staff alone."

Daniel raises an eyebrow. "Staff, huh? Then she's available to hire?" Daniel switches his gaze to hers and beams. "Your stitching is exemplary. I know I could take full advantage of your talents." His eyes roam her body as his face turns sensual.

Laughing at his blatant flirting, Emma decides she likes this man. He reminds her a lot of a couple of her packmates.

Or former packmates anyway.

"I don't think—" She starts to turn him down gently when Kade interrupts her, his voice cold and full of rebuke.

"She's mine exclusively," Kade answers for her. She turns her gaze to him just in time to see his eyes flash with power, startling her slightly. Daniel's smile doesn't waver. Instead, he ignores Kade's obvious attempt to bar him from hiring her.

He gives her an unconcerned smile. "Can she not speak for herself? Tell me, pretty, did Kade make you sign one of those horrible contracts of his? He's always trying to snatch up the most talented for himself. Greedy bastard."

"Daniel," Kade makes the name into a warning, and the man finally takes his intense dark eyes off Emma and regards Kade with a cool expression.

"Yes, Kade?" Daniel's tone is mocking, and Emma winces. He must have caught her expression because he shifts his gaze to her and gives her a reassuring smile. "Don't worry about me, sweetness. Kade and I go way back. He knows I don't curb my tongue."

"Not so far back that I can't end you if you get annoying," Kade comments. The tension in his body belies his casual tone.

"Don't pretend that would be so easy," Daniel retorts, his smile dropping away. Iridescent turquoise flashes in Daniel's dark eyes, sending a bolt of fear through Emma.

"Jinn," Emma breaths. She tries to stand up so she can get away, but she's trapped by Kade's powerful arm around her.

"Don't be afraid, little wolf," Kade murmurs to her. "Daniel's one of the civilized ones."

"Hardly," Daniel mocks. "But I'm unlikely to just gobble you up, Stitcher. I'm too eager to hire you myself."

Shuddering with fear, Emma shakes her head. Her long canines and claws slide out, ready to fight. Her skin twitches as she keeps her fur from flowing over her. Even in a dream, her wolf reactions are dominant.

Kade tries to pulse reassurance through the bond, but he doesn't understand how dangerous the jinn are, so she ignores the comfort. She might have been ignorant of mages until she met Avery and Kade, but every wolf is taught to fear the jinn—for good reason.

They're known to eat the magic of others, but it's also believed that they trap souls and torture them for amusement. The only safe way to deal with a jinn is to steer clear of them.

Why the hell did Kade invite one into her dream? Sure, mages are powerful, but jinn are deadly. The rumor is that jinn young are set against each other, and only the winner gets to eat because he's allowed to consume the lives of the defeated children. And of course, everyone knows one of their favorite foods is wolf shifter.

Reacting to her distress, the dream around them gets dark as storm clouds cover the midday sun.

"Emma," Kade reprimands, bringing her attention back to him. "Calm yourself. Daniel can't do anything here unless you let him. Even if we were to meet on the physical plane, he won't hurt you. He comes from an old jinn lineage; he doesn't need to consume the magic of others to become more powerful."

"Wolf shifter?" Daniel asks Kade, his tone and expression neutral. He's no longer trying to be friendly or flirt. He's all business now.

"Yes," Kade answers absently as he pulses assurance through the bond again. Emma can't accept it; her wolf is too wound up. She needs to concentrate on the jinn. She needs to be ready to defend herself and her alpha.

"Damn it," Daniel curses. "I thought she was a bear. Kade, you don't know shit about wolf shifters."

The jinn's harsh words make Kade suck in a breath and scowl deeply. He opens his mouth, but Daniel cuts him off. "No, don't say anything. Just let me talk for a moment. Way back in the day, jinn would keep wolf packs close at hand for physical protection and a source of food in desperate times. Each year the pack would be forced to give someone up as a sacrifice to show their loyalty. It's been thousands of years, but wolves still have a ton of old stories about how we like to eat their bodies and keep their souls in little jars for our amusement."

Emma shoots Kade a look, but he's too busy frowning at Daniel to notice. He stops pulsing the bond. She watches the two of them interact, waiting for Kade to realize how deadly jinn are and take appropriate action.

"This is ridiculous," Kade states sourly. "Only the lesser jinn need to consume magic, and only the magic of another jinn is edible to them. Jinn don't eat shifters of any type."

"In reality, that's true," Daniel says, switching his eyes to Emma. She stares back at him, unblinking. He's not going to catch her unaware. "But we made a show of pretending to eat other creatures. It made us seem more ferocious."

His gaze locks to hers, his expression sincere. "We've never actually preyed on wolves, Emma. It was legend and dramatics. We needed the wolf packs to keep us safe from the efrit. The war with the efrit is long over, and we no longer use wolf packs for protection, but unfortunately, the stories still live on."

Correctly interpreting Emma's dubious expression, Daniel continues. "Aren't there stories among fox shifters that wolves like to capture and torture them, especially kits?"

Emma can't help but roll her eyes at that. "That's ridiculous," she huffs, making Daniel smile and raise an eyebrow.

"But you did it once, or at least your ancestors did, so there's some basis in reality for that fear," Daniel points out.

"I suppose," she agrees hesitantly, relaxing minutely. "But—"

Daniel gently cuts her off. "But we're different? In this regard, we're not. We both have ancestors who did less than savory things, but that doesn't reflect on the here and now. Can we at least agree to interact with calm civility? Besides, you probably aren't aware of this, but in school Kade routinely beat me up. He can keep you safe from me."

Making a sound of incredulity, Kade gives a little shake of his head. "I hardly think besting you twice can be referred to as routine," he counters.

"Still, until you joined our school, I was undefeated. You took that hard-earned title away," Daniel teases lightly. His charming smile returns, and Emma wants to believe Daniel isn't dangerous. At least not here in her dreamscape.

"I'm no threat to you, shifter. With or without Kade here to keep you safe, I won't attack you without provocation. I don't do things like that."

Determined to appear in control, Emma nods once and schools her expression into something similar to Kade's detached interest.

"We can all be civilized," she agrees. But then she can't help but add, "You stay over there though."

Those last words don't sound confident at all, and she doesn't like the amusement in Daniel's eyes. Slowly, he sits on a nearby bench, making a production of getting comfortable and trying to look harmless. At no point does he take his intense gaze off her.

To get the men's attention off of her, she points to the dark sky.

"I didn't ask for that," she explains and then gestures to Daniel. "Did he do that?"

"The only one with power here is you," Kade explains. "He's not influencing the sky. You are."

"But you made a storm happen in my other dream," she argues. "And you made the cliff collapse."

"Only because you let me. Here, let me demonstrate."

Kade focuses on the ground at their feet, and she feels a thrill of magic emanating from him as a rosebush grows in a bare patch of dirt. It doesn't look quite right, and when it blooms there's no scent. She barely has time to take in the mutant flower. The moment the rose opens, it begins turning brown and wilting.

"That's a horrible effort," Daniel notes, and Kade shoots him an annoyed glance.

"That's enough from someone who can't even create a blank room," Kade shoots back. Daniel holds up his hands in surrender and then folds them in his lap, molding his features to be pleasantly blank.

Kade turns his attention back to Emma. "Did you feel when I created that?"

"Yes, but how would I stop you?"

"Picture a giant invisible bubble around us. The bubble is your shield. Inside of it you control everything. Now try it." Emma focuses, and although nothing in the dreamscape visually changes, she can feel the pulsing shield all around them. The dying rose bush Kade grew denigrates to ash in the blink of an eye.

"Perfect," Kade compliments her. "Now you are in total control. No one can do anything without your express permission."

"Should I attempt to grow something?" Daniel asks. "Help her get a feel for different kinds of power?"

Kade nods head. "That's—"

"Why doesn't Daniel have a smell?" Emma blurts out, making both Daniel and Kade stare at her.

"Does that bother you?" Daniel asks, surprise coloring his voice.

"Everything should have a smell," Emma insists. "If I could have scented you, I'd have known you were a jinn right away."

Comprehension dawns on Daniel's face. "Ah, shifter. Your kind is so very smell-oriented. Now I understand why this dream smells so rich. I don't know that I've ever been in a dream realm that included smell. Emma, your talent is quite impressive."

Still mildly wary of the jinn but flattered nonetheless, she gives him a tentative smile. "Thank you." Feeling more at ease, she takes a seat across from him.

"When your contract with Kade is done, there's a lot of freelance work you can do. I know stitchers who aren't half as good as you but make six-figure incomes."

Her jaw drops. "What?"

Both men chuckle at her expression. She watches Daniel concentrate for a moment; then a new scent hits her nose. Curious, she stands and takes half a step toward him, letting the smell curl through her brain. He smells like jinn, but more. Uncomfortable being that close, she backs away and retakes her seat, even though she didn't have a chance to parse out his scent.

"I'm probably the first full-blooded jinn you've ever smelled," he explains and then turns his attention to Kade. "Where did you find her, and how did you talk her alpha into letting her work with you?"

"He's my alpha," Emma says without thinking, still too caught up in figuring out the nuances of Daniel's smell.

The jinn makes a choking sound. "He's what now?"

"He's my alpha," she repeats, assuming the jinn heard something different, which is causing his startled reaction.

Her guess must be wrong because Daniel looks at her and back at Kade a few times with an incredulous expression. "Kade the loner is alpha of a pack?"

"A tiny pack," Kade acknowledges with a self-satisfied grin. He sits down next to her and lays a proprietary hand on the back of her neck. "The only one in my pack is this little wolf. I was forced to dispatch her former alpha, and she didn't handle the breaking of the bond well. Besides, she gave herself to me in exchange for her brother's life. She's mine until I'm done with her."

Pointedly gazing at the surrounding dreamscape, Daniel turns his gaze back to Kade. "So that means never?"

Both men chuckle at his words, making Emma feel uncomfortable. Being a member of a pack and helpful to the alpha is one thing, but being talked about as though she's a commodity is something else entirely. Kade must have noticed her unease because he drapes an arm around her shoulders and draws her in close.

"Easy, little wolf," he whispers to her. "Daniel and I don't mean anything by our banter."

"I'm fine," she fibs. His expression clearly shows he's doesn't believe her. He graces her with a gentle smile.

"You will be," Kade promises. "The longer you're with me the more stable you'll feel. Don't worry, Emma. Your place in our little pack is secure. And you'll come to realize I'm not abusive like your last alpha. I can make sure you're well-situated in this world. You could even end up with a hoard, just like a dragon shifter."

Snorting at that, Emma grins. "Wolves don't crave wealth like dragons do. We think of our pack as our treasure, but thanks for the thought."

"If you two are done cavorting, I have other things I could be doing with my time." There's no bite to Daniel's tone, only a slight teasing note.

"Of course." Kade pulls away, and Emma immediately misses his warmth. "Please attempt to grow something so Emma can get the feel for intruding magic. Then we'll work on twisting her dreamscape so she knows how to keep them stable even when someone puts a lot of power into damaging it."

Because there's no sense of time in dreams, Emma has no idea how long the three of them spend practicing. At some point during the training, her fear of Daniel evaporates. His subtle humor, quick wit, and absolute lack of deference to Kade makes her laugh repeatedly as both of them help her refine her stitching skills.

When they practice growing wings, her lack of fear is most evident. She gets close enough to laughingly tug at Daniel's giant crow wings in mock outrage as she struggles with creating her own.

Daniel teases her unmercifully and then praises her enthusiastically when she's finally able to coax beautiful yellow and blue butterfly wings out of her back. In his usual fashion, Kade tells her she's progressing adequately, but she can feel his delight at her skills through the bond.

Eventually, Daniel declares he really can't devote any more time to practice. His words make Emma feel genuine regret.

"Thank you for helping," she says truthfully. He holds his hand out for a typical human handshake, and Emma doesn't even hesitate to take it. The moment their skin touches she feels a flash of power move through her and her body freezes in place.

Now we can talk, Daniel's voice sounds in her head. *Don't worry. Kade can't hear us like this, but we only have a moment. I can't freeze your perfect dreamscape for very long.*

Panic fills Emma. *What are you doing? Let me go!*

I just want to make sure you're under Kade's dominance willingly, sweetness. Tell me. Do you need to be rescued. If it's money, you can make your own without Kade. I can help broker deals. If he's threatening you, just tell me. I can whisk you away to a safe spot. Daniel's voice is gentle, but that doesn't lessen her dismay at his actions.

It's none of those things. He's my alpha, and we made a pact, Emma tells him stubbornly. *And it's none of your business. Now stop this. Let me go. Let him go. Undo what you're doing!*

Very well, Daniel's tone is resigned. *I hope for your sake your faith isn't misplaced. But if you ever need me again, just call me into your dream. You'll be able to find me now.*

A familiar broad hand grips her wrist, parting her hand from Daniel's hold.

"Did you think that would work here? I have an alpha bond with her, Daniel," Kade growls out and violently flings Daniel into the air. Kade laces his fingers with hers and then draws her slightly behind him. "I hardly think it's necessary to steal my wolf away."

Daniel doesn't tumble to the ground from being flung. Instead, he swoops gracefully through the air, landing gently on his feet. With a wry smile, Daniel regards Kade.

"Sorry about that, my friend. I just needed to be sure."

"I understand the impulse behind it, especially considering what Matheus does. But, Daniel, it's an insult to think I'd be like him."

"You know as well as I do that Matheus might be extreme among mages, but his inclinations aren't unusual." The jinn's voice is full of censure. "You should be glad I'm around to keep you in check."

"I could say the same thing to you," Kade retorts. Daniel gives Kade a curt nod and then turns a genuine smile on Emma.

"I believe I've outstayed my welcome," Daniel tells her. "Remember to contact me if you need anything, Emma. It's not a trap. Unlike mages, we jinn don't look for reciprocity in everything. We believe in balance, good deeds, and all that."

"Don't believe him, wolf," Kade tells her, derision heavy in his voice. "Full-blooded jinn might not be interested in eating the magic of others, but they're still willing to use you in any way they can."

For a moment, real sadness shows on Daniel's face before he covers it with a pleasant smile.

"I'm sorry you think so," he murmurs to Kade. And then he's gone. She stares at the place he stood for a moment, feeling horribly unsettled.

"Let's go to your cliff for a little while," Kade murmurs to her, drawing her into his arms and hugging her. She burrows against him, just like she would another shifter offering her comfort. Her submissive wolf is seeking solace from a dominant packmate.

"Yes, please," she agrees readily. Visiting some place familiar and soothing is irresistible, even if it's only a recreation.

As the garden disappears, replaced with her cliff and ocean, she breathes in the salty air and thinks about Daniel's words. She's just a lowly wolf without a real pack, and she's mixed up with some very powerful creatures

If Kade abandons her, his world could swallow her whole, and no one would be capable of saving her.

They spend the next day driving back to Kade's home outside Monterey Bay. When Emma pictured his house on a cliff, she never imagined the massive sleek structure of glass and steel that rises before them as she guides the SUV up the winding driveway. When she brings the vehicle to a halt, she doesn't get out. She can't. All she's capable of doing for several minutes is staring at the house open mouthed.

"It's just a house, Emma," Kade comments dryly.

"It might be just a house to you," she retorts. "But it looks like a museum to me. Is that a pool or square pond?"

"It's called an infinity pool. It's for swimming, but I don't think anyone's ever used it."

"You live here?" she breathes.

Tired of her gawking, he gets out and looks back at her with impatience. "Of course. Now come along."

A small, thin man rushes out of the house, obviously relieved to see Kade. "*Signore* Allard, *come va*? I'm so glad to see you safe. You disappeared so suddenly with no word about where you were going. That's unusual for you, *signore*." He looks like he's about to hug Kade but stops himself at the last minute and wraps his arms around his chest in a kind of self-hug. When he sees Emma, at first he looks startled; then his eyes narrow in suspicion. When he speaks again, it's in rapid Italian. "*Ma chi e questo?*"

"*Calmati*, Franco. *Lei none e un teatrino.*" Kade responds in Italian and then switches to English for her benefit. "She's my wolf."

"I'm Emma," she introduces herself, hoping to smile past his suspicions. But her smile doesn't have the desired effect at all. The small man looks shaken and turns accusing eyes on Kade.

"A wolf?" the man squeaks. "*Lupi! Non va bene. Non va bene per niente! I lupi sono pericolosi,* Kade*!"*

Whatever he's saying sounds like a demand, probably an appeal for Kade to send her away. His tone and body language are panicky. When she shifts her body a little, he gives a skittish jerk, ready to run away from her.

Occasionally, humans will react this strongly to a shifter, but it's rare. Shifters are one of the most common magical creatures, and they blend in well with human communities. She tries to catch his scent to see if he's human or something else, but the wind is going in the wrong direction. She'd have to get closer to get a scent, but she doesn't want to upset this man any more than he already is.

"She isn't dangerous," Kade tells him grimly, giving Emma insight into what the Italian said. "Have I ever done anything but keep you safe? You need to set your fears aside. She's staying. And don't be rude, speak in English so Emma can understand what we are discussing."

Drawing himself up to his full height, which is still significantly shorter than she is, he looks up to Kade with imploring eyes. "*Signore* Allard, you can't do this to me."

"You can leave if you feel you need to," Kade tells him. His words are firm but not harsh. "I'd hate to lose you, my friend, but that's a decision you're going to have to make because, as I said, she is staying. Besides, she's not going to eat you. That's an old myth."

"I don't know if that's true. Maybe he's tasty," Emma teases, but instead of calming the stranger, her quip makes the man stumble back a few paces and pale. Feeling horrible, she steps forward and holds her hands palms out in a calming gesture. "I'm sorry. That was a joke. I didn't mean it. I don't eat anything that doesn't come out of the grocery store. Well, maybe the occasional rabbit that crosses my path, but that's it. I'd never hurt anyone for any reason but self-defense or defense of my pack."

"Stay away from me," Franco hisses. The vehemence of his sentence makes Emma frown and stop moving. Kade moves forward, grabbing the man's arm to keep him still, and then leans over to whisper in the man's ear. Whatever he's saying is calming Franco, but he still stares at Emma with distrust.

"*Allora, Signore* Allard," Franco says stiffly. "*Signora* Martin, if you will follow me, I'll show you to your room."

"Let me just get my stuff," Emma says, but Kade stops her from moving.

"Franco will see that your things are taken to your room," he tells her. "Go with him. Make yourself familiar with my house, and then I'll show you the grounds. And, Emma, no more jokes." He leans in to whisper in her ear now. "Franco's a fae-human mix. Your kind used to hunt his ancestors. I know you'll behave, but perhaps no more jokes about eating him."

Blanching, memories of her interaction with Daniel fill her head, and she feels horribly guilty. "No more jokes," she agrees. Kade gives her a half smile and strides off to disappear into the house.

"Come with me," Franco says, his body rigid and his tone cold.

"Should I call you Franco?" she asks as she follows him into the house and up a flight of stairs. Just like the outside, everything inside is bright and minimalist. "Or should I call you mister something?"

"You can call me Franco if you desire," he says, not giving an inch.

"What would you like me to call you? You can call me Emma."

"You may call me anything you wish, *Signora* Martin." He emphasizes her last name, a clear message that he's not interested in becoming friends. She's not daunted. He's reacting badly because he's afraid and probably feels like his space is being encroached upon. Soon he'll understand that she's not a threat to his position or relationship with Kade.

"How long have you worked for Kade?" she asks as Franco leads her down a long hall. One side of the hallway is nothing but glass, showcasing a view of the nearby cliff and the ocean beyond.

"I've been employed by Kade for a while," Franco answers evasively. Abruptly, he stops and turns. If not for her shifter speed, Emma would've run into him. "He has my complete loyalty."

"That's good," Emma says quickly, trying to keep her smile in place in the face of Franco's scowl. "Loyalty is important to him. He said that's why he picked me—because I'm loyal."

That doesn't appear to mollify Franco at all. "Just keep in mind, I'd do anything for *Signore* Allard. Anything!"

"Then getting along with me should be easy," Emma counters, and that seems to thoroughly confuse Franco.

"*Cosa intendi?*" She doesn't understand the words, but his puzzled expression is enough to tell her that he's asking what she meant by that statement.

"I mean, if you're willing to do anything, and by that I'm guessing you're including murder or maybe ritual sacrifice, then making friends with one amiable wolf shifter can't be all that hard. My poor taste in jokes aside, I make a pretty good friend." She's not sure, but she thinks his lips might have tried to smile before he catches himself.

"*Tieni le mani a posto,*" Franco instructs after a beat of silence. "That means don't touch anything. *Signore* likes things in just a certain way, and I don't want you to dirty anything."

Holding up her hands to show him they're clean, she nods. "I promise to shower regularly and only touch the things I absolutely have to."

With a disapproving sniff, Franco turns and continues to lead her down the hall. She absently wonders if he's part of her pack now too. If he is, at least he's just particular and not cruel. Someone with a little obsessive-compulsive disorder beats sadistic murdering bastards any day.

Her room turns out to be large and airy. Just like the hallway, one wall is made up almost entirely of windows with an ocean view. The floor is hardwood, but most of it is covered in plush rugs that muffle their footsteps.

Pointing to a door, Franco eyes her rumpled clothes. "This is your bathroom. I'll bring your items up next. Perhaps you'd like to freshen up." By the tone of his voice, she can tell he doesn't approve of her appearance. He's dressed in black slacks and a dark green button-up shirt. His dark hair is neatly styled, and his face is free of any kind of scruff. It's obvious, like Kade, appearance is important to this man. It's also obvious that at the moment, she's falling short.

Determined not to let him annoy her, she grins and plucks at her wrinkled shirt. "There was a lot of traffic, so it was a long drive to get here," she explains. "A shower sounds good."

Franco gives her a half nod of approval. "You will find basic toiletries and towels in your bathroom."

He turns to leave, but she stops him with a hand on his arm. When he hisses and jumps back, she holds up her hands, palms out to show him she didn't mean anything by her touch.

"Sorry about that," she says quickly, shoving her hand behind her back and taking a small step back. His reaction might be overboard, but then again, something in his past might have put him off being touched by strangers. No matter what, she shouldn't have done that.

She schools her expression into one of apology. "I won't do that again. I just wanted to ask a question."

"Ask," he spits out. His arms are across his chest, and his expression is more annoyed than angry.

"Do you have a phone here? A landline? There's a few—"

"No," he cuts her off, and she sees satisfaction in his eyes at being able to deny her something. "*Signore* Allard doesn't have a landline, only cellphones. And before you ask, you can't use mine. You'll have to ask *signore. Si?*"

"Right, no problem," she says hesitantly. He glares at her for a moment and then turns on his heel and starts to the door. She can't just let him leave without saying something, so she talks quickly. Her words make him pause in the open doorway.

"I know what it's like," she says to his rigid back. "I know what it's like to have someone touch you without permission. I know what it's like to be helpless. I'm sorry if I made you feel that way."

"You didn't," he responds defiantly without turning around. His voice might say he's unaffected by her words, but the tension in his shoulder eases slightly. When he speaks next, his tone is notably softer. "I'll return shortly with your things." With that, he leaves. Emma lets out a long sigh as she watches him disappear. So much for making friends.

The bathroom turns out to be luxurious, with a massive clawfoot tub at one end and a glass-enclosed shower at the other. Feeling decadent, she takes a long hot shower, enjoying the almost scentless soaps provided. Reluctantly, she finishes her shower, already thinking about spending the evening stretched out in the tub. She even finds candles as she pulls out various lotions and other toiletries from the bathroom cabinets. When she discovers a glass bottle of bubble bath, she has to stifle a groan.

"I might never leave the bathroom," she murmurs to herself, setting the candles and bubble bath next to the tub. "Later," she tells the tub. "You and I are going to have a date."

Wrapped in a fluffy bathrobe, she pads out of the bathroom to find all her things piled on and around the bed. She's still shocked at the amount of clothing Kade purchased for her.

Taking her time, she puts everything away, enjoying the unusual experience of having such an extravagant wardrobe. Before Alpha Michaels made her quit her job, she worked at the front desk of a medical office. Because she wore a uniform, she never had any reason to buy a bunch of nice outfits and no money to spare for impractical, fancy clothing.

As she puts everything away, she finds a handwritten note from Franco telling her dinner will be served "promptly at 6 p.m." The threat is clear, latecomers don't get fed.

Dressing in a pair of jeans, boots, and an emerald-colored sleeveless silk blouse, she leaves her hair loose to dry. Surprisingly, she doesn't find a hairdryer among all the items in the bathroom, only some styling gels and combs. Now dressed and groomed—well, as groomed as she can be without access to a hairdryer—she looks around her spacious room. What to do next? It's only one in the afternoon, so she has plenty of time to explore the house and grounds before dinner.

Franco pointed out Kade's room earlier, so she doesn't go poking in there, but she looks in every other door she comes across. The upstairs has two more bedrooms besides hers and Kade's. Wandering through them, she finds them almost exactly like her room, both with attached baths and only slightly smaller than hers. Having explored the upstairs, she wanders downstairs and finds a den full of comfortable furniture and an empty fireplace. She could see sitting in front of that fireplace during a winter storm, rain battering the outside of the house while the inside is warm and merry.

The next room she peeks into is an office. Kade is at his desk, scowling and talking rapidly on his phone. Intimidated by that scowl, Emma silently backs away from that door and continues exploring.

Everything in the house screams refinement and wealth. There isn't a single family or personal photograph anywhere. Perfectly lit oil paintings dominate most of the walls that aren't made out of glass.

Emma can appreciate the beauty of the art on display, but the lack of photos anywhere is disconcerting. Like most shifters, wolves live for their family and community. Her mother covered the walls of their home with photographs of family and friends. There might be family photos artfully hung somewhere else, but Emma guesses that's unlikely.

There aren't any shelves full of knickknacks and dust catchers. Display cases hold various objects that she can only assume are rare and valuable. A few shelves are even full of first-edition books that look much too delicate to read. Nothing here feels personal. As she walks from room to room, she wonders if the lack of photos and personal touches is because of the house's aesthetic or because of Kade.

While looking for the kitchen, the beating heart of any house, Emma hears items falling along with a panicked cry. Without hesitation she bounds toward the sound and bursts into the very room she's looking for.

Inside the kitchen, Franco is perched precariously on a stepstool, trying to keep hold of a large crystal vase while other items fall from the cabinet above him. He is teetering and cries out again as he loses his balance, clutching the large vase to his chest.

Few creatures out there are faster than shifters, so Emma is able to cross the room and catch him before his feet even leave the stepstool. He's an average-sized human, which puts him a few inches shorter than Emma and significantly lighter.

With ease, she plucks him off the stepstool and deposits him on the ground. Then she catches the rest of the falling items as they come tumbling out of the cabinet, setting them down on the counter next to her in the order she catches them. Once she's sure nothing else is going to fall, she turns her attention to Franco.

He's trembling slightly, still clutching the vase to his chest and watching her with wide eyes.

"*Mannaggia a Me*, you're so fast," he breathes out.

She gives him a smile without showing teeth and realizes she's standing right next to him. Wanting to make sure he feels safe, she takes a step back to give the fae-mix a little more room. The last thing she wants to do is make the Italian man feel boxed in or threatened.

"My kind usually are. Are you okay?"

"I think so," he says hesitantly and then looks down at the items that fell before Emma came on the scene. "This is horrible. *Un disastro!*" he fusses. "Those were Baccarat!"

Idly Emma wonders if Baccarat refers to the shape of the crystal goblets or who made them. Or maybe Baccarat is a type of crystal? She's woefully out of her depth in this world, but it doesn't bother her. As far as she's concerned, elaborate manners and protocol were all created by people with too much time on their hands. They serve no real purpose in a pack or the real world.

Besides, it's not as if either Kade or Franco won't be quick to correct her if she does something wrong. So why worry about what she doesn't know until it's an actual problem?

At her feet, the expensive goblets are nothing more than glittery rubbish. "I can help clean up if you like," Emma offers.

The proposal must remind Franco that he doesn't like her. His spine snaps straight, and he sets the vase he's been clutching down gently on the counter next to all the goblets she caught.

"Your assistance isn't required," he informs her coldly, making her eyebrows rise at his sudden change in demeanor. And here she thought things might thaw between them, considering she saved him from a nasty fall.

Deciding to give one last go at friendly overtures, she looks around the kitchen. "Where's the broom? I'm a good sweeper. I can get this cleaned up in no time."

The repeated offer appears to puzzle Franco, and his haughty expression slips a little as his forehead wrinkles.

"*Alora*, it's fine," he mutters. "Just go. I'll clean, and then I must call in to see if they can find any more of the Harcourt Empire pattern. I don't think Baccarat makes them anymore. What a disaster."

Not moving immediately, Emma eyes the high cupboard and then the wobbly stepstool.

She nods to the glasses on the counter. "Maybe I should put those back for you."

To her surprise, Franco huffs out a laugh. "Are all your kind this stubborn?" he asks. "I told you to go. I'll take of all this."

"Sure, I'm leaving," she says without moving. "Just let me put those back, and I'm out of here." Without waiting for his response, she grabs a handful of glasses and steps on the first rung of the stool. It takes no time for her to place the glasses back safely. Franco watches her like a hawk the whole time.

Stepping off the stool, she eyes the thing distrustfully. There's no doubt in her mind that the Italian will try to use it again and put himself in danger.

"I'll just take this with me," she announces as she folds it up and carries it out of the kitchen with her.

"*Mannaggia lupa!* Bad wolf, bring that back!" he calls out.

"No!" she shouts over her shoulder. "Make Kade buy you a better one."

She hears an annoyed huff and then something that sounds like a chuckle before she's out of the house. If he's going to act like a curmudgeonly old wolf, she's going to deal with him the same way she would deal with an elderly, grouchy pack member.

Even though Franco doesn't come running after her to retrieve his stool, she breaks it into several pieces once she's clear of the front door. Walking around the house, she finds a trash bin and ends up needing to break it into even smaller pieces to fit them inside.

Satisfied that her work is done, Emma turns to survey the estate grounds.

Except for the areas immediately around the house, it appears Kade has left his property to grow naturally. Native bushes, shrubs, and plants extend out with several dirt walking paths winding through the beautiful area. She takes the path that follows the cliff's edge. If she keeps following it, she'll end up in the nearby woods. Interested in exploring her new territory, she starts walking.

After hiking the perimeter of Kade's property, Emma settles herself on a wooden bench at the cliff's edge to watch the sea below. This spot, so much like her own in Oregon, is comforting, and she quickly loses herself in happy memories.

That's where Kade finds her, lost in thought with a small smile on her face. Whatever magic he's using to mask his scent also muffles his movement, so she's unaware of his presence until he's looming over her. Looking up, she flinches at the dark figure blotting out the sun. It only takes her a split second to recognize his large presence. That feeling of relief doesn't last long because the scowl on his face is downright alarming. What the hell did she do wrong now?

Rearing away from him, she scrambles to her feet and waits silently to see what he's going to do.

A puzzled expression crosses his face at her reaction, and then he goes blank. "Come with me," he orders briskly. "I need your stitcher skills immediately." Turning, he strides away, anger still radiating off of him. *What put him in such a foul mood?*

She jogs to catch up. Tentatively, she tests the bond between them and finds he's mostly blocked himself off from her. The only thing she can feel is a vague agitation that doesn't seem entirely focused on her. If she's not causing his mood, perhaps she can cheer him up.

"I'm just wondering why mages don't just use phones," she comments with forced casualness as she matches her stride to his. It must be hard for humans to keep up with this tall, quick-footed mage.

Giving her an inscrutable look, he doesn't slow his pace. "Phones are problematic when you're as powerful as we are. Any technology is. If I need to talk to someone else who's powerful, like another mage, jinn, or an ancient vampire, our magic tries to reach out to each other. It's almost impossible to control, even with shielding. Meeting in a dream realm allows us to talk and exchange information without burning out several phones or computers in the process."

"So no Skype, Zoom, or Facetime for you guys," she teases and is rewarded when he gives her a brief half smile.

"I can use those features, but not with other powerful creatures."

"Speaking of tech," she segues. "Do I get paid? Because I'd like an advance so I can buy a new phone."

Unexpectedly, he comes to a dead stop, and she ends up striding several lengths ahead of him before stopping and turning around to look at him inquiringly.

"What's the holdup? Aren't you in a big rush?" she asks with a cheeky grin. She's had good luck cheering people up in the past with her mildly disrespectful humor, so she goes with what she knows. "Or are we going to lie down and stitch here?" She looks pointedly down at the dirt path and the brush-covered ground around them. "It doesn't look inviting. Can I stitch as a wolf? The ground would be much more comfortable if I can shift into wolf form."

"Don't be ridiculous," he spits out, telling her the humor didn't hit its mark with the prickly mage. "We aren't lying down anywhere but in appropriately clean and furnished areas. I want to know why you need a phone."

Now it's her turn to be thrown off. That's not a question she expects him to ask.

"To call my parents and a few of my old packmates." Her answer doesn't placate him at all.

"They aren't your pack," he answers imperiously. "You shouldn't have any further concerns for them. I'm your pack. I'm your only concern now."

Cocking an eyebrow at his vehemence, Emma answers with caution. "I know that, Alpha. But I'd like to check in to make sure they're okay. You snapped Michaels' bonds pretty violently. Some might have suffered ill effects from it."

"I did all of them a favor," he announces, crossing his arms over his chest. "And I only took you after I defeated Michaels. By wolf shifter law I could claim the pack's entire coffers, including communal property, but I didn't. I informed the remaining pack to congregate and decide how to distribute the pack's wealth."

That's welcome news because many of the pack members lived in houses owned by the pack. "That's very generous—" He cuts her off before she can finish thanking him.

"I don't need your pack's paltry possessions," he announces pompously.

Shifting her eyes to take in his house in the distance, she can't help but mutter, "Yeah, our stuff doesn't go with your snob style."

"I'm not a snob. I'm discerning," he shoots back, following her eyes to view his house. "Considering the house I found you in, I wouldn't expect you to know the difference."

Eyes narrowing, she meets his gaze full on. "Ouch," she states in a dry, even tone. "You wound me with your scorn." Popping her hands on her hips, she meets his eyes with a challenging expression. "You won't let me contact Jason or Avery. You don't want me talking to my parents or my old pack. What the hell is up with that, Kade?" She wonders where this boldness is coming from. Despite all evidence to the contrary, she's decided Kade's no threat. Well, no threat to her, at least.

To her surprise, Kade's expression softens, and there's no bite to his tone when he comments. "Not so submissive right now. Are we, little wolf?"

This is such a common misconception of submissive versus dominant wolves that Emma just barely keeps the scornful look off her face.

"Submissive doesn't mean doormat. Submissives are the peacemakers. Dominant shifters, like alphas and martinets, lead and protect us. But the submissive wolves make sure everyone's taken care of. Submissive wolves are the pack's caregivers and watchdogs." The expression on Kade's face tells her this is all news to him, so she lightens her tone and keeps explaining.

"When a pack is healthy with a good alpha to lead, they have a group called the 'Council of the Just' that hears any inner pack complaints or problems. The COTJ is comprised of ten pack members, but only two are allowed to be dominant wolves. In that kind of system, the alpha's authority is bound and limited by the COTJ. That means a bunch of submissive wolves are telling the most dominant one in the pack what to do sometimes."

"Packs are far more complex than I believed," Kade murmurs thoughtfully. His willingness to listen and his change in attitude makes her irritation vanish. "I rarely deal with shifters because most of them can't afford my services. The shifters I work for most often are dragons. I've been told they aren't like any of the other groups."

"Yeah, dragon shifters are a whole other thing," Emma agrees with a grin. "But the rest of us aren't a bunch of grubby animals."

Kade's expression turns contrite. "I regret my implied insults," he grumbles, making her laugh.

"Not implied," she says and steps close enough to bump her shoulder into his. "You outright declared some of those insults. But it's all good if you're coming from a place of ignorance instead of malice."

With a small smile of his own, Kade bumps her back. "Is it a submissive trait to be so forgiving?"

"Probably," she shrugs. "Now, can I get a phone to contact people?" Kade's expression turns mulish again, and Emma stifles a sigh. They'd been doing so well.

"I still don't see the point. Even if you called them, you can't do anything to help. Contacting them and finding out someone is hurting will only make you unhappy." His words make her heart warm. He might be misguided, but he's trying to protect her like a good alpha would.

She almost "awwws" out loud.

"It's more painful for me not to know what's going on. I just want to talk to a few people and see how they're doing. My parents and my friends are important to me. And sometimes just talking to someone you love can help if they're in distress. And on that topic, you promised me we could contact Avery to see how Jason's doing. I'd like to see my brother."

A dark scowl returns to his face, and she bites her lip to keep from smiling in the face of his displeasure. More and more he reminds her of a child afraid that others might steal his precious toys.

Wanting to comfort him, she reaches out and grabs his wrist in a gentle hold. She would do the same with any other pack member in distress. The moment she touches him, something strange happens. Her meager healing power rises up. Nothing too odd there, but then it gets weird.

When she uses her limited healing gift, a slow warmth usually builds between her and the person she's touching as she searches for physical injury. This time, however, when her hand touches Kade, power zips across them with enough strength to make her gasp. Her hand tightens down involuntarily, and a strange link opens up between them.

The first thing she notices through this new link is an intense displeasure and deep frustration coming from Kade. Those are familiar feelings she got through the pack bond between them, but what's interesting is that neither emotion is running very deep. As if they're physical wounds, her healing gift goes after them, flushing them away and replacing them with a sense of peace and soft joyfulness. The whole thing happens quickly, and to Emma, it's almost like she's watching her gift work independently of her.

With those surface issues taken care of, her gift pushes deeper into Kade, looking for the real reason why contacting her pack truly upsets him. Power guides her to a deep bleeding wound in Kade's psyche. Anguish pours from the wound, almost overwhelming her.

Her first instinct is to rear back, but her need to help suppresses that instinct. She focuses on the part of her that helps her stay calm. Finding her center, she concentrates on healing Kade's mental injury. No longer overwhelmed by his pain, she can approach the center of his suffering with a clearer mind.

Disjointed words pop into her mind: *alone, unlovable, rejected.*

The emotion pulsing against her feels very much like what a child would experience. Was a young Kade abandoned by those who promised to care for him? Whatever was done to him when he was young has left him with emotional damage that never healed. Could this be why he doesn't want her contacting her old pack? There's no doubt he's got abandonment issues. Could it be that he's jealous of anyone who might take her attention away from him?

Determined to talk to him later about these revelations, she focuses on the aspect of her healing gift she's never experienced before. No longer trying to pull away, driven by the need to help, she nudges the mental wound and finds the edge of his emotional trauma.

You're not alone, she whispers as she trickles a light dusting of power over the painful and old injury in Kade's psyche. *Let this heal,* she urges. *Let the pain go.*

"No!" Kade says in a powerful voice. She feels his magic swell, and at the same time she opens her eyes, a sharp spike of pain stabs at the hand holding on to him. Pulling her hand away from his wrist, the link between them breaks. Clutching her hand to her chest, she pants as spots dance in her vision. Swaying a little, she blinks and focuses on keeping herself upright.

"What did you do?" he hisses out, grabbing her roughly by the shoulder and making sure to only touch where clothing covers her.

"I'm not sure." She shakes her head, bewildered. "I just wanted to comfort you because you seem so upset, and then I felt my lame healing power flow and then…" she trails off helplessly. "I don't know what it was, but it felt like you had a wound I needed to heal. But it wasn't to your body. It felt like a wound in your mind. As if you had a kind of bleeding cut I had to heal. But it was an emotional cut. I don't know how to explain it." Her vision is clearing, and now she can make out Kade's face. His gaze is hard as he drops his hands away from her and takes a measured step back.

"Don't touch me," he warns her. He's standing tall and crosses his arms over his chest, every inch the intimidating mage.

Utterly confused, she instinctively tries to pulse the pack bond, but his shielding is so strong she can barely tell the bond is there at all. Undeterred, she keeps battering at it, determined to get comfort from her alpha as well as give it.

"Stop acting as if I attacked you. Lower your damn shields," she demands, and Kade sucks in a surprised breath at her intensity.

"I hardly think you're in a position to demand," he counters, but she doesn't give up.

"You're fucked in the head. I get it," she says, her voice wavering a little at the remembered pain. "But we all are to one degree or another. Whatever I did just now, I didn't do it on purpose. And right now I need to feel the pack bond, or I'm going to turn into a sobbing mess. Or maybe I'll just shift and go pee on all your shoes!" Her voice is wobbling by the last threat because she feels weak and needy.

"Fine," Kade grits out, and the shielding on the bond diminishes enough for her to feel him again. A ragged sigh comes out of her when he pulses assurance down the bond.

Pulsing back contentedness and relief, she feels the rest of his shields slowly lower. She opens herself wide, removing any barrier between them. Through the pack bond she invites him in, wanting to show him that she doesn't know what occurred between them.

"You didn't mean for any of that to happen. Did you?"

"Hell no," Emma says, closing her eyes to concentrate on calming her heart rate and breathing. "That sucked. Let's not do it again." Squinting her eyes open, she regards him sympathetically.

"By the way, whatever shit happened to you when you were a kid, I'm sorry. No one should be abandoned like that." Her words make him startle.

"Is that what you found when you were poking around?" he questions. "Tell me exactly what happened?"

Concentrating, she tries to remember what happened just a few short minutes ago. Everything was so quick and instinctual. It's hard to think about it in clear, concise terms. "I'm really not sure. When I touched you, my healing gift started up, but it felt different. It was different. It kinda took over." She straightens up, feeling much better now. The alpha bond is fully open, giving her a little of Kade's power to help recover. "It's all a little bit of a blur, but something in me pushed hard to help you. To heal emotional wounds instead, just like if you had a deep cut or broken bone."

"You told me to let the pain go," he tells her. "Do you remember that?"

"Vaguely," she admits, feeling a little guilty. "Did I hurt you? I'm sorry. I honestly don't know what happened."

"You've never done anything like that before?"

Emma takes it as a good sign that his tone isn't accusing. "Never," she promises.

Shifting a little, his arms drop to his sides, and he takes a small step closer to her. He's starting to relax. He believes her. They stand in silence, the bond between them pulsing back and forth. Different expressions march across Kade's face. Most are so fleeting Emma can't name them before they're gone. When his expression settles on interest, she huffs out a breath of relief.

When he holds out his hand for hers, she doesn't hesitate. "Focus on your healing gift," he instructs. "And don't shield."

"It's pathetic," she warns him. "I can't heal anything, but I can tell what's wrong." She feels his magic press into her like a warm wave. She closes her eyes, enjoying a sensation that feels similar to the alpha bond.

"Ah, there it is," he murmurs after a few moments. "You're not a healer." Her eyes snap open to meet his bright violet gaze.

"The hell you say," she blurts out, making his lips curve up in amusement. "I know my power isn't all that amazing, but it's still there. I'm a healer."

"We need to work on your tendency to curse," he murmurs, making her growl with agitation.

"Forget my fucking cursing. What are you talking about?"

"You're not a traditional healer, Emma," he explains, ignoring her expressive language. "Your gift isn't to heal bodies. It's to heal minds. You're a soul cipher. That explains so much, especially why Avery trusted you so readily. You probably used your gift on her unknowingly to make her feel safe and protected. You probably saved your brother too because Avery didn't execute him when I broke the chain holding her magic captive. Your magic twined the two of them together."

"Soul cipher? No," she shakes her head adamantly. "I can't be. They're really rare."

"Well, my little wolf, they might be rare, but that doesn't make my statement any less true. Besides, most soul ciphers are shifters. After your illuminating explanations about what it means to be a submissive wolf, I think it makes sense. Soul ciphers are healers of the mind and soul. Caregivers, if you will." He thinks for a moment and then adds, "I was agitated when I came to find you. When you cringed away from me, my mood went from agitated to angry because you acted as if I was going to hit you. Normally, I take quite a while to come out of one of those moods. But now, I feel peaceful and calm. The only thing that happened to cause the change is your bit of magic knifing into me."

"What about the abandonment thing I felt?"

Emotions disappear from Kade's face, and he drops her hand. "Yes, well, we don't need to discuss that. It's not something you need to concern yourself with."

"I can—" She's going to offer to help him some more, but he cuts her off.

"You've done enough," he tells her in a warning tone. *Door shut, discussion over,* she thinks.

She frowns, considering his words. "Why now? I'm twenty-nine, shouldn't this have shown up earlier? I've never been powerful and suddenly, I'm a stitcher and a soul cipher? That doesn't make any sense. Are you giving me these powers?"

He scoffs at her question. "Mages can do a lot of things, but we can't 'give' people powers. You have them or you don't," he tells her, obviously entertained by her question. Now it's her turn to scowl at his condescending tone.

"But that's the only thing that explains it," she counters. "I didn't have these gifts before, and now I do. You're the only thing that's changed in my life recently."

"They were there, merely untapped," he explains. "Part of it might be this," he points to the necklace she forgot she's wearing. "Those are high-quality sapphires, and I tuned them to you. They act as a focus and amplifier. Perhaps your soul cipher gift just needed a little extra boost to manifest. Besides, you've been stitching for years, Emma. You can't tell me you haven't dreamed of your cliff many times. You just didn't recognize it for what it was."

Frowning, she touches the necklace with her fingertips, tracing one of the stones.

"Thanks," she says softly. "But I don't know how to use stones to focus or amplify."

"I can feel you used the necklace, even if you don't realize it. But you're right, the sapphires don't explain all of it. My best guess is the bond with me broke down some barrier you might have erected around your gifts to keep yourself safe. Neither of those powers would have kept you safe from your previous alpha, and both of them might have led to him selling you like a commodity. Your subconscious was probably trying to keep you from being noticed and put in danger."

"Too bad it couldn't have kept me safe from all his attentions," she mutters to herself, thinking of that one horrible night.

"Did he hurt you more than what I witnessed, little wolf?" Kade asks gently, cupping her jaw with his hand and urging her eyes up to meet his. He floods the pack bond with reassurance, making her relax a little. But no matter how safe she feels, she isn't interested in talking about that night.

"You want to keep your emotional damage to yourself," she points out. "Then return the favor and don't dig into mine."

A brief startled expression crosses his face before he gives one curt nod and drops his hand away. "Very well. You know, with a little training, you could make more as a soul cipher than as a stitcher."

It's no surprise to her that he turns the discussion to money. That's one thing the rumors got right, at least with Kade. Mages like to amass wealth. "I doubt it," she scoffs.

"I'm not exaggerating," he tells her in all seriousness. "Think about it, Emma. What would people be willing to pay to take the pain away? Healers and doctors are numerous, but soul ciphers? Your gift is almost as rare."

Suddenly anger burns through her.

"It would have been nice if this damn power showed up sooner. A lot of pack members were hurt and are probably still hurting. Manny killed himself last year because he couldn't live with the pain of losing his mate any longer. Now I find out I could've helped him? Helped all of them? This is bullshit."

Tilting his head with mild interest, he doesn't appear affected at all by her outrage. The cool, collected mage is back in full control. "You wouldn't have been able to help any of them," he states blandly. "The moment your soul cipher gift manifested, your alpha would've sold you to the highest bidder, and you would've been kept in a cage, servicing whoever could pay. There's no way he would've wasted you on his pack."

The truth in those words deflates her anger. "You're right," she mutters. Turning her attention internally, she forces the anger away. Anger and regret are useless emotions, wasting energy better served elsewhere. Feeling calmer, she opens her eyes to find Kade regarding her with a knowing expression.

"That explains so much," he states softly. "Specifically your ability to remain calm and accepting, no matter what's going on around you. At first, I thought you might be broken. That you'd been so abused you just accept anything done to you. I've met a few people like that, and they are outrageously calm, but that's only because their minds have shut down." He shakes his head in wonder. "But now I realize this ability to calm yourself is part of your soul cipher gift."

She's calm because she's a soul cipher? "What?"

"It makes perfect sense," he insists. "There's no point in having a gift that can heal mental wounds if you can't keep yourself mentally fit. You're becoming more fascinating by the day, little wolf."

"So glad to be of service," she mutters.

With a satisfied smile, he twines his fingers with hers and starts walking them both back toward the house, his pace leisurely and his shoulders relaxed.

"I can't believe I have you," he murmurs to himself. "Stitcher and soul cipher, both in one. I'm a lucky bastard indeed."

They're at the botanical garden this time. Flowers bloom everywhere, the scent hanging heavily in the air. Bright colors surround them as a gentle breeze ushers fluffy clouds across a soft blue sky. Looking around them, Kade's expression is displeased as he makes a distinctly unhappy sound.

"What?" she turns in a circle, delighted at her creation. "This is perfect." She takes a deep breath in, pulling a myriad of scents into her nose. "And it smells wonderful. Stop being such a picky bastard."

"Don't use that impudent tone with me, wolf," he warns her, but there isn't any heat in his words. He's looking over at the koi pond, frowning and then waves his hand to encompass the whole place. "I don't think this will work," he finally tells her. Exasperated, she throws up her hands.

"This is exactly what you asked for!" she huffs out, clearly frustrated by his dissatisfaction.

Realizing she's unhappy with his reaction, he places a warm hand on the back of her neck and gives it a soothing squeeze. She relaxes a little with his touch, but her aggravation is strong enough to keep her eyes open and focused on his imperious expression. "I didn't mean to be offensive, Emma. This place is lovely, have no doubts on that score. Your stitching is sublime. The problem is that this place is too enchanting."

"Too enchanting?" Emma echoes, trying to remember if she's heard anyone use the word enchanting in any context, ever.

Nope. This is a first.

Or the word sublime. Maybe she should get one of those word-a-day calendars. In about a decade, she might catch up with Kade.

"You've created quite the captivating dreamscape," he explains as he leans over to sniff at a large purple bloom.

She doesn't remember the names of most of the flowers at the botanical gardens, but she possesses very clear memories of their appearance and scent. This time around the place is even better because she's figuring out how to mix the scents together to recreate the complex aromas that filled the air at the actual gardens.

"The smell is the best part," she comments with a proud grin.

"Indeed. If I didn't know better, I'd think I was really at this place," he murmurs. Letting go of her neck, he steps close to the nearest flowering bush. His eyes become unfocused a little as he stares at the blooms in front of him. Absently, he rubs a leaf between his thumb and finger.

"But you don't like it," she reminds him.

Those words bring his attention back to her. With a tight smile, he straightens back up. "I don't like the idea of others knowing how talented you are. At least not until I've trained you better."

Pointedly, she looks around. "Trained me better than this?"

He doesn't chastise her mocking tone. "No, not training you in stitching. I worry about the soul cipher part of you." His brows furrow, as if he's debating how much to tell her.

"What aren't you telling me about being a soul cipher?" she demands, done playing his information game. He's silent, and now his expression returns to the aloof arrogance she's used to. "Don't do this, Kade," she asks softly. "Just tell me, please?"

"I don't want to scare you, but that gift paired with being a stitcher makes you vulnerable to attack," he explains with obvious reluctance.

"Vulnerable?" His words don't scare her. As a low-value healer and a submissive wolf, she lived with a constant threat of danger under Alpha Michaels. Some new vague vulnerability isn't enough to cause her concern yet.

"One of the reasons soul ciphers are so rare is that they often end up dying young. They're easily manipulated because that gift will push you to help, even if it's to your detriment."

"I'm twenty-nine," she says with a shrug. "I've managed well so far."

"Yes, but no one knew," he counters. "You didn't even know. Your gift was dormant, hiding. If someone knew, they could easily use it against you. You haven't experienced it yet, but the emotional pain of someone else can become your pain. It could cripple you. You'd do anything to make it go away, including opening yourself up. Once someone powerful is past your shielding, they could make you nothing but a puppet. Soul ciphers are as vulnerable as they are powerful."

Considering his words, she gazes around the garden she created. She's not worried about being crippled by someone else's pain. The first thing she was taught by the other healer in her pack was the skill of emotionally distancing herself from those she needs to help. But Kade's fear for her welfare fills her with a warm elation. He cares about her. He's worried for her, and she gets a strong feeling it's not just about her being useful, but that he truly cares about her well-being.

Closing her eyes, she dismisses the botanical garden and creates an endless grassy field in its place. She keeps the clouds, sky, and slight breeze, but strips the dream of everything else. She hears Kade sound a hiss of surprise and opens her eyes to find him standing in a wide stance as if startled by something.

"Is that better?" she asks, looking around at the endless green expanse meeting blue sky in the distance. It's pleasant but boring.

"You did that so rapidly," he mutters. "A warning would've been polite." His aggravated tone doesn't intimidate her in the least.

"Sorry," she says with an unrepentant grin. Irked, he narrows his eyes at her.

"Cheeky canine," he mutters. Inspecting the dreamscape, he nods with approval. "This will do."

She misses the smells so she adds the delicate scent of cut grass. Kade's nostrils flare, and he slides his gaze to her.

"You just couldn't help yourself. Could you?"

Tapping her nose, she shrugs. "Wolf," she reminds him.

Turning her attention to her clothes, she makes sure she's wearing one of the outfits Kade bought her. She adjusts the color of the blouse a little to better match the navy blue of the real one and then looks back to Kade.

"We'll need some places to sit," he informs her.

"Any preferences?" she asks.

"Not really," he answers, so she imagines the plush overstuffed chairs at her mother's house. When he snorts out a laugh at her choice, she raises an eyebrow at him.

"You said you didn't have a preference."

"I thought you meant style-wise. Could you at least make them look new?" he requests. "These look like they were bought in the fifties from Woolworths and had at least three generations of backsides using them."

Content that he's going to let her keep the familiar chairs, she concentrates on what they might have looked like when they were new. Fabric shines, dull spots disappear, and rips magically mend. Enjoying herself, she even adds a few throw pillows.

When she opens her eyes Kade is gingerly lowering himself into one of the chairs, perching on the edge as if worried the padded piece of furniture might swallow him whole if he leans back.

"We need to work on your sense of style," he comments.

"Nothing is wrong with my style," she retorts, flopping down in a chair next to him.

"It's fine for a peasant," he tells her blandly. "But you're part of the magical aristocracy now. You need to have the tastes to match."

Amused, she ignores his use of the word peasant. "Magical aristocracy?" That's a new term for her.

Pointing to himself, he says with exaggeration, "Rare and powerful mage." Then he points to her. "Rare and powerful soul cipher. In our world, the more rare and powerful you are, the higher on the food chain you are. You might not be as high as me, but you're significant enough to be in my same circle of influence. We're the magical version of royalty. We need to encourage the adoration of others by playing the part. That means living a certain way."

Wrinkling her nose in distaste, she tilts her head to the side. "You mean by pretending to be an arrogant asshole?"

"Don't be crass, Emma," he admonishes her. "Would you trust a plumber who showed up in a suit? Or a banker wearing coveralls? Every profession comes with different expectations, including ours. Eventually, you'll be dealing with actual clients. For the amount you're going to charge, they'll expect a high degree of professionalism. Appearance and demeanor are a part of that."

"Clients?" she probes.

"Once I feel satisfied that your soul cipher or stitching gifts can't be used against you, there's no reason for you to stagnate," he explains. "Using and honing your powers will only make you more powerful over time. That's something to always strive for."

His words make her feel off balance. She doesn't even know the extent of her power, and he's already talking about clients and expectations. She thought having a mage for an alpha was new and strange, but the hits keep coming.

"I can see by your expression you're feeling overwhelmed." His tone is soft and kind, and the normal arrogance on his face melts away to reveal warmth. "Don't worry, little wolf. Nothing's happening right away. We have plenty of time. For now, just be my stitcher and observe how to deal with troublesome customers."

Nodding, she's relieved to be done with this conversation for now. "Will I need to learn to call people in?"

"No, that's never the stitcher's job. You create the meeting place, and the person who hired you, in this case me, will invite others to the meeting. Your sole job as a stitcher is to maintain a seamless platform, no matter what's going on. Remember, if emotions get strong, they can disrupt the dream realm and potentially ruin a meeting. You're abnormally skilled at this, so I see no reason why you can't maintain this bland platform and observe the meeting as well."

That comment brings up another question. "What's this meeting for?"

"A client in North Dakota needs extensive wards placed around his property. Normally that wouldn't require much negotiation, but his land is in another mage's territory, so I need permission from that mage to enter North Dakota."

Now she's really confused. "Why doesn't the other mage make the wards?"

"He can't," Kade answers succinctly. When Emma continues to look baffled, he sighs and continues. "Mages don't all have the same powers. Remember? I'm exceptionally good at wards and barrier magic, but don't ask me to perform anything with the elements. The last time I tried to influence the weather, I accidentally flooded the house. Franco was not amused." His rare show of self-deprecating humor makes Emma bark out a laugh.

"So, two other people will be in the meeting today?" she clarifies.

"No, four more people. Victor's assistant, Brandon, will come into the meeting with him. And I'm sure Donal will bring his assistant Melli. Donal Olsen is the man who wants the wards. Victor Ivanov is a fellow mage."

Curious about the world of mages, Emma sits forward and rests her chin in her hand. "What's Victor's specialty?"

"Teleportation is the power he's known for. But he's also decent at elemental magic."

"Teleportation, huh? I know you can only move yourself. What can he move?"

"If he wanted to, he could move an entire small town."

"That's impressive, but he can't make wards," Emma comments, and Kade nods.

"Exactly. There's no reason he'll object to my presence in North Dakota, but before I can go there, we need to meet and set down parameters for my visit. I would do the same if someone from my territory wanted to hire him. Now, that's enough explanation. If we delay any longer, the meeting will start late, and that's highly inappropriate."

"Aye, aye, sir," she responds with a saucy grin and a mock salute.

Vexed, he makes a small, annoyed sound. "Perhaps you should be quiet during the meeting. At least until you get a feel for how to conduct yourself."

Far from taking offense, Emma laughs at his testy words. "As you wish, Alpha."

Sighing, he leans back in his chair. "I have my work cut out for me."

Emma's bored. More bored than she's ever been in her life.

At first, she listened to Donal, Melli, Kade, and Victor discussing contracts, payments, and expectations with interest. Victor's assistant Brandon remained quiet, like her, but appeared engaged in the conversation.

By hour two of the meeting, Emma's just done. Kade and Victor keep arguing about the most inane topics, including what restaurants Kade is allowed to frequent while he's staying in Bismarck. If this is how most meetings between mages go, no wonder stitchers are hard to find. She can't imagine too many people willing to let themselves get stuck in a boring stitch for hours while egotistical mages squabble.

Unobtrusively, she scoots her chair back a few feet. When no one even glances her way, she stares at the ground between her shoes. Concentrating, she imagines a flower. A bright green stem grows up from the ground, ending in a large bulb. The bulb bursts open and a turquoise flower unfolds. At the heart of the flower, stamen stalks strain upward with jewels sparkling at the tip of each.

Thoroughly enjoying herself, Emma takes it a step further and imagines an iridescent June beetle crawling up the stem of the flower.

Clumsy but determined, the beetle makes it onto the flower and starts picking up the bright jewels before decorating its hard carapace with them. Delighted, Emma creates another jewel-toned flower with gemstones in the center right next to the first one. This flower is a brilliant purple. Growing that flower to be just slightly lower than the first one, the beetle tumbles down into the center of the new flower and sets about harvesting purple gems.

Now, thoroughly entertained, she grows a short row of colorful gem-filled flowers for the insect to visit. The beetle slowly meanders from flower to flower, its carapace acquiring more gleaming gems with each move. Soon the beetle is shimmering with gems, reflecting a myriad of colorful lights on the flowers and ground around it.

Placing her hand next to the last flower, the beetle crawls onto her fingers. She lifts it to her eye level, enjoying the way sunlight refracts on her hand. But it isn't quite right. Tilting her palm, she plays with the movement of the light until it acts the way it's supposed to. A satisfied smile curls her lips at the accomplishment.

"I've never seen a stitcher do that before," a soft voice says, startling her out of her amusements. Looking up, she finds Brandon standing over her, staring at the beetle in her hand. He holds out his hand next to hers. "May I?"

"Sure." She lets the end of her hand touch his. Obligingly, the beetle crawls across her hand onto his. Lifting it close to his face, he makes an appreciative sound at the glittery beetle.

"You're immensely talented," he murmurs, poking the beetle a little to make it move. Emma doesn't like how he touched her creation, so she gives the insect wings under the bejeweled carapace and lets it fly out of his hands to land on her shoulder. Deprived of the colorful insect, Brandon hunkers down next to her chair and rubs one of the flower pedals between thumb and finger. "Even the texture is perfect."

"Thanks," she responds, unsure if she's allowed to talk to anyone in the meeting, even if it's about mundane none-meeting-related items.

Trying to be sly, she leans over and takes in a deep breath with her nose, but gets nothing. Unless someone makes a conscious effort, they don't have a smell in dreams. How can these people stand meeting with each other when no one smells like anything?

"Shifter?" he asks, and she focuses on his face to see him looking at her with an insightful grin. He caught her trying to pick up his scent. So much for her attempt at being crafty. She nods, and he looks sympathetic. "It must be hard for you here. The lack of smells must constantly bother you."

"There could be smells," she insists.

"If you think that, you must not be the stitcher here. That's funny because I thought you were. I'm sorry, but dream realms can't have scent," he counters with confidence. "Don't worry, you'll get used to it eventually."

She frowns at him. She might be a new stitcher, but she knows this guy is wrong. Hell, there was smell here before Kade made her take all but the most subtle of the scents away.

"You're wrong on both counts. I'm a stitcher, and I'm telling you that dreams can contain smell." Ramping up the scent of the grass slightly, she points down at their feet. "Can't you smell the grass?"

Wonder fills his face, and he takes a deep breath in through his nose. "That's amazing," he breathes out. "I didn't know that could be done."

Enjoying his admiration, she decides to show off a little. She grows a gardenia next to his foot and fills the air around them with its rich perfume. He plucks the gardenia and falls back, sitting on his butt on the grass next to her chair. Sliding off the chair to join him on the ground, she grows a second flower, this one a bright yellow rose with a cloying scent she remembers vividly from her aunt's house.

"See, there can be smell here," she points out. "It's not hard."

"No," he objects, looking at the rose with reverence. "It's not hard. It's almost impossible." Suddenly, he grabs one of her hands in his. Startled, she tries to tug her hand away, but he leans over and puts his face right in front of hers, his expression excited.

"I need you to do this for my mother," he tells her, his hand tightening on hers. It doesn't hurt, but it's uncomfortable. He's not her pack, so he shouldn't be touching her. But his next words make her forget all about her captured hand. "She's stuck in a hospital slowly dying, and I want her to visit her farm one more time before she dies. I live on the farm now. You could see it and then recreate it for her. I'll pay you anything. Please, I'd do anything to give her this one last visit. Anything."

"Get your hands off my wolf!" Kade's voice booms out, making Emma jump, and Brandon's eyes flash with anger. Surging to his feet, Brandon places himself in front of her as if he's going to defend her against Kade.

"Fuck off, Allard," Brandon growls out, making Emma gasp at his ferocity.

"Brandon, stand down," Victor orders, but Brandon ignores him.

"You don't own Emma. She can take on whatever job she wants to," he insists.

The blue sky is darkening, reacting to the heavy emotions filling her dream realm. It doesn't take much effort to steady the dream, but it diverts her attention for a few moments. During those moments, the confrontation between Brandon and Kade only gets worse.

"You're a guest here," Kade informs Brandon coldly, his violet eyes flashing brightly with suppressed rage. "You're not even a principal member of this meeting. You're a hanger-on. An employee. A servant. Know your place and do as I tell you. Get. Out."

"Kade, we were just talking," Emma interjects, desperate to defuse the situation.

"Get over here, Emma," Kade orders, pointing to the ground next to him. Scrambling to her feet, she tries to step around Brandon, but he neatly sidesteps and blocks her.

"You don't have to do anything he says," Brandon tells her over his shoulder. "As a stitcher, your only job is to create this place, not cater to his whims."

"She's mine." Kade's expression is forbidding and furious.

"We aren't in medieval Europe, asshole," Brandon nearly shouts. "She's an employee, not a serf."

"Brandon, I'll speak to Kade about hiring the lovely Emma," Victor says, but no one pays him any attention. Kade steps forward, hands curled into tight fists, and Emma decides she's had enough. It takes very little effort to crack the earth between Kade and Brandon. Pulling the ground apart, she creates a bottomless chasm. Everyone but her staggers as the earth moves below them. Melli gives a startled growl and grabs the arms of her chair with hands that are becoming claws. Victor curses in surprise, and she feels his power flare, but she mutes it easily. This is her place, and she's done with these men trying to disrupt it.

"Emma," Kade bites out in warning, but she ignores him.

"Sit," she orders Brandon and points to a chair.

"Emma, I—" he starts, but she cuts him off by making the ground under his feet shift and throw him off balance. Staggering, he sits down heavily in a chair, his expression a combination of hurt and surprise.

"Good girl," Kade declares with obvious pleasure. "You can cast him out. All you need to do is—"

"No," she says, slashing her hand across the empty air in front of her to emphasize her voice. "You need to finish your meeting. I'll talk to Brandon about helping with his mom. Then you and I can talk about it. Remember, hiring me out as a professional stitcher was the original game plan? Maybe Brandon would be a good first client."

Kade isn't happy with her suggestion at all. "That's unacceptable, little wolf." His tone is full of censure. "I don't trust the grendel and neither should you."

Well, that answers the question of what Brandon is. Grendels are shape changers, like shifters. But unlike her, they can pick any shape to take. The tradeoff is that their shape-changing comes with intense agony. When she shifts, her fur flows over her like water, pleasurable and satisfying. A grendel feels nothing but pain and suffering when they shift.

That knowledge only increases her sympathy for Brandon. She can't imagine what it would be like to dread shifting instead of rejoicing in it.

"Your stitcher seems to have everything well in hand," Victor calls out, his voice calm, but Emma can hear the underlying tension. His eyes are focused on Brandon, full of concern and worry. "We're almost done, and then she can dissolve this meeting, and you can have her undivided attention again. You don't need to concern yourself with Brandon. He's completely loyal to me." Victor turns his attention to Brandon, and they have a silent conversation that ends with Victor looking annoyed. "Assure him you won't do anything to hurt the stitcher, will you?"

"That was never my intent. I just wanted to hire her," Brandon growls out, casting a frustrated glace at Kade. Then she hears him mumble something about short-tempered, possessive mages, but the enraged energy coming off of him dissipates.

"We'll talk about this," Kade warns her, calming his power so she no longer needs to concentrate on keeping the dreamscape steady. "Don't think you can get away with this kind of behavior."

"Yes, Alpha," she says, deliberately using his title to placate him, but it appears to have the opposite effect. His expression turns even more menacing. She didn't even say it sarcastically.

Sometimes a girl just can't win.

"I hope you don't make me take steps we'll both regret," he warns her before turning abruptly and taking his seat across from Donal and Victor again.

Breathing out a long sigh, Emma pushes her worries aside and faces a concerned Brandon.

"Alpha?" he asks.

"He's my alpha," she confirms. "He killed my previous alpha and pack bonded with me."

"How many others are in the pack with you?" Brandon asks, worry filling his eyes.

"It's just me and Kade," she admits. "It's very new. Everything happened a few days ago. I think he feels protective because my old alpha was beating me when he showed up. He saved my life."

With a disbelieving shake of his head, Brandon regards her with something close to pity. "Oh, Emma, you don't know what you've gotten yourself into. This is so much worse than just having a contract with him."

Feeling defensive, Emma frowns. "Kade's a good alpha. He's given me clothes, a home to live in, and he's teaching me things. He might not be a wolf, but he's trying hard to be wonderful to me."

Needing comfort, she feels for their bond. He might be annoyed with her, but at her probing, he pulses reassurance through to her. That makes her smile, even in the face of Brandon's concern.

"I'm afraid of the price you're going to be forced to pay," Brandon murmurs gently, unaffected by her assurances. "Mages are a possessive group." Glancing over at Victor, Brandon smiles softly before looking back at her. "It's hard enough to deal with their possessiveness if you're on an even playing field, but if he's your alpha, that gives him a lot of power over you."

"He's a good alpha," she repeats stubbornly. "Now tell me about your mom." It's obvious Brandon's reluctant to drop the issue, but he talks about his mother anyway.

When she opens her eyes after dissolving the dreamscape, the first thing she sees is a bulky, masculine figure looming over her. It throws her back to the moment when she was lying helpless at her uncle's house with Alpha Michaels grinning cruelly down at her. A bolt of fear goes through her, and instinctively she shuts her eyes and brings her arms up to cover her face. A whimper of fear sounds deep in her chest, and she waits for a blow to land.

But no pain comes. Strong arms gather her up and cradle her to a broad chest. "No, don't do that," Kade whispers in her hair. "Don't make that sound. I hate that sound. I'm not going to hurt you. I'd never hit you, Emma. I'd never do anything like that."

"Yes, Alpha," she responds automatically, and Kade gives a heartfelt sigh.

"I've never been an alpha before. This connection between us is more… intimate than I expected," he admits softly. "I don't mean to make you afraid, little wolf, but I'm noticing I have a strong protective instinct with you. It's not something I'm comfortable with."

Risking a glance at his face, Emma tries to give him a reassuring smile. "It's okay," she assures him, relaxing into his embrace. "Good alphas are supposed to be protective of their packs."

"That's the thing, Emma. I'm not a real alpha. I'm not even a wolf. We might be able to create those pack bonds, but mages don't have packs, prides, flocks, or groupings of any kind. We are solitary creatures by nature. This is a new thing for me, and I…" he pauses and she watches with fascination as he struggles. She never thought she'd witness the eloquent mage at a loss for words.

For the second time in less than six hours, Emma feels her healing gift pushing at her to comfort the mage, to fix him. But it's not the healing gift, she realizes. It's her soul cipher power.

Giving in to the gift's demands, she lets her power flow into him where their hands join. There are no shields or barriers up, allowing her gift unimpeded access. She finds the same deep pulsing wound she felt before and runs her power along the edges. Inflamed and angry, the emotional wound throbs with pain as if agitated since the last time she soothed it.

"Emma?" Kade's voice is hushed but full of warning.

"Let me help," she begs quietly. "Just a little." As she talks, she feels along the wound and lets it speak to her.

Alone.

Unloved.

Unlovable.

Forsaken.

A clear mental picture of a small boy appears in her mind. He looks like a youthful version of Daniel—the same Daniel she met as an adult in the dreamscape. He's regarding her with a desperate expression, and Emma realizes this is one of Kade's memories.

"But he's coming back," the young Daniel insists. "I know it's been a while, but he's coming back. He wouldn't just leave me." By his size and speech pattern, Emma guesses him to be around ten years old.

"They're never coming back," Emma says in a harsh young male voice. She's in the role of angry, bitter, juvenile Kade. "Don't you understand yet? This place is the dumping ground for undesirables."

"But you're a mage. Your dad will come back for you. Maybe I can go home with you."

"He hates me," young Kade hisses out. "I'll never see him again."

Daniel is on the verge of tears and desperately trying to hold them back. "But why?"

"You're a bastard of a highborn and his mistress. I'm a murderer," Kade states harshly. Fat tears roll down Daniel's face. She can feel Kade's remorse at his sharp words, but the firm conviction that both of them need to be tough to face the world swirls strongly around her.

Got to be tough. Can't let anyone touch me. Can't care. Need to be strong.

"Murderer?" Daniel whispers, aghast. "Who did you kill?"

Don't feel. Don't care.

Don't feel. Don't care.

The words move to a strong beat, like a hammer's rhythmic blow.

"I killed my mom," Kade tells Daniel without a hint of feeling or remorse in his voice. Inside he's screaming in anguish.

Don't feel. Don't Care.

Don't feel. Don't care.

Be strong. Be tough. Don't let anyone in.

You didn't kill her. Emma wants to tell this young Kade. *She died when you were a baby. No baby kills its mother.* She doesn't know how she knows that, but she does.

"Mages do," Kade answers, his voice soft and falling on her ears outside the memory. She must have spoken out loud. She opens her eyes to find Kade looking at her, his lips twisted in a grimace. "That's why there are so few of us. We kill our mothers. We're powerful even before we're born. So much power and no logic or understanding, only raw emotions. During the birthing process we kill them, and often ourselves. I was a murderer the moment I was born."

Intense sorrow fills her. Poor Kade. Poor mages who have to pay such a high price just to be born. Poor mother who never got to hold her precious baby boy. What a cruel universe that created such misery.

"No, Kade," she argues gently. "You were lost the moment you were born."

She can feel that her power is having an effect. The edges of the emotional wound are healing and letting her get access to the open, bleeding heart of his pain. The guilt, grief, and fury are all still there but moderately diminished. The metronome of hurtful refrains is slowing with a less severe tone.

Abruptly he moves, both physically and magically. He gently pushes her power out as he sets her on the bed next to him and stands. She could fight him, but she instinctively knows that healing this kind of emotional trauma needs to happen in small parts over time.

"Are you trying to save me, little wolf?" he asks as he towers over her. She moves to stand, not wanting to remain sitting when his tall figure is on two feet. A sense of vulnerability doesn't make her get up but the idea that she wants to meet his gaze, show him she's not afraid or intimidated by his anguish.

"If you would let me," she admits. "I can feel your pain. It calls to me. I can fix it. I mean, I think l can make you feel better."

"That would be your soul cipher gift," he answers her dismissively. She watches him draw his haughty façade around him like a cloak. Standing tall, he looks down his nose at her with a remote expression she knows is a lie. He's not unaffected. Deep inside he's crying out for healing, but for some reason he's pushing her away. His next words are a revelation.

"My past made me strong. It keeps me from ever being vulnerable. You need to leave it alone. I don't care what kind of push your gift is giving you. Next time keep that impulse to yourself." He crosses his arms across his chest, looking beautiful and forbidding. "Do we have an understanding?"

"I understand," she whispers. He nods in satisfaction, as if the matter is settled.

I understand, but I refuse to agree, she thinks.

"Now, let's discuss that overbold grendel," Kade says.

Squaring her shoulders, Emma prepares to make a stand. "His mother is dying," she explains quickly before Kade can start ordering her to never interact with Brandon again. "She's stuck in a hospital bed. He wants to give her the gift of a last experience, even though she can't leave the hospital. I can do that for him. I can create a dream so real she thinks she's there. A dying woman can walk on the farm she loved so much before she crosses the veil."

That's not what Kade expected her to say because she watches him fight to maintain his detached expression. "That's all he wants?"

"She's in a hospital in the same city we are going to anyway," she explains. "It'd be easy for me to visit while you work on the wards for Donal."

A stubborn expression crosses his face. "But what if I need you there for the wards?"

"Do you normally need an assistant when you build wards?" she asks, genuinely curious. She honestly doesn't know much about how mages work. She needs to ask more questions.

"Not really, but I worry about sending you off by yourself. You're vulnerable. I wouldn't be a very good alpha if I let you get hurt." She thinks there's more to it than worrying about her being injured, but she takes a different tack. Confrontation isn't her style. As a submissive wolf, she wants those around her to be happy and content with her actions. Gentle persuasion and enticement have always been her go-to methods.

Or bold, humorous, and flippant, depending on her audience. Of course, a little flattery never hurts either.

"Who would dare touch me? I belong to the Mage Kade Allard. I can't imagine anyone would knowingly cross you just to get to me." The praise hits its mark. His expression softens, and the stiffness in his body relaxes a little.

"You're loyal above everything else," he murmurs, and she realizes something important. He isn't worried about her being threatened or injured; he's concerned she's going to run away. That thought is laughable to a wolf shifter. Other types of shifters might be quick to change alliances, but not wolves. Wolves don't leave their pack except with express permission from both their current alpha and the alpha of the pack they are joining. Wolves put family and pack first. Always.

She thinks about the emotional wound deep inside Kade. For someone abandoned, wolf shifter loyalty would be something foreign and perhaps even unfathomable. She needs to treat him a little like a pup who needs reassurance.

"I'll have my phone on me all the time," she tells him. "And I'll make sure someone's there to wake me up if you call and need me. Will that work?" She waits for a beat and then continues. "I don't know Bismarck or North Dakota very well, but maybe in the evening when you aren't working, we could go out to dinner?" She gives him a big grin. "You're turning me into a foodie. Next thing you know I'll be posting pictures of my dinner on social media and reading articles on food. Maybe I should start my blog. I'll call it 'A Wolf and a Mage Walk into a Restaurant: The Life and Times of a Hungry Shifter.'"

That makes Kade huff out a laugh. "Long title," he comments, but she can tell he's pleased that he's affecting her taste in cuisine. "Unfortunately, there isn't much in the way of food culture in Bismarck," he warns her. "But Donal has a chef, and he's rather good. Nothing award-winning, but pleasing nonetheless."

Nodding eagerly, she takes his hand. "That would be nice. I'll make sure I'm always back to Donal's compound before dinner." With an earnest expression, she squeezes his big, warm hand in hers. "Please, let me comfort a dying woman. It would make me happy to do this small thing. And I'll get to practice my stitching in ways you don't let me in the meetings. I'm sure Brandon will keep my abilities quiet, and who is his mother going to tell? She's stuck in a medically induced coma. People in comas are good at keeping secrets." Her irreverent humor hits the mark, and Kade shakes his head, smiling.

"I wouldn't think you had such dark humor in you, little wolf," he murmurs and then turns serious. "How much are you going to charge him?" With that question, she knows she's won.

"I wasn't going to ask for anything," she admits. Asking for money didn't even cross her mind when she found out what Brandon wanted.

"You have to charge him," Kade insists. "Otherwise, word will get out that you're giving your skills away for free, and everyone will demand the same."

"Oh, I hadn't thought of that." Her brows wrinkle in consternation. She likes the idea of helping people but doesn't want to get flooded with requests. "How much do you think I should charge? I don't want to be too expensive. Maybe I could ask for something instead. Something he already owns and could just give me. An old laptop or phone."

"I told you I'd buy you those things," Kade reminds her with a dismissive wave of his hand. "Besides, those things are too cheap. You need to ask for a car."

"A car?" She gapes at him for the first time since coming out of the dream realm.

"Yes, a car. I'm about to charge Donal about half a million dollars for my services. It would look bad if you didn't at least charge the equivalent of a nice BMW or Mercedes. It doesn't have to be one of the fancy ones, but it should be nice. Maybe that new Tesla."

"Tesla?" she squeaks, and he laughs.

"Don't worry, little wolf," he tells her. "I'll do the negotiating for you. You're much too soft. I'll make sure no one takes advantage of you."

The dish Franco sets in front of her smells divine, making Emma's mouth water. All she wants to do is dig in, but she restrains herself as he sets another plate in front of Kade.

She makes an appreciative sound and smiles up at the Italian. "This is amazing." She's determined to win the war of friendliness with the uptight fae-mix.

In an excellent imitation of Kade, Franco gives a disdainful sniff and hurries away from the table. Unconcerned, she picks up a fork and starts eating. She knows Franco's isn't going to be an easy conquest in her friendly war, but eventually she'll wear down the Italian and he'll warm to her.

Or maybe she'll eat him. That thought almost makes her giggle.

Although Kade hasn't said anything, the relationship between the mage and the Italian isn't one of staff and employer. Franco is wholly unintimidated by the tall mage and pushes him around without a second thought. He even admonished Kade severely for disappearing without a word and only calling in to tell Franco where he was the next day.

The Italian might be testy and as conceited as his employer, but she can tell he truly cares about Kade, and the mage seems to have a soft spot for the pretentious Italian as well. It's heartwarming to watch.

Still smiling brightly as Franco returns with several more dishes, Emma makes a point to compliment and thank him. He doesn't respond, but she thinks she might have seen a tiny smile on his face. Content with minor victories, Emma demolishes the meal, even scraping the plate clean with a last piece of bread. Pushing her plate away with a content sound, she gives Kade a broad grin.

"A wolf could get used to this," she comments, making Kade smirk.

"Give it time, and I'll have you addicted to all the finer things in life," he promises. "After all, I believe your current goal is to start your own food blog? Franco's excellent cuisine is a good way to begin your education."

"You're not wrong," she murmurs as Franco returns carrying dessert. It's some kind of many-layered chocolate cake and just by the smell alone, she knows it's going to be delectable. "Did you make all of this, Franco?" Emma asks. "You're an amazing cook."

"Chef," he corrects her, his voice dripping with contempt. Damn, she flubbed that one.

"Chef," she repeats cheerily, ignoring his tone. Picking up a clean fork, she concentrates on the dessert. "You're an amazing chef." Setting a slice of the cake in front of Kade, Franco fills his hands with dirty dishes and disappears back into the kitchen without another word, his normal disgruntled expression firmly in place.

"We need to talk about traveling to North Dakota," Kade tells her, ignoring his cake. "We'll be taking a chartered plane so you don't need to be concerned with packing too much. Franco can help you pick the appropriate outfits."

"Sure." She's distracted by the rich chocolate confection she's eating, so his words take a moment to register. When they do, she swallows hard and meets his detached gaze with her own worried eyes. "What? Did you say plane? As in flying?"

Quirking an eyebrow, he regards her with mild interest. "Of course. We certainly aren't going to drive all the way to North Dakota. Don't worry. I own my own plane. We won't need to be stuffed into a commercial flight like cattle."

Appetite gone, Emma straightens up in her chair and tries to keep anxiety from taking over. "Uh, wolf shifters don't do planes," she tells him firmly. "We don't handle it well at all." That's a gross understatement if ever there was one. Wolf shifters never fly. Ever.

Well, okay, they occasionally flew if sedated to the point of unconsciousness. She knows of a few examples where wolf shifters were drugged and stuck in magically reinforced cages before being loaded into planes. She doesn't want to do that.

Curious now, Kade sets his glass of wine down and leans forward. "Do tell."

"Our animals don't like to fly. We lose control. It isn't pretty," she admits with a little cringe. "I don't personally know any wolf shifters who've ever flown. Maybe I should just sit this adventure out."

Frowning now, Kade shakes his head. "That's not acceptable, Emma," he warns her. "I travel a lot for work. I can't set up wards from a distance. We're going to need to find a solution to this issue."

Now the anxiety is making her stomach roil. She hopes she doesn't lose all the wonderful food she just filled her belly with.

"I guess you could drug me." And stick her in a box. Fuck, what kind of life is she going to have now? This new development is going to make her life hell.

"Is that what your kind does when they need to fly? Use drugs?"

"On the rare occasion one of us has to fly, they drug us until we pass out. Then they stick us in a double-walled, magically reinforced cage in case we fight past the drugs, which usually happens. During times of stress our metabolism kicks into high gear, and we burn through any drugs they give us. A panicked wolf shifter stuck in a small space is never a good thing. If the cage holds, we just damage ourselves. If a shifter gets free of the cage, well, things get ugly fast."

Kade's eyes widen briefly at her explanation; then he sits back with a thoughtful expression.

"This issue is going to take some thought. I'm not strong enough to teleport both of us at the same time or to send someone without me. Victor could do it, but then I'd owe him. I don't like the idea of owing another mage. Besides, I'm not about to ask Victor to transport you every time I need to travel."

"I could just stay here while you go," she offers again. Not being able to help Brandon's mom is depressing, but she consoles herself with the fact that she might be able to pull the woman into a dreamscape from a distance with Brandon's help. The scape might not be great because she wouldn't get to see the farm beforehand, but she could create something beautiful for the woman anyway.

"Absolutely not," Kade says, surprisingly animated. "I want you with me on these trips. I find your presence soothing, and besides, I might need to take meetings while out on assignment. You're my wolf, Emma, my own personal stitcher. That means I want you available no matter where I'm traveling."

"Yes, Kade," she sighs, closing her eyes briefly and concentrating on quieting her fear. It takes several breaths, but she manages to draw from the deep well of calm she's always possessed. When she opens them again, he's watching her with a calculating expression.

"You have amazing control over your own emotions. Do you think between that and the alpha bond, you could stay calm for a flight?" he asks. Her first reaction is to say no. No way can she be trusted to keep her wolf restrained, but his next words make her reconsider. "I can push a lot of power into the alpha bond. With me there to help keep your wolf under control, do you think flying is possible?"

"I don't know," she replies honestly. This is an entirely new scenario. Wolf shifter alphas have to deal with their own inner wolf going crazy on a plane and have no reserves to help a subordinate pack member. But Kade doesn't have an inner wolf to deal with, so he could concentrate on helping her through the ordeal.

"Here's what I propose," he says, setting his wine glass down with a soft click. "We see if you can handle flying by circling the airport a few times. If you start having issues, we can land right away." Accurately reading her expression, he gives her a kind smile. "Don't worry, Emma. I'm powerful enough to keep you from hurting anyone, including yourself. But let's see if we can keep that from happening."

"If that's what you want to do," she agrees and feels her stomach attempt to rebel again. She can't believe she's agreeing to get on a plane.

"Trust me, little wolf," Kade says with confidence. He pulses control down the bond, and her stomach calms. Feeling much better, she takes a deep breath.

"I do," she promises. "I trust you."

It's after midnight by the time Emma gives up trying to sleep. Her wolf is agitated and needs to run. The last time she shifted was weeks ago, and it's no surprise after the excitement of the last few days that her inner beast needs to be let loose.

The moonless night outside is calling to her, and she debates waking Kade. She needs to shift and run, but he told her not to leave the house at night without permission. She doesn't know what wards Kade has set up on his home, but considering that's his specialty, they're probably strong enough to fry her if she tries to leave on her own.

She could shift and just pad around the house, but that doesn't sound like much fun, not with the expanse of grassy cliffs surrounding the house and the nearby woods. Crossing her fingers that she isn't about to upset Kade too much, she walks down the long, dark hall to his room.

The door is cracked, and it easily swings open on silent hinges with just a little push. Kade's sleeping on his side with his back to her. Not wanting to approach her alpha from behind, she moves to the far side of the bed, crouches down, and calls out his name.

"Sir, Kade—"

His eyes roll open before she's even finished, and a long arm snakes out and grabs her, hauling her roughly into the bed. His big body pins her as the bond between them flares to life. Entranced, she watches his handsome face wake up from the fog of sleep. She doesn't fight, just lets him recognize her.

"Emma," he grunts, rolling off of her. "What are you doing?"

"I'm sorry I woke you up," she whispers.

Blearily, he picks up his phone from the nightstand and taps it awake. "It's almost one in the morning. You should be asleep, little wolf, not traipsing around the house."

Dropping his phone back on the nightstand, he sits up and rubs his face. Taking her cue from him, she scrambles off the bed to stand a respectful distance away.

"I need to go outside," she explains.

"Outside?"

Tapping her chest, she pointedly looks out one of his picture windows.

"My wolf needs to run. You told me I couldn't go outside at night without your permission." Comprehension dawns on his drowsy features.

"Ah, I understand." He pulses the bond between them, and she sags a little at the feeling. "It's good you woke me. If you tried to leave the house after I set the nightly wards, you could've been hurt. I can teach you to dismiss and activate the wards, so in the future you can leave the house at will. And I'll set the passive wards to recognize you so you can come and go from the property without me. But for now, I'm glad you came to me."

He pulls the blankets away from his body, and Emma notices he's not wearing anything on his upper body. His lower half is covered by loose pajama pants, but his muscled chest is bare.

As a shifter, she's used to nudity, but that doesn't keep her from admiring his physique before courteously dropping her gaze. Out of the corner of her eye, she watches him yawn and reach for a deep blue sweater. Tugging it over his head, he stands and moves to an expansive closet to fish around. Finally, he pulls out a pair of hiking boots and thick socks, and then he sits on the bed to pull them on.

They look brand new, and she wonders if he's ever worn them before. She's getting the feeling her mage isn't one for hiking. Or camping, probably. She can't imagine he'd ever be content with a meal cooked over a campfire. The thought of him roasting marshmallows almost makes her giggle.

It belatedly dawns on her that he's getting dressed to go outside with her.

"You know, you don't need to come out with me," she assures him, worrying about the health and comfort of her nonshifter alpha. "It's probably pretty damp and chilly out there."

"I can't leave my shifter unprotected," he counters and then gives her a small grin. "Besides, I want to see your wolf."

With long strides, he leads the way out of the room and down the stairs. "Don't worry. We mages are a stalwart group. A little misty night air won't bother me. Let's go, little wolf."

Hurrying, she catches up just as a burst of power comes from him. She feels a strange pressure in her chest. Her ears pop, and then it's gone. He opens the front door and marches out.

Stopping a few yards from the house, he turns to watch her approach. A little nervous, she fumbles with her sleeping shorts and shirt. The moment her body's free of the clothes, she pulls at her wolf.

Shifting makes the rest of the world, even the large and intimidating mage watching her, disappear. Fur flows over her like water, and a rush of pleasure hits her. She feels no pain, no discomfort. Everything that's human moves aside as her wolf emerges. In a fluid blurring of lines, her wolf takes over. She falls onto four padded feet with a soft grunt of relief.

"You're beautiful," Kade breathes. He's regarding her with an awed expression. Unexpectedly, he drops to his knees next to her and sinks his fingers into her lush gray fur. "I've seen shifted wolves before, but you're by far the most stunning."

Preening, she rubs her body against his. No one's ever admired her form before, probably because among the pack her wolf isn't particularly striking. Except Kade thinks she's beautiful, and who is she to argue with a mage?

His stroking fingers make her wish she was a cat and could purr. He keeps petting her as he talks. "I'd say we need to hire a photographer to get pictures of you, but I'm sure they'd never do you justice." He keeps caressing her neck and back, making her want to lean into him and whine with pleasure.

Standing up abruptly, he sweeps an arm out. "Go on, run. I want to see you in full flight."

Happy to oblige, she bunches her muscles and leaps off into the night. She's acutely aware of Kade plodding along the footpath behind her. Running full out, glorying in the feel of her legs flying over the rough ground, she makes a big circle, ending up skidding to a halt in front of Kade.

"Done already?" he asks with a quizzical look. Tongue lolling out, she ducks down in a play bow and sprints off again to the sound of his laughter. She does that for a while, pretending to stalk Kade and then running off when he spots her. He keeps a sedate pace along the trail, making no effort to mask the sound of his movements from her keen wolf ears.

She's about to pounce on him again when the scent of a rabbit catches her attention. Dashing off, she gives chase to catch the fleeing animal. Clamping down she breaks its neck quickly, ending its suffering. The little body dangles limply from her muzzle as she proudly trots back to her alpha.

Stepping out in front of him on the path, she lowers to her belly and crawls toward him, dropping the rabbit at his feet.

"Is this a gift for me?" he asks.

She yips with happiness when he picks up the dead rabbit by a hindfoot and holds it up for inspection.

"Thank you, little wolf. I'm sure this will taste wonderful in a stew."

She wants him to rip into it while it's warm and fresh, but that need pales compared to the deep gratification she feels from her alpha's approval. Racing off, she hunts down another rabbit, eager for more of his addicting approval. This time he laughs as he accepts the rabbit.

"Another rabbit for the stew pot," he comments, holding it up to examine the thin prey animal. "You're a magnificent hunter, Emma," he tells her. "But I think that's enough rabbits for now."

Mildly disappointed, she whines. She caught the scent of at least two others she can hunt down and bring to him. Her alpha's a big male. He'll need a lot of meat to keep his belly full. It's too bad she can't scent any deer in the area. A good-sized doe would feed her alpha nicely.

"You don't need to provide me food, little wolf," Kade tells her, as if reading her canine thoughts. "I consider these gifts and treats, not sustenance. Now run to the tree line and back for me. I enjoy watching you fly over the ground."

Eager to please him, she scampers away, sprinting to the nearby woods. By the time she returns, the exertion has calmed her wolf, and she can pad beside him as they both walk to the cliff edge. Taking a seat, he pats the bench next to him.

"Climb up, wolf. Watch the stars with me."

Clambering onto the bench, she awkwardly pushes her head under his arm until she's resting half her body on his lap and his hand is stroking her fur. She sounds a contented huff and lets her eyes drop closed.

"I never star gaze," he murmurs to her. "I never take time to just admire the view I paid so much money for. I'm always too busy." He grasps a handful of the loose skin at the scruff of her neck and gives a gentle tug, making her grunt with pleasure. "But now that I have a wolf, I guess I'll need to find the time for excursions like this."

She doesn't know how long they stay that way. In shifted form she's horrible at telling the passing of time. But she knows this is the most content she's ever felt. She wants this moment to last forever.

"I think I just saw a shooting star," he tells her absently as he pets down the length of her side. He keeps talking to her. He tells her about his work and the things he owns. Then suddenly, his grip tightens a little.

"I know part of the reason you needed to shift is because you fear flying tomorrow. You needed to run to help with the anxiety."

His words hit her like a bucket of ice water. She tenses up and tries to slide from his lap, but he holds her still.

"Shhh," he soothes her. "I just want you to know that everything will be fine. I protect what's mine."

Although, once again, he's referring to her as a possession instead of a person, she finds the words comforting. Maybe tomorrow won't be so bad after all.

Or he might be forced to turn her into a cockroach to keep her from ripping apart his plane.

Emma doesn't know of any shifter that's ever suffered a heart attack, but with the way her heart is trying to beat out of her chest, she might be the first. Clutching a small carry-on to her chest, she stares at the shiny plane and fights the impulse to shift and run.

Sweat drips down her back, soaking her blouse as a shudder of terror shakes her. Overhead the loud whine of a jet coming in for a landing all but deafens her. The smell of fuel burns her nose. People, luggage trams, maintenance vehicles, and planes move all around her. So much is going on that it's hard to focus, and all of it is hurting her sensitive shifter senses.

A cart towing several wheeled platforms full of luggage sluggishly moves past her, but she barely notices. All her attention is taken up by the stairs in front of her. It's not a far climb to get into the plane, but she can't make her foot move. She's frozen in place, staring up at the plane.

Her wolf makes a high keening cry of fear in her mind.

No, she can't do this. She'll do anything else to please her alpha, but not this.

"Emma?" Kade's deep voice doesn't even penetrate her growing panic. A broad warm hand lays itself across the back of her neck, a thumb rubbing the spot just below her ear. That helps a little. Fear roils inside her, but at least now she's able to pull air into her starved lungs.

She didn't even realize she'd stopped breathing until that moment.

"Climb the steps, little wolf," Kade orders. She wants to obey the voice, but her legs won't listen. The muscles in her thighs tremble as she fights with herself.

"It's a private plane," Kade reminds her. "No one else will be in there. We'll have the entire cabin to ourselves. Just us and the pilots."

That's nice. She won't be in danger of accidentally mauling anyone but Kade.

"Pick up your right foot and place it on the first step," he demands, his voice hard and uncompromising. She wants to do what he says, but when she tries to lift her right leg, her whole body collapses.

"Oh hell," Kade curses as he swoops down and picks her up. "I didn't think it was going to be this bad."

"S-s-sorry," Emma stammers, feeling tears prick her eyes. She doesn't want to fail her alpha, but she's a wolf shifter. She can't fight the other half of herself.

"Don't cry," Kade says as he mounts the stairs, holding her securely against his chest. The sternness is gone from his voice, replaced with tenderness.

"Where is all that amazing soul cipher emotional control now?" he asks. His question is full of remorse rather than reprimand. "I was so sure your soul cipher gift would rear up and you'd be able to self-calm."

His admission is a revelation for her. She assumed he just didn't understand how bad flying was for wolf shifters, but in reality, he thought she was stronger than other wolf shifters. That makes her feel like even more of a failure. She is special among wolves, and she should have more control over herself than this. Reaching deep into herself for the calm acceptance that's come so easily for most of her life, she's dismayed to find it won't be drawn out. Kade must sense her growing agitation because he makes a soothing sound as he maneuvers the two of them through the hatch of the plane.

"I'm going to try something," he tells her as he takes a seat on a small couch that runs along one side. "Try to be still and don't claw my face."

His tone is teasing, but in truth she's holding back her shift with everything in her. Her concentration is so absolute that talking is prohibitive. Whatever he's going to do, he needs to do it soon because the only thing keeping her from absolutely losing her composure is the small bit of outside she can see through the open hatch.

"Are we ready to take off, Mr. Allard?" a female voice asks. Emma wants to see who's talking, but she can't tear her eyes away from the slice of sky and concrete still visible.

"I'm going to need a few minutes, Captain," Kade replies. His arms tighten around Emma slightly. The powerful hold feels good—like his arms might help hold all her emotions inside and keep them from exploding out of her in a fit of destructive violence.

Her outfit is soaked in sweat now, and she feels alternately hot and cold. She clenches her jaw to keep her teeth from clacking together. How can she feel desperately chilled and overheated at the same time?

"If we wait too long, we'll be stuck on the taxiway," the captain warns him.

"Then we get stuck," Kade responds, brusque and indifferent.

"Is she sick?" the woman's voice is full of concern now. She must have just noticed Emma. How she could have missed the six-foot, whimpering, shaking shifter in Kade's arms before now is a question Emma wishes she could ask.

"She's none of your concern," he snaps. "Leave us. I'll call out when we're ready."

"Very good, sir," the captain responds with stiff formality.

Emma vaguely hears her walk away and then voices talking. She wants to call the woman back and explain that Kade's being rude because he's concerned. She wants to smooth ruffled feathers and most of all, make sure the captain isn't upset because she's going to be flying the plane!

But she can't do any of that. She's much too busy trying not to hyperventilate. Kade ordered her to breathe, but now she can't seem to stop the gasping pants.

"All will be well." She feels his hot breath on her cheek as he whispers to her. "I'm going to make sure you're safe."

Then everything changes.

Kade's scent fills her nose. Whatever magic he's used to keep his smell at bay is gone, and the rich smell of him surrounds her. Just like in the dream, it takes all her attention. She's still panting, sweating, and panicking, but her fear subsides minutely because of his delicious scent filling her nose and making her want to rut.

While his smell triggers her lust, his power pushes hard inside of her, flooding her with his magic. The alpha bond surges, making her gasp and twist in his arms.

"Don't fight it," he orders. She wants to tell him that it's too much. Alpha bonds aren't supposed to be this way. Alphas take power from their subordinate shifters; they don't send power back. Not unless the shifter is on the brink of death, and even then, they never share this much. It's not that shifter alphas are greedy, but they don't possess very much magic to share.

"Look for your soul cipher gift now, Emma." His words are a compulsion she can't refuse.

Despite how overwhelmed she feels, she obeys. It takes her a moment to compose herself enough to even start looking for her calm. Finally, she's able to dig deep, able to pull forward the part of her that's helped her maintain peace and serenity. It unfurls inside her, warm and soft. Kade must be able to feel it through their bond because he thrusts power at it. It's not a painful feeling, just a sensation of suddenly being too full. Backed with Kade's immense strength, her soul cipher gift overwhelms her panicked wolf.

With a sigh of relief, her wolf stops urging her to run and settles down within her. Taking her first deep breath since getting to the airport, Emma lets her head thump against Kade's shoulder.

"There now," he murmurs with satisfaction. "There's my wolf."

Looking up into his face, her breath catches for a whole new reason. With his delectable smell filling her lungs and his warmth surrounding her, she finds herself unable to tear her gaze away from his mouth.

Driven by the need to taste him, she lifts her head and puts her lips to his. He stiffens at her touch, startled. But then his lips soften and his mouth opens. She thrills at the feel of him. Just like with the rest of her life, he takes command of the kiss. She eagerly acquiesces, letting him set the pace of the intimacy.

When he breaks the kiss and pulls away, she whines and tries to chase him. "This isn't a good idea," he breathes out.

"But it is," she insists. Before, her panic was taking up her entire world; now Kade is. Everything around her fades to nothing as the mage fills her senses. There's no doubt in her mind. She knows he is her mate.

She wants to sing and dance. She wants to simultaneously jump up and down in joy but also hump the hell out of Kade. Between her earlier panic, the intense feeling of mellowness imposed by the Kade-backed power of her soul cipher gift, and the intense joy at finding her mate, Emma goes perfectly still.

Mate. The word just sighs through her mind, making her brain tingle with pleasure as Kade's scent fills her lungs. *My mate.*

Mine, mine, mine. The words sing inside her, a happy refrain. *My mate, my mate, my mate.*

She needs to tell him. She needs to explain that he is hers and she is his. Her mind is jumbled with emotions and thoughts, but that one sticks out clearly. Her mage needs to understand what it means to be a mate. Then a female voice intrudes before she can form a coherent sentence.

"Sir?"

Turning her head with a growl, Emma feels her jaw readjust as her canines grow. This human is an intrusion and potential threat. Her wolf's protective instincts rear up as she flashes fangs at the stranger. The captain gives a startled exclamation and jumps back, grabbing the back of a seat to keep from falling.

"Fuck," she shouts with wide eyes. Then she brings herself back under control, straightens her shoulders, and looks to Kade. "Is she feral? Do I need to get the authorities in here?"

Caging her with his arms, Kade huffs out a laugh. "No, she isn't feral. You just startled her."

Emma doesn't fight against Kade's hold. She has no intention of attacking the human unless she tries to get any closer to Kade.

The captain looks dubious. "Uh, sir, she's still growling at me."

It's true. A ticking growl coming from deep in Emma's chest fills the cabin with menace. Kade's not afraid or worried. His alpha bond is strong inside of her and she can feel his amusement and affection. Her inner wolf relishes his reaction.

"Ignore her," Kade instructs. "We're ready to get underway now."

"You didn't tell me we were going to be transporting a shifter," the captain says with apprehension as she eyes Emma. "Is she a wolf shifter? There are regulations about wolf shifters flying. She needs to be in a magic reinforced double-walled cage with tranquilizers on hand along with a keeper who can put her down if she gets out of the cage."

Instead of answering her, Kade asks a question of his own. "Who owns this plane?"

Stiffening, the captain glares at Kade. "You do, sir."

"And who pays you?"

"Also, you, sir. But I can't go against regulations. I could lose my pilot's license."

Kade isn't swayed. "I believe those regulations only apply to commercial flights. As this is a private plane, we can dismiss those rules."

"With all due respect, Mr. Allard," the captain continues, undaunted. "Those laws are in place for a reason. I've seen footage of wolf shifters flying. It isn't pretty. She could slaughter me and my copilot in seconds. Then the plane crashes, and you get to die too. I'm trying to keep all of us safe." Her words are firm but not confrontational. If Kade's scent wasn't sending her brain into a tailspin of protectiveness and lust, Emma might feel sympathetic toward the captain.

"I know you've only been working for me for a few months, but do you remember what I do?"

The captain is taken aback by Kade's question. "I know you're a mage, Mr. Allard."

"You don't seem impressed," he says with a quirked eyebrow. "You must not know much about mages. Very few magical creatures out there are more powerful than mages. A few of them are referred to as deities. That's how powerful I am." Kade swipes a hand in the air, and the plane around them shakes slightly.

"Captain!" a voice shouts from the cockpit. "We're moving!"

"What the hell?" the captain curses. Her stiff professional demeanor disappears as she scrabbles to the hatch to look outside. "We're a foot off the ground," she breathes out, looking back at Kade with awe and a little bit of fear.

The plane shakes again, and Emma feels it settle back on the ground. "If I can do that, I can certainly keep one wolf shifter contained." His words are casual, but Emma can feel how much effort it took for him to lift the plane. Strain quakes down their bond, and she stops growling to nuzzle at his neck and chin, trying to comfort her exerted mate.

"You've made your point," the captain grinds out, straightening up and pulling the hatch door shut. "We'll be underway soon. Just keep your pet out of my cockpit."

"Excellent," Kade responds as she strides away. Once the cockpit door closes, he drops his gaze to Emma. "Now it's just us."

She and her wolf couldn't be happier.

Now that the human's gone, Emma turns all her attention to the lust raging inside her. There's something important she should tell Kade. Something about being mates, but that gets pushed to the far reaches of her thoughts. Her current mood can only concentrate on one thing—claiming her mate.

Clambering onto Kade's lap, she pushes her mouth to his again and gives a little whine of pleasure when he opens his mouth for another kiss.

His broad, warm hand grips the back of her neck and squeezes a little, stilling her. Breaking off the kiss, he tugs her back so he can see her face. His expression is one of concern, and the way he's holding her away causes a spike of anxiety to go through her.

"Easy, little wolf," he murmurs. "I know the alpha bond is a strong one, but I need Emma right now. I need to make sure this is a willing coupling, not something I inadvertently caused with my power." She's trying hard to understand him, but desire is making it difficult to think. All she wants is to taste every part of him—put her hands on his bare skin and feel his hands on her.

Magic flares off him, and suddenly his scent is gone. She opens her mouth to howl in distress, but his hand clamps down on her mouth to keep her from wailing. "Let's try not to scare the crew any more than we already have. Shall we?" His tone is careless, but she hears an underlying tension in his voice. Losing his smell is like being dunked in cold water, a shock to her system. But once the initial reaction is over, her mind clears a little.

The desire is still there, roiling through her, but her human mind has enough control to form words. Reaching up, she taps his hand to indicate he can remove it from her mouth. With a cocked eyebrow, he does.

"Ready to make conversation?" he asks sardonically. Under normal circumstances, she might be annoyed by his tone, but she can feel his lust through the bond and knows his words are nothing more than a way to cover his own need.

"I want to smell you. Bring back your scent," she demands, her voice low, rough, and animalistic.

Expression softening, he takes a deep breath. "I will," he promises. "But I need to know you understand what's going on here. I've never been the alpha for a wolf shifter, and this bond is more powerful than I expected. I don't want to overpower you with my magic. I don't want to make you a willing rape victim."

Dropping her head down a little, Emma's hair flows in front of her face as she takes in a few ragged breaths and tries to figure out how to assure Kade that she wants this too.

"I've never wanted anyone as much as I want you."

His grip on the back of her neck tightens a little. "Are you sure?" he demands. His tone isn't composed any longer. There's a slight edge to his voice. Through the bond she can feel that his control fraying a little. He's as affected as she is but doesn't want to admit it, even to himself.

If she was in her right mind. If they were on the ground instead of stuck in a tin can with engines. If she wasn't depending on Kade to help keep her wolf in check. If all of that wasn't happening, she might use her soul cipher power to soothe Kade and explain that he's her mate. The scent is there. Without a doubt, she doesn't just want to have sex with him; she wants to bind their hearts together like shifter mates do.

But those words don't come out. Instead, she fills her lungs and forms the few words she can get out. "You're mine. I'm yours. I knew since that one dream, before you took your scent away. I wanted you then and want you now. Please, Kade?" Her words started out as growls, but by the end she's whining.

Throwing open all her shields, she pulls at him through their bond. Her soul cipher gift rears up and sets up internal barriers to keep him from going too deep, but it's easy for her to draw him to the surface of her thoughts. She pulses the lust she's experiencing, tries to show him what the smell, taste, and feel of him does to her. He jolts, unfamiliar with experiencing the world like a shifter.

"How extraordinary," he murmurs as his eyes drift shut. "I never realized how much input you get from your senses. I've always been so reliant on magic, not something so base as smell or touch. But there's so much here. Everything's rich to you."

"Please," she begs. "That's why you need to bring your smell back."

"The bond isn't doing this to you," he says, opening his eyes. Their color has changed to a slightly deeper violet than normal, bordering on bright purple. Not only are they a different color from lust, but they're also glowing with power.

"No," she agrees. "Need you."

"I can feel your ardor, ravenous and demanding," he whispers, awe in his voice. "You really want this. You really want me. It's not the money or power. It's only about me."

An Emma who wasn't out of control with hunger might've rolled her eyes and said, "Duh." But right now, all she has the brainpower to do is agree with him. Leaning forward, she nips and licks at his lips, like a wolf might do to a dominant pack member in the wild. He gives a little gasp at her movement, tightening his hand on the back of her neck, but he doesn't pull her away.

"No crying later," he tells her firmly. "When this is all over, I don't want to see any tears."

"No tears," she agrees, although she doesn't understand what he's talking about. Why would there be tears later? What she wants to do with him should just make them exhausted and content, not cause them to bawl.

"You take the lead, little wolf," he orders her, letting his hand drop away from her neck. "I'm big, and I don't want to accidentally hurt you."

She wants to assure him that wolves are difficult to hurt, but then he withdraws the magic that was hiding his scent and what few words she might've said are gone. More than anything, she wants his naked skin against hers. She tugs at his clothes, only to feel his disapproval through the bond. Whimpering slightly, she looks at his face, her own showing puzzlement and apprehension. She thought he felt the same way, but maybe she's mistaken.

"Easy," he murmurs. "Let me take off my clothes. No need to tear them off."

Oh, right, her alpha likes his clothes. Shouldn't damage them. Need to be a good wolf. With more patience, she brushes away his hands and starts unbuttoning his shirt with shaking fingers. If she could talk through the lust raging through her system, words would be pouring out of her to compliment his fine form. The shirt parts to reveal his beautiful chest, broad and muscled. He has just a hint of soft hair on his pecks and stomach, and a line of hair disappears into his pants as she rubs her cheek on his belly, enjoying the texture.

The smell of him is perfect, filling her nose and making her sex weep with need. Opening her mouth, she nips at the flat skin of his stomach, enjoying the way he jumps.

"Watch those fangs," he warns her, but there's no real upset in his voice. She can feel his erection pressing against his pants and the inside of her thigh. It feels huge, and she wants to free it.

When she can't seem to unbuckle his belt, she hisses with frustration. His hands push hers out of the way, and he manages the buckle without issue. Popping the button off in her haste, she ignores his sound of censure and unzips the pants. It feels like she's won a grand prize when she draws his stiff cock out of his underwear. Leaning over, she gives the tip a quick lick, loving the salty taste of him.

"Emma, you don't need to—" he starts, but his words stop when she wraps her lips around him and swallows him down. She gags just a little, trying to get his full length in her mouth, eager for his taste. Regretfully, she backs off a little and uses her hand to cover the part of him she can't take in.

With a satisfying moan, he shifts against her. "That feels amazing, little wolf," he whispers. She grins around the hard flesh in her mouth and runs her tongue along the underside. He twitches a little but doesn't protest.

Feeling needy, she reaches down with her free hand and bunches up her skirt. Wiggling the crotch of her panties out of her way while keeping Kade's thick cock in her mouth is a challenge, but she manages it. Then she slides her fingers into her own wetness, finding that nub of flesh that's throbbing with need.

With a firm hand on the back of her neck, Kade pulls her away. "Oh, no, you don't."

"No," she whines, struggling slightly against his grip.

"Get your hand away from that pussy. That's mine to play with," he orders. Grabbing her under her arms, he hauls her up onto the couch next to him. She yelps with surprise as he reaches under her skirt and roughly tugs at her panties until the fabric rips. Then he pushes his fingers where hers had been a moment before. His touch is firm but not harsh, and it's a pleasurable sensation, but she was enjoying the position she was in earlier.

Then magic rolls off him and the hand between her legs feels like it's imbued with a kind of electricity. The pleasure is so intense she might have screamed if Kade didn't cover her mouth with his free hand.

"Shhh," he whispers as he works his thumb on her clit and eases a broad finger inside of her. "Not all mages can do this," he explains. "You should consider yourself lucky to be with one that can."

She can't talk. She can't think. Gasping, she strains against him, thrashing and panting. Prepared for her violent reaction, he uses his magic to hold her down while he works his hand over her. She's not fighting him because she doesn't want him to stop, but the pleasure is so intense she can't remain still.

"Kade," she whimpers behind his hand. He smiles against her cheek.

"Most don't react this strongly," he whispers to her, his voice heavy with arousal.

"Shifter," she mumbles as her eyes roll back in her head. He chuckles and then gives a little moan of his own when her soul cipher power rises and caresses him back. She isn't trying to do anything. There's no conscious thought, but a bolt of fear goes through her. What if she loses control of her gift and Kade stops?

"Easy, little wolf," he soothes, easing his power back and bringing her pleasure down a few notches. Disappointment fills her, but Kade pulses the alpha bond reassuringly. "I'm not stopping, but you need to understand what I'm about to say. Open your eyes, Emma."

Reluctantly, she opens her eyes to see Kade's face. He isn't smiling, but he isn't scowling either. If she put an emotion to his expression, it would be restrained—heavily tested restraint.

"Your soul cipher power might partially feed off pleasure," he explains. She tries to move, to push aside his words and kiss him. She wants more of the bliss from before, and her soul cipher gift isn't shy about wanting it also.

Kade's expression turns hard and all the wonderful sensations cut off abruptly, leaving her bereft. She moans low, tears forming in her eyes. "Emma, focus," he orders sharply as he pushes power through the alpha bond. That steadies her, and she finds she can concentrate now.

"Yes, Alpha." Blinking, she watches Kade's face soften.

"Good," he grunts, and then places a chaste kiss on her cheek. "I hope you realize this is hard for me."

A small smile curls her lips as she wiggles a hand into his lap to his gorgeous cock. "Yes, it is, Alpha." Her actions make him choke out a laugh, and then his magic is moving her hand away from him. She frowns until he rubs his cheek against her in a wolf shifter fashion, and her smile comes back.

"I know you want me," he explains to her. "I don't doubt that. But from what little I know about soul ciphers, they can feed on strong positive emotions. It should drain you to heal the negative, but it should fill you with power to experience positive feelings, like joy and passion. I need you to keep your gift out of me, Emma. This is important. It can be part of the passion, but don't let it get away from you."

Brows furrowed, Emma feels for her gift. When Kade triggered her power back in Monterey it felt like a compulsion to heal. A deep need to help and mend. Right now, her gift doesn't feel like that at all. It feels like her wolf during a pack run, playful and exuberant. The wound in Kade is there, healed around the edges but still throbbing with pain. Right now, her gift isn't pushing her to heal, only to enjoy.

"I'll try to control it," she answers hesitatingly. "I can't promise."

"That's understandable," Kade allows with a sigh. "It's new, and you're young yet."

Wiggling, Emma gives him a hopeful look. "Is the talk done now?"

With a quiet laugh, Kade doesn't say a word. Putting his lips to hers, he presses his hand between her legs. The amazing pleasure from before returns, so intense it borders on pain. He works his fingers inside of her while he deepens the kiss. Unprepared for him to hit her with the full force of his heady magic, an orgasm steamrolls through her, making stars appear behind her closed eyelids.

Not only is this climax the most intense she's ever had, but it keeps going. The combination of his magic and her gift creates a feedback loop, making her convulse with the force of her orgasm as it crashes within her.

Her soul cipher gift greedily absorbs everything deep inside her as a place of power grows in her chest. The sensation is strange but not unpleasant, and she intuitively knows she can pull from that reservoir of power any time she needs to and then refill it just by having sex again.

When did life get so good?

"Yes, you can recharge with sex. But sex only with me," Kade growls out. He must have felt her thoughts through the open and vibrating alpha bond. "Right now, little wolf, you're mine only. I know shifters have a liberal view of sex and sexuality, but you're mine. I don't share."

Slowly, he pulls his power back, letting the strong orgasm finally settle. Instead of feeling wrung out, she feels energized. When he removes the magic holding her body still, she rolls herself into his lap, her shifter grace making the move appear languid and effortless.

His erection presses into her stomach, hard and needy. Pushing as much of her body against his as she can, she presses her lips to his and tries to reassure him with a kiss. He responds with a small moan of lust, his hand grabbing her ass and pulling her even harder against him.

She wants to tell him wolves might sleep around, but once they find their mate no one else will turn their heads ever again. Wolves are intensely loyal to their mates. Other species often envy the bond. He's her mate, and she'll never want another again. But she knows he's not ready to hear that, so she breaks the kiss and pulls back just a little, smiling reassuringly.

"Then you better keep me sated."

Freezing for a heartbeat at her words, she watches his normally aloof expression go through a myriad of emotions. His feelings echo through their alpha bond, jealousy, insecurity, and, finally, a hint of love. Then he shuts down everything but the lust.

"Far be it for me to deny my little wolf anything," he retorts and squeezes his hands on her ass again. He lifts her a little and then lowers her onto his throbbing cock. Her eyes flutter closed at the sensation. The soul cipher part of her is downright giddy.

"That's nice," she moans as he slowly enters her, making her feel deliciously full. When she's finally fully seated and her sensitive clit rubs on his pubic bone, she can't help the gasp that escapes.

"That's not all," he murmurs cryptically. Before she can ask what he means, his dick thrums pleasure through her just like his hands did earlier.

"Oh fuck," Emma whines as the power builds inside her again.

"Don't worry, little wolf." He uses his grip on her ass to move her up and down his shaft. "I'll make sure both of us are well gratified."

Although he started the rhythm, she quickly picks it up, making his need to move her superfluous. He lets go of her to bring his hands up to her breasts, cupping her and kneading the flesh there gently.

"More," she pants, so he rolls her nipples with much harsher pressure. The sensation is all she needs to go over the edge again.

This time, instead of making her want to thrash with the intensity, her climax nails her in place, making her freeze and whine. She cries out and feels Kade coming as well.

His pleasure shines through the alpha bond, making her reel with happiness as her chest grows heavy, both from the accumulation of power and from the intense love she feels for her mate.

The open alpha bond hums with magic, tenderness, and affection pouring from Kade. Soon, she's sure, love will be there too.

"Mages don't love," he murmurs to her, sensing her thoughts through their bond.

Undaunted, she collapses against his chest as they both pant and recover. "That's fine," she responds out loud. She knows she's got enough patience and affection for both of them while he learns that even mages can love.

She tugs at his shirt. "Can we be naked for round two?"

With a wide smile, he reaches for his shirt buttons. "Absolutely."

"We are on final approach," the captain announces over the intercom. It's the third announcement she's made in the last hour, and unlike the first two, this one spurs Emma into action.

Not wanting to be caught with her pants down, literally, she pulls on her clothes. Chuckling at her frantic haste, Kade dresses at a much more leisurely pace.

"You have plenty of time, pet," he tells her, but she just glares at him. Or tries too, anyway. It's hard to be angry with a man who just gave you the best sex of your life.

Wolves are normally randy creatures. It's not surprising considering shifters don't get STDs and can't get pregnant outside of a mating bond, so there's no reason for wolf society to develop the same cultural taboos as humans regarding sex. Unfortunately, under alpha Michaels, the pack was subdued and fearful. It wasn't the environment for impromptu liaisons between willing, unmated wolves. But now, Emma has her mate, and she's eager to make up for lost time.

With her skirt and blouse on, she jumps on Kade's lap. With a startled *harumph,* he takes her weight and wraps his arms around her.

"Happy wolf," he comments as she nips at his lips.

"I want to do that again," she demands. His face lights up, and his mouth curls up in an uninhibited grin. For a moment, he isn't the arrogant, aloof mage. He's just a male pleased to have a female interested in him.

"Do you now?" he murmurs. The alpha bond pulses strongly, his affection coloring the feel of the bond in a way she's never experienced. It makes her want to wrap her body around Kade and never let go.

"I liked sex before," she confides in him. "But you make it even better!"

"I'm honored to receive such high praise." His eyes glint with humor.

"I'm going to leave you a fantastic Yelp review," she teases.

"You're making me feel like a servant," he says, his grin still firmly in place. A hard impact jolts the plane, and his smile disappears. "But, alas, I believe we've just landed."

Gently, he sets her on the couch next to him. He might not be a shifter, but the way he's able to just pick her up and set her down means mages must have shifter-level strength. She loves it.

In fact, she and her wolf love everything about this mage. It only takes a moment of debate before she decides to lay her cards on the table.

"When you're ready, I'd like us to mate." She throws caution to the wind and tells him exactly what she wants. "We should twine our souls with a mating bond."

She's never seen Kade put a foot wrong. He never uses unnecessary movement. Every action he takes is economic and purposeful, as well as elegant and sure-footed. He wears his self-assurance not just on his face, but with his whole strong, sculpted body.

Yet, at her words, he stumbles forward while in the process of standing up. He makes an inarticulate sound of surprise and reaches out to grab a tall-backed swivel chair to steady himself.

Or he tries to, anyway. The chair moves under his grip. It's bolted to the floor, but pivots around so Kade's momentum isn't checked at all. Flaying, he goes down in an ungraceful heap, hitting the side of the chair on the way. He ends up on the floor in a very undignified heap.

"Kade!" Emma exclaims as she rushes to his side. He's already sitting up with a very un-Kade like dazed expression. "Did you hurt yourself?"

"I don't trip," he mutters, his face melding into indignation. He looks at her with something akin to exasperation. "You made me trip."

Biting her lip to keep from smiling, she drops her gaze. "Sorry?"

With a sigh, he puts a hand under her chin, bringing her gaze back up. "I can't be your mate, little wolf. I can only be your alpha."

"And lover," she counters. "It's not much farther down the path to mate from there." It's a lie, but one she's sure will comfort him. Shifting forward, she rubs her face against his shirt-covered chest. She doesn't need to scent mark him because they are both thoroughly covered in each other's scent already. But the action feels right, and the impulse is too strong to ignore.

"You're my mate," she tells him bluntly. "Now that you're not hiding your scent anymore, it's obvious. I can wait for you to realize it too. Don't worry. I'm patient."

"I'm afraid you'll be waiting a long time," he states grimly and pushes away from her with enough force to make her tumble back. Physically she's unhurt, but his action is an emotional blow.

From her seat on the floor, she watches him stand and straighten his clothes. His expression is back to its normal imperiousness with the body language to match: spine ramrod straight, shoulders back, and movements economical and exact. He even partially blocks the bond with her, limiting what she can feel through it.

Disappointed fills her even though she knows his rapid backpedaling is her fault. She should've taken the whole thing slower. He might be powerful and worldly, but emotionally he's young and fearful.

When he extends a hand out to help her from the floor, she accepts it, fighting to keep her face neutral. "I'm sorry if I hurt your feelings," he tells her, accurately reading her. "But anything less would be dishonest. Mages can't love. And we don't mate."

"But you had a mother," she protests.

"Ah, I forgot wolves need to be mated to produce offspring. No, little wolf, that's not how mages work. We are always fertile and can impregnate just about any other magical creature. We don't need love and commitment to reproduce; we just need a woman to sacrifice."

Remembering what she'd learned about what happens to the mother during birth makes tears gather in her eyes from sympathy and sorrow.

At her look of sadness, his expression softens and he pulls her into a tight hug, pulsing comfort through their bond.

Rubbing his hand down her back, he makes a soothing sound. "Don't worry. I promise to keep you safe, even from me."

The whine of the airplane engines cut off, and before Emma can say anything else. Then the captain is there, opening the hatch and then stepping far away as she keeps a wary eye on Emma.

Kade turns to lead her out of the plane, but she grabs his arm and tugs him back to her. "You can love," she states.

The alpha bond between the two of them is more intimate than any bond she's had with any alpha or other pack member. Between that bond and her soul cipher gift, she knows a lot more about Kade than he realizes. One thing is certain. He is capable of love.

The deep desire to love and be loved is there, waiting and yearning. The emotional wound she's slowly healing is keeping that love from fully forming, but she knows without a doubt that once he's healed, he'll be able to love her.

"Don't speak so confidently of things you know nothing about," he responds testily. Unperturbed, she gives him a small smile.

"I can wait," she states again. "I love you and I can wait until you're ready to pull your head out of your ass and realize you love me back. Then we can be mated."

Shock, fear, frustration, and longing all cross his face, but he settles eventually on impatience. "Enough of this drivel," he says, tugging her along. "We're here on business. Act with decorum, or I'll leave you locked in a room all day." She knows the threat is empty. He's just lashing out and making her think of a scared teenager. Willing to indulge him for now, she schools her features and attempts to appear professional and subservient to him.

The airport isn't very large. Kade's plane is the largest one there. A shiny black SUV is parked close to the plane with three men standing next to it, waiting. Taking a careful sniff, Emma can pick out the scent of bear. All three men are bear shifters, probably grizzlies if her nose isn't mistaken.

Wolf and bear shifters get along because they mostly ignore each other. This will be the first time she's deliberately interacted with bear shifters outside of walking past one on the street or in a store.

All three men are as tall or taller than Jason, which isn't a surprise considering the beasts they house within their bodies. Two of the men stand a little back while a third man waits with a pleasant and expectant expression. She recognizes the man in front, Donal Olsen, alpha of the Olsen Sleuth. He participated in the dreamscape meeting, but the other two are strangers. All three are dressed casually in jeans and shirts, which probably bothers Kade to no end.

No sooner does that thought cross her mind then she feels Kade's annoyance through the bond, making her giggle.

"They're not trying to insult you," she tells him. "They're shifters. We aren't into clothes like you mages."

"Still, they could've made an effort," he mutters back.

"They are," she says. "They smell like very clean bears, so that means they showered today. Just for you." Kade hides his grimace at her words, and she's forced to stifle a laugh. He might act like she's annoying him, but she can feel his amusement through their bond and it only encourages her.

Once they're close, Donal steps forward with an extended hand in a typical human greeting.

"Welcome, Mr. Allard."

"Hello, Alpha Olsen, it's a pleasure to meet you in person instead of the dreamscape."

It feels odd to watch a shifter shake hands. When two shifters meet for the first time, they don't touch. Instead, they take turns standing upwind from each other so that they can know each other's scent. Kade doesn't have the shifter sense of smell or all the instincts that go with it, so perhaps he usually goes with human greetings.

"And it's a pleasure to meet you in the flesh as well, Miss Martin," Donal says, shifting his attention to her. He doesn't hold out his hand. He takes a small step sideways, putting his back to the slight breeze. The smell of bear fills her nose, and she gives a slight nod and moves to put her own back to the wind. She doesn't get far before Kade snakes out a hand and grabs her arm.

"What do you think you're doing?" he asks. His tone is conversational, but there's no mistaking the hard glint in his eyes.

"Greeting the bears," she explains. His expression turns puzzled, and she realizes he doesn't understand how most shifters greet each other.

"Mr. Allard, we can forgo our usual welcoming ritual if that would make you more comfortable," Donal says, his forehead wrinkled in concern.

"Fine, you can finish your shifter meet and greet," Kade concedes, letting go of her arm. Frowning, he addresses Donal. "Don't hurt my wolf."

"Of course not," Donal says, not reacting at all to Kade's claim on her. Emma steps around until her back is to the wind and Donal and his other two bears are in front of her. Like following the leader in a children's game, Kade follows her, obviously trying to puzzle out what they're doing.

"I'm Emma Martin of the Allard Pack," Emma tells Donal now that they've both gotten a chance to scent each other. As she stands upwind of them, she knows they can smell Kade and sex on her, but that's not something shifters care about.

"I'm Donal Olsen of the Olsen Sleuth. Me and my sleuth welcome you," Donal replies.

She continues the traditional greeting when entering another group's territory. "I promise to be respectful of you and your sleuth."

"And we promise you no harm," Donal concludes. The two bears next to him grumble out greetings as well.

The tallest of the three inclines of his head. "Hello, Emma. I'm Gus. Welcome to my sleuth."

"And I'm Cory," the last introduces himself. "Welcome to my sleuth."

Greetings finished, Emma grins up at Kade's bewildered face. "Sleuth?" he asks.

Chuckling, Donal explains. "Canine shifters live in packs. Cat shifters are prides. And bears live in sleuths."

"Ah, I thought all shifters referred to their groups as a pack or pride. Is that a typical greeting between shifters or is that a bear thing?" Kade asks, directing his gaze at Emma. She's a little surprised he's so ignorant of shifter protocol.

"It's typical of most shifters, not just bears. Well, except for dragons and water shifters. They're a little different," she elaborates. "Dragons are stuffy and formal. And water shifters aren't as scent orientated, and those greetings are done at a much greater distance."

"That's because water shifters are grumpy as hell," Donal scoffs. "There's no such thing as a friendly kraken."

Ignoring that comment, Emma pointedly looks up toward the rapidly darkening sky. "Perhaps we should be on our way."

"You're probably right. The weather's been foul on and off for the last few days," Donal concedes as he turns and indicates they should follow him. Instead of getting into the car, Cory and Gus stride off.

Watching them, Emma pauses at the open door of Donal's vehicle.

"Where are they going?" she asks as Donal settles himself into the driver's seat.

"They only let one vehicle drive onto the airport at a time, so Gus and Cory's vehicles are parked in a lot just past the terminal," he tells her.

"We all could have fit in here," Emma comments as she climbs into the backseat of the SUV. She assumes Kade will want to ride up front with Donal and discuss business. But when she turns to close the door, Kade is right there. He muscles his way in, making her squeak with surprise as she has to scoot over to make room for him. With a proprietary air, Kade slings his arm around her shoulders as he makes himself comfortable on the bench seat of the large vehicle. He's not glaring exactly, but his expression isn't open and welcoming either.

She catches Donal's grin in the rearview mirror at Kade's antics.

"Kade requested a large vehicle with only a driver, no other passengers," Donal explains. "It's in the contract. You were there when we negotiated it."

Blushing a little, Emma slides her eyes over to Kade, who casts her an amused look. "Sorry," she mutters. "I guess I wasn't paying attention."

"No, you were much too busy growing bugs and flowers," Donal pipes in. "I have to tell you, Emma, I've never seen such a talented stitcher before. The way you broke the ground between Brandon and Kade as if it was no effort at all was impressive too."

"She has a singular talent," Kade agrees, and she warms at the pride in his voice. "Although she still lacks discipline."

"I'm not the one who tried to start a fight in the last stitch," she points out primly. An embarrassed feeling comes through the bond, and Kade clears his throat.

"You're still naïve," he grumbles. "I was just trying to keep you from being taken advantage of."

"Speaking of impressive feats, I'm surprised you got her on the plane, Kade," Donal comments. He directs his next question to Emma. "Are wolf shifters better at flying than bears?"

Adamantly shaking her head, she gives a jittery chuckle. "Absolutely not. I guess I can fly because Kade's my alpha, but not a shifter himself. He used the pack bond with me to keep my wolf in check and distracted."

"I can smell it was a pleasant distraction." Donal's tone is teasing, but Kade stiffens and glares.

"That's inappropriate," he bites out and then looks astonished when both Donal and Emma burst out laughing. Baffled, he turns to Emma. "What's so damn funny?"

Shrugging, she grins and just says, "We're shifters."

Going by Kade's expression, that doesn't explain everything as much as she thought it would.

"I know that," Kade reminds her, his tone acidic. "I don't see how Donal commenting on our private life because he can smell our earlier liaison is amusing to either of you."

"In our world sex isn't something to be ashamed of or kept hidden," Donal tells him gently. "It's joyful. Something important and meaningful, even if it isn't between mated couples."

"We smell like each other and delight. That's not embarrassing." Putting one of her hands on his, she squeezes. "I like that you smell like me and pleasure. I'm a wolf. I want to roll in your scent, and I want to make sure you're covered in mine."

"Mission accomplished," Kade mutters. He sounds disgruntled, but delight is pulsing down their bond. He likes her possessiveness. If he's never let anyone get close before her, this might be a novel experience for him.

"During the original negotiations, you requested two rooms. But I guess you two will only need one room now," Donal mentions as he maneuvers the large vehicle down the road. Most of the fields they pass are bright green, filled with plants soon to be harvested. She wonders what the endless fields would look like covered in snow.

"I still want two rooms," Kade objects. "But they need to be right next to each other. If there's a connecting door, then all the better."

Giving him a startled look, Emma tries not to feel hurt. "You don't want me in your bed?"

"Of course I do, little wolf," he tells her. His words are gentle, but his posture is still formal and cool. "But it's better to have choices."

She wants to object. Once a wolf sets on a mate, there's no going back. She's chosen Kade. He's her mate. No doubt, no questions, no uncertainty.

But he's not sure yet, and she needs to set aside her confidence and let his affection for her grow. She might know they're mates, but he's going to be slower to accept it. If two rooms will make him more comfortable, she won't argue.

He better not try to lock her out, though. Wolves don't do barriers between mates.

"We're set to have a formal dinner tonight," Donal mentions. "Victor and Brandon will be there as well as the alpha and several wolves from the local pack. I wanted to make sure Emma is known to them, so she's not accosted when she leaves the compound."

"That's very thoughtful of you," Emma murmurs. "Thanks."

"After the amazing job you did stitching for our meeting, I'm happy to make your stay comfortable so maybe I can hire you myself in the future," Donal admits.

"She's not for hire," Kade interjects.

"Not yet, anyway," she counters and then catches his ominous expression. "Let me guess," she says with a grin. Then she does her best Kade impression, "We'll talk about this later, little wolf."

Donal laughs, but Kade isn't amused. It doesn't matter. She's entertained herself at least.

After a shower and a change of wardrobe, Emma makes her way into Kade's room. She finds him sitting on his bed and tapping away at his phone. Their rooms are right next to each other, and while her wolf doesn't like Kade in a separate bedroom, Emma's human side knows she needs to pick her battles. She won't object to her luggage in one room and his in another, but there's no way she's sleeping alone. Like it or not, Kade's going to find himself with a wolf shifter wrapped around him tonight.

"You look lovely, Emma," he tells her, taking in the simple, long-sleeved, royal blue cocktail dress with matching shoes. Before they left, Franco set out all her outfits and explained what to wear and when to wear it. He was terse and impatient, but she let that go because he was showing great concern for her. To Franco, dressing in the wrong outfit would put her at a disadvantage. His explanations might have been delivered with unnecessary severity and acrimony, but the intent behind them was obvious. He cared enough to want to prepare her for visiting the Olsen Sleuth.

He even included pages of detailed instructions on each outfit. It was probably the most helpful thing he did for her because once she started pulling out outfits, she wouldn't remember anything he lectured her about the previous day. Now, standing in one of Franco's ensembles, she sends a silent thanks to the fae-mix.

"Thanks," she says, smiling demurely at Kade's simple words of approval. Then Kade's forehead wrinkles and his lips turn down slightly as he continues to gaze at her.

"What?" she asks, glancing down at herself. Nothing's changed. No sudden stain appeared or crease developed. What could he possibly be frowning about?

"It's nothing you did," he assures her, standing up and crossing the distance between them. He leans over slightly, his gaze locked on the necklace at her throat. The low neckline of the dress puts it on display nicely, but he doesn't seem pleased.

"You told me not to take it off," she reminds him.

"You did just right, and the sapphires go well with this dress. But perhaps we should invest in several necklaces so you can have some variety in your wardrobe," he muses. "You should be able to match your jewelry to your outfits. I'm surprised Franco didn't say anything to me before we left."

"I like this one," she states, worried he'll take away the stones he imbued with magic. She's come to rely on her newly awakened soul cipher gift and fears that losing the enchanted sapphires will diminish her access.

Accurately reading the apprehension in her face, his expression softens, and he pulls her into a tight hug.

"I'll make sure all the jewelry you wear is attuned to you," he assures her. "I wouldn't deny you something so important."

"If it's true you wouldn't deny me, when can we contact Avery and Jason?" she asks. "They're far more important than a few bits of gems and precious metals."

She expects him to get upset with her, as he has every time she brings up the topic of her brother and the other mage. It's unexpected when he looks mildly intrigued instead.

"Some would disagree with you," he says thoughtfully. "Many would say riches are far more important than any familial or emotional attachments. Happiness, love, and desire can be fleeting and hard to quantify. But wealth and power are tangible and easily measured."

She doesn't respond right away. Her soul cipher gift rises up at his words and sinks into him through their bond, feeling around his wounds for a new opening to slide into and heal. He's dropping his shields with her more readily today, giving her an opening to slip into the part of him that's so badly damaged.

"I can feel what you're doing," he murmurs, startling her. "I'm not sure I approve, but I can't find the will to thrust you out again."

"You need to interact with shifters more," she pronounces.

"I assume you have a point to that non sequitur," he mutters. It's hard for her to talk while she's trickling power along his wound, trying to draw out the long-festering pain there.

"We don't care about money," she tries to explain. As if she's sinking fingers into a deep festering gouge, she prods inside Kade. Healing the edges of this wound won't do much good. She needs to find the core and lance it. As if sensing her intention, the bond between them thrums with power. None too gently, he pushes her probing gift out.

"Enough of that." His voice is mild, as if telling her to stop fidgeting. As much as she doesn't want to withdraw, she takes it as a victory that he let her do anything.

Patience is going to be the key with Kade—patience waiting for him to understand love and patience in healing him.

"Now explain your comment," he insists. "When you say, 'we don't care about money,' do you mean shifters?"

"Yes, shifters. Don't get me wrong, we like our creature comforts. When we went on pack camping trips under Alpha Julia, several people towed campers to the state park."

That makes Kade smirk. "Campers?"

"We like soft beds too," she mutters, thinking of her own family and the leaky air mattresses that plagued her parents one year. "Anyway, do you want me to explain, or do you want to keep making fun?"

The smirk disappears, replaced by a detached, indifferent expression. Emma regrets her words, but when she tugs at the bond between them, his answering pulse of power is reassuring.

"Money is worthless if you don't have friends and family to share it with," she states. "That probably sounds naïve and unsophisticated to you, but for us, people are the real wealth. You give me things like these nice clothes because you want to show that I have value to you. But for me, the better way to show it would be to let me contact Jason and Avery. My concern and affection for my brother doesn't diminish my feelings for you. Love doesn't work that way."

"I wouldn't know," he responds with icy disdain. "But you've made your point. If I want to keep you content, I'll need to allow you access to your family. I can pull them into a dreamscape tonight. Will that suffice?"

Overjoyed, she hugs him tightly enough to make him whoosh out a lungful of air. "That's perfect. Thank you!"

About twenty people sit around a large banquet table, chatting and eating. Kade sits to Emma's right and talks avidly with Victor about modern art and collecting. Victor is across the table from her. It doesn't come as a surprise to find Brandon sitting far down the table instead of next to Victor. The sour look he shoots Kade occasionally tells her all she needs to know about the seating arrangement. Victor looks amused while Kade seems satisfied, even though he scowls at Brandon every time he catches the grendel's eye.

Kade might let her visit Brandon's mother in the hospital, but that doesn't mean he's interested in interacting with the grendel socially. She can tell one of the biggest obstacles she faces with Kade is teaching him that other people are not a threat to his relationship with her.

Donal sits on the other side of Kade, at the head of the table, and bear and wolf shifters occupy the rest of the seats. Gus is sitting to her left and introduces her to everyone at the table as the food is being served.

"I hope you like the grub," Gus says as he scoops up a mouthful with an oversized spoon. "Donal told the chef to be extra fancy today because Kade's here, but I was worried about you. I don't know if some wolf shifter digestion is sensitive, like the big cat shifters."

"Not sensitive at all," she assures him. "We're like bears, omnivores and opportunists. And this is good." That being said, the difference between wolf and bear shifters is notable at the moment.

The bears around her might be dressed in refined clothes and eating excellent food, but they're still bears. They need to eat an incomprehensible amount of food to keep their shifter bodies strong, so everyone is shoving large amounts of food in their mouths. She always thought wolves ate a lot, but not compared to these guys. At the moment, she feels downright dainty, and that's not an experience she's ever had before.

"I was talking to Donal while we waited for your plane. He says you're the most skilled stitcher he's ever met," Gus comments.

Not sure she wants to talk about stitching, or any of her powers, she demurs when the smell of bear cub hits her nose. Distracted, she looks down to find a child, probably around six, wiggling himself between her and Gus.

"Ethan, what are you doing down here?" Gus asks and moves to pick the cub up. But with an adorable little growl, Ethan squirms away and clambers onto Emma's lap. Scooting her chair back to accommodate the cub, she lets him get situated.

"Sorry about that," Gus says, looking around. Emma follows his gaze to see a harried woman hurrying over. She looks exasperated and apologetic.

"Megan, what's going on?" Donal asks, bringing everyone's attention to their end of the table.

"I'm so sorry, Alpha," Megan says with a huff of frustration. "Ethan's restless, and I thought I'd sneak him out for a run in the woods, but he got away from me on the stairs."

"What are you?" Ethan whispers in Emma's ear. "You don't smell like us."

"I'm a wolf," she whispers back, keeping one eye on Donal as she talks. Just like wolves with their pups, bears are very protective of their cubs and the last thing she wants to do is to be perceived as a threat.

"Wolf!" Ethan announces a little too loudly, turning heads and making Emma wince. "Want to run with me? Megan's going to take me outside to play. Come play with me."

"Emma's in the middle of dinner, Ethan," Donal tells him gently as Megan makes her way around the table. She tries to pluck Ethan off her lap, but the cub wraps his little arms around Emma's neck and holds on.

"Ethan, let go," Megan demands and tugs at him. Emma makes a strangled sound, and Megan stops trying to pull the cub away.

"Ethan." Donal's warning is clear in that one word, and Ethan's little body shrinks against her. He turns his head to look at his alpha, his eyes filling with tears and his lower lip trembling. Emma's heart melts.

"Hey now," she murmurs, rubbing his back. "None of that. I'd love to go out and play. My wolf loves running at night. I bet your little bear legs can't keep up with her."

The challenge has the exact effect she's going for. Indignant, Ethan lets go of her neck and sits up.

"Bears are way, way, way faster than wolves!" he announces, making several people at the table chuckle.

"You don't need to do this," Donal tells her with a smile. "Ethan's usually wary of strangers, but he's been having nightmares recently, so maybe the stitcher in you is calling to him. It's not something you can do anything about."

Now she understands why Ethan sought her out. Her soul cipher gift must attract those in distress. With self-assurance she's far from feeling, she smiles confidently at the sleuth's alpha.

"If it's okay with you, I'd like to go outside with Megan and Ethan. I could use some animal time after the plane ride today."

A few murmurs sound from those at the table. Apparently, not everyone was aware she flew into North Dakota. Maybe they thought she and Kade teleported. It would make sense because their local mage, Victor, has such a powerful teleportation magic.

"What was it like to fly?" Megan asks, he face pale.

"It was pretty nice," Emma says, and Gus chokes out a laugh.

"From what I smelled when you got off that plane, it was much better than nice," he teases as she extracts herself from the chair and lets Ethan slide down to the floor. She expects Kade to get upset at Gus's words, but when she looks over, his expression is calculating instead of agitated.

"Nice is rather a banal description," he chides her. "I'll endeavor to change that adjective next time."

"Improvement is a worthy goal," she counters, surprised at how much she sounds like him at that moment. His eyebrow wings up, and he barks out a laugh.

"Indeed," he agrees and then sobers. "Don't wander too far. I'm here to set wards because of previous incursions from a local blood witch coven. As long as you stay close to the manor house, you should be safe."

A coven of magic-wielding humans isn't a group Emma wants to mess with, especially if they're involved with blood magic. If the coven is intruding on shifter land, it's probable they want shifter blood for their spells. That makes them powerful and dangerous. No wonder Donal will pay so much for Kade's wards. It might be the only way to keep the blood witches out and the sleuth safe.

"I'll be careful," she promises and lets Ethan take her hand and lead her away. Megan falls into step next to her.

"Did I hear that Kade is your alpha?" the woman asks. Emma nods, and Megan looks impressed.

"I didn't know mages could be alphas. How many others are in your pack?"

"Uh, maybe one more?" Emma answers, thinking of Franco. "But he's part fae and part human, so I don't have a pack bond with him, only with Kade."

"Doesn't it feel weird?" Megan asks, wide-eyed. "Not to have a pack, I mean? I don't know if I could handle only having Donal and not having my family. What about pups? Will Kade let another wolf into the pack so you can have pups?"

Absently, Emma toes out of her shoes and leaves them in a small pile of shoes in the mudroom Ethan led her to. The flats were surprisingly comfortable, but she's still happy to be barefoot. With the opportunity to shift presented, she's more than eager to strip down and slide into her fur.

"I want to have pups, but I'm not sure Kade's interested in that," she hedges.

Megan stumbles a little at her words and looks at her, aghast. "Are you and the mage mated?"

Raising an eyebrow at her horrified tone, Emma keeps her displeasure in check. "Not yet, but we will be," she states confidently.

The woman grips her arm and gives a little shake. "You can't do that. You just can't. Mages don't mate. Emma, it's a death sentence for you. That's why they don't have wives or mates or families. They send their children away to be raised by others. Everyone knows mages kill anyone close to them eventually. You need to get out, Emma."

Huh, that's a new one.

Waving a dismissive hand in the air, Emma pulls out of Megan's grip. "No, they don't. Honestly, all these rumors about mages are ridiculous."

"Are we gonna shift?" Ethan calls out, standing in the open doorway. He's already stripped out of his pajamas and is shuffling from foot to foot impatiently. Unlike wolf shifters who don't start shifting until their early teens, bear shifters can shift to animal form at just a few years old. Too eager to remain in control, Ethan's hands are already turning into little bear paws and fur is sprouting on his forearms.

"We're coming!" Megan calls out, stripping out of her clothes and placing them in a convenient cubby above the shoes. Emma follows her example and once both women are naked, they shift. Now she understands why all the doors in this place are huge, otherwise Megan's bear form wouldn't be able to leave the house.

Emma trots out the door after a shifted Ethan and Megan, and they lumber into the night. The cub is adorable as he tries to sprint to the nearby woods. Emma pretends she can't quite keep up with him and enjoys the way the cub dances in delight at winning their race to the tree line.

Pretending to charge her, Ethan growls and swipes a paw at her head. She easily ducks away from him and bumps him with her hip so he topples over. Enjoying the game, he gets back up and charges her again. Megan joins in, letting the bear cub take swipes at her and pretending to be intimidated by his ferocity.

As they play, Emma lets her gift ease into Ethan. If he's having nightmares, maybe she can help with her soul cipher powers. Because he's young and doesn't have any shielding, she slides into his mind with ease and searches for the cause of the cub's distress. She finds fear throbbing inside of him, like a raw burn, easily irritated and difficult to heal.

The experience is so fresh that the memory comes to her with very little coaxing. The images of him out with his parents are as clear as a movie on a screen. The three of them are cavorting in a shallow stream when they're attacked by several coven members. A dozen adult bears were nearby and rushed to lend aid to the couple, saving the family's lives. But Ethan saw all of it, including his father being grievously injured during the fighting.

Soothing the burn, Emma pushes forgiveness into the cub. The poor boy feels like the whole attack was his fault. She finds a memory of his mother telling him the attack wasn't caused by him. Strengthening the memory, she emphasizes the soft tone of his mother's words and her warm, loving embrace. Then she links the feelings of comfort and love with the memory and pushes that to the front of his mind. The emotional wound is still there, but it's healing now.

Distracted by her work, she doesn't notice when Ethan's swipes get a little too close until his claws catch her shoulder. Letting out a yelp, she dives away just as Megan swats the cub in typical matriarchal bear fashion. The claws of her big paw don't touch Ethan, but she sends him tumbling.

Shifting, Emma examines the claw marks with a grimace. She's not truly hurt, but Kade's not going to be happy with her carelessness.

Also shifting to her human form, Megan stands next to her trying to see the marks herself. "I'm so sorry, Emma. Are you okay?"

"It's nothing," she waves off Megan's concern. "It's my own fault. I wasn't paying attention."

"Emma?" Ethan's shifted back to human form now and is standing on her other side, tears in his eyes. "Are you mad at me?"

"Of course not, cubling," she assures him with a smile. She shows him her shoulder. "See, it isn't even bleeding. Nothing to worry about." She crouches down next to him. "You are just so much faster than I was ready for!"

Responding to her praise, his tears dry up and he puffs out his little chest. "I'm really fast."

"You know," Emma continues, finding the thread into his mind she lost when his claw caught her. "You've worn me out. I don't suppose bears like chocolate? Maybe we could go back to the house and make some hot chocolate?"

Peering at Megan, Ethan tries to look commanding. "We need to get Emma hot chocolate. She's probably cold because she's only a wolf and not a bear. And she said she's tired."

Keeping a straight face, Megan nods with exaggerated seriousness. "You're probably right. Would you shift back and lead us to the house? I think I might be a little turned around."

Feeling important, Ethan stands on his toes and sniffs a few times. "This way," he points and then shifts before charging off. Exchanging laughing looks, Emma and Megan shift and follow him.

Emma admires Megan's skills at juggling as she handles a mug of hot chocolate, a pastry, and a snoozing Ethan without spilling anything. Having a snoring cub in one arm has slowed her down, so Emma polished off several pastries before Megan's finished even one. Thankfully, there's plenty more.

Unlike Franco, who yells at her when she wanders into his kitchen looking for a snack, Kieran, the Olsen Sleuth chef, made them welcome and even put together several plates of treats as well as serving up the best hot chocolate Emma's ever had.

With Ethan asleep, Megan gives Emma more details about their current issues.

"Alpha Donal sent formal requests for them to stay away and even filed grievances with the local authorities," Megan explains, making Emma snort with derision.

"Like the human authorities care about what happens to shifters," Emma mutters. "They'd only care about a bunch of blood witches if they started killing humans instead of shifters."

"Yeah, that didn't do any good," Megan agrees. "But at least it's on the books that we tried to do this peacefully. The attack on Ethan was the last straw. They want a young shifter for their magic, and nothing we've done has kept them away. We could lock the cubs up in the house, but that's no way to live."

"No," agrees Emma. "Shifters can't live like that, especially young ones. So, your last resort was to call in Kade?"

"He's our second to last resort. If his wards don't work, we'll go to war with the blood witches. Hunt them down one by one and wipe them out," Megan explains grimly. "We discussed moving, but that would make us look weak and draw other blood magic witches to prey on us."

Although she's never had to deal with blood witches, Emma understands the importance of being thought of as strong in the magical world. Those who are perceived as weak are prey. Being prey never ends well.

Unaware of Emma's snooping into Ethan's mind, Megan tells her about the attack on the cub's parents. It happened only the day before Donal contacted Kade. That attack pushed Donal into trying out Kade's wards and made him willing to pay exorbitant amounts to get the mage to North Dakota on such short notice.

That makes Emma curious about the Olsen Sleuths' finances. "How can you guys afford Kade? He told me how much he's charging. I've got to be honest. My old pack wouldn't ever have been able to pay that."

"Oh, our sleuth is rich," Megan explains blithely. "We created and maintain AltShifter."

Emma knows her mouth is gaping open, but she can't seem to control it. AltShifter started as a website for all things shifter. Now it's the premier website for all magical creatures. Anything you might need to buy, know, or find is on AltShifter. Even Emma, who's never been particularly into social media or buying items online, uses AltShifter. Several other websites have tried to copy its success, but none are even close. One wolf called it Facebook, Instagram, Amazon, Wikipedia, and Alibaba all rolled into one.

It's also the main reason shifters have a strong presence in Congress at the moment. AltShifter helps promote shifter-sympathetic candidates. They run virtual fundraisers and protests, keeping the shifter world apprised of what's going on legally and politically. Many other magical communities are doing the same thing using AltShifter's platform.

The Olsen Sleuth isn't just rich. They're filthy rich.

"Fuck," Emma breaths out, making Megan laugh.

"Your expression is priceless," Megan chortles, and Kieran joins in with a laugh of his own. They all stop when Ethan grumbles and moves around a little on Megan's lap. Once he's settled and fully asleep again, Emma nods down at him.

"Is he having nightmares every night?"

"Bad ones," Megan confirms. "My sister, his mom, is caring for his dad. Ben's going to be fine, but one of his legs got badly mangled, and it's going to take some time before the intense pain subsides. Lauren doesn't want Ethan to see his dad like that, so I'm taking care of him, but he won't sleep. At best, he'll go down for a few hours, but then he always wakes up screaming." She gives Emma a tired look.

"Take him to be with his mom and dad," Emma says firmly. "He'll do better if he's with them."

"But Ben's still being healed, and we both know how intense that is," Megan argues. But she bites her lip as if considering Emma's suggestion.

"It doesn't matter if Ben's in pain. Ethan can handle that. What he can't handle is thinking his parents are rejecting him because he caused an attack."

Gasping, Megan tightens her hold on the slumbering cub, making Ethan mumble out a sleepy protest. "Sorry, bud," she whispers. She waits until Ethan settles back down before turning her angry eyes to Emma.

"How can you know that?" Megan hisses.

Crap, now she's in sensitive territory. "I just know," she hedges.

Any hope she had that Megan would just accept that vague statement is dashed when the other woman's eyes narrow.

"What did he say to you, wolf?" she asks, determination hardening her jaw. "What did Ethen tell you?"

Sighing, Emma gives up. "I might be a soul cipher," she whispers.

It sounds so farfetched when she says it out loud that she wants to call back the words. After a moment of silence, she keeps talking.

"At least that's what Kade thinks. I don't really know. I do know that I get these feelings, and I can tell when people are hurting." She taps the side of her head. "When people are holding on to their pain here." Then she taps her chest, over her beating heart. "And here. I can help them. Urge the pain to heal. But from what I felt, Ethan is drowning in guilt. No matter what everyone's telling him, he's sure the attack was his fault. He needs to be with his parents, no matter how much pain Ben's in. He needs to be part of the healing process or he won't heal either."

Now it's Megan's turn to gape at her. "Soul cipher?" she squeaks out, loudly enough for the chef to hear. He drops the knife he's holding. Cursing, he jumps back so the tool lands harmlessly on the floor with a loud clatter. Ignoring the knife, he turns to Emma.

"You're a soul cipher?" It's more of an exclamation than a question. His eyes are unblinking as he stares at her, his body tense and his voice halfway to a growl.

Feeling uncomfortable and exposed, Emma shrugs. "Maybe? I don't know. I've never met or talked to one. I can only go by what Kade tells me."

"If Kade says you're a soul cipher, you are one," Kieran insists adamantly. Emma's not prepared for him to cross the kitchen and grab her in his large hands, giving her a violent little shake.

"Do not tell anyone else! Do you understand me?" he demands. His emotions are intense enough to make his eyes flash with power. His jaw moves a little, popping and trying to reform as his bear pushes to be let loose. Long teeth slide out of his upper gums and claws start forming, pushing painfully into her skin.

"What the hell?" Emma cries out as she pushes forcefully against him. Looking down at his hands, he realizes he's losing control. Letting go of her, he backs away. He's sweating lightly from the effort to control himself.

"I'm sorry," he says quickly, lowering his eyes respectfully. Then he pins Megan with a hard glare. "Do not speak of this. She's helped Ethan with no request for reciprocity. You will not ruin this by telling everyone what she is. No posting on AltShifter and no entries into the soul cipher database or resource catalog. Nothing!"

Shaken, Megan gives a little nod and slides off the stool she's perched on so she can move away from the intense chef. Coming to a stop when her back hits a nearby wall. Kieran shuts his eyes for a moment, taking a few steadying breaths. He unclenches his fists and finally opens his eyes to look at her. His claws have retracted, and his teeth are human again. His gaze is still intense, but no longer crazed.

"My sister is a soul cipher, and she was kidnapped. We never saw her again. I don't know what happened to her, because we were so careful. But she was taken anyway." Deep sadness crosses his face. "Her absence is a gaping wound in our sleuth. I'd save you and your loved ones the same pain. Tell no one. Don't let it be known what you can do."

Emma gives the chef a gentle smile, finally understanding why Kieran is acting so oddly. "I'll keep it a secret," she promises.

A full-grown female bear shifter is not easily kidnapped. Sure, there are drugs or spells, but they're expensive. And the fact that this rich sleuth still can't find her says a lot about the wealth and power of those who took her. Or perhaps those who took her are just that clever and sneaky.

The last thing she wants is to disappear like Kieran's sister. The thought sends a bolt of fear through her. "What's your sister's name?"

"Cathleen," Kieran tells her. "She's the kindest person you will ever meet. A soft-hearted soul, you know? She was always bringing home prey animals to heal and release." His sadness eases, and his voice softens as he loses himself in the memory. "We learned to put markers on the animals she rescued so we didn't accidentally kill and eat them while shifted." He smiles, and Emma gets a clear picture of a woman with long chestnut hair shaking her finger at a young Donal.

"That happened once. Donal ate a deer she raised from a baby. She cried for days. We all felt horrible. Donal had just gotten his driver's license the month before and convinced his parents to let him drive halfway across the state to get the saltwater taffy she liked best." His eyes mist with emotion. "She was our heart and now we've been forced to live without her for over a year."

Unable to resist, Emma leans over the high counter that separates the kitchen and places a hand on Kieran's shoulder. Unlike all the other times she's let the soul cipher in her loose, this time her power isn't subtle. It hits Kieran with force, making both of them gasp. It's not a wound the soul cipher gift wants to heal. No, her power wants to share knowledge.

Power flows, and hope flowers inside Kieran.

She's out there. She's alive. She misses you.

She will be back.

Choking out a sob, Kieran sags against the counter between them. His expression is haunted but optimistic. "I would know if she had died," he whispers to Emma.

"You would know," she agrees. "The sibling bond is there, just weak and fragile. But I can feel it. Don't give up hope or she might lose the bond. That might truly be the end of her."

His expression turns determined as he gives a sharp nod. "No, I won't give up."

Emma pulls her power back, fatigue making her slump onto her stool. Kieran straightens up, full of energy and purpose. "If you'd be willing, I need you to talk to Donal about this. No one else needs to know, but he's gotten lax about looking for her, and I think this is just what we need to keep the search going."

"I can do that," Emma agrees. "But tomorrow."

"Yes, of course. I'll arrange a meeting between the two of you after dinner," Kieran tells her.

"Kade needs to be there," Emma insists. There's no way she's going to admit to anyone else that she's a soul cipher without Kade there. Hearing the story of Kieran's sister is bringing home the reality of her value as a commodity.

"Of course," Kieran agrees. "That's easily arranged. Let me walk you to your room. I think you might have done more than your fair share of healing today."

"Agreed," Emma says and then bids good night to Megan after getting the bear to promise that Ethan will be with his parents no matter what they say.

It's good that Kieran leads her through the labyrinth of corridors. Fatigue is tugging at her, making all the hallways look alike. When he finally stops and points to a door, she doesn't even recognize it as her own.

The next door down opens, and Kade stands there, his violet eyes full of annoyance. "Did you enjoy your late-night snack?"

Eyeing the displeased mage with dislike, Kieran wishes her a good night and leaves.

Focusing on Kade, Emma summons a tired smile. Ignoring his scowl, she walks to him, wraps her arms around his tall body, and nuzzles her face into his muscled chest. The sensation of holding him makes her hum with contentment. He's wearing cotton pajamas, but only the bottoms, leaving his top half free for her to lick and kiss.

Huffing out a chuckle, he hugs her back. "I guess you missed me."

"Tired," she mutters, leaning her body weight against him. The bond between them thrums for a moment, and Kade sounds a resigned sigh.

"You've overtaxed yourself," he mutters, leaning over and picking her up. "You've been a naughty wolf and using your soul cipher powers. You shouldn't do that, Emma. You don't have any training yet."

"It's the stupid gift's fault," she complains, sounding like a petulant child. "I'm not trying to use it. The thing just flares up."

"I know, little wolf. That's one of the reasons soul ciphers need to be closely guarded. I'll do a better job from now on."

"Don't need guarding," she grumbles. "I just need some sleep."

Kade sets her on her feet in the bathroom. "Get ready for bed," he orders as he leaves and shuts the door behind him.

Later she'll wonder why her toiletries are in his bathroom when he'd insisted on separate bedrooms. For now, she concentrates on brushing her teeth, washing her face, and using the facilities.

He's waiting on the other side of the bathroom door when she opens it, his expression equal parts concern and affection. Guiding her to the bed, he helps her to stay upright and strips her out of her dress. Once she's naked, he pulls the covers back, and she practically falls in.

The bed is warm from Kade's body heat and smells like him. Wiggling a little, she moans with pleasure. When Kade lies down, she wraps her limbs around him and decides this moment is the most perfect moment she's ever experienced.

"Are you a wolf shifter or octopus?" he teases, snuggling her close.

"Shhh," she whispers, already falling asleep. "Let's go talk to Jason."

His sound of confusion doesn't even register as she slides them both into her stitch.

Cool, crisp sea air fills her nose as a pelican effortlessly glides overhead, disappearing into the azure sky. The day is cloudless and warm sun rays keep the sea breeze from being chilly. The waves below crash hard against the cliffs, creating a muted roar that eclipses all the other sounds around her.

"I missed this," she murmurs to herself, smiling. With a little concentration she creates dolphins cavorting in the distance. A few seagulls call to each other farther down on the cliff.

There, now it's perfect.

"I'm a fan of cliffs and oceans, but I like the botanical garden better," Kade tells her as he takes a seat next to her on the short, spiky coastal grass. "This place feels so raw. It's too real to be believed. Your botanical garden has a surreal feeling because it's too perfect, not a plant out of place. It fits in the dream realm. This place," he waves a hand to indicate the surrounding dream. "This is much too accurate."

It's hard to be offended when someone's complaining that your skills are too good to be true. Grinning at him, she wiggles closer until their sides are touching.

"Hi, Kade," she purrs. "Have you ever had sex in a dream?"

Raising an eyebrow, he smirks at her. "Blunt canine," he accuses without heat. "Who knew such a little wolf would have such a large sexual appetite."

"The keyword in that statement is wolf," she tells him. "And the only person I look little next to is you, or one of those bears. I tower over most of the humans, especially the females."

"Does my height bother you?" he asks with genuine concern.

"Hell, no," she answers with a grin. "I like you all big and manly."

"That's good." Then his expression turns sly. "There's much I need to learn about shifters. I plan to do an in-depth study of wolf shifter sexuality. I'm going to make you my case study. I look forward to all our *interviews*."

"I'm glad you're so diligent in your studies," she murmurs. Breathing in deeply through her nose, she beams. "Thanks for bringing your scent in with you. Now that I know your smell, it doesn't feel right to be near you without your scent."

"My pleasure," he responds, wrapping an arm around her shoulder and nuzzling her. "It's a small thing." He runs his tongue gently over the shell of her ear, making her quiver at the sensation. She might be enjoying herself, but she needs to see to another matter before indulging.

"Before we go any further, can you bring Jason in? We can play after he visits."

His arm tightens to the point of pain, and a sound of annoyance fills her ears.

"No," he snarls, surprising her with his vehemence.

"I just want to talk to him briefly and then we can have some fun," she wheedles. She strums at the bond between them, trying to figure out why he's having such an intense reaction. Resentment is easy to pick out, but the surprising emotion coming from Kade is fear.

Pulling at her soul cipher gift, she eases her way into him.

"Stop it." His tone is soft and his words have no edge to them at all. He doesn't put up shields or do anything to keep her out, so she ignores his order.

The resentment is easy to follow right back to the throbbing emotional wound that colors so much of his reactions. Right now, possessiveness and jealousy are weeping out of the wound like puss from an infection—poisoning and painful. Sweeping in her power, she cleans out the new infection to an old wound.

I'm right here.

I'm not leaving you.

I can love Jason and you.

He won't take me away from you.

Each statement eases the wound until it's no longer ragged and painful. Knowing that if she tries to do anything more Kade will start pushing her away, she pulls her power back. She does it slowly, giving him plenty of time to adjust.

"If you can do that without any formal training, I'm both eager and afraid to see what you can do once you know how to harness your gift properly," Kade murmurs.

She opens her eyes to regard him. His eyes are still closed, but his face is relaxed, and the bond between them is serene.

"The gift seems to know what to do," she says with a little shrug. "And it feels good to use it." Someday she hopes Kade will be comfortable enough to let her help those from her pack who were badly traumatized by Alpha Michaels.

"I can hear your thoughts," he tells her. "The bond is open and strong between us right now. How can you always think of others? You should be thinking about hiring yourself out to the highest bidder. You could make tens of thousands of dollars an hour, but all you can think about is helping your pack? Emma, we need to work on your priorities."

"I think you need help with the whole priorities thing," she counters, sending affection down the bond. "Money is nice, but knowing that I can help those I love is more important. Besides, there's no reason I can't hire myself out at the same time I help my old pack and family on the side."

"It's not just about the money," Kade counters. His brows furrow and she can feel concern flowing from him. "If people find out you give away your gift for free, there'll be no end to the requests. You can't help every person with a sob story."

"Maybe not, but I can help those I know and love," she argues and feels his resignation wash down their bond.

"We'll work out a schedule," he tells her. "After you're trained, we'll create a list and schedule people so they can't overwhelm you. Don't fight me on this, Emma. It's for your own safety."

"Yes, Alpha," Emma says obediently. It doesn't occur to her to argue with Kade over a schedule. She knows herself well enough to know that Kade's accurate when he talks about her being overwhelmed. Saying no to family and pack is next to impossible for her. Even trying to say "no for now," and not an absolute "no" would be difficult.

He gives her a sour look at the use of alpha, but doesn't comment. Instead, he gives her a quick squeeze.

"I'll need to disappear for a moment to find Avery and Jason. If they aren't asleep, I won't be able to bring them here. I don't have the kind of power that can force people into the dream realm if they don't want to go," he warns her.

"He'll be asleep." She knows she's smiling like a fool, but she's so eager to see Jason that she can't imagine he won't be asleep. He just has to be because she needs him here.

With a last look of affectionate skepticism, Kade disappears, leaving her alone with her favorite dreamscape.

To keep herself entertained, she brings in a flock of cormorants and quiets the crashing waves so the birds can fish among the rocks far below. Taking it a step further, she creates bright silver fish for the birds to catch and carry back to their nests on the cliff. She's so engrossed in her dream manipulations that she doesn't realize she's not alone any longer until she hears another voice.

"Emma!"

Looking over her shoulder, she sees Jason running toward her, an elated smile on his face. Jumping to her feet, she runs to meet him, only to skid to a halt when Kade appears in front of her. Without a second thought, she moves to go around him, just in time to watch Jason fall to the ground as if tripping on something invisible. Her brother tries to get up, but his legs won't cooperate.

Fearful, Emma starts toward him again, but now Kade's grabbing her and swinging her up into his arms.

"Keep your distance," he warns her.

Scowling, she meets his concerned gaze with her irritated one. "What the hell are you doing?"

"Not me," he explains quickly and nods. She follows his gaze to find Avery gliding to Jason, casting suspicious glances at her and Kade.

"Damn it, Avery," Jason yells, looking at her over his shoulder. "We talked about this!"

"I'm sorry," she coos to him but doesn't take her distrustful eyes off Emma and Kade. "Be patient, my heart."

My heart? That must be good. Right? If Avery is claiming Jason as a mate, he's safe.

Except Emma doesn't like the look on Avery's face. In this dream realm, she should look beautiful. She should appear as the best version of herself, yet the woman striding toward them is much too pale and thin with bloodshot eyes. Emma sniffs at the air, but Avery didn't bring any scent into the dream realm with her.

"I'm sorry, Emma," Jason calls out to her, looking frustrated and helpless but not scared. "She can be overly cautious."

"I don't know what that's like at all," Emma quips, rolling her eyes to meet Kade's amused ones.

"I guess you and your sibling bring out the possessive monsters in mages," Kade comments wryly.

"What do you mean by bringing us here?" Avery demands, coming to a halt in front of Jason as if shielding the larger man with her much smaller body.

"Avery, let me up," Jason demands.

"In a moment, my sweet beast," Avery calls back to him without looking.

Smirking at Jason, Emma wiggles in Kade's grip. "Sweet beast?" she chortles. "I can't wait to tell cousin Jack!" Kade lets her slide to the ground. Once on her feet, he wraps his arm around her and keeps her caged tightly against his chest.

"Shut up," Jason grumbles, red flaring up his neck.

"Whatever you say, sweet beast," Emma says in a sing-song voice, making Jason groan. Her teasing comes to an abrupt end when Avery's power flares up around them.

"You do not speak to him that way," Avery hisses at Emma. It takes all of Emma's concentration to keep her dream stable and to mute Avery's influence.

"Avery, this is Jason's sister. Don't you recognize her?" Kade bites out, his power flaring. If Kade unleashes in this dream, Emma's not sure she'll be able to keep it secure. The power of two mages battling it out will probably overwhelm her dreamscape.

"Who are either of you to call my Jason here?" Avery questions, her voice dripping with outrage.

It's apparent Avery isn't emotionally stable. If her dream projection is anything to go by, she's still recovering physically, which is no doubt affecting her mental state as well.

"Jason, you need to calm Avery down," Emma calls out, keeping her voice low and soothing. "Has she formed a pack or mating bond with you?"

"Mating bond," Jason replies, eyes becoming unfocused as he feels for his bond with Avery. "But her emotions are all over the place sometimes." Jason pales and his eyes meet Emma's. "Shit, I can feel her powering up to level a city right now."

"Feel for the bond," Emma instructs urgently. An unstable mage is the last thing anyone needs. They might be far enough away from each other that Avery's overt use of power won't hurt her or Kade, but there are no doubt innocent lives near their physical location.

"I can feel it, but she's pushing power out so much I can't push anything back," Jason tells her. Avery's eyes light up: violet, glowing, and volatile.

"He's mine!" Avery shrieks.

"Avery, get control of yourself!" Kade orders. His power swells, pushing against Emma and making it hard to concentrate.

"Find me!" Emma instructs as she pushes power out to rebuild the sibling bond Avery broke. Without thinking about the broader implication, she reaches for Kade's power to help her reform the bond with her brother. She feels a moment of hesitation, but then the alpha bond between them opens wide, and his immense power flows into her.

Tugging at her soul cipher gift, she probes for her bond with Jason. Because they shared a womb for nine months, their bond is stronger than most and easy to rebuild. Once she re-establishes the bond, she's able to push her gift into her brother. Now she searches for Jason's mating bond with Avery and finds it glowing in Jason, bright and throbbing with power.

Delicately, Emma moves her power through Jason and Avery's mating bond.

"If you're going to do something, you need to do it soon." Looking up at Kade, Emma sees lines of strain on his face. A quick check of their bond tells her he's managing to contain Avery both in the dream realm and the physical realm, but he won't be able to do it much longer. Especially with Emma pulling from him.

"Follow me," Emma calls out to Jason and pulses his mating bond with Avery. Jason closes his eyes. She feels him with her, moving power up the mating bond. The farther they move, the more Emma feels something fundamentally wrong with Avery. Her mind isn't working as it should. There isn't just emotional damage here; there's something else amiss. Something physical.

Alcohol and drugs, Jason whispers to her through their bond. *Avery's an addict.*

Pain from their short but tumultuous relationship trickles through to Emma. The addiction explains a lot of what she's feeling in the bond between her brother and Avery. As a group, mages seem to end up with abandonment and affection issues, but adding any kind of addiction along with their level of power is a recipe for disaster.

Tell her you love her, she whispers urgently to Jason. *Tell her you'd never leave her. Talk about wolves mating for life. Call her mate. Keep repeating those things.*

A constant murmur of words starts flowing from Jason to Avery, both through their link and out loud.

"Avery, my mate, please come here. I need to hold you. My wolf needs you. Please, my love, listen to me." Jason's voice is a combination of worry and demand, and Emma can feel it's hitting a good spot in Avery's mind. She wants to respond to Jason's pleas for contact and comfort, even if the other part of her wants to eliminate what she sees as a threat to her relationship with Jason.

Emma stops paying attention to what Jason's saying to Avery and concentrates on manipulating their bond. Now that she knows what's wrong, she focuses on shutting Avery down instead of trying to soothe her. Only Jason can calm the mage's agitation, so she pumps power into Jason's mating bond.

Knowledge about manipulating sleeping minds flows into her from Kade, so she's ready. The moment Avery relents and turns her attention to Jason instead of Kade, Emma leaps into her mind. A roar of rage sounds from the diminutive mage, but Emma's already shutting down her consciousness and sending the mage into a dreamless sleep state.

Avery's body goes still; her expression becomes blank; and then she disappears from the dream before her body can fall to the ground.

"Emma, what did you do?" Jason calls out, horrified.

"She's fine," Emma assures him. "Feel the mating bond. See, it's strong. I just put her into a different kind of sleep." Jason concentrates for a moment; then his body relaxes, and a tired smile forms on his face.

Stumbling to his feet, he walks to her with open arms. She pulls away from Kade and accepts the hug. "I missed you! After Avery and I disappeared, I was so scared for you."

"I might have missed seeing your stupid face too," Emma murmurs, and Jason chuckles. Feeling Kade's displeasure at the continued embrace, she reluctantly pulls away from her brother. "It's good to have the sibling bond back. It was weird not being able to bug you with it."

Making a face, Jason shoves at her playfully. "Whatever, brat."

Happy to fall back into familiar patterns, Emma grins as she insults him. "Car chaser."

"Hello, Jason," Kade says as he pulls Emma back into his embrace, interrupting their sibling banter.

Jason's friendly expression never wavers. "Hi there, Mr. Allard. thanks for saving us." He shifts his gaze to Emma, and she feels his questions through their sibling bond. Jason can feel the lack of a mating bond between her and Kade. She gives a slight shake of her head. She doesn't want to talk about Kade yet. Respecting her wishes, he doesn't ask her.

"Where are you guys?" Jason says. "You know, in the real world."

"North Dakota," Emma says. "We're staying with the Olsen Sleuth."

"Bears, huh," Jason says thoughtfully and then rubs his face with an exhausted sigh, as if this polite conversation is suddenly wearing him out. "I never thought we'd find ourselves like this. I don't even know where I am right now. When I'm gone too long Avery goes insane with worry."

Without Avery clogging everything with her immense and fiery magic, it's easy to read the state of Jason's mind and body through their sibling bond. His exhaustion is bone deep, and he's plagued by worry and doubt. The entire time she's been enjoying herself with Kade, Jason's been fighting to save Avery's life. Withdrawal symptoms on top of the trauma she suffered from her captivity sent her into a downward spiral that could've killed them both.

Even now, evidence is strong that Avery's suffering isn't finished. Emma caresses the mating bond between Jason and Avery, using it to assess the mage's damage. Even in the dream realm and working through a mating bond to get to a third person, it seems she can be effective. She finds none of Avery's wounds are as deep as Kade's, but she has so many of them they take her breath away.

With the added benefit of Kade's power, she soothes several of the worst ones. Not surprisingly these fears revolve around Jason. Her fear that Jason will abandon her. Her terror that she won't be able to keep him safe. Self-doubt that she's not worthy of his love.

Can you feel this? she asks him, guiding him to those painful places in Avery's mind.

Jason's pain at her suffering is palpable. *I'd never leave her. How can she think I would?*

They aren't wolves. You need to remember that, Emma explains gently. *From what I've learned from Kade, they don't have families when they're young, let alone a pack to keep them safe and make sure they know they're loved. I've done what I can for now. Keep doing what I'm showing you. If we can all be together again, I can do more.*

"How are you able to do this at all?" Jason asks out loud. Emma opens her eyes to see her brother regarding her with a quizzical expression.

"Turns out I'm a soul cipher," Emma says with a little shrug.

"The hell you say!" Jason exclaims, making Kade chuckle behind her.

"I see the family resemblance," Kade comments, amiably. "It's good to see that both you and Avery are doing well."

Both siblings gape at him, and Jason shakes his head. "Avery was on the verge of decimating a city, and that's doing well?"

Raising an eyebrow, Kade gives them his best arrogant look. "The city is fine. Jason's alive. Avery's alive. They could be dead, along with possibly several hundred thousand bystanders. I say they're doing well."

"Put like that," Emma mutters. "Just about everyone's doing well."

"I'm glad you understand, little wolf," Kade says, deliberately ignoring her tone.

"You know," Jason says with so much forced casualness that it makes Emma roll her eyes. "Avery and I have a mate bond. So, I guess what everyone says isn't true. Mages can form a mate bond. They don't have to be alone."

Kade stiffens at Jason's words, all good humor bleeding out of his face. "Is that so?" His tone doesn't invite any further conversation on the topic.

"Leave it, Jason," Emma says, trying to keep her tone light. "We're fine."

"Sure, no problem." Jason casts a wary glance at Kade's forbidding countenance. It's obvious he wants to say more, but to Emma's relief, he keeps any thoughts on Kade and Emma's relationship to himself. He glances over to where Avery was before she disappeared from the dreamscape. His expression turns worried. "There might be some fallout from you putting Avery to sleep like that."

"Probably, but Kade can keep me safe from her wrath," Emma reassures him. "And eventually she'll come around. You'll need to be patient. She wants to heal, and she's got a strong will. But to be honest, she's got a lot of damage. It could take some time."

"That's fine." Jason sighs. "She has my heart, so by default she owns my time also."

Tugging Kade's arm off her shoulders, Emma gives Jason a last hug. "I'm going to help," she promises him. "All that I can."

"Emma," Kade says in a warning tone. She's surprised he's been quiet this long. Undaunted, she turns fierce eyes on him.

"No, Kade, this isn't negotiable. We help family. Period. If I'm your wolf, Jason's your family now. And Avery. We help them no matter what."

The silence between them stretches for several minutes, Kade's face like stone and the bond between them muted. Her submissive wolf wants her to drop to her back, expose her belly, and whine for forgiveness. But the human part of her knows she needs to draw this line in the sand and make sure Kade knows what's important in life, because so far, he's been woefully mistaken on that score.

Finally, he gives one small nod and forcefully pulls her back into his arms. "Very well," he says, a strange finality to his voice. "As long as you're mine, I'll include Jason as important."

"Kade, this is excessive." Pointing at the three massive bear shifters standing next to an equally massive SUV, Emma makes an irritated sound. "It's broad daylight, and I'm going to be with Brandon. He's a grendel. He can keep me safe. Besides, I'm a wolf shifter. I'm not helpless."

"I'm sure you can be perfectly deadly when you wish to be," Kade responds in a tone that tells her he doesn't believe a word he's saying. When her expression turns sour, his smile becomes placating. "You could be kidnapped in broad daylight. And that damn grendel is one of the reasons you're getting an escort. I don't trust him, Emma. I promised you could help his mother, but I still don't want you alone with him. You either accept the guards, or you don't go."

"That's not fair," Emma whines, throwing up her arms like a dramatic teenager.

Lips twitching, Kade's expression softens. "You wouldn't want me to worry about you all day. Would you? The wards I'm setting up are tricky, and if I'm distracted, I could accidentally hurt myself."

"Low blow," Emma mutters and then rolls her eyes. "Fine, they can come with. But they have to stay outside the hospital room while I'm stitching."

"In that case, you'll keep the room door open," Kade bargains. Emma can see that's as much as he's willing to concede, so she grabs him in a hug.

"Sure, the door can stay open," she agrees, wrapping her arms around him tightly. After everything that happened in the dream last night, she finds she can't touch Kade enough. They slept together, and when he tried to get up in the middle of the night to go to the bathroom, he was forced to wake her because she wouldn't let go, even in her sleep.

If she wasn't so eager to help a dying woman see her farm one last time, she wouldn't leave his side.

"I love you, mate," she whispers to him. As usual, his body stiffens, and his expression turns stony.

"Don't say that."

"Too late. I already said it. And I know I'll say it again, so you should just accept it," Emma says with forced cheerfulness.

Instead of answering, Kade returns her hug. He can't even acknowledge love, so she knows better than to expect the words. It's okay. They have time, and she's confident he'll come around.

"I'll be back for dinner," she promises.

"I'm not worried. The bears will make sure of it," Kade says. "They know who's in charge of you." She ignores both the tone and the words because she knows they're coming from a place of insecurity. He wants to convince himself that he's possessive of her because she's a possession, not because he's rapidly losing his heart to her.

Pulling away, she gives him a smile. "Be careful."

"Always." With that, he turns on his heels and strides away. Emma watches him disappear back into the house before she heads to the waiting SUV.

It takes the bears almost an hour to drive her to Brandon's family farm. By the time they arrive, she knows all about Greg, Amos, and Ken, as well as their mates, cubs, and hobbies. Amos even promised to give her an archery lesson if there's any daylight left after dinner.

All four of them grow quiet as the SUV slowly makes its way up the long, straight drive to the farm house. "I feel like this should be a movie set," Ken mutters, and Emma mutely nods in agreement.

The house itself is a modest single-story structure made of stone. Smoke is even curling out the chimney. Colorful shutters frame the windows and a big welcome sign hangs on the front door. Flowering bushes line the path from the drive to the front door and a big bushy tree in the front yard shades half the house.

Just behind the house is a giant red barn with fenced-in areas on either side. On one side, horses are grazing, lazily swishing their tails to swat at flies. On the other side are half a dozen cows and a few calves roaming around. One calf bounds over to the fence line and watches them park with large, curious eyes. Chickens scatter as a few dogs come running up, barking and wagging their tails.

"Any moment now Dorothy is going to come around the corner of that barn, singing about rainbows or some such shit," Amos mutters, making Emma snort out a laugh.

"Should we get out?" Greg asks, eyeing the dogs. None of them are afraid of the dogs, but they don't want to end up hurting a beloved pet if the dogs decide to be aggressive. Dogs can get weird around shifters.

"Maybe we should wait for someone to come out of the house," Emma suggests.

"I could honk the horn," Greg says, his hand hovering over the center of the steering wheel.

"Ah, don't do that. Horns hurt my ears," Ken protests.

Before the discussion can go any further, Brandon bounds out of the house, calling to the dogs as he goes. "Bread, Butter, sit!"

The dogs stop barking and plop their butts down. Tongues loll out the sides of their snouts as they pant and look up at Brandon with adoration.

Amused by the names and impressed by their obedience, Emma unlatches her seatbelt and reaches for her door handle. She's eager to talk to Brandon and see the farm, but Amos grabs her before she can open it.

"No, no," he objects, all earlier teasing and fun gone. "You don't do anything first. You stay here with Greg. Ken and I get out, check around, and then come back for you. If you try to get out before we get back, Greg will lock the door and leave. We're under strict orders. You follow protocol or we take you right back to the sleuth house."

Brows furrowed, Emma huffs. "That's a little extreme. Don't you think? It's not like Kade has cameras around here to see what's going on. You can ease up on the protection. I won't tell him."

Amos's expression doesn't change. "It's not harsh, Emma. It's an appropriate level of caution," he tells her gravely. "And this has nothing to do with Kade at all. We need him to set those wards, but he's not the only option. I don't even like the guy. I advocated for war with the blood witches, but I was outvoted."

Emma is surprised by Amos's animosity. If she had to guess, she'd bet the coven hurt someone very close to him and he's still dealing with the aftermath. Her soul cipher gift rears up, but she ruthlessly forces it down. The effort makes her break into a sweat, and by the time she's done, her breathing is ragged.

Opening eyes she didn't realize she'd closed, she finds all the men watching her curiously. Ken has his phone out and fingers poised over the screen.

"You okay?" he asks. "I can call Victor or Kade if you need someone."

"Victor?" she breathes out, unclenching her hands from the seat in front of her. She needs to get some training because fighting her gift isn't fun at all. She wonders briefly about going into a hospital where people will be suffering emotional pain all around her. That's going to be a major test of her restraint.

"He can teleport," Ken explains. "Get you to a hospital or just away from a place quickly if necessary."

"I don't need anything like that," she assures the bear. "I just needed a moment to compose myself."

"I triggered it. Didn't I?" Amos asks gently.

Unsure how to respond, Emma gives him a shaky smile. "Nothing to trigger. I'm good."

"You don't need to lie to us, Emma," Greg tells her gently.

"My mate was attacked by the blood witches," Amos explains. "She's alive but still recovering. The magic they hurt her with is taking her a long time to heal from." He lets out a long breath. "I feel responsible." That must be what made her soul cipher power flare. Amos is probably suffering some serious guilt and shame from not being able to keep his mate safe.

"I'm sorry that happened—" Emma starts, but Amos cuts her off.

"We know what you did for Ethan and Kieran," he tells her. "We know you're a soul cipher like Cathleen. Kieran told us everything. I didn't mean to make you fight your gift."

"Fuck," Emma cusses, thoroughly annoyed. Kieran made such a big deal about not telling anyone, and then he went blabbing to his entire sleuth. "So much for keeping it a secret."

"It is a secret," Amos insists. "Only our sleuth will know about it."

"Now do you understand why our protectiveness isn't about Kade?" Ken asks. "You're like Cathleen. You're a gentle, kind soul in a world of monsters. You helped Ethan and Kieran without regard to yourself or your safety."

"We all talked last night, the whole sleuth," Greg explains. "Donal knows Kade as well as anyone can know a mage, and he's sure you were told not to use your power. But you did anyway, for strangers who aren't even wolves."

"We've decided to offer you a place," Ken adds. "The three of us were picked to be the emissaries for the sleuth. We want you to join us. Be a part of our sleuth."

"But I'm a wolf!" Emma protests, both touched and astonished by the offer. Outside of mating, shifter groups don't accept members that don't match their animals. It just isn't done.

"Doesn't matter. You helped two of ours with no request for compensation. You gave freely a gift you could have hoarded and bargained with. You acted with generosity, just like our Cathleen would have. Kieran's willing to take you as his sister in our sleuth. Donal told us to make sure you know Victor is our close ally, so we can keep you safe, even from Kade."

"Guys, that's all amazing, but Kade's my mate. I'm not leaving him," Emma tells them gently and gets three matching scowls for her troubles.

"He told Donal that he isn't your mate," Amos tells her. Worry and displeasure radiate off him. "After we found out about your soul cipher gift, we consulted with Victor before deciding to ask you to join us. Victor told us that Kade is a very traditional mage, so he won't ever take a mate or spouse or anything like that. You're never going to be more than a convenience for him, Emma."

"You don't know what you're talking about," she insists stubbornly. "He might be a mage, but he's my alpha, and soon he'll be my mate." The three bears' expressions go from scowls to pity in the blink of an eye. Tired of this conversation, she points to where Brandon is patiently waiting for them to get out of the vehicle. "Go check what you need to so I can get out of this damn car."

"Promise you'll at least think about our offer," Amos requests.

"I will," she says. There's no harm in promising that. "But don't get your hopes up."

"Too late," Ken says with a grin as he gets out of the car.

Watching them greet Brandon, Emma contemplates the bizarre path her life has taken. Never in her wildest dreams did she ever think one of the richest sleuths in America would ask her to join them.

"I'm not a stray dog that needs a home," she mutters to herself, but Greg, with his shifter hearing, answers her.

"No, definitely not a stray dog," he agrees, giving her a quick grin in the rearview mirror. "And from what I heard about wolf shifters, I think your wolf will love running with our bears. Especially my grizzly." The hint of desire in his expression catches her off guard. "I know my bear already likes you."

Thankfully Amos is opening her door, ending her need to respond.

"It's perfect," Donna whispers, an expression of pure delight on her face. In the dream realm, Donna isn't the sallow, sickly human in a hospital bed. Here, she's healthy and vibrant, striding through the house and touching everything. Emma notices a rug is missing in the living room and quickly adds it as Donna picks up a picture frame from the fireplace mantel.

Brandon stands next to her, a massive smile splitting his face. "You can ride a horse too, if you want," he tells her. "Emma met Dyno and saw all the tack. She can make it so that you can ride."

Donna turns to her son, and love and joy pour out of her. "I can't believe all this," she tells him. She opens her arms up, and Brandon folds his much bigger body around the slight woman, enveloping her in a hug.

"Anything for you, Mom," he says, his voice choked with emotion.

"None of that," Donna says briskly as she extracts herself from the hug. "No tears or sadness here." She turns her attention to Emma. "Is my garden here? I want to see my snapdragons blooming. Oh, and my nasturtiums!"

"Of course," Emma says, thankful for the gardening crash course Brandon gave her earlier that day. "They're all there." Because she wants to make the experience as vibrant as possible, Emma ratchets up the color and smells in the garden.

When she hits a wall of strong perfume walking out the back door, she winces. She might have gone a little overboard. She's about to tone down this part of the dream realm when Brandon taps her shoulder.

"Human," he reminds her. "This might be strong for us, but it's probably just right for her."

His words are proven true when Donna gives a little squeal of delight and flutters around her garden, burying her nose in flowers, touching vines, and talking nonstop about her favorites. Emma can easily see what the woman was like before she became so ill. On the ride over to the hospital, Brandon explained that his mother is suffering from a rare auto-immune disorder and because she's human, magic can't help her. Now, on a ventilator and forced into a medically induced coma, Donna has days left to live with nothing to mark the passing of time.

Emma can give the woman one last walk in her garden, the ability to say goodbye to her son, and a place to make peace with her mortality.

They gather flowers, making crowns and wreaths. Emma brings in butterflies, making them flitter and dance around the three of them, delighting Donna. When the woman requests birds, Emma creates small jewel-toned birds. Then she goes a step further and has them landing on Donna or dropping flowers in her lap.

"I feel like a Disney princess," the woman crows out, petting a bird that just landed on the ground next to her.

"Right now, you're anything you want to be," Emma tells her. This dream might not be her usual style, but the happiness radiating out of Donna and Brandon is energizing her, pushing her to stitch something perfect and wonderful.

Eventually, they move to the pasture next to the barn. The bay horse called Dyno nickers as he runs to Donna. Murmuring endearments, she hops onto the stocky horse's back without saddle or bridle and lays herself over his withers. Wrapping her arms around his neck, she breathes in deeply.

"It's just right," she breathes out. "He smells right too. Fur, sun, and grass. Just like I remember." She strokes his glossy coat and chuckles to herself. "But he was never this clean." She throws Emma a grin. "He was always rolling in mud. Damn horse could find mud no matter how dry the weather."

It only takes Emma a small effort to put a few patches of dried mud on the horse's sleek coat. When Donna feels the crusty dirt, she cackles out a laugh and almost falls off Dyno's broad back.

"There it is!" she sings out, grabbing a handful of her horse's mane to steady herself.

There's no sense of time in the dream realm. The sun never moves in the blue sky as Donna rides her horse while Emma and Brandon watch.

"She's human," Emma comments absently.

"So was my father," Brandon says. Neither looks at each other, both of them focusing on Donna laughing as she jumps Dyno over an old broken wheelbarrow.

"How do two human parents give birth to a grendel?" Emma asks.

"Grendels rarely raise their children," Brandon explains. "You've heard of changelings. Right?"

"That's when a fae sneaks in and takes a human child, replacing it with their own fae child," Emma responds. "I thought that was a myth."

"It's not a complete myth. The fae never did things like that, but grendels used to replace a human baby with one of theirs and then discard the human child somewhere deep in a forest or in the ocean where the body wouldn't be found. Most grendels can't be bothered to raise their own children. Kind of like cuckoo birds that put their eggs in the nests of other birds so they don't have to go through the effort of raising their own young."

That horrifies Emma. "How can parents just give away their children?" It makes her think about Kade being abandoned as a child. Children in the magical community are routinely discarded and unloved. The idea is devastating.

"We're shape changers," Branden explains. "Not shifters. We don't have the same instincts as you guys."

Waving her hands to indicate the dream around them, Emma frowns at him. "But I can tell that you love your mom. How can you say you don't?"

"I'm an anomaly among grendels," Brandon says. "I think it's because I was raised surrounded by so much love. But most of my kind aren't interested in intimate relationships of any kind. They're like mages in that respect, all about money and prestige."

"Why bother having children at all?" Emma asks.

"Female grendels will get a biological drive when they get to their forties. If they don't bear a child, it can shorten their lives. The woman who birthed me didn't even want to know the name of the man she slept with to get pregnant. I'll never know who my biological father is."

"Does that bother you?"

"Not in the least. I'm one of the lucky ones. Now an organization specializes in placing grendel children with families, just like the human adoption programs. I was placed with Donna and her husband, Ed. They loved me as if I was their own but never made me hide my grendel side. They even hired a grendel tutor to teach me how to shift and use my powers."

"Where's Ed" Emma asks.

"He died about ten years ago. Stroke," Brandon explains. "It was fast, and I don't think he felt any pain. He just collapsed one day."

"I'm sorry, Brandon. It must be hard to have fragile human parents," Emma says softly.

"I wouldn't trade my life with them for the world," Brandon assures her. "A lot of grendel babies get adopted by humans who want to change them and make them more human. I lucked out and got parents who only wanted me to be happy."

"I'm glad we went through the effort of drugging Dyno," Emma comments, watching Donna wheel the horse around, using only pressure from her legs. When Brandon tried to introduce her to the actual horse in the real world, the poor animal panicked the moment he got a good whiff of her.

Forced to give the horse a large dose of calming drugs, they finally got him to stand long enough for Emma to inspect him. Emma felt bad for putting the old horse through so much stress, but Brandon was adamant.

"I knew this would be Mom's favorite part," he admits. "She owned Dyno's dam. She was there for his birth and did almost all his training. He can't be ridden anymore, so she hasn't been on him for years, but here she can ride him. They can both be young and pain-free. You've created an amazing thing here, Emma."

"It's my pleasure," she says honestly. Stitching this place stretched her skill in fun ways, and watching Donna's joyful reactions made her own heart feel warm and full. She should look into doing this for other people. It might take some convincing for Kade to agree, but it could mean so much for those dying in hospitals or on hospice, far from everything familiar. She could give many people one last moment of joy.

As if thinking about Kade summons the man, he appears next to her. The grendel hisses and pulls Emma behind him, making her gasp at the sudden move.

Kade reacts swiftly, grabbing the grendel and tossing him through the nearby barn wall. Blinking at Kade, she sends a little of her power to make sure it's him and not a figment created by her unconscious mind.

"It's me," he growls out, crossing his arms and glaring at her.

"What are you doing here?" she asks, but before Kade can answer, Donna's there, charging Kade down with Dyno.

"Don't touch my son!" she screams out, leaning low over Dyno's neck as they barrel down on Kade.

Annoyed that this lovely dream went downhill so suddenly, Emma stops Dyno's charge and pulls Brandon out of the barn, repairing the wall once he clears it. Kade makes a move toward Brandon, so Emma lifts him into the air and holds him there in a giant bubble he can't break out of.

This is her dream and in here she has all the power.

"Emma!" Kade calls out, furious with her.

"Quiet," she orders, ignoring his anger and floating him out of the pasture to the gravel area in front of the barn. Then she turns her attention back to Donna and Brandon, both of them watching her with wide eyes.

"You guys keep enjoying yourself," she tells them, giving Donna control of Dyno again. The horse tosses his head and whinnies. Donna strokes a hand down his neck to soothe him.

"Who was that?" she asks, casting a wary glance at the irate mage.

"He's with me," Emma explains. "I need to go talk to him, but I can keep this area steady while I do that. Please don't mind him. Keep riding. Brandon told me you taught Dyno a bunch of tricks. I'd like to see them when I get back." Mutely Donna nods, and both of them watch her climb over the pasture fence and stride to where Kade floats a few feet above the ground.

"Damn it, Kade," she hisses. "What the hell are you thinking?"

He remains unrepentant. "He touched you."

"He thought you were a threat. He was trying to protect me," Emma counters, her annoyance evaporating as she realizes Kade's insecurity was in control of his actions.

"I don't like him touching you. I don't want anyone touching you."

Popping the bubble, she lets Kade drop back down to the ground. He makes a small, surprised sound as he stumbles, but he quickly rights himself. Straightening, he crosses his arms over his chest again and glares down at her.

"You're late," he declares, making Emma blink in confusion.

"Late?"

"Right now, three anxious bears are standing out in the hall trying to figure out how to wake you up. They're all scared that if they do it wrong, they might hurt you," Kade explains. "It's five thirty in the evening, Emma. You've been here for six hours."

Now it's her turn to be surprised. "Really? That long? Sorry, Kade. I didn't know. We were having so much fun."

Expression softening, he lets his arms drop to his sides. "I figured. They finally called me and asked what to do. That's why I'm here to wake you up."

"Are you at the hospital?"

"No, the alpha bond means I can drop into your dreams despite distance or shields," he explains.

"Do I really need to stop?" Emma whines, looking over to where Donna is galloping Dyno around the circumference of the pasture. "She's having so much fun."

Pulling her into a hug, his scent fills her nose, familiar and comforting. "Tender-hearted wolf," Kade murmurs into her hair.

"Can I come back tomorrow? Please?" Emma asks. "You'll still be doing wards, so you don't need me to stitch for you."

Sounding a long-suffering sigh, Kade tightens his arms around her. He's silent for a few minutes, as if debating with himself. When he talks, his voice is resigned. "Fine, you can come back tomorrow."

Emma smiles up at him. "Thanks, Kade. We should probably plan on you telling me when it's time to wake up in the future."

He huffs out a rueful chuckle. "No doubt. Six hours is a little excessive, Emma. Even for you."

"It's not," she counters, nodding her head to the pasture. Dismounted, Donna is standing in the ankle high grass with Dyno on one side and Brandon on the other. "We're fitting all their last moments into these hours."

"We need to work on your compassion," he tells her. "Caring is a fast way to get hurt."

"And not caring is a good way to die before your body stops breathing," she shoots back.

"Enough philosophy," Kade mutters. "Wake yourself up. Dinner will be delayed because of you, so you need to be quick about getting back to the sleuth's compound."

"Yes, Mr. Allard," she says with a saucy grin. "I miss you too."

"Troublesome wolf." Kade tries to sound annoyed, but a reluctant smile forms on his face. "Fine, I feel your absence keenly.

Hurry back." With that, he disappears, leaving Emma holding nothing. Dropping her arms to her side, she grins at the empty air.

"Everything okay?" Brandon calls out, and Emma turns to them and gives a thumbs up.

"We're good, but I have to end the dream now," she explains as she walks to the pasture fence. Brandon looks sad but resigned. Tears fill Donna's eyes.

"But I don't want to say goodbye yet," she whispers.

"We'll be back tomorrow," Emma says quickly. "But I need to go back to have dinner with Kade and the bears. It turns out we've been here for six hours, and we're making everyone a little nervous. No one wants to tell Kade that his stitcher died of hunger."

As intended, that makes Donna and Brandon laugh. "Well, if you're anything like my Brandon, you're probably ready to eat an entire cow by now," Donna says, and then she ducks between the rails of the fence. Wrapping small arms around Emma, Donna gives her a fierce hug. "Thank you for this, Emma."

"It's a small thing for a person so loved," Emma tells her, hugging the woman back.

Brandon beams at her. "Kade said you could come back tomorrow? Even though I pissed him off?"

"Everyone pisses him off. You're not special," Emma says dryly. "But we need to get going. Close your eyes. I'm going to end the dream."

"See you tomorrow, Emma," Donna says, closing her eyes. Emma dismisses the dream and feels both Brandon and Donna retreat into their own minds. Opening her eyes, she looks around to find Brandon already getting up from the chair he was sitting on, groaning and stretching. Her own body feels intensely stiff from staying in the same position for so long. She makes a few pained sounds as she stands. The cot the hospital staff provided was better than the floor, but by no means comfortable.

The moment she's on her feet, the room floods with anxious bears, offering helping hands and trying to hurry them along.

"We're late," Ken states. "Can you walk? Should I carry you? I've never heard of a stitcher spending so much time in the dream realm. I guess Brandon and his mom had a lot to talk about."

"Mom spent most of the time riding her horse, Dyno," Brandon tells them with a fond smile. "She's been sick a very long time, even before she ended up here, so she couldn't ride. And Dyno has been too old to ride for years. It was amazing to watch her. She used to win competitions. She and Dyno were state pole bending champions once." All the bears freeze at his words and turn astonished eyes to her.

"What?" she asks, wrinkling her brow at all of them. They're stopped in the hall, blocking the staff and patients, but because of the massive size of the bears, no one's trying to make them move.

"Uh, horse?" Amos asks.

"That's why we went to the farm," Emma says, puzzled. "I needed to see the farm to recreate it in the dream realm."

"But stitchers can't do that," Ken protests.

Understanding dawns, making her want to roll her eyes at the bears. "I'll explain on the way back to the compound," she says. "Didn't you guys say we're late?"

That gets them moving, and she and Brandon exchange an amused look as they're hustled down the hall.

Emma can feel Kade's exhaustion pulsing through their bond. She can also feel the effort he's making to keep everyone from knowing how tired he is. Victor and Brandon have joined them again for dinner as well as several more of the sleuth members, pushing the dinner attendees past thirty.

The conversation is lively, and everyone has questions for Kade concerning the wards. He answers all of them in detail, only becoming impatient when a question is repeated. It only takes one glare from him to make the questioner shut up and focus on his food.

It's a revelation to Emma that Kade can be fatigued. It makes sense. Even someone as powerful as he is can only possess so much power. But he controls so much that Emma forgot her mage has limits too.

"Slow down," Kade murmurs to her, putting a restraining hand on her arm. "There's plenty of food. No one's going to take it away."

Blushing, Emma straightens in her chair. "Sorry," she mutters.

It's not that she's starving. She's eating fast so the meal will end sooner. Kade's fatigue is pulling at her, making her want to tuck him safely in bed with her wrapped around him. But he's eating at a leisurely pace, outwardly unconcerned with ending the meal. It's one of the many ways Kade tries to convince the world he's invulnerable.

Deciding to use the tactic her dad successfully uses on her mom, Emma leans over and rests her head on his shoulder.

"I'm dead tired," she whines. "Are you done eating yet?"

Raising an eyebrow, he glances down at her plate. "You haven't finished eating. But if you're that drained from today, you can excuse yourself and go to bed."

Well damn, that backfired. She catches Victor's smirk. Lifting her head from Kade's shoulder, she frowns at the mage sitting across from Kade.

Still smirking, he gives a little shrug. "You need to be blunt with Kade," Victor tells her. "It's best practice to be blunt with all mages."

"Blunt but respectful," Kade corrects him with a little frown of his own. He settles his gaze back on Emma. "What aren't you telling me, little wolf?"

"She wants you to go with her to bed," Victor announces, loudly enough to make several of the bears chuckle.

"Lucky mage," Greg grumbles, making another gust of laughter travel down the table. To her surprise, Kade doesn't glare at Greg or anyone else at the table. His gaze is fixed on her.

"Is that the truth?" he asks. "You don't want to go to bed without me?"

It's easy to be honest, so she lets a cheerful grin curve her lips. "Of course."

"Then why didn't you just say that?" he huffs out. "Let's finish our food, and then we can retire to my room."

Happy to see him eating with a little more alacrity, she applies herself to finishing her meal. She listens with half an ear to the conversation around her.

She's not involved in the conversation at this point. Earlier she spent a great deal of time explaining first to Amos, Greg, and Ken about her stitching abilities and then again at the beginning of the dinner. When several bears asked her to stitch for them, Kade quickly put the kibosh on that by telling them the only stitching he's willing to let her do while in North Dakota is for him or Brandon.

There were disappointed faces, but no one argued with him, and secretly Emma's grateful. She enjoys stitching, but doesn't want to spend her time here lying on a bed and building dreamscapes for everyone. Stitching itself doesn't wear her out; if anything she wakes from it refreshed. But the way her body remains motionless while she stitches results in an unhappy body when she needs to wake up and move. Even hours later, she's still stiff and sore from stitching so long at the hospital.

At least the happiness at the table is a distraction from her discomfort. Just like wolves, the bears are loud, talkative, and convivial. She can tell Kade's not used to this kind of rambunctious conversation. He isn't quite able to cover his wince when the laughing gets boisterous. She thinks the diminished ability to handle raucous bear interactions might be a symptom of his fatigue.

"How long until you let Emma pick her clients? A stitcher of her caliber could command quite the price, especially if what Brandon's told me is true," Victor asks out of the blue. His question wasn't particularly loud, but the entire table goes quiet as all eyes fly to Kade.

Emma's not sure why everyone's watching the two mages with such interest. Victor's question seems innocent enough, but the look on Kade's face tells her something more is going on between the two mages that she's not aware of.

"Not that it's any of your concern, but Emma's still in training," Kade answers, his tone full of censure.

"I doubt that," Victor responds pleasantly. "Brandon told me all about the dream she stitched. You and I both know that level of skill is unprecedented. I also remember her handling you and Brandon quite well at our meeting with Donal. It seems to me that she has all the skills she needs. The only thing left is to learn is how to negotiate. Especially how to negotiate with pushy individuals. No one here wants to see her taken advantage of."

Ah, there it is. Emma finally understands. Victor and the bears aren't happy with the way Kade's treating her. The faces around her are all looking at Kade with expressions ranging from disapproving to outright hostility.

Now it's Emma's turn to be annoyed. She can excuse Victor for thinking he might swoop in and rescue her from servitude under Kade, but the bears have no excuse to treat Kade with such suspicion. They know about her soul cipher power, so they're fully cognizant of what a tempting target she is. Considering Cathleen was kidnapped for that very reason, they shouldn't be so upset about Kade's caution.

"Wolves are easy to abuse," Donal comments, his tone casual, but his words seem to have weight to them. "It's easy for bears to leave and join another sleuth if they don't like what's going on, but wolves don't. They're loyal to a fault. It's their best and worst quality, especially submissive wolves."

Comprehension dawns, and she wants to groan at the misunderstanding. Now she sees why the bears are casting disparaging looks at Kade. Bears don't have submissive or dominant members in their sleuths. The title of alpha is more of an elected position as opposed to someone who holds strong magical bonds with all the bears. Because she's a submissive wolf, they all think she's being taken advantage of.

"Guys," she says, rapping her knuckles on the table to get everyone's attention. She wishes the wolves who joined them for dinner yesterday were here today. Their alpha could help explain wolf dynamics. Unfortunately, she's the only wolf here right now. "I might be a submissive wolf, but I'm not helpless. Besides, Kade's a good alpha." Warmth flows through the alpha bond, and she looks over to Kade.

"You don't need to defend me," Kade tells her gently, placing a warm hand on hers. That makes her realize she's gripping her fork tightly enough to bend it. Dropping the damaged utensil, she twines her fingers with Kade's.

"They don't understand that you're trying to protect me." She regards the rest of the table. "I enjoy stitching, but I don't know if I want to do it for money," she explains.

That's when Victor's pleasant expression disappears. He turns accusing eyes on Kade.

"Really?" Victor manages to put an impressive amount of reproach in that one-word sentence.

"Don't take that tone with me. I'm not keeping the money. It's in a special account I opened for her," Kade responds, meeting Victor's accusation with chilly disdain.

"What's going on?" Emma asks, moving her gaze back and forth between the two mages.

"I'm paying you," Victor tells her, his bright violet eyes meeting her own. "I'm paying you very well. Kade negotiated the contract for you. Little did I know the money wasn't going to you, but to Kade. How do you feel about your alpha now?"

A blast of air whooshes through the room as Kade's anger manifests along with proof of his tiredness. Emma's never met someone as in control of their power as Kade, yet here he is releasing magic by accident.

"I don't need to steal her money," he hisses to Victor. The cool, controlled Kade is gone. In his place is a man with rapidly fraying patience. "I have plenty of my own. That's why it's in a high-yield account. I provide everything she needs right now, so she doesn't need to use her earnings. That money will be there for her when our arrangement is terminated."

"Terminated?" Emma whispers, tugging her hand out from under Kade's hand. She couldn't care less about the money, but the idea that Kade's already planning for the end of their relationship sends a shaft of pain through her chest.

Dealing with Kade's possessiveness, emotional distance, and arrogance was acceptable because she believed it was only a matter of time until they were mated. But she's only deluding herself if he's already planning for their separation.

He doesn't try to capture her hand as she pulls away from him and regards her with an indifferent expression.

"All things eventually end, Emma," he tells her. "I wouldn't expect our affiliation to be any different. Once this arrangement isn't mutually satisfactory any longer, I expect you'll wish to explore on your own. With the money in that account, you'll have the means to do that."

"You want me to leave?" she asks, clumsily standing up and knocking her chair over behind her. Everyone in the room is silent, captivated by the drama unfolding. The hurt must show on her face because Kade's expression softens a little.

"Of course not," he responds, his tone still remote but less frigid. "But eventually you'll realize there's nothing between us, and you'll want to acquire a real mate."

"Oh, Kade, my old colleague. How can you know so little about wolves?" Victor murmurs, genuine sympathy on his face. "Emma, is he your mate?" When she nods, the room fills with hushed voices.

"Poor Emma!"

"How could he?"

"Do you think she'll recover?"

"Can wolves mate a second time?"

"What can we do?"

"Maybe Victor can help her. He's a mage too."

"I don't think she can just trade one mage for another, not if her wolf picked Kade."

"But there's got to be some kind of magic to help."

The voices all flow together, creating a background noise that doesn't match the roaring in her ears.

"But you're my mate," she whispers, looking back at Kade.

"As I've told you, I'm not," he answers. His stern face forbids argument. He glances around the room, taking in all the bears with an expression of disgust. "Ignore them. We can figure this out between us."

This time she violently shakes her head and steps away from the table, almost knocking over a bear who's standing right behind her. She flinches and pulls away, but the bear is fast and throws an arm around her shoulder. It's Melli, Donal's assistant.

"It's okay," Melli tells her. "Just come with me." Mutely, Emma lets the bear lead her off, ignoring Kade's demands that she return to the table. She hears Victor talking just before the heavy door swings shut behind her.

"You're throwing away something important," Victor tells Kade. "Only a fool would let go of Emma."

Melli leads her outside. The moment the frosty night air hits her skin, the impulse to shift is much too strong to ignore. She strips, noticing the bear is doing the same thing. Both of them leave their fancy dinner clothes in a small pile just outside the door and then take a few steps away from the house.

It's a relief when her fur flows over her, and the wolf part takes over. Without a backward glance, she lopes off into the night, Melli trundling behind her. She can smell other bears in the woods, but only Melli stays close enough for her to see. When her wolf feels far enough away from the house, she sits down, looks up at the starry sky and starts howling.

In the distance, a few wild full wolves answer her lonesome song. It feels good to harmonize with them, letting her distress pour out her muzzle into the dark night.

Emma. It's Kade's voice in her head. He's pulling at the alpha bond but not so hard that it's painful. Ignoring him, she stops howling, gets to her paws, and pads deeper into the night. Away from the house. Away from Kade.

We can hear you howling. Emma, stop this absurd behavior. Come back right now.

So now her broken heart is absurd? Well, it probably does seem foolish to someone like Kade, who keeps their softer emotions on lockdown, never to see the light of day.

Unsure how to talk through their pack bond, Emma sends the image of a sturdy brick wall to him. She can feel his puzzlement flow down the bond to her.

What do you mean by that? You're being childish.

She's being childish? How dare he cast such aspersions? She sends the image of the brick wall again, this time with a chain-link fence in front of it.

Are you trying to bar me? he asks. *You can think about all the fences and barriers you want, but you can't keep me out. I'm your alpha.*

But she wants him to be so much more. She wants his love not just the alpha bond. Hampered by her inability to send words back through the link while she's a wolf, she screams silently in her head. She wants to cry on his shoulder and rage at him all at the same time. She's hurt and angry at his dismissive words.

Is this about the money? I promise I wasn't stealing it. It's in an account with your name on it. I'm putting money in it as well. You're getting a percentage of this job. And you'll get a percentage of all my jobs while you're with me. I meant to tell you but forgot.

She sends an image of money burning in a fire.

She notices a feeling of surprise from him and then an uneasy silence. She thinks that last image might have ended the conversation. She finds a place to sit so she can gaze up at the starry sky while she nurses her broken heart. When he speaks again, his tone is soft and pleading.

Please come back, Emma. I'm sorry I kept the money from you. I didn't tell you about Victor paying because I knew you'd refuse. I don't want anyone to take advantage of you. It's important to be tough in this world, even if it's a front. You're too gentle, little wolf. Too kind. Everyone has a sob story. Everyone has a dying family member. People of this world will suck you dry without even meaning to.

She doesn't send him any images, but she thinks about his words. The next time he talks, the tone is a little more frantic with even a hint of desperation.

No matter what you decide, I'll make sure you have plenty of funds and all the wards I can fit into the necklaces. But can you come back? Please? For a little while longer? Be with me a little bit more? I'm sorry I kept things from you. I only mean to protect you as best I can.

Genuine remorse and desperation accompany those words, and a revelation hits her. He's talking about her leaving, about her going off to find a mate. Never once in all those little speeches did he say he's going to push her away.

This isn't about him ending the relationship. This is about him trying to be ready for when she abandons him. The money is his way of showing love. It's as if he's saying, "Even if you leave me, I'm going to take care of you."

Victor's right, she thinks. Kade doesn't know anything about wolves.

Her mind is calmer from a combination of Kade's words and her wolf's activities. Her soul cipher power flares up, soothing and serene. With that power coursing through her, she can think more clearly. She's not sure what she's going to do about Kade's absolute refusal to acknowledge her love, but now she knows it's going to require her to be more than passively patient. She's going to have to push him, and it might not be pleasant.

Her bear escort follows her back, and she finds Kade sitting on the front steps of the mansion, his head in his hands and shoulders slumped. She's never seen him look so defeated. Trotting up to him, she wishes she had a rabbit to offer. But the look on his face when he sees her emerge from the dark tells her a rabbit would be superfluous. Her presence is all he wants.

"Oh, little wolf, you had me worried," he tells her, opening his arms. Without hesitation she snuggles her wolf body in his arms and shifts. He cradles her naked human form and puts his lips to hers. The kiss is tender, and she feels the bond between them spark with relief and affection.

"Please don't do that again," he whispers. "Please don't leave like that again. Talk to me. Yell at me. Hit me. Anything. Just don't leave."

"I won't," she promises, wondering if he realizes what he's asking.

As he holds her, keeping her furless body warm, she sinks her soul cipher power into him, healing just a little more of his wound and uncaring if he notices. She's done being patient. She's done waiting. Now it's time to be more aggressive with her powers.

Kade doesn't know it yet, but she's not the same wolf that galloped out into the dark.

Absently playing with the color of the flowers in her section of the garden, Emma tries to stay unobtrusive as Brandon and his mother say goodbye. This is the third and last day for her at the hospital, scrunched up on a too-small cot while she stitches. Next to her cot is the hospital bed holding Donna's emaciated and atrophied body. A dozen different machines beep as they keep Donna alive. The smell of antiseptic, diseased flesh, and despair is strong in the room.

But none of that is touching them right now as they inhabit Emma's dreamscape. For the moment they're surrounded by color with the warm sun shining down on them and the smell of the garden in their noses.

Yesterday Brandon told his mother about the state of her health. That she's being kept alive on life support with no hope of recovering. He offered her a choice—stay on life support or be taken off and die sooner. There was no judgment in his voice when he gave her those options, only a deep and abiding wish to do whatever she wanted.

Showing an intense strength of character, Donna asked important questions about the cost of her hospital stay, how Brandon's finances are doing with all the added expense of her care, and his emotional state. He dismissed all her questions, making sure she understood that all he cared about was what she wanted.

Watching their exchange made Emma's heart swell with feeling. Finally, Donna requested one more day of stitching before Brandon had the doctors take her off life support. Emma agreed without a second thought.

Now, Brandon and Donna are hugging each other, after spending a day walking the farm and reminiscing. Their time is coming to an end. Kade already came and went from the dream to tell them it's been nearly five hours. To Emma's relief, he was quiet and respectful when he entered the dreamscape, staying only long enough to make them all aware of the time and then leaving without causing any distress.

Kade has been treating Emma with kid gloves since the disastrous dinner at the sleuth. The morning after, he woke her a little earlier than necessary so he could go over her bank accounts. He explained in detail the investments he made on her behalf and how to access them if she wanted to.

Through the alpha bond, she can feel his deep need to show her everything, to prove that she can trust him. She remained quiet through the financial lecture. She interrupted only to ask questions to show him that she was paying attention.

In all honestly, if asked about it today, she wouldn't be able to give any details because everything he said fell on deaf ears. She was much too busy sinking her soul cipher power into him to pay attention to his lecture on her finances. At one point, he gave her a mildly frustrated look but then continued talking. He knew what she was doing but wasn't going to stop her. It was another sign that he didn't want to lose her.

"Emma?" Donna's voice brings Emma out of her thoughts. Both Donna and Brandon are standing in front of her, holding hands. Tears are streaming down Donna's face, but her expression is calm and resolute.

"I'm so sorry." Emma's heart is breaking because all dreams must come to an end.

"Don't be sorry. You've given us a gift," Donna tells her, dropping Brandon's hand to throw her arms around Emma's broad shoulders. "I can't thank you enough. I only wish you could have brought Victor in so I could say goodbye to him."

Puzzled, Emma slides her glance up to Brandon. "Victor?"

"The terms Kade negotiated said only me and Mom in the dreamscape," Brandon explains.

She isn't confused by the limit Kade put on the participants allowed in the dreamscape. That strikes her as a very Kade thing to do. But why would Donna want to see Brandon's boss Victor before she dies?

Before she can clarify her question, Donna looks up at Brandon and gives him a content smile. "I want you to take good care of yourself. Don't stay on the farm if you don't want to. Sell.

Go explore. Or stay there. I don't care as long as you do what makes you happy."

"Mom," Brandon chokes out, grabbing her in another hug.

"I mean it," she insists, clutching him back.

"I know you do. You and Dad were the best parents a grendel could have."

"I might not have given birth to you," she states fiercely. "But you were my son the moment I saw you. Never forget that."

"I won't. I love you, Mom."

"I love you too."

They both look at Emma, who's fighting her own tears. "Close your eyes," she whispers, her voice thick.

They both shut their eyes, and she dissolves the dream. When she opens her real eyes, the farm is gone; only stark off-white hospital walls surround her. She's got a little headache, and her body aches all over. Three days of stitching have taken their toll. With a moan, she tries to sit up. Every joint in her body is registering displeasure after so many hours of being so unnaturally still.

Then Kade is there, helping her stand and trying to pull her out of the room as a doctor and nurse come in. She digs in her heels. "No, Kade. I need to stay. Brandon shouldn't be alone."

"He won't be," Kade promises, nodding his head. She follows his line of sight to see Victor standing next to the sobbing Brandon. Pulling the grendel into his arms, the mage looks up to the medical staff in the room.

"We're ready," he states, and the doctor nods. He and the nurse turn off the various machines keeping Donna Myborn alive. Brandon tries to stand, but his legs collapse under him. Victor wraps his arms around the grendel, holding him up so he can watch his mother take her last breath.

Emma never realized the amount of noise the machines in the room made until they're all turned off. Now, with only the heartbeat monitor on, the sounds in the room seem discordant and unbalanced. When the heartbeat monitor stops beeping, Brandon shuts his eyes and leans his head against Victor's shoulder. The mage kisses the top of Brandon's head and murmurs soothing words.

That explains why Donna wanted to say goodbye to Victor. The mage and the grendel aren't employee and employer. They're a couple. That also explains why Victor paid for Emma's services instead of Brandon, and no one thought it was odd.

Feeling better now that she knows Brandon has someone to comfort him, Emma lets Kade lead her out of the room, her own eyes swimming in tears.

"Please don't cry," Kade begs softly as he walks her down the corridor. "My tender-hearted wolf, your tears are making me feel things I don't want to feel."

"Tears aren't always a bad thing," Emma tells him as they make their way out of the hospital.

"How can such suffering not be bad?" he scoffs, his gentle hold on her never wavering.

"Pain from loss means we knew love and joy," she tries to explain, but she knows her words are probably falling far from the mark. "We grieve deeply because we love deeply. Brandon's childhood could have been so different, but he got lucky. The man and woman who adopted him sincerely loved him as a son and a grendel. They made his happiness their own. He mourns now because the love and happiness he felt with them was so strong. I know he wouldn't trade his life for another, even if he's suffering right now."

The look Kade gives her can only be labeled as dubious. She knows he wants to argue, but he's still in appeasement mode, so he simply leads her out of the hospital. Several SUVs are waiting for them in the pick-up and drop-off zone, so they walk to the closest one.

"Kade," Donal calls out, pulling their attention to the first vehicle in the line. Emma gives him a watery smile, and he smiles back. They all know why she's been here today, so she's sure they'll give her space to shed a few tears for Donna and Brandon.

"Could you please look at this?" Donal asks, holding up a laptop. "Manny says there might be a flaw in one of the wards."

"That's highly unlikely," Kade grumbles, but he moves to walk the two of them to the front vehicle.

Emma feels a tug on her leg. Looking down, she finds Ethan standing there with an expectant expression on his adorable face.

"You go talk to Donal," she tells Kade, wiping away a last tear and pulling out of his hold. Bending over, she sweeps Ethan up in her arms for a hug. "I'm going to get my cub cuddle fix."

"Fine, but as soon as this is sorted, we're leaving this forsaken place," he growls. He strides impatiently to Donal. Bears pile out of the second and third SUV, all wanting to hug her and wish her well. They ignore her tears and talk to her with kindness and camaraderie.

She didn't mean to, but she's made a lot of friends in the sleuth over the last few days. Using her soul cipher powers, she helped Ethan's parents deal with the trauma of the attack and also did another session with Kieran and Ethan. Half the sleuth managed to fit in just a few SUVs so they could all see her one last time. It makes her heart swell and also brings a deep longing in her to have a pack again.

They also have gifts for her. "This is from all of us," Ethan tells her as he hands her a crumpled drawing.

It's a picture full of stick figures. Each figure has been labeled with a name added by an adult. "See, Mom put names next to each person so you wouldn't forget us. She said sometimes people forget names, so I wanted to make sure that didn't happen."

Touched by his gift, she hugs him a little tighter. "I love it, kiddo," she tells him sincerely. "I'm going to frame it and hang it up on the wall."

"That will look nice next to Kade's postmodern artwork," Rachel rumbles out, making a few of the bears laugh. Rachel, almost as big as her male counterparts, won Emma's affection when she agreed to go hunting with her. They didn't manage to take anything down, but Emma had more fun in her wolf form than she'd had in a long while. When they get back to the coast, she's going to need to talk to Kade about letting her run with a wolf pack occasionally. Her animal needs a community.

"We're going to miss you," Megan says, holding out her arms to take Ethan. The cub is reluctant but allows Emma to transfer him.

Kieran thrusts a heavy paper bag into her free hand. "I made all your favorites for the plane trip," he explains. "There's enough for Kade if you want to share, but I know some of the items I included are much too philistine for him."

Clutching the bag, Emma looks at him hopefully. "Did you put—"

"Yes, there's fleischkuekle in there," he cuts her off with a chuckle. Yesterday, he casually offered her the meat-filled pastry as a snack. She liked them so much, she ended up polishing off an entire platter of them. She made herself a little sick, but they tasted too good to bother with regrets.

"You're the best," she says with a wide grin.

"I know," he says with an answering grin. "But if you want any more, you'll have to come back and visit us."

"I'll do my best," she says. With Kade as a big unknown in her life, it's better not to make any promises.

Then Melli is there, pushing a phone into her hand. "Take this too," she whispers as the bears close ranks to block her from Kade's sight.

"That's sweet of you guys." She tries to hand the phone back. "But I'm sure I can get Kade to buy me a phone."

Crossing her arms over her chest, Melli is everything stubborn. "No, you're keeping it. It's already programmed with our numbers. And I loaded the AltShifter app on it and created an account for you. Your account is already linked to us, so we can all communicate through the app too," Melli explains. "We noticed you don't have a phone. Even if Kade buys you one, it won't have our numbers or information. You're important to us, Emma. We want to make sure you can contact us if you want to."

A rumble of agreement sounds from many of the surrounding bears. Touched by the gift, she hugs it to her chest. "I'd love to keep in touch."

"It's more than that. We want to make sure you're not trapped," Ken tells her. "Remember, you're not alone. And you don't need to rely on a wolf pack for help."

"And we included Brandon and Victor's numbers too," Greg tells her. "If you ever need to get away from Kade, you just call Victor. He can transport you to our sleuth, and we can keep you safe from there."

"That's fine then," Donal announces loudly. That must have been some kind of prearranged signal because the bears around her all shuffle backward.

"I'm happy and safe," she promises everyone in a low voice before giving them all a confident smile. "And I'm going to miss you guys too. Maybe I can come back and visit someday. Hunt down an elk with all of you," she teases in a louder tone.

That makes them laugh as Kade claims her hand, relieving her of the bag of food Kieran gave her.

"Bears are too lazy to hunt," he comments. "They just wait for their prey to wander too close."

Donal huffs out a laugh. "That's not entirely accurate, but we do enjoy foraging more than running after fleeing animals."

"But we can play," Ethan says, his eyes big and hopeful. "I liked playing with you."

"Me too," Emma agrees, leaning over to give him a last kiss on the cheek. He makes a mildly disgusted face, causing her to chuckle.

"Be good, cub," she orders, and he nods. All too soon, she's sitting in the first SUV with only Donal. Instead of taking the front passenger seat, Kade crawls into the back with her just like the day they arrived.

As Donal drives off, Kade plucks the phone from her hand. "What's this?"

"A phone," she teases. "I would think that's obvious."

"I can see that," he grunts. "But where did you get it?"

"We gave it to her," Donal answers for her. "It's a gift from the sleuth for helping Brandon and Donna. Besides, she didn't have a phone, and she's made a lot of friends among my bears. They want her to keep in touch."

"Oh, well, that's fine then." He hands her back the phone. "As long as it's not some kind of strange shifter courting gift, or some such thing."

"We give food as courting gifts," Emma tells him. He gives her an indulgent smile. When he realizes she's being serious, his expression turns oddly blank.

"Rabbits?" he questions, and she takes a moment to make the connection. When she does, she blushes a little.

Embarrassed, she ducks her head. "They aren't much of a courting gift. When I get the chance, I'll bring you something better, like a deer or an antelope. Proper-sized gifts."

After a moment of silence, he finally responds. "The rabbits are enough."

Because she can't read his expression, she feels along their bond. All she gets from him is intense concentration. He's brooding over something and isn't ready to talk about it.

"Whatever you're thinking about, I might be able to help if you talk to me," she tells him. He gives a quick, humorless smile.

"I'm sure you would try," is all he says, making her feel disquieted.

Naked and draped over Kade's much larger form, Emma gives a contented yawn. The moment the captain and copilot were locked in the cockpit, Kade flared the bond between them. They were naked and making love before the plane even took off. If the captain hadn't made a few announcements over the intercom, Emma might not have even noticed they were in the air.

Several orgasms later, she snuggles against Kade, her nose filled with the mixed scents of them and sex.

"I'm going to have a bed installed on this plane," Kade comments, his voice languid and content. They ended up on the floor because the couch just couldn't contain their two bodies. Kade made them as comfortable as possible, finding every pillow and blanket on the plane, but Emma knows the only reason she's so comfortable is because her body is mostly on top of Kade. He makes an excellent bed.

"That's not a bad idea," she agrees. "I like the way you keep me calm on planes. I think I might want to travel this way all the time."

A laugh rumbles out of him. "Lustful wolf."

"I believe putting those two words together is redundant," she quips. He angles his head so he can look down at her.

"So apparently is putting loyal and wolf together," he mentions. "Donal talked with me yesterday about wolves and mating."

"Oh?" she tries to be casual, but her body goes still and tense, giving her away. "What did the alpha of a bear sleuth tell you about wolves?"

"Is it true wolves only mate once?" he asks gently. She closes her eyes and lets her head flop down on his chest.

"We know who our mates are," she says without really answering. "The scent tells us. I've never heard of a wolf taking another mate after finding their one and truly, even if the mate dies."

"Emma, I can't be your mate. I'm not a wolf." There's no mocking or censure to his tone, only gentle compassion.

"It doesn't matter. If a wolf's mate is not a wolf, so be it. It's more on the rare side, but wolf shifters can end up mated to humans or other shifter breeds."

"I didn't know," he says simply, bringing a broad hand up to stroke down her back. "I'm sorry if I was cold to you. I'm not familiar with this kind of affection. I'll try to be better. I can't love you as a mate, but I can take good care of you, little wolf."

"I'm willing to accept that," Emma tells him boldly. "For now."

"That's all I have to give," he responds, his arms tightening around her. She sends soothing emotions across their bond.

"Give it a little time," she whispers. "Don't shut down what's healing and growing inside of you. I know you can love, Kade. I know you can be a true mate. I can feel the potential, but I need you to trust me."

"That part is easy," he says with a little sigh. "I trust you more than I've ever trusted anyone, little wolf. You've breezed past all my barriers."

"I wouldn't say I breezed past," Emma snorts.

"Steam rolled?" he offers.

"More like clawed," she retorts. "You've got some tough shells."

"Not anymore," he murmurs.

They fall into a companionable silence. Emma's drifting to sleep when Kade speaks again. "We were only with Donal and his people for four days, and you spent most of that time in the hospital, but they love you. I don't understand."

Genuine confusion colors his voice, and Emma's heart goes out to the mage.

"You will someday," she promises. He sounds a *harrumph* noise of disbelief, making her smile. "We'll visit the sleuth again, and you'll understand."

"We'll see," is his only response.

Stomach rumbling, Emma sits up, causing Kade's arm to fall off her back and to his side.

"Kieran packed us food." She spies the bag on a nearby seat. Leaning over Kade, she ignores his hand reaching up to cup her breast as she snags the bag of food off the chair. She settles down into a sitting position on the floor next to him. He watches with interest as she opens up the bag and pulls out a few items.

When he sees the fleischkuekle, his lips twist in disgust. "How can you eat those things?"

Laughing at his appalled expression, she bites into the pastry with relish. She takes her time before trying to talk again.

"It's good," she insists. Then she breaks off a corner and holds it to his mouth. He accepts the morsel with reluctance.

"No," he argues after swallowing, his expression never wavering. "It's still revolting."

"Well, you like raw oysters, so I don't think you have a leg to stand on in the gross food department," Emma points out, shoving the last of the pastry into her mouth.

Nine more are in the bag, but she wants to save them for later. Who knows when she'll have access to fleischkuekle again? Better to make what she has last as long as possible. She digs around in the bag a little more and unearths a carefully packed box of fruit and cheese. Pulling it out, she waits until Kade's sitting up before she hands it to him.

"Ah, this is much better," he says, accepting the food. As they eat, they chat about inconsequential things. It's the most relaxed she's ever seen Kade. She can only hope this isn't a fluke but a direct result of her soul cipher power and the blossoming of his trust in her.

"We're on final approach," the captain calls out over the intercom. "Please stay seated for the remainder of the flight."

Giggling, Emma gets up and pulls her clothes on. "Do you think they know what we're doing in here?"

"I don't know," Kade answers blandly, donning his clothes. "It wouldn't matter if they did. For what I'm paying them, we can indulge in just about any proclivity without fear of it being commented on."

"Let me guess. They signed strict contracts too," Emma teases affectionately.

"Quite right," Kade replies with seriousness.

Bumping him with her shoulder, she gathers up their impromptu bedding and piles it into a convenient chair. She flops down on the couch and watches him finish dressing. Fastidiously, he tucks, tugs, plucks, and finagles until he looks just like he did when they left the mansion that morning. No one would ever guess he tumbled a wolf on the floor of his private jet as they winged their way through the skies.

"Hey," she says suddenly, sitting up. "I'm a member of the mile-high club now!"

Chuckling, Kade sits down next to her, drawing her to his side with one arm around her shoulders. "Should we do anything to commemorate such a grand achievement?"

"Let me think about it," she answers with a small laugh. "We should contact the Guinness people. I'm pretty sure it's a first among wolf shifters."

"Just tell me when you're ready," he says. The plane jerks a little as they land, making her anxiety spike out of nowhere. He floods their bond with assurance. The anxiety evaporates, and the warm post-coital afterglow returns.

As they taxi, she idly wonders about asking Franco to make fleischkuekle. Probably not right after they get home, but maybe after he's warmed up to her. Or at least thawed a little more.

Her thoughts are cut off when the copilot comes out to open the hatch. As the curved door opens, hot humid air full of unfamiliar scents fills the cabin. Even before they exit the plane, her nose tells her they aren't in California. She grips Kade's hand as she sends him a questioning look.

"We're in Florida," he tells her, satisfaction radiating from him. "I found Jason and Avery. I'm going to take you to them now."

Emma has a hard time staying still while they drive. The town car and driver waiting for them at the airport said the trip would take about an hour. Even though she knows they can't be close yet, she keeps peering out the window.

"What's wrong with Avery?" she asks.

"Avery's weak," Kade begins but stops and raises a surprised eyebrow when Emma growls at him.

"Don't do that," she orders. "Don't call her weak. She might be a lot of things, but the woman I met is a survivor. That makes her strong, not weak."

"Very well," Kade says cautiously. "Avery has several addictions that make her vulnerable. The one I know about for sure is alcohol, but she probably has others. Years ago, we talked in-depth about the repercussions of her wea… uh… dependence on these substances."

"How do you know Avery?"

"We're both mages and there aren't a lot of us. We all know of each other in passing. Because Avery's based on the West Coast too, we've had to meet over the years to negotiate territories and mutually beneficial exchanges of clients. Avery's a gifted manifester. She created my house for me. In exchange I warded several of her homes."

"Would you call her a friend?" Emma asks.

Kade's brow wrinkles as he thinks about his answer. "How does one define a friend? She's a colleague and compatriot. We talked at length once about having a child together. Because she's a mage she would survive childbirth. I could do her the service of keeping her guarded while she's pregnant and less able to defend herself. It might have been a mutually beneficial arrangement."

"You wanted to have a kid with her?" The thought makes Emma feel a little sick to her stomach.

"No," Kade answers promptly. "We decided against it. She wants children, but she's strangely emotional for a mage. She decided she wants to have feelings for the father of her child." Unconcerned, he shrugs his broad shoulders. "I was only mildly interested in reproducing, so her decision wasn't particularly disappointing for me."

"It's not strange to want to love the father of your child," Emma tells him gently.

He casts her a derisive look. "Emma, how many times do I have to explain that mages don't love. What Avery wants might not sound strange to you, but it's very abnormal among our kind."

Emma explores a little. "If women who aren't mages die during childbirth, how many mages have parents to raise them?"

"We aren't raised by parents," he answers with a dismissive wave of his hand. "Mages never raise children."

"Does that mean your kind are like the grendels? You give your children up for adoption?"

He casts her an appalled look. "Certainly not. Mages are much too rare and powerful to just be given to anyone. We are raised in specialty schools with a staff trained to deal with powerful children. At five years old I could have leveled a city block during a temper tantrum." His tone gentles as Emma's expression turns horrified. "We aren't like other creatures, Emma. We're dangerous from the moment we're born. That's why mages don't raise their children. It's a full-time job to keep a mage child in check. As adults we're much too busy to dedicate so much time to offspring."

"That's just not true," Emma huffs out. "With your money, you could hire powerful nannies. Staff could help. There's no reason a child should be so cruelly separated from a loving family and raised in cold isolation."

"That's not our way," he states firmly. Obstinately she shakes her head.

"No, Kade, that *was* your way," she insists, emphasizing the past tense. "That's all going to change now. I'm realizing that it's not just you who needs me but your entire community."

"We aren't a community," he scoffs. "There's no name for a group of mages because we never congregate. There are no packs, prides, sleuths, or flocks here. You need to curb this impulse, Emma. And before you point out Victor and Brandon, I'll remind you of what I said yesterday. Victor doesn't love Brandon. He just feels some affection for him. Their relationship won't last. This notion that you can change mage culture isn't only ridiculous. It's dangerous."

"We'll see," she says, taking a page out of Kade's book and keeping her answer noncommittal and vague. His disgruntled expression tells her he doesn't like it when the tables are turned.

"We certainly will," he mutters. "But this discussion needs to be tabled for now. I believe we've arrived."

The town car pulls into a quaint seaside neighborhood. The adorable bungalows around them all look well-maintained with small lawns in front and welcome signs on their front doors. Except for one.

The bungalow Kade's looking at is run down. The lawn is an overgrown jungle. The door sags slightly, and it looks like one of the front windows has cracks running through it and is being held together with duct tape. The roof desperately needs repair, and it looks like there might even be a hole in it.

Emma meets Kade's gaze. Magic is coming from the house. Even this far away, she can smell it. "She's there," Emma confirms. "The place reeks of power."

He gives her a concerned look. "I wish we could've pulled the two of them back into a dreamscape so we could discuss this with plenty of distance as a buffer. Unfortunately, we'll have to do it this way. I need you to remain in the car. Avery will be protective of her territory and Jason. I'll need to negotiate entry with her before you can come in."

The mental image of the shifters with their heads exploded back at her uncle's house fills her mind. She clutches his hand anxiously. "Will you be safe?"

With a humorous laugh, he extracts his hand from hers. "I'll be perfectly safe. Avery can't hurt me. But she could hurt you or Jason by accident. Remain here and let me speak to her. Never fear, my wolf. I'll gain you access to Jason."

Before she can protest further, he's out of the car and striding to the house. She watches with fear as the front door flings open before he even gets to the stone path that leads up to the dilapidated bungalow. Avery appears, hovering a few inches off the ground, her power sparking around her.

"Holy shit," the driver mutters.

"Fuck," Emma breathes out, agreeing with the driver.

Floating over the threshold, Avery advances on Kade, her body gliding through the air with no apparent effort from the mage. Kade stands his ground, his power making the air glimmer around him. To Emma, it looks like broken bits of shimmering glass are floating around his tall frame, refracting light all around him. The floating mage stops before the bending, bouncing light Kade's producing can hit her.

"You're not welcome here," Avery announces. "Not you or that bitch." Her face is contorted in a cold rage, but Emma can feel something else going on. She feels fear there—deep biting fear.

Now that she's physically closer to Jason, she can feel a great deal more through their link than before. Avery's muted emotions are coming to her through Jason along with his concern for his mate.

Images of the mage from Jason's mind fill her head. Avery vomiting into a bucket, too weak to even make it to the bathroom. Her body covered in sweat as she twists and jerks in her sleep.

Face pinched with pain as her body is denied the substances she's come to rely on for too many years.

Along with each image is Jason's feelings of helplessness and love. His unwavering loyalty and his desperate hope that Avery will get better soon are apparent. His willingness to do anything to help her, including risking his own life to wake her from nightmares. Her uninhibited power threw him through a wall.

Now, inspecting the mage floating a few inches above the lawn, Emma notices her pallid complexion, gaunt body, and haunted expression, not unlike the dream version. Starting with the day

Alpha Michaels kidnapped her, Avery's been through hell, and her body is clearly showing the signs.

Emma plucks at her sibling bond with her power. Recognizing her, Jason opens wide. Not only does he drop all the barriers between him and Emma, but also anything barring access to his bond with Avery. That gives Emma a circuitous but unhindered path to the damaged mage. No longer stymied by Avery's shields, Emma pours her soul cipher power into the mage.

"How dare you!" Avery screams, but she's not looking at Kade. Her focus is on the town car and Emma.

A shock of outrage hits Emma. Even though Emma's trying to help, Avery views her as a threat. She doesn't snap the reestablished sibling bond between her and Jason because she doesn't want to hurt him, but that doesn't mean she's happy about it. Possessiveness and fear pour from the mage as she glares at the car.

Magic fills the air, making it thick and heavy. Even the human driver is aware of it. Fearful, he starts the car and tries to pull away from the curb, but it won't move. The tires screech and the smell of burning rubber hits Emma's nose, but the vehicle doesn't advance at all.

Resigned, Emma opens the car door and steps out. She can't stay in the car and risk Avery hurting the human.

"Emma, no!" Kade calls out, casting a hand at her. The same shimmering that shielded Kade from Avery is now surrounding Emma. With a panicked sound, the driver gets out and runs. None of them pay him any attention. The human is irrelevant either as a threat or protection.

"Avery, please don't," Jason calls out. He steps out of the front door and tries to walk to her, but within a stride his feet leave the ground and he is hovering too. Unlike Avery, he doesn't move through the air. He floats several feet above the earth, stationary and trapped in whatever magic Avery's using to suspend him.

"Avery, let me down," he begs. "Let me hold you. That's my sister. Feel our bond. She would never hurt me or you. Please, Avery, try to listen to me."

The sibling bond is giving Emma clear information on the state of Avery's mind. The mage is recovering, but her thinking is still colored from pain and withdrawal. To her, Jason is the bright spot in a dark world full of agony.

Emma's happy to find that although Avery doesn't use the word love, she associates affection and safety with Jason. Crafting her healing along those lines, Emma dumps power on the most current raw wounds—the part of Avery's mind craving the numbing effects of alcohol. There's too much to heal all at once, just like Kade, but she can diminish the cravings plaguing Avery. Through the sibling bond, she feels Avery's thinking become a little clearer.

It's a good sign when Avery doesn't scream at her to stop. She turns to face Kade, effectively ignoring Emma. That, along with the fact that she's keeping the bond with Jason open, makes it appear that the mage is giving Emma tacit permission to continue. She could shield herself from Jason and effectively cut Emma's access, but she doesn't.

Bloodshot eyes narrow in suspicion and anger as Avery confronts Kade. "What the hell are you doing here?"

"Emma wants to see you and Jason," he states. Both his tone and his body language are calm and mild. "That's all. I have no interest in anything but that. We aren't here for nefarious purposes." Emma winces as the alpha bond screams with worry for her, but none of it shows on Kade's face. If she didn't have a bond with him, she'd think he's as composed as he appears.

"Why should she care?" Avery asks suspiciously, casting a glance over to Emma.

"Avery, Emma is my sister. My twin. She loves me," Jason tells her. "She could come to love you too if you'd give her a chance."

Scoffing at his words, Emma feels the woman push back against the soul cipher power. Drawing from Kade, Emma gives up on subtlety and floods Avery with love. She pushes images of Jason as a child into Avery's mind. Images of them with their parents. She even risks sharing Jason's memories of caring for the sick mage. Her haggard appearance filtered through his love and devotion.

Jerking like she's been touched with a live current, Avery twists around to stare at Jason. "Is it true, sweet beast?" she breathes, floating herself a little closer to the trapped shifter.

"You're my mate, Avery," he says simply, and for a wolf shifter, it is that simple. She feels Kade jolt at Jason's words, so similar to the ones she's repeated to him.

"But…"

"There's no but, Avery. You're my mate, and that is everything." He taps his foot in the air and pointedly looks at the ground. "Let me down, Avery. Let me hold you."

The magic makes a swooshing sound as Avery dismisses it and Jason drops a few feet to the ground. Moving with shifter speed, he snatches Avery out of the air and cradles her to his chest.

"I love you," he whispers, turning his back to Kade and Emma. "And I'll keep telling you until you finally believe me."

Avery doesn't answer. She whimpers instead, her body flagging from exertion. Emma marvels at how much like Kade the female mage sounds.

Body sweaty and shaking, Avery is still weak and recovering. The amount of magic she just poured out was more than she could stand to lose. With a surprised grunt, Emma feels Kade pushing his power hard into her. When she looks over, he dips his head to indicate Jason and Avery.

"Share with her," he orders, and Emma shuffles the magic through her bond with Jason into Avery. The woman gives a soft sigh of relief as her body greedily absorbs what's being offered.

Murmuring sweet words of devotion, Jason carries Avery back into the house. At a discreet distance, Emma and Kade follow but stop at the doorway. They watch as Jason walks to the couch, sits down, and situates Avery in his lap. When Jason looks up, he gives them a tired, thankful smile. They both look at Avery, who's watching them with wary interest.

"Come in and have a seat," he offers. "I think everything is going to be okay now."

They're all sitting in the bungalow's small living room, Jason with Avery on his lap on the short couch. Kade sits on the only chair with Emma perched on his lap. She tried to settle on the spot of ancient carpet between his legs. It wouldn't be the first time she's sat on the floor when too many wolves tried to crowd into a small space, but he made an upset sound and pulled her into his lap instead.

"I was fine on the floor."

He mutters something about filthy floors and hovels before wrapping muscular arms around her waist and hugging her to his chest, not unlike what Jason's doing with Avery.

Now that she thinks about it, a strange kind of reverse symmetry is happening. A mage with a wolf on his lap in the chair, and a wolf with a mage on his lap on the couch. The humor must have shown on her face because Avery's expression darkens.

"Do you think my condition is funny?" she asks, the threat heavy in her voice. Emma shakes her head quickly.

"No, I wasn't thinking about that," she explains. "I just thought it was cute that two wolves ended up with two mages."

"Don't look for threats where only friends are sitting,"
Jason chides her gently. When she looks up at Jason, Avery's face
softens, and her mouth even curves into a smile.

"She's your sister," Avery acknowledges. "I'll be nice for
you."

"Do you remember me?" Emma asks. "I was in the house
with Jason when you were first captured."

She keeps half of her attention on Avery's emotions through
her sibling bond with Jason, trying to gauge the mage's reaction to
both her and Kade. She's poised and ready to flood the mage with
more soul cipher power if necessary.

Avery frowns as she studies Emma's face, this time without
rancor.

"You tried to help me," she murmurs. "And you stitched a
dream for me. Kade was there, and he caused a storm." Avery's eyes
flash with derision. "It was a good stitch, but you lost control of it
too easily."

"Emma's much more skilled now," Kade defends in a mild
voice, but Emma can feel the tension radiating from him. "And you
should know. Those first stitches with the cliffs were created
without the benefit of any formal training."

"Quite the talent," Avery acknowledges.

"How are you feeling now?" Emma asks, wondering if they
should try to get a healer to visit Avery.

"Much better now," the mage says with a dismissive wave
of her hand. "Back to full strength."

"She's weak," Jason says, speaking over her. "And she can't
keep food down. She's lost weight, and I'm scared."

"Jason!" Avery reprimands.

"They aren't going to take advantage of your current state,"
Jason assures her.

"Absolutely not," Emma agrees.

"I could," Kade adds, making both Jason and Emma glare at
him.

"Kade!" Emma admonishes. The bond between them snaps
with her irritation. A brief flash of hurt comes through their bond
from him before it's smothered.

"I said I could, not that I would," Kade retorts stiffly. "I
didn't realize we weren't being honest now."

"Honest yes, threatening no," Emma mutters and then
focuses back on Avery. "I have a little healing ability. I could try to
help, but you'll have to let me touch you."

The suspicious expression is back. "Make him go away first," she insists, pointing a shaking finger at Kade.

"No," Kade responds quickly, adamant and scornful. "You're not going to separate me from my wolf so you can alpha bond with her. I know you. I know how your mind works."

"I'm sure she wouldn't do something like that," Emma tries to reason, but Jason cuts her off.

"He might be accurate, Em. I think she was thinking about doing something like that," Jason says ruefully. "I've missed you. And after you helped in that dream, I wanted you here. It's been rough. I've been thinking of how you're always so calm and know just what to say to make everyone feel better." He eyes Avery with a hint of frustration. "She might try to break Kade's bond so she can keep you here because of me. I can feel her wanting to make me happy by doing something along those lines."

Vindication from Kade flows through their bond, making Emma roll her eyes. She meets Jason's worried gaze with a wry smile.

"Do you ever feel like the latest fashion accessory?" She mimics talking into a microphone. "Having a wolf shifter is just sooooo in right now. Every stylish mage is collecting one."

"Or two." Avery's voice is so staid that Emma doesn't realize it's an attempt at humor until Jason chuckles softly.

"You only get one," he tells her and nuzzles his face into her hair. "Don't be greedy."

"Does that mean you'll let Kade stay without raising a fuss?" Emma asks. Raising a fuss sounds like she's talking to a recalcitrant toddler, not a mage that has the same destructive capability of a small volcano. But Avery doesn't take offense. She nods as her eyes droop. She's at the end of her energy, and sleep is dragging at her, even with Emma sending her power through Jason.

"Jason's going to keep holding you. I'm just going to touch your arm," Emma tells her, sliding from Kade's lap.

Displeased with this situation, Kade sounds a soft hiss and tries to hold her back. She doesn't struggle. She stands between his legs and cups his cheek with her free hand.

"I'll be right back," she assures him. "And you'll be right here. I know you'll keep me safe."

"Always, little wolf," he says and reluctantly lets go of her arm. "If you feel her touch our bond, you need to pull away." His voice is authoritative and confident, but she can feel his fear.

"I will," she promises.

Stepping away from Kade, Emma kneels next to Avery and Jason. Gently taking the mage's hand in her own, she's shocked at how cold Avery's skin is. The moment they make contact, her soul cipher power flares, but she pushes it down. She needs the limited physical healing she can conjure right now. Avery won't have a mind to heal if her body dies.

To her surprise, Emma finds that her healing gift is mildly better than it was before. It helps her figure out that Avery's nerve endings are misfiring, causing an unpleasant tingling sensation in her limbs. Her muscles are unnaturally weak, even taking into account her lack of nutrients. Her stomach is a mess, her liver has mild cirrhosis, and neither kidney is functioning quite right.

This woman needs a real healer and soon.

Letting go, Emma gives Jason a meaningful look. "I can tell you that she needs a thiamine supplement and a lot of fluids," she says softly. "But the thing I'm most worried about are her kidneys. Something is wrong there that I can't even figure out, let alone help fix. I was able to set her stomach right, so she can eat little bits of bland food and keep it down. But that's all I could do. We need a healer much more skilled than me."

"My love, would you let me find you a healer?" Jason asks. "You're sick, and I'm scared."

Half opening her eyes, Avery tries to give him a comforting look. "I'll keep you safe." She sighs, making Emma wonder how much Avery can understand. Her mind is muddled from fatigue.

Casting a worried glance at Kade over her shoulder, she finds him frowning at Avery.

"This is unacceptable," he announces, making both Jason and Emma jerk with the severity of his tone. Avery doesn't flinch. She just slants her eyes in his direction, her expression turning sour.

"Your rebuke is unnecessary," Avery whispers. Except for the total lack of force behind those words, she sounds just like Kade.

"How could you let yourself fall into such a state?" Kade continues. "You're a mage. Our kind are above petty issues like physical weakness."

"Kade!" Emma hisses as she stands up. She grabs his arm and tries to tug him out of the chair, but he won't be moved.

"Hush, Emma," his expression and voice are full of condescension. "The mages are talking." Avery sounds a breathless chuckle, and Jason makes an irritated sound.

"He sounds just like Avery," Jason grumbles. "Arrogant and patronizing."

With a commiserating look, Emma meets Jason's eyes. "Humility is not their strong suit." This time Jason snorts out a laugh.

Neither mage looks at the wolf shifters. They're much too busy having some kind of meaningful, silent conversation that seems comprised of exchanging disdainful expressions.

"What would you do if I tried to take Jason away from you right now?" Kade asks, breaking their silent dialogue.

"I'd fight you," she answers without hesitation.

"But would you win?" Kade counters. Triumph covers his face when Avery's expression turns blank and remote. "You know the answer to that. Now stop being obstinate and let me find a healer. I might not want your wolf, but if you don't get well soon, someone else might steal him."

It's obvious that Jason's not happy about being discussed like a possession, but he doesn't object because Kade's words are having the desired effect. Her expression turning resigned, Avery lets her eyes close and sighs out a breath.

"Fine," she mumbles. "Find a healer. But whoever it is, they need to be distinguished. I don't want just anyone touching me."

"Of course not," Kade says, affronted. "I'll find the best in the area. I would never hire anyone with less than illustrious credentials."

Comforted by Kade's pompous words, Avery lets her head lull back against Jason's shoulder. Her breathing evens out, and her body goes lax. Jason shifts her weight a little, so he can better support her.

"She needs a healer who specializes in the effects of long-term alcohol abuse," Emma tells Kade in a low voice to keep from disturbing Avery.

"I'm already searching," Kade tells her, his phone out and his big fingers rapidly tapping the screen.

"I'm sorry I got upset earlier," Emma apologizes. "I didn't realize why you were pretending to insult Avery."

Kade gives her a quizzical look. "Pretending?"

"All that stuff about mages not being weak, that was just to convince her to see a healer. Right?"

A hard look crosses Kade's face. "No, Emma, that's real. Mages are apex predators with a lot of enemies, many of whom are waiting for us to stumble so they can take advantage. We can't afford the luxury of any kind of weakness. I've warned Avery in the past that her drinking could prove to be her downfall. The state she's in now is a direct result of her lack of willpower, nothing more."

Blinking at the vehemence of his words, Emma's not sure how to respond. She could argue—make a case for empathy and compassion versus judgment and indifference—but something tells her Kade isn't ready to hear that yet. He's come a long way in the short time he's been with her, but like Avery, it will take a while before a lifetime of attitude is re-trained.

"Wolves don't work that way," is all she says. She's proud that her voice is gentle but firm, even though her heart hurts badly for the two mages in the room. "We're a community, and the weakest members are cared for, not discarded."

"We aren't wolves," Kade points out dryly, but Emma's not affected by his tone.

"You are now," she states with conviction. "You have me, and Avery has Jason. Our two packs might be small, but that doesn't matter. We are still packs. In a real pack, like under Alpha Julia, no wolf is left behind. No one suffers alone or goes without. We might not be as powerful as mages. We might not have your money or influence, but for wolves, those things aren't as important as caring for our pack. It's something both Avery and you will eventually learn."

The effect of Emma's speech is notable. Kade looks dumbfounded, as if she just started speaking to him in an ancient language. That's when she realizes Kade expected to mold her in his image, teach her to be more like an imperious mage. Now he faces the startling and very real prospect of being pushed into a more wolf-like mindset.

It's obvious the idea doesn't sit well with him, but she takes it as a good sign that his expression is one of surprise, not distaste. Deciding she's made her point, she focuses on Jason and Avery, noting Avery's tangled greasy hair. She still has marks on her from the dirty basement floor, and the sour scent of old sweat and sickness clings to her skin.

"Would you like me to help bathe her?" Emma offers. "I'm sure she'd like to be clean and presentable when the healer gets here."

"Please," Jason agrees. "I've been afraid to bathe her alone, but with an extra set of hands, I think we can do it and keep her warm."

"Not a problem," she assures her sibling. "We're here. You don't have to struggle on your own any longer."

"I wish I could set up an IV line," the healer tells them with a rueful smile. "But since I can't, you're going to need to push fluids orally."

"Why can't you use an IV?" Emma asks, gesturing to Jason. "He can monitor it and change the bags out."

"You can't perforate mage skin," Kade explains. "That's why mages don't have any tattoos or piercings. Our skin reacts without our control. Whatever pierces our dermis ends up being reduced to particles."

"Well, that's inconvenient," Jason mutters, casting a frustrated glance at Avery. "I'll try to get her to drink more. But she's always mumbling about tap water and pushing the glass away."

"I included several cases of good, bottled water with the groceries I ordered," Kade tells him with a smirk. "You're caring for a mage, Jason. She's going to have high standards. You can't expect her to drink water from the faucet like a peasant."

Exchanging a glance with her sibling, both of them end up biting their lips to keep from laughing at Kade's outrageously patrician attitude. But Kade's not done yet.

"I'm surprised she found this house acceptable." Looking around the room, he makes a disgusted face. "This place is a hovel. Barely fit for barn animals."

In this instance, Emma can't argue with him. All the furniture is decades old and worn, the carpet is bare in patches with stains, and the walls desperately need a fresh coat of paint. Little things are broken everywhere. A cupboard door hanging off its hinges, a doorknob that won't latch, and a window with a broken pane of glass are just a few items Emma can see from where she's standing. The place has potential, but even she has to admit that in its current state, it's grimy, dreary, and in sore need of repairs.

"From what little I know, she has some kind of history with the house," Jason tells them, looking around the dingy living room, obviously also unhappy with the accommodations. Wolves don't mind minimalist living, but they like to keep their dens neat and clean. This place probably hasn't been cleaned in years.

"I can feel Avery waking up," Jason says, craning his neck around to see into the door of the equally shabby and small bedroom. "You should all probably leave. I want to keep her stress levels low."

"Good idea," the healer notes and heads for the front door. "I'll be back tomorrow at this time to continue the healing. Make sure she takes those supplements and eats a lot of small meals. Also, get as much fluid in her as you can."

"You need to eat too," Emma murmurs to Jason, giving him a last hug. Now that Avery is on the road to healing, she turns her attention to her worn sibling. She didn't notice earlier, but Jason's dropped weight and looks haggard. Not only isn't he eating properly, but Avery's probably pulling a lot from him through their mate bond to keep her own depleted body going.

"I made sure there's plenty of meat in the groceries," Kade tells both of them. "And I've set up for daily dinner deliveries from a local restaurant. They'll continue until you call them to cancel."

Jason is still wary of Kade but graces him with a thankful smile. "Your generosity is appreciated." He casts a quick look at Emma. "For helping me, Avery, and my sister. You saved our lives."

"Emma is paying your debt, so don't thank me." Kade's words feel dark, and they make Jason's smile disappear.

"Maybe after Avery's better we can—"

"No," Kade cuts him off. "Avery can't induce me to trade for Emma's debt. She's mine. You might be her sibling, but I'm her alpha. And if Avery tries to take her away from me, it will end badly for both of you."

Jason doesn't assume an aggressive stance at Kade's words. He doesn't growl or posture. Instead, he regards Kade thoughtfully. Like Emma, Jason is a calm wolf and won't react to Kade's forceful proclamation with belligerence. For all his size, Jason's a gentle soul.

"Helping one moment and threatening another," Jason murmurs. "It must be a mage thing because Avery did that a few times, too. Be at ease, Mage Allard. I'm not going to steal my sister's affections for you. She has a heart big enough to love a sibling and you."

Kade doesn't look remotely pleased by his words. It must confuse Kade, who expects Jason to react offensively with hostility or retreat in fear. But he's doing neither, and that has to be bewildering for the mage. She can also feel he's comforted by Jason's words, even though he'll never acknowledge it.

Trying to rally, he gives Jason a triumphant look that Emma knows he doesn't feel. "As long as we are clear on who owns Emma."

"I'm very clear about the relationship between you two," Jason tells him with a small smile. "I'll enjoy talking to you in the future when you better understand the relationship yourself."

Those words make irritation flare from Kade. To cover his annoyance, he shifts to a mocking expression.

"I find myself bored with this childish conversation. I believe we've overstayed our welcome. Shall we be off and let the wolf take care of his debilitated mage?" He gestures for the healer to precede him out the door.

Emma suspects that was the most insulting thing he could think to say, but it doesn't affect any of the parties who can hear him. Wolves are set up to care for their weakest pack members, and healers deal with the infirm, injured, and incapacitated all the time.

Emma and Kade follow the healer out. She isn't surprised that Kade is eager to leave, tugging her along impatiently and breathing easier once they're outside the shabby house.

He hid the tension he was feeling, but now she notices the telltale indicators. His shoulders relax, the wrinkles around his eyes disappear, and the bond between them is open and flowing again. Distracted by Avery and Jason, Emma hadn't noticed all these things, but now she realizes how much of a strain Kade was under.

She lays a comforting hand on his arm. "It's okay. Avery wouldn't ever be able to steal me. I'm your wolf, not hers." The bond tells her those were the exact right words to say.

"I'm so glad you're alive!" the driver shouts with relief as he gets out of the town car. He's a little rumpled, but other than that he looks fine. Beaming at them, he hurries to open the back door so they can climb in. "When that lady made it so I couldn't move the car, I was sure she would kill you both."

Smiling at him, Emma pauses before climbing in. "We're all fine. I'm glad you took yourself away from the situation. And I'm doubly glad you were brave enough to come back." She hears

Kade make a scoffing sound, but she jabs him in the gut with her elbow and he quiets.

"My sister married a fae guy, and he always told me that if any magic started happening to just hightail out of there," the driver explains. "I can't wait to tell him about what happened today!"

Then Kade is there, leaning over Emma and getting in the driver's face. "You'll not speak of this to anyone. Do we understand?" His voice is low and dangerous. The driver pales a little and nods quickly.

Emma shoves Kade, who just ignores her. She might have shifter strength, but Kade has mage strength, which is apparently much better.

"N-n-no," the driver stammers, shrinking back against the side of the car and ducking behind the open door a little. "I'd never speak about clients."

"Kade, get in the damn car," Emma growls, hungry and tired of dealing with conceited mages.

"Language, wolf," Kade reprimands as he straightens away from the driver. Climbing into the car, she tugs him in after her and listens to the driver close the door and scramble around the vehicle to get into the driver's seat.

"Where would you like me to take you?" he asks. His voice is shaky, but his hands are steady at least.

It's late afternoon, and Emma's starving. "Can we get dinner?" she asks. "I know you want to freshen up, but I'm starving."

"Of course," Kade answers readily as he tugs at the bond between them and then gives her a concerned look. "You're positively famished. You should have said something sooner."

"What are you in the mood for, miss?" the driver pipes up. "I could make a recommendation."

Pulling out his phone, Kade waves off the driver's offer. "Unnecessary." Then he says something about not trusting the opinion of a serf as he taps his phone. Both the driver and Emma remain silent as Kade explores options on his phone.

"Council Oak seems to be acceptable," he announces. When the driver's eyes go a little wide, Emma knows the restaurant must be expensive.

"Where are you two staying?" the driver asks. He's just trying to be friendly, but the unwelcome look on the mage's face makes the driver busy himself with getting the car started and checking traffic before pulling out on the quiet street.

"I believe I have a reservation at the Epicurean," Kade answers. "Will that be a problem?"

"No, sir, not at all," the driver says hastily as he steers the town car toward a nearby freeway. "I've heard a lot of good things about both Council Oak and Epicurean."

Satisfied, Kade smiles at Emma. "Food soon, little wolf," he promises, and she feels a little jolt of joy come down their bond. He's excited at the idea of feeding her. It must be her wolf rubbing off on him. Pack members feeding each other is a way to show affection, not only when courting. Of course, fresh meat is always best for courting.

She's going to need to hunt him down a deer when they get home.

Belly full, Emma follows Kade through the lobby of their hotel when a man only a few inches shorter than Kade steps in front of them, abruptly halting their progress. The man's violet eyes flare with power, and Emma watches with fascination as the same familiar contemptuous expression covers the stranger's face.

"Kade Allard, what are you doing slumming in Tampa?" the man asks. Kade tugs her behind him as he draws his body up tall to face the new mage.

"Hello, Matheus," Kade greets the man with no warmth in his voice. He sounds almost dismissive. "I might ask you the same thing."

Laughing with no actual humor, Matheus tilts his head thoughtfully. "I'm here on business, as I'm sure you are as well. Why else would we bother visiting such a forsaken place?"

"Indeed," Kade replies. It doesn't escape Emma's notice that neither of them is giving the other any information. She thought Kade and Avery's interactions were bad, but this is a whole new level of chilly civility.

"Are you working for the Mendoza Clan?" Matheus inquires.

"Perhaps. Can I assume you're not?" Kade responds. She can't see Kade's face, but she can tell his eyebrow is lifted with that question because of the lilt of his voice.

"Perhaps," Matheus echoes mockingly. Peeking out from behind Kade's broad back, she examines the man. Unlike Kade, he's classically handsome instead of strikingly beautiful. Along with violet eyes, he possesses pale, flawless skin, sharp cheekbones, and a strong jaw.

What's striking is that he's so much colder than Kade. Their eyes might be the same color, but Matheus's eyes have no humanity to them, no capacity for compassion or kindness. Nothing is there but selfishness and cruelty. When his eyes settle on her, dread washes through her.

"And who do we have here?" With his question, she ducks her head back behind Kade, realizing her folly much too late.

"No one of consequence," Kade tells him as he sends her a quelling look over his shoulder. Through their bond, she can feel his tension and concern. There's no question that Matheus is dangerous. He has even the powerful and arrogant Kade worried. That alone might make him the most terrifying person she's ever met.

"Nevertheless, I'd like to make her acquaintance," Matheus insists.

She feels power close in around her and gives a strangled gasp as her hand is ripped from Kade's grip. She's dragged out from behind him, the power holding her bringing her to a halt in the air between the two mages. Encased by Matheus's invisible hold, she can't move at all and can only breathe in rapid, shallow pants.

"Really, Matheus, was that necessary?" Kade's voice sounds bored, but his fury and fear are pulsing through their bond. And then the bond shuts down. It's so abrupt, Emma would've stumbled if she wasn't being held by Matheus's power. She can't move at all, not even to turn her head to look at Kade. All she can do is stare straight ahead at Matheus. His face is a veneer of pleasantness, but she can see the hard calculation and brutality underneath.

With the bond between her and Kade shut down, she feels like part of her is missing. She wants to retreat behind her mage, hug him around the waist and demand he open their bond back up. She wants to feel the reassuring weight of his hand on the back of her neck and hear his deep voice in her ear. But more than anything, she wants to hide from this frightening man who wields enough power to make Kade uneasy.

But all she can do is keep her eyes on Matheus and wait.

Smiling at Emma, Matheus addresses Kade. "Friends share toys."

"Mages don't have friends."

"True," Matheus agrees in a mild tone as he takes one of Emma's hands in his. "But I still want to meet your latest acquisition." She isn't surprised when her soul cipher power flares at his touch, but instead of reaching out to Matheus, it retreats deep inside of her, trying to hide behind her much weaker healing gift.

Cold power washes over her, alien and completely opposite of Kade's warmth. Matheus's power pushes into her like her shields are made of crepe paper. The pain of his entry is enough to push the breath out of her lungs. Clenching her teeth, she works on dropping her shields and mitigating the pain as much as possible. His power pours through her, flipping through a few of her most recent memories and feeling out her healing gift, but thankfully it doesn't find the soul cipher power.

Staring into her eyes, Matheus's smile turns genuine. "Submissive wolf. I had one of you once. I kept him for a few years. He was quite diverting."

"She might be submissive, but she can be rather stubborn." Kade's voice is heavy with annoyance, making it sound like she argues with him all the time. If she didn't realize he was trying to make her unappealing to Matheus, she might be tempted to protest.

Following Kade's lead, she rolls her eyes and takes on a petulant expression.

"I don't argue all the time." Her voice is thready and much weaker than she likes. She wanted to sound challenging, but instead she sounds whiny and childish. When Kade makes his familiar irked sound, she decides it was the right thing to say, even if it didn't come out as she intended.

"See what I mean," Kade huffs out.

"But you keep her," Matheus remarks, quirking an eyebrow at her and then Kade. She feels another wash of power go through her. "Ah, I understand now. Her stitching ability is quite profound." Memories of stitching for Brandon and Donna fill her head. "The bears adore her. She must be valuable when dealing with shifters. Their kind can be distressingly emotional."

"She's of limited help. Her soft heart gets in the way," Kade answers.

"That's easily solved," Matheus counters, and she feels a sharp strike of power hit her in the gut like a fist. The unexpected blow makes her jerk and cry out. "I find that pain is an excellent teacher."

She struggles uselessly against Matheus's hold on her until another blow lands. This one's harder, pushing the air out of her lungs and stunning her into stillness.

Matheus looks pleased. "Now then, you wouldn't dare to disobey your owner. Would you? Not when we have so many delightful ways to cause pain."

"No, sir," she grits out. "Never."

"Oh, I like that. Sir indeed." He regards her with delight. "I think she might have some training already. It won't take much to break her."

Sweat rolls off Emma's body as fear fills her. Without a doubt, Matheus is a psychopath. A faint feeling of sexual excitement emits from him. He's turned on by scaring her. Hurting her. What did he do to the poor wolf before her? The question is too horrible to contemplate.

"Breaking her might lessen her stitching gift," Kade tells him. She can hear the edge of rage in his voice, but Matheus seems oblivious.

"I don't care about that. If I break this one, there are always more toys to collect," he answers dismissively. "I'd like to acquire this one. Shifters are always so big and ungainly, but she's not too ugly. Her face is nice enough. Her healing gift isn't anything of worth, but I can feel resilience in her." His smile turns a little more predatory. "Do you know that it can be harder to break the submissive wolves? The dominant wolves don't know how to hide anything. It doesn't take much skill to break them. But the submissive ones are very good at hiding their true feelings, and they're consummate actors. They can be quite convincing, and you think you've molded them to your will. Then they try to escape. It's always entertaining."

Reaching up, he grips her chin in his hand and forces her head back. "But don't worry. I know better than to ever let a pet off-leash." Letting go of her face, he turns his smile to Kade.

"What would you like for her?" Because she's expecting Kade to say no outright, she can't help the gasp of betrayal that escapes her at his next words.

"I can't sell her until tomorrow. I have three meetings scheduled for today and tonight." There isn't even a hint of anger or denial in Kade's tone, only calm negotiation.

"I see," Matheus murmurs, looking her up and down. "I guess I can wait a full day. I'll collect her tomorrow evening."

"As far as price goes, I want your condo in New York," Kade demands without hesitation. Matheus doesn't look surprised or concerned.

"I know you've had your eye on that place for some time, but that's much too rich for one wolf shifter, even one that's going to be so much fun. I'm willing to pay $1.5 million or something of equivalent value in trade."

"I'll agree to the $1.5 million if I get first right of refusal when you decide to discard her," Kade counters. Matheus's eyes narrow.

"Why would you want a broken toy?" Matheus asks with obvious suspicion.

"Perhaps I'm looking forward to playing with her after you're done breaking her. I saw what you did to Samantha Li's fae. He still won't talk, by the way." Kade's tone sounds slightly amused at this, as if whatever trauma caused the fae to go mute is interesting instead of horrific. "Anyway, while she wasn't thrilled by the changes in her fae, I might appreciate it in this wolf."

Surprise registers on Matheus's face; then he appears thoughtful. "That's not something I expected from you."

"I don't like to advertise my proclivities," Kade demurs. "I do so hate public attention."

"Ah, there's the Kade I know," Matheus says with a slight nod. "Can I assume this right here," Matheus waves it at where she's floating between the two of them, "is bothering you as well?"

"You have captured everyone's attention," Kade points out. Rolling her eyes, Emma can see a ring of onlookers watching them. Some are filming with cell phones; others are simply staring with wide-eyed shock.

Kade makes a disgusted sound, and power emanates from him. Several cell phones make loud crackling noises, and the people holding them gasp and drop them. "I do hate it when the humans get nosy."

"You never did like to be the center of attention. That's so un-mage like of you, Kade. Very well. Let us meet for dinner tomorrow and discuss this wolf's purchase."

"My name is Emma."

She has no idea why she felt like trying to say anything at all. When Matheus's gaze rests back on hers, she knows it was the wrong thing to do. His face is mildly annoyed, as if he's dealing with an abnormally chatty person on an elevator.

Power gathers against her skin, and pain crashes into her. She wants to scream, but there's no air in her lungs for that. When her vision starts to go black, the agony abruptly stops, along with the power that was holding her in the air. She tumbles gracelessly to the floor and lies there panting. The wolf in her screams for her to get up and run. Shift and sprint away. But the human part of her knows she needs to remain docile for now and trust Kade.

She remains on the floor, panting and waiting, his feet right in front of her face.

"That's your first lesson," Matheus tells her, his voice mild, but he's licking his lips with pleasure at the sight of her distress. He nudges her with the toe of his shoe until she looks up at him. "You don't speak unless I expressly tell you to. Push that limit, and I'll take your voice away. Eventually, you'll understand that's the least of what I can do to you." With a weak nod, Emma closes her eyes and lets her head thump against the tile floor.

"The price will go up if she can't perform her stitching duties today," Kade tells him blandly.

"Shifters are rather robust; she should be fine. But I'll take that into account when I calculate my offer. I'll bring the paperwork tomorrow," Matheus agrees.

Paperwork! How often has he bought someone? Emma knows that buying and selling of nonhumans happens, but is it so common that they have standard contracts? She's about to find out.

"Very good," Kade agrees. "Shall we meet at Malios?"

"It's the only acceptable place," Matheus agrees. "Will seven tomorrow be agreeable?"

"That should work."

Curling up into a ball, Emma squeezes her eyes shut and wishes this was a dream she could control. She'd decapitate Matheus and throw Kade through the nearby picture window.

"Does she have a suitable wardrobe? I find that the shifters don't dress appropriately," Matheus inquires. His toe nudges into her shoulder. When she doesn't respond, he nudges harder until she rolls back over and opens her eyes. He's staring down at her, but in an assessing way, not meeting her gaze. "She's not bad looking, for one of them. At least she isn't a bear. They're entirely too bulky. With the proper garments she might be passable enough to take out in public. Especially if I starve her for a while. I like them thin. Lean. They look so lovely when they're emaciated."

"She has a wardrobe, but perhaps I should leave her home for our meeting." Kade's voice is heavy with sarcasm. "If you don't like the outfits I've chosen."

"You'll need to bring her because I will have plans in place for after dinner. And I didn't mean to insult your choice, but it's obvious you let her dress for comfort. She shouldn't be able to move well. Shifters can't stand that. The little things help break them. Find out the everyday things that will make them uncomfortable or mildly ill and use it against them." Matheus sounds like he's lecturing Kade on the intricacies of torture. His tone lowers, and he leans a little closer to Kade.

"I have this lovely little cage specially made for the last shifter I owned. He would rather I cut off a finger or toe than go into the cage. It came to be my favorite thing to do to him, and honestly, I think that's what broke him. I'll use it more sparingly with this one because I want her to last longer."

Now Emma can see Kade's expression. She sees mild disgust but also interest there. "I'd ask where you get a cage that can hold a shifter, but I find I don't have the stomach for the process. But I want to have access to the final result."

The laugh that comes out of Matheus is downright evil. "That works out perfectly. Once they're broken, I have no further use for them." Looking down at Emma, he puts his foot on her chest and stands on it slowly, daring her to move or try to wiggle out from under him. "Enjoy your last night with Kade. Tomorrow you and I will play."

Meeting his eyes, she glares at him. "I'll be dead before then," she promises. Kade hisses out a breath at her words, but Matheus's grin gets wider.

"No, you won't. But I can promise you that you'll wish you were dead," he corrects her. Taking his foot off her chest, he regards the growing crowd with a slight frown. A news van is pulling up outside. "We really should depart. This is getting out of hand. I don't mind the average imbecile gawking at my presence, but I detest the news. They always make me look bad, and I can't do anything because most of them are human."

"I can see where that would be a nuisance," Kade agrees, eyeing the van. "If only we could kill humans with impunity, but their governments won't ignore that. Until tomorrow, then."

"Tomorrow." With that, Matheus turns on his heels and strides away. Several figures emerge from the onlookers to follow Matheus into the bar of the hotel. One of them is a woman with a blank expression. She's an average height for a human and impossibly thin. Even the heavy makeup she's wearing can't cover the bruising on her face or the telltale dark circles under her eyes. And no amount of cosmetics can change the haunted look on her face.

She casts a glance over to Emma, still on the floor. Her expression holds both pity and relief. Emma suspects she's going to be taking that woman's place as Matheus's favorite toy.

"Over here," Kade calls out to a man who's already hurrying across the lobby. It's the concierge, who looks deeply flustered.

"Do you need me to call an ambulance?" he asks, gazing down at Emma with worry.

"I need you to lower your voice," Kade tells him in a stern whisper. He hasn't even glanced down at Emma yet, and she wonders if she should try to run away now? Can she even stand? "Get me a town car right away." Pulling several hundred-dollar bills out of his pocket, he shoves them in the concierge's hand.

"But, sir—" the concierge argues, eyeing Emma. Kade's eyes blaze with power; the man gives a little whimper of fear and stops talking.

"Did I stutter? Were any of my instructions unclear? Also, that money is for your discretion. If anyone asks, we are taking a meeting at La Meridien."

"No, sir. I mean, yes, sir. Right away, sir." He's already hurrying away with those words, practically diving behind his tall crescent desk and reaching for a phone. When Kade's eyes drop to find hers, she's relieved to see concern flash across his face. Then his expression is one of deep displeasure. When he talks, his words are harsh, and his tone clipped.

"Can you get up, or do I need someone to haul your carcass to the car?"

The bond between them is still closed. Emma reaches out with her power, pushing at the bond, desperate to feel Kade's warmth and caring. The stone wall of power she meets makes her want to howl until the slightest brush of his power caresses her. One word floats into her mind. A word she didn't think to hear from him. It's a whisper, a promise, and an embrace.

Getting to shaky legs, she stands without help while Kade taps away on his phone with fierce concentration. To any casual observer, it would seem that he isn't paying attention to her at all, yet she can feel his power watching her, even if his eyes aren't. He might appear focused on his task, but she can feel him checking her balance when she stands and sways slightly as her equilibrium adjusts. His arm is tense, as if ready to reach out and grab her if she topples over.

Matheus didn't do any permanent damage. Mostly she's wrung out from the pain he caused her, but otherwise her body feels fine. Looking up from his phone, Kade scowls. "Can you walk? We're late for the next meeting." His voice is unnecessarily loud for her sensitive shifter hearing, but one of Matheus's followers is standing at the entrance to the hotel bar.

"I can walk, Alpha." Her tone is deferential and meek. With a cavalier flair, Kade turns and starts striding away.

"Then be quick about it," he barks. Following, she's proud that she keeps her head high and her stride mostly straight though her clothing is mussed, her hair is falling around her shoulders in disarray, and there's a rip in her shirt.

Only when they're walking out the grand doors of the Epicurean does she notice she's missing both her shoes. They must have dropped off her feet when Matheus used his power to lift her, but what's amusing is that no one bothered to tell her about them. Even now, they're probably sitting in the middle of the lobby.

Considering how few mages are in the world, Kade and Matheus meeting in the lobby of a hotel in Tampa is an attention-gathering event, just like a major celestial phenomenon. Those two alone would draw anyone's attention, but adding the drama of her writhing on the floor means a pair of shoes isn't going to be noticed by those watching. Even Kade, who cares so much about such little things, isn't aware of her missing footwear.

Even if someone notices, who would want to risk getting close to the mages to return them to her? Not that she blames them. If she was an onlooker, she'd think twice about messing with these mages. Kade's kind gentleness toward her and Avery's obvious love of Jason lulled her into a false sense of security around the powerful creatures. Mages are not to be trifled with.

A town car is waiting for them with a smiling but nervous-looking driver holding open the door. Kade puts a hand on her back, giving her a little shove into the car. The driver makes a distressed sound as Emma tumbles inside. She's recovered enough that her shifter reflexes take control and she lands softly on her hands and knees, flipping over gracefully to sit on her butt on the seat.

"Drive the damn car," Kade snaps at the man as he folds himself inside, forcing her to slide across the seat to accommodate him. The moment the doors shut and the metal and tinted windows sit between them and the outside world, Kade snatches her off the seat and hugs her tightly to his chest.

"I'm so sorry, Emma," he whispers over and over again. "I'm so sorry. I'm sorry. Sorry, sorry, sorry. My sweet wolf. If I could have done anything to spare you that, I would have."

The bond opens, and a flood of emotions hits her with enough force to make her a little dizzy. Fear, regret, shame, and dread are just a few of the things Kade's dealing with. He showers her face with kisses as he rocks her in his lap.

"If he knew how I felt, he might have killed you right there. He likes to do things like that. That's why he took Samantha Li's fae. He found out she felt affection for him, so Matheus took the poor man. Kept him for almost an entire year. Getting him back cost her almost everything she had, and she got back a shell of the man he was."

Shivering at his words, Emma clutches at him, scared for her future. "But you're not going to sell me?"

"Never," Kade promises as his phone rings. He lets go with one arm to answer it, putting the phone on speaker so he can toss it down to the seat next to them and resume hugging her.

"*Signore* Allard," Franco's voice sounds frantic. "What's happened?"

"Matheus wants Emma," Kade spits out. Franco makes a hissing sound.

"No! *Assolutamente no*! That *cagacazzo* can't get past your wards here at the house, *si*? We must get you both back here. Back to safety."

"That's why I'm contacting you. Is my plane ready?" That explains who Kade was texting while pretending to ignore her earlier. A wave of relief goes through her. Her mage is already figuring out an escape plan.

"No and *si*. I couldn't get ahold of our pilot, but I found a replacement. The plane is being fueled as we speak. It should be ready to take off by the time you get there. The new pilot will take you as far as Albuquerque. No other pilots are qualified to fly our plane the rest of the way, so I've arranged for a different plane to fly you from Albuquerque to Monterey." After a brief hesitation, Franco rushes to say the rest, his voice apologetic. "The plane on your last leg isn't up to your normal quality. *Mi scusi*, but it's all I could do given the time frame."

"Getting Emma to safety is far more important than comfort right now." No disdainful sniffs, no contemptuous expression. All she's getting from Kade is urgency and anxiety.

"I will be there to pick you up when you land, *signore*," Franco continues.

"Pick us up in the Jaguar. It has the best wards," Kade instructs. "And double check all the ward anchors around the property. Make sure nothing is out of place. Matheus is powerful enough to take advantage of even the slightest crack."

"I'll do the entire perimeter, *subito*," Franco promises, his voice tight with tension and anxiety. "Both along the fence line and the house itself. We'll make sure he can't get to her." Harsh, barely suppressed rage fills his voice. "After what that monster did to Armond, he should've been executed. Killed with *nessuna pietà*."

"I concur." Kade's voice is tired. She can feel depression and resignation through the bond. Kade hates Matheus and has wanted him dead for a long time, but he's helpless to make that happen. For someone like Kade, that must be nearly unbearable. "But killing him just isn't an option for us."

"*Si, signore*, I know." The sadness in Franco's voice matches Kade's. "Message me when you're on the plane, *si*? I'll contact the hotel in a few hours and have your things packed and sent here."

"I don't know what I'd do without you, Franco," Kade breathes out.

"First you would starve, *si*? And then your house would be irredeemably dirty," Franco teases, surprising Emma into a light laugh. His tone is so different from the acidic one he's used with her, or the preferential one he uses with Kade. "Ah, I see my humor found its mark, *molto bene*. Breathe easy, Emma. We'll keep you safe." The fae-mix who seemed to hate her so much hangs up before she can respond to his kindness.

"It's official. Franco's adopted you," Kade tells her, resting his cheek on the top of her head.

"That's nice?" she says hesitantly.

"It can be. But it can also be quite aggravating. Franco adopts people, and then you can't get rid of him," Kade explains. "I never hired him. He just showed up at my door and demanded entrance. Then he told me what his duties would be. We argued over his salary for hours, but he finally let me pay him." This is revealing a whole new aspect to the grouchy Italian fae-mix to Emma.

"Why?" she asks simply. It would never occur to her to walk up to someone as dangerous as Kade and demand to be employed. Franco is far more courageous than she's given him credit for. Or foolish. Or Both.

It's probably both. She can understand both. Hadn't both she and Jason done courageous and foolish things since meeting Avery? Maybe mages just bring those qualities out in people.

"Armond is his cousin. I'm the one who got him away from Matheus. I was too late, but he still sees me as the savior." A quiver of revulsion goes through Kade. "The things Matheus did to that poor man were abominable. There's not a chance I'd let him take you, not without a fight. I'm sorry if I hurt and scared you, little wolf, but I needed to play a part. Matheus is too strong for me to go head-to-head with. I had to buy us time to run."

This is also news to her and explains Kade's actions. "Mages can be more powerful than each other? You picked up a plane. You turned Michaels into a cockroach. How can he be more powerful?"

Kade takes a deep breath, and she feels reluctance through their bond. Whatever he's about to tell her, he doesn't want to talk about. But he's going to, anyway.

"There are two types of mages, full-blooded and half-blooded. Full-bloods are uncommon because female mages are rare. Full-blooded means both parents were mages. Half-blooded are like me, Avery, and Victor. Our mothers were something else and our fathers are mages. Matheus is one of the rare full-bloods and damn powerful even for a full-blood. I think only a mage named Hadiza Musa, and maybe my father, are powerful enough to challenge him."

He draws her away a little so he can look her in the eyes. "My father is a selfish man. I'm going to ask him to kill Matheus, but the answer will probably be no. Not because he's scared but because he can't be bothered to do something so drastic unless it affects him directly. He already considers me a disappointment; I doubt anything I can say will push him to help us."

"But I'll be safe at your house in Monterey?"

"Not even Matheus can get past my wards," Kade assures her, pride coming through both his voice and their link. "That's why I can demand top dollar for my wards. They are impenetrable and undefeatable. My wards have been keeping several individuals safe from Matheus for the last few years. He wanted both of them as toys, so Franco brought them to me for wards. Matheus either lost interest or couldn't get past the wards—probably both because those men are still free. That means I can keep you safe, too. We just need to get back home before he realizes we left Tampa."

"That's good," Emma murmurs, snuggling her head into the side of his neck. "And I heard you before. I love you too."

"I never said I loved you," Kade objects, but his voice lacks conviction.

"You did," she insists gently. "While Matheus held and hurt me, you told me. You whispered to me."

"You're imagining things," he grumbles, making Emma grin tiredly.

"I might have imagined the word love," she concedes. "But just in case you sent it to me on wisps of magic, I want you to know I love you back."

Travel weary but glad to be so close to home, Emma lets Kade carry her off the plane without protest. After pulling her into his lap in the car outside the Epicurean, Kade has refused to let go of her. At first, she objected. It's embarrassing to be carried like a child in public, even if it's through a small private airfield just outside of Tampa. But when his fear of losing her pulsed through their bond, she stopped trying to get him to set her down. He carries her not because she's weak but because of his sense of helplessness when facing Matheus.

Franco is there, waiting for them with the heavily warded car. The potent smell of magic coming off the vehicle tickles Emma's nose. Without a single word of greeting, Franco ushers them into the backseat and then practically dives into the driver's seat. No sooner do the doors of the Jaguar shut, and Franco is speeding away, mumbling curses in Italian.

As if trying to set a speed record, Franco zooms through traffic. He dodges cars and shakes his fist at drivers who dare get in his way. Despite the rough ride and Franco's uncouth behavior, Kade doesn't reprimand the small Italian fae-mix. He clutches Emma and concentrates on his magic. He's been that way the entire trip. Pouring his power into personal wards that keep them both hidden from Matheus.

"Almost there, *signore*," Franco calls back. They're out of town now, and the scenery outside is moving by in a blur. She's amazed they haven't been pulled over by the police, but perhaps whatever kind of magic Kade's doing to keep Matheus from seeing them is also keeping the police from noticing Franco's excessive speed.

"Have you heard anything?" Kade asks Franco. The fae-mix shakes his head with a frustrated expression.

"Nothing." Franco's tone is angry and she can feel hatred seething off him. "He's a *bastardo,* no? No care for others, like most of you mages."

Kade sounds a tired sigh. "We have to try, at least."

"Who's the bastard?" Emma asks, and Franco snorts out a derisive laugh.

"Just about all mages except for this one and sweet Samantha," Franco tells her. "*Bastardi,* every single one. Even that Victor."

"In this instance, the specific bastard we're discussing is my father, Gerard Allard," Kade explains as Franco whips them around a corner. "But it seems as if my dear father isn't interested in talking to me."

"That's…" Emma searches for a word but fails. She already knows mages aren't close, but not even to bother to return a child's call for help is an anathema to her as a shifter. She literally can't think of a word bad enough to describe it. "Maybe he's busy and hasn't gotten your messages yet?"

The look Kade gives makes her wince. "Until a few years ago, my father kept playthings as well." That simple sentence makes Emma's stomach drop. Kade nods at her obvious unease and explains.

"He's not as bad as Matheus, but he could easily compel others to love him. One of his powers is mind control. If you're human, he can make you think or do anything, even kill yourself." Kade takes a deep breath and then continues. It's obvious this isn't a topic he enjoys discussing. If he's telling her about it, it must be important for her to know.

"Real fucking winner there," Emma mutters with sarcastic disgust. This time Kade doesn't reprimand her for her language.

"I met a few of his human, uh…" Kade pauses, searching for a word. "I guess we could call them companions. They were all intensely beautiful. Models, actresses, and the like. Most of them were just held in his thrall, but a few fought him constantly, and he would overpower their minds. He enjoyed it. He'd let the magic fade just enough so they could do small independent acts. He'd let them think they might escape, and then he'd reinforce the magic. He loved making them do things they abhorred. Nothing illegal like murder, per se, but if a person didn't like to kiss, he'd make them kiss everyone at a party."

The more Emma hears, the more she wants to sink her claws into Kade's father. What kind of men are these who use and abuse without thought to anyone's suffering? Now that she knows so much about mages, she's amazed Kade grew up with any compassion at all.

"Gerard can't influence anything nonhuman. When he can't use his power, he uses bribery or threats. My mother was a bear shifter, a very distant relation to Donal Olsen. I've been told that my mother was mated with another shifter when she caught my father's eye. I don't know what he did, probably threatened to hurt the sleuth. They were a small group with little money and no powerful connections. He took her away from her family. Getting pregnant with me was an accident, but he did nothing to help her during the birth."

That doesn't shock her. Unlike wolves, bears don't need to mate to get pregnant. "Poor woman," Emma murmurs. Being taken away from her family and sleuth and fearing for the lives of everyone she loved must have been horrible.

When he pauses, she looks up. Their eyes meet. His face is full of regret and sorrow. His need for reassurance pulses through their bond. Without hesitation, she floods him with affection. His face clears a little, and he kisses the top of her head.

"That's why I'm a murderer," he tells her, fully opening their bond so she's witness to his self-loathing. "Being born upsets normal babies and because mages are powerful at birth, we tear our mother apart with our magic. He might have helped her, at least alleviated the pain, but he deliberately decided to be out of the country during her last weeks of pregnancy."

Abhorrence seeps through their bond, and Emma releases her soul cipher gift. She pushes hard into him, expecting him to ask her to stop. He doesn't. He keeps talking instead.

"The absolute worst part is that deep in the babies' minds, they fully understand what's going on but are powerless to stop themselves."

That breaks Emma's calm. "No, a baby doesn't fucking know it's killing its mother," she nearly shouts at him. She twists in his lap and grabs his face, forcing him to meet her eyes. "As a baby, you might understand someone being hurt, but there's no way you could understand what was going on."

"How can you be so sure?" he demands.

Instead of answering him, she stabs her gift into him. She's too upset to bother with being gentle or nuanced. She shuffles through his memories until she finds some of the earliest. It shocks her to realize that one of the memories she uncovers is of him in the dark, listening to the muffled sounds of voices.

It's him in the womb listening to his mother talk to someone.

Interesting, but not the one she wants. Exploring, she finds the one she wants and pulls at it.

Baby Kade, the world around him full of chaos.

Screaming. Loud voices. Bright lights.

The room is so heavily imbued with magic that he feels like the walls are pressing in on him. He reacts with force, instinctively throwing out magic wildly, but the only thing his magic affects is the woman who carried him in her womb.

Men and women hurry around the room. Their voices are tense as they deliver the baby and fight to preserve the mother's life.

He can't get them to understand that he wants to stay inside her.

He tries to hold on to his mother with his magic. His infant brain can't understand why he's being ripped from the warm comfort of her womb. He doesn't want to go. He clings so strongly that he rips her soul out of her body as hands physically separate mother and child.

"I love you, baby boy," the bear shifter whispers as she breathes one last ragged breath and goes still. Baby Kade screams inconsolably as he's placed in a warded incubator. He feels unprotected. Helpless.

No wonder mages are a fucked-up bunch. No one should be able to remember their birth, especially if their mother dies during it.

With this memory, Kade's deepest wound erupts with revulsion and self-hatred.

Determined to stop these self-destructive emotions, she pours power into him.

Your father is not you.

Your mother loved you even before you were born.

She loved you even as you hurt her.

It wasn't your fault.

Babies can't be at fault. They're babies, innocent of right or wrong.

You aren't a monster like your father.

You're loved. You're not alone.

To her absolute shock, the wound closes a little. He doesn't just accept her gift. He pulls her into him, opening himself to her power and laying himself bare. It takes her a moment to realize he's not just opening himself up to her soul cipher gift, but he's dropped every single shield or barrier. She could easily end his life right now.

It's as if he's asking her to judge him worthy or not.

"Does he still do these things?" she asks gently. "Does your father still take people? Hurt them?"

"I stopped him," Kade tells her. His expression is dull and his words listless. He's done fighting her and himself. Now he's just waiting for her decision. It's not lost on her that when they first met, he held the power of life and death over her, and now their roles are reversed.

"It took years, but I finally found a way to make him stop. I did the best I could. Every time he discarded one, I would find them a place to live and a community to support them, but it would take years or decades for them to recover. Many were never the same. I tried to track down the one he had before I was old enough to help. Most of them were dead—suicide of some kind or another. Drinking themselves to death or behaving recklessly. One put a bullet in her brain."

"How did you stop him?"

"I promised him a baby," Kade explains simply. "Sometime in the next ten years I need to have a child or he'll start up again. That gives me ten years to figure out how to stop him before he realizes I won't live up to my end of the bargain. I'll never have a child. I'll never do to anyone what my father did to my mother."

"I can't ever see you enslaving anyone," Emma soothes, but he's not comforted by her words.

"Not enslave," he counters. "I'll never condemn anyone to death because they're unlucky enough to get pregnant with a mage's child. Only female mages like Avery could survive giving birth to a mage child. If no female mage is willing to carry my child, then having one is out of the question. After Avery and I decided against having children, I had a powerful spell put on me so I could never get anyone pregnant." His words don't surprise her, but they make her a little sad. She would've liked to have had children.

"You're an honorable man," she whispers to him, hugging him close.

"I'm a coward," he responds. "I should've challenged my father the moment I understood what he was doing. There's a slight chance I could've won, and he'd be dead. He deserves to be dead. Most of us mages do. We're an abomination on this earth."

"No," Emma counters, dumping all the reserves she has into her soul cipher gift. "You're not an abomination. Avery isn't an abomination. Victor isn't an abomination. You are mages, and as children, you had no choice about being conceived or not. What matters is what you do with this life you have, and right now you're acting with great courage and integrity."

She lowers her lips to his, kissing him until he comes out of his stupor and kisses her back. Hope flares across the bond between them. When she breaks the kiss and opens her eyes, he's watching her with cautious optimism. "That part of your life is over," she tells him. "You'll never call yourself that ever again. Do you understand me?"

You are loved.
You are loved.
You are loved.

"Such fierceness, my wolf," he whispers. His words are an attempt at teasing, but his eyes are clearing of anguish.

"I'm your wolf," she agrees. "And you're my mage. I might give my loyalty to whoever my alpha is, but you have my heart as well, and that only goes out to those who are worthy."

"Then I shouldn't have it," he tells her firmly.

"Only you should have it," she counters with determination. "Just try to make me leave. You're my alpha, my pack, and my mate. I'm your wolf, your family, and your mate. Get used to this, Mage Allard. There's no getting rid of me."

She sees a single tear sparkle in his eye before he pulls her too close to him to see his face any longer, trapping her in a tight hug.

"I'll keep you safe," he promises. "No matter what, I'll keep you safe."

He might not say the word love, but he's pouring the feeling through their bond. Being more careful with her soul cipher power now, she checks on the wound that burst as he talked. It's more than half-healed, making him well on the way to forgiving himself for something he had no power over.

She withdraws her power, finding both of them exhausted. Her fatigue directly results from strenuously using her gift. But for Kade, it's brought on by the emotional maelstrom he just experienced. He's in a fragile state, and she should let him rest before attempting any more healing. She's confident that if he doesn't fight her, it will probably only take another two or three sessions for her to finish healing the deep trauma in his soul.

A fissure of magic tingles her skin. Looking up, she sees they've just passed through the gates of Kade's property. A sigh of relief goes through him, and she smiles as tension eases from her shoulders.

"It's good to be home," he murmurs and lets his head drop back, eyes closed. The magic he's been holding for hours disappears, and bone-deep weariness filters through their bond.

Depleted, Kade is barely able to make it out of the car, and it takes both her and Franco to get him into the house, up the stairs, and into bed. He's asleep the moment his head hits the pillow.

Standing over the bed, Emma catches Franco smiling softly down at the slumbering mage.

"I'll get him undressed," she tells the fae-mix.

"And you'll stay with him, *si*?" he asks her, fretting. "He shouldn't be alone. He punishes himself for the sins of *suo padre*. But he shouldn't. He's not like the other mages. He's not like that *bastardo*. He's a good man and hurts himself by staying alone. You're the first one he's ever brought here to stay for more than a night."

Jealousy rears up in Emma. It's so unfamiliar it takes a moment for her to identify the emotion. She can't help the question that pops out of her. "He's brought many women here?"

Chuckling, Franco gives her a half shrug. "And men too. Sometimes a few at the same time. He's got a large appetite, but these mages do, *no*? But all the others, they'd stay for a night, and I'd drive them home the next morning. He wines them and buys them baubles, brings them home, enjoys them, and then leaves before they wake. It's my job to see that they are gone before he returns. I thought I'd be taking you away too after that first night, but you're different."

"I guess I am," Emma agrees, jealousy evaporating as she looks down lovingly at her stubborn mage.

Franco shuffles a little. "You're not so refined as the bed partners he normally picks. Not sophisticated." The insult makes her growl, but when she meets the fae's eyes, she sees nothing but good-natured humor there. She huffs out a laugh.

"We can't all be born with sticks up our asses," she says with a playful shove. They trade a few more insults until Franco suddenly sobers. He takes her hand in both of his and holds tightly.

"We're family now," he tells her, his voice serious. "I guess you would say we are pack now. We'll keep you safe. You need to stay on the property, *si*? Don't leave for any reason unless Kade is with you. Matheus is powerful. I think he might even be more powerful than Kade's *padre*."

Shivering at the memory of meeting Matheus, Emma adamantly nods. "You don't need to tell me twice. I won't leave."

With an approving nod, Franco gestures down to Kade. "Now get in bed with this one. He's going to wake up hungry in more ways than one. I'll be in the kitchen preparing a feast for us." With that, he turns on his heels to leave.

"Will you sit at the table with us like a proper packmate?" she asks before he leaves the room.

"No," he retorts, turning his head and giving her a half smile. "But I'll sit at the table with you as a proper family would."

It takes several weeks, but the three of them develop a routine. In the mornings Emma helps Franco prepare a light breakfast and clean up the kitchen afterward. Then she helps Kade in his office if she can. Because he's reluctant to leave the property, he's taking a lot of meetings in the dream realm, so Emma often spends quite a few hours a day stitching for him. Not only does it make her feel useful, but she also enjoys it. When the meeting is only attended by someone he's familiar with, he even lets her create the botanical gardens or something else equally elaborate.

But never her cliff. Never the place they first met. He told her that's special to the two of them, and no one else should get to see it. That warmed her heart until he also added that "your seagulls are also just too realistic. My clients will think they're about to get defecated on, and that's a horrible environment for a meeting."

Just for that in the next meeting, before he pulled the clients in, she made a gull appear out of nowhere and leave a nice slimy white mess on his pristine suit. She giggled for hours over the look on his face.

She also got to visit with Jason a few times in the dream realm. He never gave her much information, but he promised her that both he and Avery were doing better. She learned to be content with that.

Lunch is informal, with either a quick sandwich or a plate of antipasto left in the fridge by Franco. Dinner, she quickly comes to learn, is where Franco likes to shine. She enjoys watching him prepare the elaborate meals he serves them, and although he occasionally starts cursing in Italian, he never asks her to leave the kitchen. The cursing, he explained once, helps to flavor the food.

An entire month goes by with no contact from Matheus. Franco tells her that's surprising. He expected the mage to at least contact Kade with a threat. Perhaps his interest in Emma wasn't real. They can only hope he's dismissed her. But none of them are taking any chances. Kade checks the wards every morning and evening. Neither Franco nor Emma leave the property, only Kade. They have everything, including groceries, delivered although Franco pouts at not getting to pick the produce himself. Emma learned to steer clear of the kitchen on days the groceries arrive because Franco is never happy with what they send. Other than that, everything is going reasonably well for all three of them.

"I have a job in Chicago," Kade tells them one morning over coffee, interrupting Emma and Franco's conversation about a movie they saw the night before. "It's going to take me at least two days to do, but I'm coming home each night."

"Can you teleport and work within the same twenty-four hours?" Franco asks, concerned. "That's a lot of power to use."

"I can if Emma lends me a little of her power," he says with his eyes on her. Emma's first emotion is delight. He so rarely asks her to do anything. But her second thought is one of disappointment.

"I'm not powerful," she points out. "You can take whatever I have, but not much is there."

Kade's eyes go wide for a moment and then narrow. "I'd thought you realized what you are by now, but apparently not."

Stiffening, Emma gives him a puzzled look. "What are you talking about?"

"Your soul cipher gift allows you to maintain a reservoir of power, little wolf," Kade explains. "Right now, you're brimming with it. I'm going to need to teach you to pull in your aura because you're shining with power right now. If we're ever able to take you out in public again, you'd be a beacon."

"What?" Emma gives a startled gasp and brings up her own hands to stare at them, expecting to see bright light emanating from her skin. But her hands look normal. When Kade chuckles, she drops them into her lap and glares at him. "That wasn't funny."

"I forget wolves rarely have magic users," he murmurs. "I'm not amused at you, exactly, but at your naivete." Getting up, he walks around the table and takes the chair next to her. Then he grabs her chair and turns it so that they're facing each other. She doesn't help him at all but just continues to glare. She keeps her hands limp as he picks them up into his own. "Look down at your hands again." She doesn't, and he gives a little sigh. "I'm sorry I laughed. Now please focus. I want you to be able to see auras."

"Fine," she grumbles and looks down at her hands. "They look normal."

"Let your eyes un-focus," he instructs. "Feel inside yourself for your soul cipher gift. Feel for that reservoir of power. If it helps, you can use your gift on me, but only a little. I don't feel like having an emotional breakdown and then falling asleep right now," he tells her wryly. "So just try to gently probe me with your gift like you did that first time."

"What does it feel like when I use my gift on you?" she asks curiously as she draws on the soul cipher power.

"Like you're shoving a hot poker into my mind," he tells her blandly. His words make her lose her concentration, and she looks up at him, startled.

"It hurts?"

"Intensely," he confirms. "If your gift hadn't been pouring power into me at the same time you were mucking about with my emotions, I wouldn't have been able to maintain the wards. Your healing in the car ride from the airport was one of the most painful things I've ever endured."

Devastated, Emma practically jumps in his lap and wraps her arms around him, hugging him tightly. His chair rocks back from her impact, but his large body keeps it from going over. "I'm so sorry," she whispers as she shoves comfort through their bond. She didn't know her gift caused pain. "I won't do that again. I didn't mean to cause you pain."

"Shhh," he soothes, bringing his arms up. "I guess I should tell you that when I woke up from that nap, I felt calmer than I have my entire life. What you did to me made it feel like a weight was suddenly gone from my chest. Do you remember what I said to you when I woke up?"

Emma bites her lip to suppress a grin. "I believe it was something along the lines of 'why are you wearing clothes?'"

"Oh, yes, but after that," Kade says with a chuckle.

She has to think about it for a moment. "I didn't know what it was like to walk in the sun until you." She pauses, thinking. "I thought you were quoting something."

"No, Emma," he tells her gently, bringing up one of her hands to kiss. "I woke up, took a deep breath, and felt free of a pain I'd lived with for so long I didn't even notice it until you took it away. I've always known soul ciphers were powerful, but I never really understood what form their power takes. I haven't had a single nightmare since you've been in my life. Not one. When I dream of my childhood now, it's only the enjoyable moments with

Daniel. I can…" He pauses, taking several breaths before finishing. "I can almost see what it would be like to love."

"But—"

"Yes, I know there's more to heal," he cuts her off quickly. "But you're going to need to give me a little more time. I'm not exaggerating when I say the healing hurts."

"I can go slower. I can do a tiny amount at a time," she promises, pushing her power into him. She drops her gaze down to where their hands are joined, only to see the skin of both their hands are glowing. Fascinated, she brings their intertwined fingers up higher to examine them. Kade's skin glows just a little, but hers is lit up like a bright light is hidden under her skin. "Oh, wow," she breathes.

"Very good," Kade says with approval. "You can see it now. Do you feel the power you've stored?"

This is the first time she explores the gift inside her while not trying to actively help someone. Manipulating her formidable gift without focusing on healing someone feels strange. Power vibrates in her, responding to her exploration as if getting ready to heal. It feels eager and ready to jump into Kade. It takes a conscious effort to keep the power in check.

How had she never noticed it before? She's brimming with energy, and when she lightly taps at it, a spark of power shoots out and makes her skin tingle. "Fuck," she mutters, and both Franco and Kade laugh.

"I felt that," Kade tells her. "To draw from it, imagine a siphon gently releasing power that you can direct to me. Your gift won't like the idea of drawing power for anything but healing. It shouldn't hurt, but it might feel odd."

Imagining a small waterfall in her mind, she directs the power to Kade through their joined hands. It's not a pleasant experience. The only thing she can compare it to is getting a series of static shocks, but it's not so horrible as to make her stop. Kade sighs with pleasure as the power trickles into him.

"Emma," he whispers, "that feels amazing." She checks in with the alpha bond and finds that the power is having a very titillating effect on Kade. Opening her eyes, she looks at his lap and notices an erection straining at his pants.

Now that she knows power exchange can be erogenous, she vows to explore this further in the future. She cuts off the power exchange and puts her lips to his. They kiss until Franco obnoxiously clears his throat.

"It's noon," he points out primly. "And we're in the dining room. Do you two consider this appropriate?"

Grinning, Emma breaks the kiss and looks over at the disgruntled fae-mix. "You sound like him."

"Thank you," he responds sincerely, making Emma laugh.

"You're correct," Kade says as he stands, holding Emma securely against him. "The dining room is unsuitable for a romantic dalliance. We'll retire to my room for the afternoon. If Emma's going to be lending me her power, it's only right that I make sure she's well stocked herself."

"I'll see you at dinner then," Franco responds, his expression stiff, but there's a hint of a smile on his lips that makes Emma giggle as Kade carries her out of the room.

"Indeed," Kade calls back.

To her surprise, when they get to the bedroom, Kade tosses her on the bed instead of setting her down. With a gasp, she bounces and then hops off to tug off her shoes. While she's balancing on one foot and pulling off her left shoe, Kade grabs her and tosses her back on the bed. Both shoes go flying.

"I put you there, so you stay there," he growls out. His actions and words make her skin flush and her heart pound. Putting a knee on either side of her hips, he leans over and nuzzles against her neck. Then he deliberately opens his mouth and bites down. Eyes fluttering shut, Emma moans.

He doesn't break the skin but bites hard enough to leave a bruise. When he tries to release her neck and sit up, she grabs the back of his head to keep him there. "More," she begs. Obligingly, he bites her again, this time a little lower on her neck. After the third bite, she is panting and undulating her hips.

Rising, Kade grabs her jaw and moves her head to the side so he can see his handiwork. "You're going to have bruises," he murmurs, running his thumb over her skin.

"Good," she breathes, letting her eyes stay closed.

"I called an acquaintance," he tells her as he wraps his hand around the back of her neck. The hold is gentle and light, but just having his hand resting there makes her feel centered and happy. "He's an alpha out in Colorado. I asked him all about keeping a submissive wolf happy. He gave me detailed instructions." Reaching down, Kade rips her blouse open. "Very detailed."

Even if Emma could respond, she wouldn't know what to say. The sound of ripping fabric and his forceful actions coupled with the affection coming through the alpha bond are putting her brain in a very happy place. Her panties are already soaked and she feels overheated and needy. She makes a little desperate sound.

"That's right," Kade coos as he tears at her clothes. "This is what you need. My friend told me to keep it rough. Rough enough to bruise. He said to be heavy-handed. I worried I might hurt you, but I can feel that you like this through the bond. You needed this, my little wolf. You need me to take control. To show my strength so your submissive side can feel safe."

It's true. Wolves like to play rough and although Emma's been enjoying Kade's gentle lovemaking, she missed how roughly another wolf would take her. Two dominant partners will even fight throughout sex. One time she and Jason came home to find the living room in shambles because their parents decided to "enjoy" an evening with the house to themselves.

On the other side of it, submissive wolves are passive and want to be roughed up a little by their partners, just like Kade is doing to her now. The last bit of cloth he tears away are her panties, and he takes a moment to sit back and admire the flesh he's revealed. The approval on his face makes her feel special and cherished. The lust in his eyes makes her feel damn sexy.

"You know, it's not uncommon for wolf packs to own kink clubs. We're kind of famous for it," Emma tells him with a grin.

Realization dawns on his face. "I knew that. I've invested in a few sex clubs owned by the Cruz Pack. I always thought it was because wolves loved sex in all forms. Now I know it's because you're all suffering from species-wide kinkiness."

That distracts her enough to make her bark out a laugh. "Could be. My parents were both dominant wolves. Their bedroom was in the basement so they could knock each other around and the neighbors wouldn't hear."

Distaste crosses his face. "That's a fact I didn't need to know, Emma." That makes her chortle until he grabs a handful of her hair. The hold is strong but not painful and he uses it to keep her head still as he kisses and bites at her lips and along her jawline. Her heartbeat picks up again as he nips at her skin.

Emma goes still under Kade's onslaught, caught up in the wonderful contrast as he alternates between his kisses and bites. She makes a small sound of distress when he pulls away, but it turns to a moan of pleasure when he flips her onto her belly and sits on her thighs, effectively pinning her down. Running his hand down her spine, he settles it on her bare backside to squeeze. As if reading her mind, he slaps a hand down on her ass with a nice loud crack. She gasps and wiggles from the sharp bite of pain followed by the delicious burn.

"My alpha," she whispers, her eyes shut and panting. *My mate.*

"My wolf," he answers her and leans over to bite her shoulder. She wiggles under him, not because she wants to get away but because she can't possibly be still. Rough hands grab her, alternately pinning her in place and petting her heated flesh.

"Do that thing," she pleads. "That thing you can do with your hands. Please!"

"No."

His denial makes her whine louder and struggle under him. He drops his weight on her back so his body is almost entirely covering her, and she goes still. The bulk of him feels delicious pinning her down.

"Greedy wolf," he murmurs and nips the shell of her ear. "I'll do what I want to you when I want, and nothing you do or say can change that." His words send a bolt of lust through her. He must feel it through the bond because he chuckles evilly. "I never thought I'd enjoy this kind of interaction, but you're bringing out all kinds of instincts I didn't know I had."

Not sure what to say, she just makes needy sounds and moves a little under him. He holds her there, nipping at her neck until she's mewling with need. Sitting up, he grabs her legs in a harsh grip and forces them up and apart. When she goes to rise on her elbows and bring her shoulders up, one of his hands slaps down on the back of her neck and forces her head against the mattress.

"Stay," he growls out. The position is delightfully submissive, and her wolf whines with the pleasure of it. The hand leaves the back of her neck and starts roaming over her breasts and then her belly. Fingers tease the curls at the apex of her legs but then move back up. That makes her growl with frustration. Kade ignores her and continues to grab, tug, massage, and pinch her flesh in a random pattern that has her jumping, purring, or yelping.

"Bastard," she mumbles into the mattress.

"What was that, little wolf?" His tone is dangerous, and she winces.

"I love you?"

A startled laugh escapes him, making her giggle. His stiff cock is resting heavily along the crack of her ass and she wiggles her hips to get his attention.

"Such a needy pet," he murmurs. Moving his hips, he places the tip of his cock at her entrance but doesn't push in. She tries to wiggle back, but that only gets her another smack on the ass. It's not a deterrent, but she stops moving anyway. One of his hands moves to her neck to hold her upper body still, and the other one glides down her belly. She thinks he's going to tease her again, but instead he pushes those blunt fingers between the swollen folds of her sex and starts rubbing on her clit.

With a violent push forward, he surges into her at the same time he hits her with pulsing magic from his fingers. The two sensations at once make her scream and thrash under him. His tight hold on her keeps her from getting away, and all she can do is passively accept all the pleasure he's pumping into her.

She comes hard, crying and gasping with the intensity of it all. He thrusts himself a few times, and then she feels him climaxing as well. Breathing hard, he collapses to the side, bringing her with him. He's still lodged deep inside of her, but neither of them seem to be in any kind of rush for him to pull out or to get themselves cleaned up.

A huge grin curves Emma's mouth as they both get their breath back. "Thank you," she whispers.

"Oh, no thanks necessary," he tells her, hugging her tightly. Both she and her wolf luxuriate in being satiated and curled up against their dominant alpha lover. "I didn't know it could be like that."

"It's always like that between mates," she assures him, and although he stiffens, he doesn't contradict her. She counts that as a victory.

When Emma's phone rings, it startles her. Feeling mildly restless, she decided to walk the path around Kade's property but ended up sitting on a convenient rock to stare out at the ocean. They may not be her cliffs back home, but they're similar and just as nice.

Looking down, she finds the phone in her hand. Funny, she doesn't remember bringing it out with her. The number on the screen is unknown, but that's not unusual. She's just now getting all the contact information from her old pack.

Curious, she answers the unknown caller.

"Emma! I need you!" Jason's voice is high-pitched and panicked, and that makes her panic as well. He almost never panics. Like her, he is calm and measured. Only one thing could make him panic right now, Avery.

"Jason, what—"

"I need you here!" he cuts off her question. "Can you get here fast? Please, Emma, I don't want her to die!"

It's just after one in the afternoon, and Kade isn't due home for another four or five hours. She can't leave the property until he gets back.

"Are you still in Florida?" she asks.

"Yes, the same place," he tells her. "Avery can transport you here, but you need to leave Kade's property first. She said she can't get past his wards."

"I can't just leave, Jason. Kade's not here," she argues and then hears a cry of pain in the background. It sounds like Avery. "Have you called the healer?"

"The Healer's dead," he tells her grimly. "That's why I need you."

"I really shouldn't," she tries to explain. "It's dangerous for me to leave the property without Kade." She hears another distressed cry in the background.

"Emma, it's me," Jason says, his voice full of anxiety. Torn, she bites her lip and listens to Jason plead with her. "This can't wait for Kade to get back. Avery can't wait another ten minutes. I need you now."

There's no choice to make. If Jason and Avery need her, she can't say no. "Give me five minutes, and I'll be off the property, and Avery can teleport me to you," she tells him.

"You need to take off that necklace Kade gave you," Jason instructs. "It will keep Avery from being able to find you."

"I don't think—" A scream from Avery cuts her off. "Yes, I'll leave the necklace."

"Hurry!" Jason demands and then hangs up on her. Emma dials Kade's phone with one hand as she tugs at the necklace with the other. His phone goes unanswered, no surprise considering he's probably working. She leaves a brief message.

Setting her phone down on the ground next to the boulder, she struggles with the clasp with both hands. The necklace hasn't come off since Kade put it on her. Maybe he had it modified somehow because it doesn't seem to want to come off.

In frustration, she gives up and just pulls until a link breaks and it falls into her palm. Something amorphous breaks around her and she feels a shaft of unease go through her. It doesn't feel right not to have the necklace on anymore.

Discarding her feelings of foreboding, she sets the necklace down next to her phone. She's not sure why she leaves the phone, but it seems like a good idea for some reason. Standing up, she jogs back down the path. The spot where she was sitting is almost at the farthest point on the property from the front gate, but it seems to take her no time to get to the front of the driveway and slip through the small side gate.

The moment she steps out of the gate, everything changes. The bright sun disappears, and the night sky full of stars glitters over her. She isn't in jeans and a blouse; she's wearing a small pair of sleep shorts, one of Kade's undershirts, and her feet are bare.

What is going on?

A figure walks to her from the darkness. Normally with her shifter vision, the dark wouldn't be an issue, but she's having a difficult time figuring out who the person striding toward her is.

"Avery?"

"I'm afraid not," a man says. The darkness around him clears as if it's a fog. Fear makes her catch her breath as Matheus appears before her, a cold smirk on his face. "Hello, Emma. It's been a little while. But you're mine now, so I'll forgive you for the delay. I have such lovely things planned for you."

"No," she whispers and turns to run. The side gate is hanging open. All she needs to do is jump through it to be safe, but it might as well be miles away instead of a single stride because she doesn't even finish her turn before Matheus's power wraps around her and jerks her off her feet.

"No, no, none of that," he admonishes as he floats her to where he's standing. "I've had to work harder to acquire you than any toy in the past. I'm certainly not going to let you slip away so easily."

Emma can't talk. She can barely breathe. All she can do is watch as he gets closer to her, the glint in his eye making her quake with fear.

Bringing his hands up, he reveals some kind of metal collar. With a flourish, he snaps it around her neck. Magic snaps and crackles over her skin as the mechanism to the collar clicks closed.

"There now." He steps back with an approving nod. "Now you look like a proper dog." The magic holding her up releases, abruptly dropping her to the ground. Gasping, she doesn't hesitate. Using her natural speed, she tries bolting for the gate again. She doesn't even make it to her feet before a wave of pain makes her crumble to the ground as Matheus chuckles.

"There's a lot of magic in that collar," he explains. "That's what it does if you try to leave me. If you attack me, the collar kills you. It's also tied to my emotions, so if I'm not happy with something you've done, the collar punishes you. Isn't that a nice little gift? It was quite expensive, but nothing's too good for my toys."

Emma reaches out to the alpha bond with Kade but finds she can't pulse anything through it. The bond is still there but blocked by the collar. It's a horrible feeling, and she fights against it, straining against the collar and getting shocks of pain for her troubles. By the time she stops trying to get through to Kade, she's sweating and panting from the effort and the resulting agony. Looking up, she finds Matheus smiling down at her.

"Have you finally figured out you can't reach anyone? The collar also means you can't use your healing or stitching gifts." He giggles and rubs his hands together. "Even under Kade's ownership, you still haven't learned to hide your emotions. Everything shows up on that face. You think you'll kill me in my sleep. Or escape someone how. Or maybe you think you're dreaming. Well, no time like the present to dissuade you of all that nonsense."

Leaning over, he touches her shoulder with his fingertips. She feels dizzy for a moment, and then the world around them changes. Now they're in a dimly lit room, full of elegant antique furniture, bookshelves, and a roaring fireplace.

"Ah, home sweet home," he murmurs as he straightens up and strides over to a fainting couch. Emma remains on the floor, watching warily as he sits down. Looking over at her, he gives a little frown. "Unacceptable," he tells her and snaps his fingers, pointing to the ground at his feet. "Get over here now."

There's no point in rebelling until there's a clear avenue of escape, so Emma gets shakily to her feet. He snaps his fingers again. "No, crawl over here, like an obedient dog."

Flushing with humiliation, Emma crawls on hands and knees to the spot on the floor where he indicates. When she sits, he makes another displeased sound, and this one comes with a bolt of pain.

"Stay on your knees unless I tell you otherwise," he orders her. "I can see you haven't had any real training at all. Kade has been much too lenient with you." He grabs the back of her neck, but unlike Kade's touch, Matheus's fingers dig into her flesh and send pain shooting down her spine. A whimper escapes her, and he smiles. He gives her a little shake, sending more jolts of pain through her body. She doesn't fight him.

"You didn't beg for me to stop. That's good," he tells her with satisfaction. "I'm sure you'll learn quickly. First lesson: Never beg for the pain to end. The pain is how you prove you adore me." He sits up and waves a hand in the air. A ring sounds somewhere in the house.

"Let's go over the rules," he says. "You're my dog. You will answer to Dog. Like a good dog, you don't talk unless I tell you to. You don't walk upright unless I tell you to. You never look me in the eye. You do everything I tell you to do without hesitation." Emma drops her eyes to the floor to make sure she doesn't accidentally meet his gaze.

"Good Dog," he says and strokes her hair. His touch makes her skin crawl, but at least he isn't causing her pain. The door to the room opens, and the woman from the restaurant walks in. All she's wearing is a negligée and slippers, and Emma can see healing burns all over her arms and legs. She wasn't wearing a collar at the restaurant, but she has one on now. Keeping her eyes downcast and her hands clasped behind her back, she comes to a stop in front of Matheus.

"You called for me, Master?"

"Strip," Matheus orders and she doesn't hesitate. She pulls the skimpy negligee off and drops it to the floor next to her. Emma hisses as she sees the skin of the woman's stomach. It's covered in burn scars. "Turn around and let Dog see your back." Obediently, the woman turns, showing a back that is nothing but scarred flesh. It looks like she's been whipped until her skin was ripped bloody and then allowed to heal, only to be whipped again. She smells human to Emma, so that kind of damage would take years to accomplish.

"Isn't she pretty?" Matheus murmurs. "She's one of my prized possessions. It took some time, but I've molded her into a lovely little plaything." The woman doesn't react to Matheus's words. She just waits calmly for the next order. "I made her hold still once; then I broke her leg. I had a healer fix it right away; then I broke it again. Her screams were delightful, but the best part was that she let me do it repeatedly and never tried to move away from the pain. She just lay there and let me hurt her."

He sighs with pleasure, as if the memory is one of his favorites. "Even with the healer's intervention, she walked with a limp for months. I loved that limp. Perhaps we should do that again, and I can ask the healer to leave you with a limp permanently. Face me and tell me what you think of that idea."

Turning, the woman keeps her gaze down and bows her head a little. "I live for your pleasure, Master," she murmurs, no hesitation or hitch in her voice. Emma can feel terror radiating off the woman, but it isn't showing on her face. "Would you like to me go to the playroom now and wait for you?"

"You're my perfect girl," he tells her with a smile, and then he looks down at Emma. "When I first got her, she called herself Daria. Tell Dog your name now?"

"Idiot," Daria replies without a change in her tone. "Until Master gives me a different name."

"Yes, you were Whore first; then I got a new Whore so I let you be Idiot. I've been so generous, letting you move from one spot to another."

"Thank you, Master."

"Dog, I want you to emulate Idiot. I know it will take time and a lot of lessons, but eventually I want you to be like her. If you end up perfect enough, perhaps I'll keep you. Wouldn't that be nice?"

Although her insides are screaming to say no, Emma nods. She knows how to play this game from the years of being under Alpha Michaels' control. This man might be more powerful than her old alpha, but he has a similar, sadistic nature.

"Very good answer," he tells her. "Idiot, go fetch a drink and some food appropriate for our newest addition." Turning to leave, Daria moves quickly to do Matheus's bidding, not even pausing to put the negligee back on.

"You know, I didn't think I'd be able to capture you before the new year," he tells her idly as he tugs painfully at her hair. "Kade's wards are rather good, but then I hit on the idea of using your stitching ability against you. I've been in your dreams, Dog, for the last week, observing what you dream about." He snorts out a derisive laugh. "You're dismally soft-hearted and it was apparent quickly that the easiest way to capture you would be by using your brother. You stitched that dream; I just linked your physical body to your dream world, so when you moved in your dream you moved in reality as well. It's easy to do normally, but Kade's wards were rather irksome." He makes an irritated sound, and pain hits her system again. It appears her collar is very responsive to his mood. He smiles knowingly when he sees her jolt. "I can see you're already receiving lessons from your collar. As I was saying, it took me weeks to figure out how to manipulate you. I've never had to spend so much time to do something so simple."

His little speech explains what happened, and she curses herself for not learning more about her stitching gift. It never occurred to her that it could make her vulnerable. Kade must not have known that either, or he would've trained her to better guard herself.

If she ever gets out of this situation with her faculties intact, she's going to find herself the best stitcher she can and get lessons on how to protect herself.

"If only Kade wasn't so greedy," he mutters. "Then I wouldn't have had to go to such lengths to get you. Now he's never getting you back. When I'm done with you, I'll kill you. Or perhaps I'll keep you around to entertain others once I'm bored with you. But whatever I decide, he no longer gets to have you after I'm done. Troublesome half-blood. His father could've done so much better than a bear shifter. I guess heritage will always shine through, no matter what kind of school or training one receives."

Daria returns then, holding a silver dog bowl in each hand. She walks up to them, kneels with effortless grace, and then sets the bowls down on the ground in front of Emma. One bowl appears to be full of water and another has actual dog food in it.

"There now, how perfectly appropriate for Dog," Matheus says with approval. "Well done, Idiot. You may take your clothing and retire for the night."

"Must I leave you, Master?" Her words are full of pleading. If Emma didn't know any better, she might think Daria's sincere about wanting to stay with Matheus. If she was Daria, she'd be out of the room the moment Matheus gave her permission to leave.

"I'm afraid you must," Matheus tells her. He lets go of Emma, and she thinks he's going to pet Daria, but instead he slaps her hard enough to make her head turn. A trickle of blood appears at the corner of her mouth. Daria gives a little startled gasp but otherwise doesn't react to the blow.

"Leaving you is more painful than a blow," Daria murmurs, and Emma realizes this is a script Matheus has developed. What happens to Daria if she doesn't ask for the blow by begging to stay when she's dismissed? If she's willing to beg to be hurt, the alternative must be so much worse.

"Poor Idiot, you just don't know what to do with yourself when you're not in my presence," Matheus murmurs. He stands up and starts unbuckling his belt. "Lean over the desk."

Rising, Daria drapes herself over the desk, reaching her hands out to grab the far side of the wide, imposing piece of furniture. She spreads her legs a little so her belly and chest are flush with the wood top. It is obvious this is a familiar scenario, and Emma watches with dread as Matheus steps up behind Daria.

"How many blows would be more painful than leaving my side?" he asks her, his tone teasing as he wraps the buckle end of his belt around his fist.

"There is no number," she responds, her voice flat, her eyes closed, and her expression braced for what comes next. Without another word, Matheus brings the belt down hard against her back. Daria cries out but doesn't move her body. This is how her back ended up with so many scars.

After about a dozen blows, Matheus pauses. His breathing is heavy and his face is flushed with enjoyment. "Is that pain equal enough?" he asks her.

Sobbing now, Daria shakes her head. Matheus rains down more blows. Surprisingly, the skin hasn't split yet, but Emma can see it's only a matter of time before the belt strips off skin.

He stops when there isn't a part of her butt, back, or shoulders that isn't red and swollen from his blows. "Kneel," he orders, and Daria slithers off the desk and down on her knees, her head bowed and her hands locked behind her back.

"Thank you, Master," she whispers. "May I stay with you now?"

"Perhaps," Matheus says and turns to Emma. Snapping his fingers, he points to the spot next to Daria. Emma's been kneeling for so long, her legs have gone a bit numb, but she clumsily crawls over and take the position indicated by Matheus. He frowns at her, obviously displeased by her lack of grace, and a painful jolt of magic from the collar hits her.

"Idiot will need to give you lessons," he says. "You're deplorably clumsy. And much too fat. But that can all be fixed. Now, I think we should have a competition to see who loves me more."

Fear spikes through Emma as she accidentally raises her eyes to look at his face. He hisses in displeasure. The collar reacts to his disapproval and knocks her over with a blast of pain. While she's panting on the floor, he casually steps over and kicks her in the stomach. "Back on your knees," he orders. "How dare you move when I didn't tell you to?"

Scrambling back to her knees, she keeps her gaze down and even puts her arms behind her back the way Daria is doing. Grunting with approval, he dangles the belt in front of her face.

"Now then." He uses his free hand to grab Emma's jaw and force her gaze up. "What if I told you to leave the room?"

Slowly, Emma moves trying desperately to find a position that doesn't put pressure on any of the bruises or wounds that cover her body. She's not sure how long she's been under Matheus's control, but she thinks it might be around five days. Each one of those days has been a marathon of pain and humiliation. She can't remember the last time Matheus let her walk on two feet or consume anything other than what he offers her out of the dog dishes.

By the second day she was so hungry she ate the dog food. Every last, dry, disgusting morsel of it. Matheus patted her head like she was a real dog. She wishes that was the most degrading thing he's done to her. Matheus is teaching her a whole level of degradation and agony can be inflicted on a person, and she has a strong suspicion he's only getting started.

Right now, she's lying on the floor at the foot of his bed, her collar chained to a bolt in the floor with only a few inches of slack. The first night he chained her like this she made the mistake of moving too much, causing the chain to rattle and disturb Matheus's sleep. He unchained her from the floor and took her to the playroom, his word for the torture chamber on the third floor. Once there, he secured her arms over her head and left her standing on her toes for the rest of the night.

It was just another example of no matter how horrible or uncomfortable she is, he can always make it worse. The mage loves giving her the choice of *bad* or *worse*. She's learned quickly that he loves it when his toys beg for the *bad* so they don't have to experience the *worse*.

Enduring the pain of the bad is her entire world. The longer she stays with Matheus, the more she realizes she's getting off lightly.

At least for now.

What had he threatened Daria with to make her be still while he repeatedly broke her leg? It's hard to even contemplate.

Grabbing the links of the chain so it doesn't make any noise, Emma wiggles until she's on her back. The wounds on her back protest, but at one point yesterday he dislocated both her shoulders then had them popped back into place, so lying on either side of her tortured body is very painful.

Her shifter healing abilities could have healed these wounds, but she hasn't been allowed much food for the past five days. The pain of hunger is slight compared to everything else that hurts, but more than the pain is the fact that she's dizzy and nauseated all the time from lack of sustenance. That makes it hard for her to jump to Matheus's commands. Her lack of speed gets her punished.

She needs to learn to endure the hunger along with everything else.

A slight noise draws her attention to the open bedroom door. Matheus rarely shuts doors. He doesn't believe in privacy, probably because he owns everyone in the house. There isn't a single soul here who doesn't bear scars from him. And all of them wear the same blank, obedient expression as Daria.

Emma's learning to copy the same expression.

Rolling her eyes, she sees someone crawling through the open door. Shock hits her first. She can't imagine anyone in the household coming into Matheus's presence without strict orders.

As the figure gets closer, Emma sees that it's Daria. She has something in her mouth and her eyes are on Emma, pleading. Closing her mouth, Emma stays perfectly still, telling Daria she won't do anything to alert Matheus.

It takes ages, but Daria finally reaches Emma. Then she realizes the woman is holding a sandwich in her mouth. Carefully, she hands the food to Emma, but not before she taps the side of it.

Taking it, Emma looks to find words have been written on the bread.

You're not alone.

Those simple words bring tears to Emma's eyes. Daria isn't so broken as she lets Matheus think.

Cramming the food into her mouth, Emma eats the entire thing in three bites, enjoying the feel of having food in her belly. Daria is turning to leave when Matheus moves in the bed.

"Dog, are you mucking about down there? Do I need to teach you another lesson about being still?"

Emma's eyes fly to the cage in the corner of the room. The night spent in that was one of the worst so far. The cage is so tiny she was forced to sit with her legs drawn tightly to her chest and her head lowered against her knees. The bars felt like they kept getting tighter and tighter. By the time Matheus took her out the next morning, she was sobbing and begging to be chained at the foot of the bed again.

Seeing the terror on Emma's face, Daria moves quickly. She crawls to the edge of the bed and slithers up, disappearing from Emma's sight.

"Master, may I please you? I miss you."

A slap sounds and then a gasp.

"That's not your job any longer, Idiot. What have I told you about seeking me out?" Matheus asks, but Emma can hear the delight in his voice. "But I'll let you pleasure me, just this once. But it will cost you dearly. Is that what you want?"

"Yes, Master. Anything to be close to you." Emma hears the hitch in Daria's voice. She can't see what Matheus does to Daria, but by the end of the hour, the stoic woman is sobbing from pain. When he's finished, he pushes her out of the bed and she lands in a heap on the floor. "As a reward you can sleep there tonight," he tells her.

"Thank you, Master."

Curling up into a ball of misery, Daria shoves her fist in her mouth to quiet her sobs. It's a bad idea to keep Matheus awake when he wants to sleep. They both stay still until Matheus's breathing is even and they know he's gone back to sleep.

Slowly, carefully, Emma extends her hand out, under the bed toward Daria. The woman opens her eyes and stares at Emma's open hand for a while, tears silently rolling down her face. Finally, she uncurls one hand from around her legs and moves it out to grasp Emma's hand.

Since the moment Matheus put the collar on, her soul cipher gift has been buried deep inside of her, hiding from the sadistic mage. Now, with direct contact with someone suffering so much, it cautiously unfurls, tentatively testing Daria for a reaction.

The collar doesn't let her stitch or heal, and it blocks her bonds with Kade and Jason, but there's no barrier to her soul cipher power. When she doesn't make a sound, Emma lets it flow a little more and soon the gift is fully activated, flooding Daria with soothing words. The wounds are many and deep, but she has a core of strength and resilience that Matheus hasn't broken yet.

Emma does what she can, but she's much too depleted to do more than bolster Daria's natural inner strength and partially heal one of the more minor emotional wounds. Reluctantly, Emma withdraws her gift and lets it tuck away, deep inside of her. But even though she can't do any more healing, they remain holding hands for the rest of the night, only letting go when Matheus stirs the next morning.

Just before Matheus gets up and kicks her out of his way, Daria meets Emma's eyes. The message there is very clear, and Emma gives her one quick nod to tell the other woman she understands.

Daria hasn't given up hope. If she can have hope, so can Emma.

Matheus likes to keep his new toys close at hand. For the first week, he kept her in the house. When he left to attend a business meeting, he either restrained her in the playroom or shoved her in the cage in his bedroom, but he's decided it's time to take her out in public.

"Shift," he orders her as he checks his appearance in the mirror next to the front door. Without hesitation she lets her fur flow over her skin, enjoying the feeling of letting her wolf out after not being allowed to shift for so long. The collar shifts with her, adjusting to her larger wolf throat and giving her a bolt of pain once she finishes shifting. The pain drops her to her belly and makes her pant. He must have done that on purpose to keep her from shifting at will, then he orders her to change shape even though he knew it would hurt. Asshole.

Leaning over, he attaches a leash to the collar. "There, now you look appropriate." She wants to glare but keeps her eyes focused on the floor in front of her. Moving back, he yanks on the leash, making her yip with surprise.

"Now, we're meeting a client for lunch, and you'll be on your best behavior. When I sit, you lie down at my feet. When I walk, you keep pace beside me. You don't acknowledge anyone else unless I permit you. If you're good, I'll reward you."

A reward could mean food or pain. It's impossible to tell with this vicious mage. He keeps them all starving and sleep-deprived, and she knows her thinking is getting punchy. Sometimes she's slow to act on his orders, but it only took a few punishments for her to realize that's part of Matheus's game. That's why all of his staff are thin and exhausted; none of them are allowed proper sleep or enough food. It's just another way to hurt them with the added benefit of keeping them weak.

Leaning over, he grabs her muzzle in a brutal grip and forces her gaze to meet his. "Show me how happy you are to spend the day with your master."

Puzzled, she stares at him until he pointedly looks at her tail. Obediently, she swishes her tail back and forth, making him smile.

"Good dog," he murmurs, and it's all she can do to keep her hackles down.

A short, hollow-eyed young man opens the door for them and bows as they walk through. Over the last week, Emma has met the dozen individuals who make up Matheus's staff. All of them have scars, both inside and out. It seems Matheus doesn't hire people; he buys or abducts them.

"Boy," Matheus purrs as he gets to the door. The man flinches a little but remains still. "I feel like I've been neglecting you. Perhaps when I get back, I should make time for you. Would you like that?"

Nodding, Tommy keeps his eyes downcast, his body tense. "I've missed having your focus on me, Master."

From his smell, Emma knows Tommy's a fox shifter. Most of the staff are kept minimally clothed while serving in the house, except for Tommy. He's wearing a tight bodysuit. Whatever the thing is made of, it's uncomfortable. When Matheus isn't watching, Tommy tugs and pulls at it, trying to get relief from the irritating fabric.

Emma remembers Matheus telling Kade about making sure everyone's always uncomfortable. He makes sure their world is nothing but pain, discomfort, hunger, and exhaustion. This sick bastard seems to feed off of their misery.

"My sweet Boy," Matheus says with a wide smile. No one has names anymore. Tommy is Boy, Emma is Dog, Daria is Idiot. She doesn't know what the real names are of the woman Matheus refers to as Whore or the man he calls Dirt. It's just another way to degrade them. Just another way to break them down.

Reaching out, Matheus runs a hand down Tommy's cheek. "I'll give you all my attention when I get back. Why don't you retire to the playroom and wait for me? You know how I'd like you to wait, don't you?"

Tears gather in Tommy's eyes as he nods. "Yes, Master. Right away."

Scrambling away from him, Tommy heads to the stairs. They're going to meet a client, so that means whatever horrible position Matheus expects to find Tommy in when he returns, the poor fox shifter will need to maintain it for hours.

Stepping out the door, Matheus jerks on the leash and Emma hurries to fall in step with him. When Matheus takes his toys out into public, he dresses them in more socially acceptable clothing, or in her case, covering naked skin with fur. The man Matheus calls Dirt is holding the door to the car open, standing with slumped shoulders and staring at the ground in front of his feet. He's wearing an old-fashioned chauffeur's uniform that looks much too tight and constricting to be comfortable. If he wasn't so gaunt, his face would be handsome, with high sharp cheekbones and beautiful hazel eyes.

He's holding his left arm at an odd angle for the past few days, so Emma assumes Matheus did some serious damage. It's another thing the mage likes to do, make them work injured and pretend they're slow because they're lazy instead of hurting.

Daria, wearing a tight evening dress and impossibly high heels, follows them out to the car. Matheus gets in first, folding himself into the backseat with a sigh of pleasure. When Emma jumps in, she lands at his feet, expecting he will want her to lie on the floor. With a swift kick, he hurls her back out of the car. Yelping from both the kick and the pain from her collar, Emma lands hard on the cobblestone drive.

"Dogs don't ride in here," he tells her and then addresses the driver. "Dirt, put her in the trunk."

Resigned, Emma slinks to the back of the vehicle with Dirt right behind her. By his scent, Emma knows he's mostly human with a little jinn thrown in, but not enough to have any actual power.

The trunk pops open. Dirt steps around the car and waits for her to jump in with an ungraceful leap due to the lack of food making her uncoordinated. She sees a quick look of sympathy from Dirt before he shuts the trunk. The car jostles a little when Dirt gets in; then they're underway.

Matheus might think making her ride in the trunk is a punishment, but in reality, it's a stolen moment for Emma to relax.

Curling up on her side, she closes her eyes and lets her mind and body enjoy this calm moment out from under Matheus's merciless attention.

She has no sense of time in the trunk, just the gentle movement of the car around her. It's a little hot and stuffy in here, so soon she's panting, but still content. She lets her thoughts drift to Kade, Franco, Jason, and Avery.

She misses them so very much. Sometimes it's all she can do to keep herself from ending her own life. It wouldn't be hard. There are knives in the kitchen, and she has the freedom of the house now. One swift plunge and she could spear her own heart. Her limited healing ability gives her an excellent understanding of physiology. Her pain could be over in less than a minute.

But then she thinks about Kade. She holds on to a thin thread of hope that he'll wait for her. If she can just survive Matheus with her sanity intact, he'll wait for her. Her soul cipher gift is helping her to accept a situation she can't change and pushes her to look toward a future where she's free of this pain and degradation. Free of fear and terror. Free of Matheus.

When she has a moment like this, she makes up scenes in her head. Returning to the Monterey house. Walking up the driveway to find both Franco and Kade waiting for her, both of them wearing warm, welcoming smiles. Maybe even tears. She'll hug Kade, jumping into his arms and wrapping her legs around his waist. Kissing him. Never letting go.

She can almost taste him on her lips again.

All too soon, the car is coming to a gentle halt, and the trunk is opened. She takes a moment to blink the spots out of her eyes as sunlight hits her face. Then she leaps from the trunk and stumbles. Dirt steadies her with a hand on her shoulder. She thanks him for the small kindness by butting her head against his leg as he walks past.

Matheus and Daria are already out of the car, so she hurries to put herself next to Matheus. He reaches down to grab the leash that's still attached to her collar and gives it a little tug. "Come along, Dog."

She knows she's in Chicago from a delivery vehicle she catches a glimpse of. Unfortunately, she isn't familiar with Chicago or Illinois at all, so she doesn't recognize the grand hotel they're walking into. A concierge hurries up to them, eyeing Emma unhappily until he recognizes Matheus. Stumbling to a halt, he gives an awkward half-bow.

"Mr. Greer, it's so good to see you again. I saw you're taking a catered meeting in one of the suites, but I wasn't aware you were bringing a pet with you. We have excellent dog care personnel on staff if you'd like to make use of them while you're here." To the man's credit he only stumbles over the first sentence. After that he speaks smoothly with just the right combination of fawning and authority.

"Dog will stay with me," Matheus informs him in a voice that isn't up for arguments. "Have the others arrived yet?"

"Certainly, sir. They're waiting for you." The concierge snaps his fingers and a member of the staff hurries over, wide-eyed with fear.

"T-t-this way, Mr. Greer," the guy stammers and leads them away. Emma absently notices the stares they get as they walk. Unlike the first time she met Matheus in Tampa, when he had at least five of his toys with him, right now he only has her, Daria, and the concierge escorting him. Dirt got to stay with the car.

Soon they're ushered into a room where three other people are waiting for them. Emma stumbles when she realizes Victor is one of the three. As he looks down at her, she expects him to frown, but he must not recognize her wearing her fur because there's no empathy or kindness in his expression. He smirks as he looks back up at Matheus.

"New pet?" he asks as they shake hands.

"Very new," Matheus says, releasing Victor's hand to lean over and unclip the leash. "She's still in training."

"Can Anna meet her?" Victor asks, gesturing to the woman standing behind him grinning widely.

"I sure do love dogs!" Anna enthuses before going down on one knee and snapping her fingers at Emma. "Come here, girl." Afraid to move without permission, she looks up at Matheus.

"Go on," he says and gives her a little kick that almost knocks her off her feet. Victor makes a displeased sound, and Anna frowns, but no one reprimands Matheus.

Of course, they don't. No one would dare stand up to him.

Padding over to the woman, Emma gives an obligatory sniff to Anna's hand, as if she really was a dog, and then lets this stranger pet her. It's not a horrible feeling. Anna's gentle and only touches her face and neck.

"She's just glorious. She looks like she might have a little wolf in her. Do you know her pedigree?" Anna asks Matheus. Later, no doubt, Matheus will chuckle about Anna's questions, but for now he just shrugs.

"I guess pedigree doesn't matter," Anna murmurs as Victor introduces Matheus to the third man in the room, Steven Tolard, a businessman from Dallas. They all sit and discuss the reason for the meeting. Except for Daria, who stands at attention behind Matheus, and Anna, who stays crouched on the floor next to Emma, still petting and cooing at her.

As far as she can tell, Anna and Steven are human. Steven, Victor, and Matheus engage in an intense discussion immediately, but Anna stays on the floor, all but ignoring them. The woman's touch is pleasant, so Emma permits herself to enjoy being touched by someone with no intention of hurting her.

Then something strange happens. Anna's fingers rest on the collar, and a slight buzz of magic tingles along her skin. Nothing painful, more like a light pressure playing out from the collar. Anna's eyes darken for a split second, and her mouth turns down in a frown.

The touch of magic doesn't feel anything like Matheus's, telling Emma that Anna is not human and must have something in place to cloak her power. Unsure what this woman's end game is, Emma remains perfectly still, fearful of giving anything away. There has to be a reason that this woman's trying to pass for human, and the last thing Emma wants to do is draw Matheus's attention to this stranger.

Just because she thinks Emma's a dog doesn't mean she deserves what Matheus might do if he found out he's being tricked.

"Anna, dear," Victor calls out. "I know you love dogs, but perhaps you can join us? Steven needs you to explain the timeline for our project."

Frown disappearing, Anna straightens up with a last pat on Emma's head and takes a seat next to Victor at a table laden with food. The smell of it makes Emma's stomach cramp, but she doesn't whine as she slinks over to Matheus and lies down next to his feet.

"She's so well-trained," Anna compliments as she fills her plate with food. "Would you ever be interested in selling her? Is she fixed? I have a lovely Bluetick Coonhound stud I'd like to breed with her. They'd make gorgeous pups."

Matheus chuckles because he's probably delighted at the idea of forcing Emma to have sex with a dog, but he shakes his head and reaches down to grab a handful of her scruff to shake it.

"I'm afraid I'm rather attached to Dog," he tells her. "I've no plans to give her up any time soon."

"Pity," Anna says, watching with narrowed eyes as Matheus finally lets go of the painful grip he's got on Emma. "Well, if you ever change your mind, please call me. I'd love to add her to my stock. I raise and train hunting dogs back home. She looks like she'd make a fine hunter."

"I'll keep that in mind," Matheus assures Anna, and all Emma wants this woman to do is stop drawing attention to her.

Their conversation moves on to contracts, costs, and fees. She lets her mind drift, thinking about Franco's amazing food. Then a familiar name brings her attention back to the people at the table.

"Kade?" Victor says thoughtfully. "I haven't seen him for a few months. I think he's in Russia right now, working. Last I saw, he had this new assistant. Pretty little thing. I think she's a Diwata-human mix. She's trading work for protection. You know those Diwata don't like it when their members mix with other species. There's probably a price on her head because they consider her an abomination. Anyway, she seems a little meek to me. I like those around me to have a little more backbone."

"Indeed," Matheus murmurs with a satisfied grin. "I'm sure Kade is doing what he needs to do so she remains sufficiently loyal. I thought he was rather taken by his last pet. I didn't realize his affection was so fleeting." Sending a significant look down at Emma, he pats her head. "But most of us know one pet is just as good as another. Isn't that right, Dog?"

Feeling sick, Emma lets her head hang. Does Kade already have a new lover? Has she been replaced in both his bed and his heart? A new low hits her. She thinks about those knives in the kitchen again.

No, that's not the way to think. Even if Kade isn't waiting for her, Jason and Avery will be. They probably don't even know she's been kidnapped yet. That gives her a little hope. Avery's powerful. Maybe, when she's recovered, Jason can convince her to come to Emma's rescue. Or at least try to buy her.

The meeting draws to a close, and everyone stands and shakes hands. With a last look at Victor, Emma walks out at Matheus's side. It was nice to see a familiar face, but the pain of leaving them without Victor even knowing who she is makes her want to howl.

At least she has the entire ride home in the trunk to calm herself before facing whatever Matheus decides to do with her later today.

Several days later Emma and Dirt are left alone in the playroom. Matheus restrained Dirt on a large table behind Emma so she couldn't see what he was doing to the poor man. She heard pained grunts and pleas from Dirt that he just wanted to be close to Matheus, the familiar refrain whenever Matheus feels like torturing his toys.

Then he left without doing anything to her, which was a surprise. Normally he likes to take several victims to the playroom together so one can be tortured while the other person is forced to listen and fearfully imagine what he'll do to them next.

Instead, he put Emma on her knees, secured her hands behind her back, and then attached them to a chain from the ceiling. This position put her arms up so she's forced to awkwardly bend forward on her knees. It's not the most painful position he's left her in, at least not yet. But if he leaves her like this overnight, her arms will be useless tomorrow. Maybe that's the plan?

Her ears pop, and she hears scuffling to her right. It reminds her of when she stands too close to Kade when he teleports. Looking over, she blinks but doesn't react because she must be hallucinating. That can't be her tall, proud, and beautiful Kade standing less than two yards away from her with a familiar scowl on his face.

He's looking around the room, and when his eyes find hers, his expression is a combination of relief and fury. Hurrying over, he drops to his knees in front of her and puts his face to hers.

"K-k-kade? Is it really you?" Or has she gone mad?

"We need to get her unchained." A second man is there, and it takes Emma a few moments to remember his name. "Victor?"

"She's so thin," Kade mutters brokenly, gathering her up in his arms as best he can. He feels so warm and solid. Hope for freedom and peace floods her. "You're so cold, little wolf. I've got you now. I'm going to get you out of here. You're going to be safe. I promise." Emma can't make any words come out of her mouth. Tears pour out of her eyes and she has a lump in her throat as too many emotions flow through her. With a little sob, she nuzzles closer to Kade, uncaring about her numb hands and throbbing shoulders.

"I can't transport her while she's chained," Victor tells him. "We need to get her free and get that collar off."

"Right," Kade says, reluctantly letting go of her. His face is fierce as he looks around. Bringing his eyes back to her, he cups her cheek. "Do you know where he keeps the keys?"

She looks to the narrow cabinet on the far wall. Without another word, Victor strides over. Soon he's behind her, freeing her from the restraints. Her arms dangle uselessly at her sides as she tries to straighten her back but ends up slumping to her side instead. Kade catches her and picks her up, cradling her high against his chest.

"Get us out of here," he tells Victor, but she makes a sound of protest and tries to wiggle out of his grip. "Shhh," Kade soothes. "You're safe. This is Victor. You know him. He's going to transport us out of here. We'll be home in the blink of an eye."

"Can't leave them!" she whispers, her voice cracking. After so many days spent being silent, using words feels wrong. How long has it been since she's talked? Days? Weeks? She pushes those thoughts aside. She has more important things to focus on right now. "We can't leave the others. He hurts them too. We need to save all of them."

Kade doesn't argue. "How many?"

"Ten more beside me and him," Emma says, nodding her head to where Dirt lies unconscious.

"We can't wait," Victor hisses to Kade. "We've only got a few more minutes before the masking charm fails. We need to get her collar off and escape while we can." Victor points to Dirt. "We can take this guy too, but trying to find the others is asking to get caught. Once the masking charm isn't working any longer, he'll feel me teleport."

"Then take him and leave me," Emma demands, making both Victor and Kade draw back in surprise.

"No," Kade grinds out, hugging her tightly.

"All of us or I don't go," Emma insists. Part of her wants to leave and ignore the other people suffering under Matheus. After all, even if they're able to free all the current "toys," Matheus will just go out and collect more. Won't he? Why does it even matter?

But it does matter. These people matter. Especially Daria. She can't leave without Daria. Once she's freed these people, maybe she can bring attention to what's going on here. Rally the magical community. Shame the government into doing something. She has hope they can stop him in the future, but right here, right now, she needs to save the others trapped in Matheus's brutal grip.

"We'll get them," Kade promises and starts lowering her to the ground. He steadies her until she can stand and turns to Victor.

"He might not notice us even after the charm wears off," Kade points out. "There's no reason for him to think anything out of the ordinary is happening. He probably doesn't scan his house or grounds very often. Who would even attempt to enter here without his permission? He's Matheus Greer, one of the most powerful magical creatures in the world. Besides, you said he bought the idea that I had someone else in my life and was off working like normal. He shouldn't be suspicious at all."

Grumbling, Victor turns to unlock Dirt. "This is such a bad idea. If I get killed, I'll come back and haunt you."

"If he kills you," Kade tells him bluntly. "That means I'm already dead."

A grunting gasp alerts them that Dirt is coming around. He startles at seeing two unfamiliar faces hovering over him but is much too well-trained to make any other sound. Feeling is returning to Emma's hands, so she reaches for Dirt to help him sit up. His face is badly swollen with only one eye visible. It looks like his jaw might be broken, and she knows his right arm is dislocated again from the way he cradles it. Blood seeps slowly from a dozen puncture wounds on his chest and abdomen. His breathing is shallow and pained, so he's probably got a few cracked or bruised ribs. A small hammer lies nearby, Matheus's weapon of choice for Dirt's torture earlier. The claw side is probably what made the puncture wounds while the mallet side caused the broken jaw and cracked ribs.

"We're getting out of here," she tells him. "Tell me your name."

"Dirt," he replies, looking at her warily as if this is a trap.

"No, your real name."

He's quiet for a while, as if trying to figure out what to do. Then finally, in a voice so quiet there's almost no sound, he whispers, "Brian."

"My name is Emma, and we're going to get out of here, Brian. We're going to get free." Turning to Kade and Victor, she straightens her shoulders. "I'll go down and bring the others up here."

"No!" Kade hisses vehemently. "Absolutely not!"

"You don't know the house; you don't know where they are. It will be faster for me to get them. If I shift, I can be stealthy. My wolf was the best stalker in my pack. I can do this."

"She's right," Victor interjects. "We need to get this done now, and she'll get all of them here faster than we can. Hell, we can't even use magic in here until it's time to leave, so we'd be going down there blindly. She can use her sense of smell and superior eyesight as a wolf to keep away from Matheus."

Putting a hand on Kade's forearm, she meets his gaze. "I can do this," she insists. "I have to do this." She ignores her trembling body and spotty vision. She'll move through that. She's stronger than that.

She has to be.

"Fine," Kade grouses and then grabs her before she can turn to leave. "Hold on a moment." He rubs his hands on her collar, closes his eyes, and concentrates for a moment. She feels the unmistakable sensation of magic flowing and then the collar snicks open. Drawing it off of her, Kade casually breaks it in two at the hinge and sets it on a nearby bench.

Rubbing her bare throat, Emma stretches her neck around and finds she feels incredibly light. Energy floods into her, making her downright giddy. "Goddess be praised. Anna's magic worked," Victor mumbles.

"Anna?" Emma questions.

"The meeting you attended was a setup. We needed Anna to feel the collar so we could figure out how to get it off of you. I tried to have the meeting here, but that damn Matheus is paranoid as hell. Anna's a powerful earth witch, and between the three of us, we were able to cloak her so she appeared human. She set a spell up to track you and also figured out what kind of magic to use to pull the collar off without doing permanent damage."

"Track me?"

"We needed to know exactly where you were before we teleported in," Kade explains. "We couldn't risk teleporting in and having Matheus standing right next to you. We would have been here sooner, but it took extra time to unravel some of the magic around this place so we could get in."

"There's no other woman? You never went to Russia?"

"There's a woman, and I went to Russia," Kade explains impatiently. "But it was part of the ruse. I needed Matheus to think I didn't care after he had you. Otherwise," he stops talking and his face shuts down.

She hugs him tightly. "Otherwise, he might have killed me to hurt you."

"We need to get these people all in one room and get out of here," Victor reminds them, an edge of panic in his voice.

"Right," Kade points to the hall. "We'll be right there at the top of the stairs. Shout if you're discovered." Shouting would just draw them quickly to their deaths, so Emma vows to herself to remain quiet. Kade must have read her expression because he doesn't release his grip on her.

"You promise to shout for us or I'll have Victor get us out of here right now." His expression is as pleading as it is demanding.

"I'd rather die than bring you to your death," she whispers.

"I feel the same, little wolf," he responds. The alpha bond between them flares to life now that the collar is no longer blocking it.

The bond feels so good she doesn't notice right away that there's an added facet to it. Twined with the alpha bond is a mate bond, warm and steady. "Wolves mate for life," he murmurs. "That means my life is over when yours is, so you might as well call for help when you need it."

"What have you done?" she whispers. With a mating bond between them, Kade will probably die if she does. The mate bond she feels right now is a complete one, lending her Kade's strength and in turn making him vulnerable. Their lives are now irrevocably bound together.

"I'd rather die here and now with you than live a long life alone. You taught me what it's like to bask in the sun. I can't go back to the darkness," he explains. "Go rescue your friends, my soft-hearted wolf. Then I'm taking you away from this place and never letting you out of my sight again."

Determined, Emma nods. Without another word, she lets her fur flow over her skin and hurries out of the room.

The playroom takes up two-thirds of the third floor, and the last third is used for storage. Pausing at the top of the stairs and listening intensely, Emma tries to figure out where everyone is, but it's hard to hear over the thundering of her own heart. Her wolf form is large, but her fur is dark, so she blends well into the shadows of the old house.

As she silently makes her way down the stairs, she realizes she's not even sure the time of day. She thinks it's late afternoon, which means Matheus could be anywhere. He doesn't keep any kind of structure to his afternoons.

The closest and safest place to look for people is in the bedrooms assigned to them on the second floor. Three bedrooms house the twelve of them. She knows at least two should be in the rooms, recovering from beatings they received the day before.

Just like the rest of the house, none of the rooms have doors on them. Right now, it's helpful because Emma can creep into the first and second room soundlessly with no squeaking door hinges to give her away as she searches. The third room has two sleeping forms, Tommy and Jenna.

Shifting to her human form, Emma wakes Tommy up first. He goes perfectly still at the sight of her, puzzled and then alarmed.

"We're getting out of here," Emma whispers to him. "Get to the playroom. Two mages are there to rescue us—Kade and Victor. But you need to be silent and don't give anything away. Do you know where everyone else is?"

"He'll find us," Tommy whispers, tears forming in his eyes. "He'll just find us and bring us back. That's what he did to Mariah. He brought her back, and he took her arms and legs from her. And her tongue. Then he made her crawl around the house. She was like that for months."

"Shhh," Emma hisses and grabs Tommy's shoulder, pushing her soul cipher power into him. She doesn't have the time to be gentle. She finds the part of him that wants to believe her, a spark of hope that Matheus hasn't extinguished, and she shoves power at it.

"Kade will keep us all safe. He has wards Matheus can't get through. He's powerful, and he'll protect us." Her words echo the emotions she's bolstering in Tommy until he nods and starts getting up. "I know Cook's in the kitchen and Dirt's in the playroom, but other than that, I don't know where anyone is."

"Tobin, Savannah, and Angela are all in the gardens working," Jenna whispers. She's sitting up, her face scared, but her eyes shine with defiance. "Matheus decided he wanted the Japanese garden replaced with roses. Cassy's probably cleaning, but don't try talking to her. She'll fight you to stay with Matheus. Her mind is that broken."

"I'll stay away from Cassy, and I can get to the gardens from the back-room window. That means I should be able to get them all into the playroom without being seen."

"Lauren and Leah are helping cook," Jenna tells her, giving her the locations of the last of the staff, except for one.

"Daria?"

Jenna's mouth turns down. "Daria's with Matheus in the library."

"Fuck," Emma breathes. She'll save Daria for last and hope she can come up with a plan by then. Maybe a distraction? "Get upstairs. I'll gather the rest."

Without wasting another moment, Emma shifts back to her wolf form and slinks down to the first level. Getting to the kitchen is easy. Convincing everyone there to go to the playroom is a little harder.

Cook noticing her lack of a collar finally convinces them. The only way it could be taken off is because someone powerful besides Matheus removed it.

"If this is a trap or it fails," Cook tells her in a whisper. "Our deaths are on you."

"No one's going to die," she promises.

Once she escorts them to the stairs, Emma sneaks to a back bedroom and out the window. It takes her no time to sprint across the lawn to the garden. Her wolf form startles several of them as she comes to a skidding halt.

"Dog?" Savannah whispers. "You're supposed to be in the playroom. Does master need us?"

Shifting, Emma takes Savannah's hand and gestures for the rest of them to gather close. Assuming she's under orders from Matheus, they do her bidding, but soon incredulous looks cover their faces as she tells them it's time to escape.

"You can't be serious," Tobin hisses. He holds up his left hand that's missing all the fingers except for his index finger and thumb. "All I did was sneak some food, and he did this to me. What do you think he'll do if we try to leave?"

Emma doesn't argue with him, just points over her shoulder. "We've got powerful people to save us," she states with bravado. "If he tries to hurt us, we'll take *his* damn fingers this time."

They all hesitate, staring at her neck with wide eyes. "I don't want to live if he catches us," Savannah states softly. "I don't want to live through what he'll do to me."

"He won't catch us," Emma assures her.

"But if he does…" Tobin argues.

Emma says the only thing she knows will comfort them. "If we're about to be caught, I'll kill you myself before he can get to you."

Usually the threat of death makes people uncomfortable, but her words make Tobin's expression turn relieved. "You'll make it quick?"

"I know how," she promises, feeling sick to her stomach. "But it won't be necessary."

"You'll do the same for me?" Savannah asks.

That makes Emma realize they're so desperate to end the suffering that the promise of a painless death is just as welcome as the offer of escape.

"If it comes down to it, I'll make sure none of us suffer," Emma vows. "But that's not going to happen. We're getting out of here. When we are all safe, we're going to figure out how to make Matheus pay."

With expressions made up of equal parts fear and hope, they all hurry off to join the others in the playroom while Emma goes in search of Daria.

Cassy is working in the laundry room, so it's easy for Emma to avoid her. Following the sound of Matheus's voice, she crawls around the house on her belly until she's right under the library window. She listens until she gets the feeling for his movement in the room and risks a peek in the window. His back is to the window, so she has a moment to take in the scene.

Several other men sit in the room with him, drinking while he talks. They're interested but intimidated. These men must be the reason her torture was delayed.

The pungent scent of Matheus's magic fills her nose through the small crack in the window, so she can't figure out what these men are, but from the look of them she'd say human. They must be rich humans if Matheus invited them into his home. That must also be why so many were sent to help cook. Matheus no doubt wants to serve his guests an elaborate multi-course dinner. He loves being impressive.

Daria is here, wearing a tight dress and kneeling on the floor between the two men. Occasionally, one of the men looks down at her appreciatively and then back up at Matheus. She gets up to refill the smaller man's drink as Emma watches. The man reaches under her short skirt, grabs her butt, and grins. Daria doesn't even flinch, just pours, returns the crystal decanter to its spot, and then takes her place back on the floor.

How the hell is she going to get Daria out of this room? Maybe a disturbance? It would need to be something she could set up and then leave, so Matheus would investigate. Then she could grab Daria and run before he realized what was going on. Maybe she could set fire to one of the cars parked in front of the house.

She watches them as she thinks about the best way to set a car on fire when a shriek sounds behind her and an impact against the side of her head sends her toppling to the ground.

Holding a shovel, Cassy looks down at her with angry contempt. Emma was so focused on planning their escape that she didn't even hear the woman approach.

"What do you think you're doing, Dog? How did you get loose? I know Master left you chained in the playroom. Don't you understand what a privilege it is to have Master's attention? He never takes me into the playroom anymore. You don't know how lucky you are."

"I'll take you to the playroom all you like, Trash," Matheus states pleasantly as he appears next to her. Before Emma can react, Matheus puts his foot down on her neck, trapping her on the ground. Her head is throbbing from Cassy's blow, and she's seeing double. It's taking a lot of effort to keep her pain hidden from her bond with Kade.

Fuck, they're all in trouble now. If he drags her up to the playroom, he'll discover everyone hiding up there, waiting to escape.

Foot planted against her throat, Matheus casually reaches out and grabs a handful of Cassy's hair. He drags her to him and places an almost affectionate kiss on her forehead. "You've done well here, Trash. You've certainly earned my attention. Once I've dealt with Dog, I'll devote hours to you."

"Thank you, Master," Cassy beams. Faces appear in the window above her as the two men lean out to see what's going on. Matheus ignores them as he digs the toe of his shoe into Emma's throat.

"Now, Dog, would you care to explain to me what you're doing here?" Matheus questions but then he frowns. "And where did your collar go? You can't get it off yourself, so someone must have been bold enough to sneak onto my property." She feels him expand his power, searching for the intruders. That makes her panic and forget to block, causing her emotions to bleed into the bond with Kade.

Her ears pop, and suddenly Kade and Victor are there, using their magic to shove Matheus away from her. Laughing, he stumbles back, looking at the two other mages with something akin to delight.

"How perfect." He claps his hands together once. "I thought today would be special, but I never thought I'd have this much fun."

"Let me take her, and we'll leave you in peace," Kade offers. His power makes his aura light up the air around him, just like when he faced off against Avery in Florida. If Emma wasn't so busy being worried that everyone is about to die, she'd admire the sheer magnificence of his aura when his power is on the rise.

Later, she thinks, *if we all survive, I'll have to tell him how beautiful he is.*

Matheus laughs as if Kade just said something hilarious. "Do you think even with Victor at your side you're up for challenging me? Two half-bloods don't equal a full-blood. But I must say, I'm impressed with your audacity. Really—"

Before Matheus can continue, Kade throws up a hand and magic punches out. With a movement that's almost languid, Matheus dissipates the magic blow. Kade continues to attack and Matheus neutralizes him, his face twisted into mocking boredom.

"This is ridiculous," Matheus taunts him.

Emma wonders why Victor isn't attacking. Looking behind Kade, she meets Victor's eyes. He looks down at the ground next to him and nods ever so slightly. If Emma wasn't watching closely, she might've missed it. Kade is distracting Matheus to give her time to get to them.

She's not sure how the other women ended up outside, but Daria is kneeling right next to her, wide eyes watching Matheus as her fingers dig into Emma's thick fur. Shifting back to her human form, she grabs the woman's hand and moves to drag her to Victor. She doesn't even make it to her feet before Matheus's power grabs her. He picks her up, then slams her down on the ground.

The suddenness of the action makes Daria cry out, but Matheus ignores her. Now that Emma's dazed, Matheus uses his magical hold on her to lift her high into the air, her feet kicking uselessly as she dangles. She watches helplessly as now both Victor and Kade throw magic at Matheus, who doesn't seem to even feel it.

"Did you think you could take her from me, Kade?" Matheus asks, keeping the same mocking tone as before. "How utterly romantic and irrevocably stupid. And you, Victor. I thought better of you than to throw in with this emotional half-blood. You might be half-blood too, but you always struck me as far more intelligent than this fool."

"The fool is your father for not drowning you at birth," Victor grinds out as he's pushed back a few feet from a wave of magic Matheus flings out.

"Childish," Matheus denounces. "I would think you'd have better insults."

Emma can see that both Victor and Kade are losing ground to the powerful Matheus. Through their bond, Emma can feel Kade losing strength as he hurls blow after blow at Matheus. She senses no plan in his mind, only determination. Sweat is dripping down their faces, and both men are breathing hard while Matheus doesn't even look like he's using the same amount of effort it would take him to climb a flight of stairs. This mage is just that powerful.

"Do you honestly think your puny efforts would accomplish anything?" he continues to ridicule. She can tell by his expression that he's growing bored, losing interest in toying with the two other mages. With a casual gesture, he sends a tidal wave of magic back at the two men, knocking them off their feet. Victor goes still where he falls and gives a little moan. Kade lands hard but staggers back to his feet and brings his hands up, ready to face Matheus.

"Let her go," Kade demands, and Emma feels the bond between them grow warm.

It doesn't make sense. The bond should weaken as Kade exhausts his power, but instead it's growing stronger and more solid. The reserve from her soul cipher gift fills with Kade's magic, and strength returns to her limbs. Her head stops hurting, and her eyesight sharpens.

That's when she sees Kade slump a little.

"No!" she screams, but any further sound is cut off when Matheus tightens his hold on her. Kade is giving her all his reserve power. He's filling her with whatever he can send to her through their bond.

He's giving her his life.

Screaming in her head, she focuses all her attention on Matheus. To save Kade she needs to stop him. All she needs to do is distract him. Scratch him. Knock him over. Anything to take the focus off Kade so he can teleport to safety. But she can't make any part of her body move.

His hold on her is too strong, and no matter how much she fights, she can't even move her arm. Tears pour down her face as she watches Kade fall to his knees, losing ground to Matheus's superior strength.

Then Daria is there, taking Cassy's shovel away and bringing it down hard against Matheus's back. It's obvious she tried to bring it down on his head but fell short. Still, her blow causes him to fall forward with a startled cry. All the magic stops as Matheus hits the ground with a loud thump.

He never expected any of his toys to attack him, and Daria is prepared to take full advantage while he's stunned. She raises the shovel again to bring it down on the back of Matheus's head when Cassy tackles her to the ground.

Daria might be out of the picture as she fights over the shovel with Cassy, but it doesn't matter now because Emma is free. Shifting seamlessly back into her wolf form, she lunges at Matheus with her fangs bared determined to rip out his throat and end all this torture.

Rolling over, he sees her coming, and his eyes widen. He throws out a hand, but the power only brushes against her left side, harmlessly ruffling her fur. Then she's on him. Triumphantly, she clamps her jaw closed, only to feel his magic stop her with her canines just pricking the skin of his neck.

She screams in her mind. She was so close to killing him. So close to saving them all. Only a second or two longer and he'd be choking on his own blood.

Matheus's power closes in around her, crushing her chest. Instinctively, she reaches for the last weapon she ever thought to use, her soul cipher gift. He can't block her because she's got one fang buried in his neck. Vaguely she remembered that she shouldn't be able to pierce his neck, but whatever magic allows her to be a soul cypher seems to be imbuing her with the ability to overcome that aspect of a mages natural defenses.

There's no barring her with that kind of physical contact. She shoves her gift into him, looking for any weakness to exploit.

His mind is nothing but dark sickness. He loves nothing. He cares about nothing. She can't find a single trauma, wound, doubt, or worry to exploit. Nothing is there but twisted perversion. Desperately, she jabs her soul cipher gift into his power, thinking she might siphon enough off to weaken him and strengthen Kade, but it doesn't work like she expects it to.

Instead of just skimming some of his power, her gift opens a channel between her and Kade, pulling Matheus's power from him and pouring it into Kade through their link. She feels puzzlement come from Matheus, and he focuses his power on crushing her.

That's when things start feeling strange.

All her terror evaporates, replaced by calm. In her mind's eye, she sees Matheus's gift like shining globes of power. In a move that feels almost leisurely, she reaches in with her power and takes hold of one of those shining globes deep in Matheus. Then she rips it out.

The evil man howls in pain. He tries to put up shields, but she brushes them away. She grabs another globe from Matheus and plucks another gift out of him. Fear is flowing from him now as he wails.

"No! No! Stop! I'm your master. You have to stop!" His pleading and demands fall on deaf ears. He shrieks, alternately begging for mercy and threatening her. His words have no effect. His voice is nothing but an insect buzzing in her ears.

Even as he begs, a part of him tries to amass enough magic to hurt her. With ease, she strips that from him too. But the wolf in her isn't happy because the man under her is still there. Still breathing. As long as he lives, no one she loves is safe.

Without hesitation, she keeps digging until she feels the part of him that links him to his soul. With a calculated thrust of magic, she snips the link and feels the body under her go lax.

Unhinging her jaw, she spits Matheus's neck out of her mouth and rolls away from him. The last image she sees are his sightless eyes staring up at her, his face contorted in agony and fear—a fitting end for such a monster.

Closing her own eyes because the sun is too bright for her now, she pushes the last of the power she pulled from Matheus into all the people surrounding her, healing and helping as much as she can. She hears some gasps but doesn't open her eyes.

It's strange, but she can feel them. She's always been able to smell magic on others, but she's never been able to feel their magic. Now, it's like she has some kind of magical radar, and everyone around her is pulsing with life.

No, that's wrong. She isn't feeling their magic; she's feeling their souls.

Emotions from the dozen people around her flood into her mind: fear, relief, anxiety, joy, disbelief, hunger, gratitude, and so much more. There's too much, so she erects barriers to better shield herself from the flow of emotions. The moment she does, all she can feel is Kade. She sighs with relief as she feels her arrogant mage, beautiful inside and out.

"Emma?" Strong arms pick her up and cradle her against a broad chest. She squints her eyes open to see Kade's relieved face. "I don't know how you did it, sweet wolf, but you killed one of the most powerful, full-blooded mages on the planet."

Shifting back to human, Emma blinks up at him and smiles, "Good." Her mind feels like it's floating right now. Nothing hurts. Nothing is scary. Everyone's safe. She's in Kade's arms, and everything's going to be fine.

As her eyes focus on Kade's face, she watches his expression morph from relief to alarm. "Victor!" Kade calls out. Emma frowns and pets the side of Kade's face with a clumsy hand. Goodness, her limbs feel heavy.

"It's okay," she soothes him. "I killed the asshole."

"Oh, Emma," Victor breathes out as he drops to his knees next to them and looks at her face. "What did you do?"

Is she disfigured? Did Matheus somehow maim her as he died and she didn't feel it? Why are both Victor and Kade looking at with such incredulous expressions?

"I felt her pulling power from him and giving it to me," Kade tells Victor.

"Maybe she pulled more than power from him," Victor says.

"What's going on?" she asks and then yawns. Her yawn makes Kade chuckle.

"Only you would want a nap after all this happened," he mutters, but she hears no censure or rancor in his tone, only mild amusement. Love floods through their mate bond, making Emma hum with happiness. Both mages are still looking at her with concern, although Victor looks a little intimidated as well.

"Why do you two both look so worried?" she asks lazily. Matheus is dead, and Cassy is alive but unconscious from being hit by Daria. The nice thing is that Emma doesn't even need to look to know. She can feel these things, so there's no reason for Kade or Victor to be so distressed.

"Better to show you," Victor says as he reaches down to pick up a hand-sized rock. Concentrating on it for a moment, magic shimmers and solidifies into a reflecting surface on the flat edge of the stone. Victor holds the rock-turned-mirror up to her face, and she stares at a reflection that should belong to her but doesn't look quite right.

"My eyes are violet," she murmurs, touching her cheek with her fingertips. She should probably panic right now, but the earlier calm remains, making her interested instead of terrified. She looks at Kade and smiles. "I match you now! I hope I get to keep them."

People laugh, and she looks around to find everyone's gathered around them, all of them regarding her with expressions ranging from gratitude to fear. Looking at them, she decides they are part of her pack now. They're all going to need help to recover, and who better to give it than a soul cipher.

A soul-stealing soul cipher.

"You're all going to come home with me," she declares. "We're all going to eat, rest, and talk. And when you're ready, you can leave and start your new lives." Without needing to touch any of them, she sends out her soul cipher power, giving all of them the feeling of safety and hope. Wrinkled foreheads smooth, smiles appear, and hands reach out to touch her.

"How did she do that?" Victor mutters. "I've never felt anything like that. She just breezed right past my shields as if they weren't there."

"I believe we are looking at a wolf shifter who has mage-level power," Kade states thoughtfully.

"And pretty violet eyes," Emma interjects as she sends another wave of reassurance to those around her. At the same time, she checks in with Kade to see how he feels about this latest development. All she feels is love. He's not disgusted or afraid of her. That's good. She doesn't want him to be afraid.

"Oh, you love me so much," she murmurs, closing her eyes and enjoying the high from feeling such a strong bond with Kade.

"Never doubt it," he agrees, testing the mate bond with a little power. Love and lust sing between them, and Victor gives a gasping choke.

"If you two are going to do that, could Emma release the rest of us first? Emma's pretty, but I'd rather not be feeling lust toward you, Kade."

Opening her eyes, Emma smiles ruefully at Victor. Instead of cutting off everyone, she calms the mate bond with Kade and pushes more reassuring feelings to everyone else.

"Let's all go home now," she orders. She feels a power in her, whispering that she can be home in a blink of an eye. She unleashes it and her ears pop as she teleports them all back to Kade's house. They appear in the area between the infinity pool and the house. Well, almost all of them, anyway. Victor ends up in the pool, splashing and spluttering before he finds his feet and climbs out.

"Emma!" Kade says, turning astonished eyes on her. "How?"

"I don't know," she admits with a grin, suddenly feeling much too tired to keep talking. "We can figure it out later."

"What's going on here!" Franco calls out as he rushes to them from inside the house. Emma turns her violet eyes on the Italian and smiles.

"Hiya, Franco. We're all safe. Matheus is dead, and I'm a mage now. Oh, and I'm exhausted."

She hears someone snort out a laugh as she relaxes into Kade's arms and falls into a dreamless sleep.

Screams echo all around her.

Multiple voices cry out in pain. Emma opens her eyes to find herself in Matheus's playroom surrounded by Daria and the rest of the servants—bloody, broken, sobbing, and begging.

"Keep your eyes open and watch, Emma," Matheus tells her, his magic holding her high in the air so she has a view of the entire room. Blood flows in thin rivers from all sides of the room down to the drain under her. Matheus walks over to Daria holding a large, serrated knife. She whimpers but doesn't move at all as he grabs her hand and slowly starts sawing off her right thumb. "You can serve me just as well without thumbs," he tells her with a cruel smile.

She screams but doesn't pull away from him. He looks back up at Emma but never stops cutting. "Watch me do this or I cut off all her fingers and we can watch her serve me with just her palms. Won't that be fun?"

"Emma."

It's Kade's voice. Frantically she looks around the room, fearful she'll find him bound to the wall, waiting for Matheus's vicious ministrations.

"Emma, it's not real."

No, it is real! She can smell the blood. Can feel the despair pouring off everyone in the room except for Matheus. From him, she feels glee and joy. He's radiating with pleasure.

"No, my love, it's not real. Calm yourself. Shut your eyes. Look inside yourself. Follow me."

"I can't," she whispers. "If I look away, Matheus will punish me."

"Matheus is dead. Close your eyes, little wolf. Trust me."

"I trust you." A high-pitched wail sounds from behind her, and Emma closes her eyes. She feels for Kade through their mate bond and finds him, familiar and reassuring. The bond floods with love. The cries of pain disappear, making her sag with relief. A salty sea breeze brushes her hair back as a broad, warm hand gently closes over the back of her naked neck.

No collar is there. Only the soft touch of a large, familiar hand soothes her.

"Easy, little wolf, I've got you." Opening her eyes, she finds Kade looking at her with a mix of concern and love. "That was a bad one," he murmurs.

Looking around, she sees that they're on the bench near the cliff on his property in Monterey. "I'm dreaming," she breathes, her body shuddering a little with relief.

"You were having a nightmare," he agrees. "But I caught it early this time." Now that she's no longer trapped in a terrifying dreamscape, memories of previous dreams that made her flail and scream in her sleep flood back into her mind.

"I'm sorry," she whispers, her eyes pricking with tears. She hates this. It's been months since they killed Matheus, but she's still having nightmares. Even trying to leave the property gives her anxiety attacks.

"Don't apologize. You're healing," Kade tells her, gently pulling her into his lap. "You're doing far better than everyone else we rescued."

"I wasn't under his power anywhere near as long as the rest of them," Emma points out as she curls herself against him. "I love you, Kade."

"I love you too," he murmurs in her ear. "Let's sit here and watch the ocean. Shall we? No more nightmares tonight."

Good to his word, they spend the rest of the night sitting on that bench, watching the ocean crawl and crash under them as sea birds wheel in the azure sky above.

"Emma?"

The voice is so quiet Emma's not sure she heard anything until she opens her eyes to find Tommy leaning over her with an anxious expression. Fox shifters and wolf shifters rarely get along, but ever since rescuing the twenty-two-year-old from Matheus, Tommy clings to her as if he's a young kit and she's his mother.

Occasionally she'll wake up to find him curled up asleep under their bed. Instead of complaining, Kade instructed Franco to put a sleeping mat down there with blankets and a pillow. Tommy's healing, but at least once a week he needs the comfort of sleeping close to her.

"Kade told me I should wake you up so you can eat breakfast with everyone," he explains, dropping his gaze. She can tell he's fighting the urge to drop to his knees, so she won't put more pressure on him by reminding him to look her in the eye. One battle at a time. Most of the people they rescued still find her violet eyes disconcerting, so she never gives them a hard time for not meeting her gaze.

Reaching out, she rests a hand on the top of his head and lets her soul cipher gift flare between them. The eleven people they rescued have so many emotional scars it will take years for them to heal, even with Emma's help, but that doesn't deter her from working on them every chance she gets. With her increased soul cipher power, she can help them without needing to touch them, so every day is filled with her gently reaching out to each of them with her power and doing whatever she can to help.

"Lauren won't come out of her room. It's been two days. And last night she didn't eat the dinner we left for her." Fear makes Tommy shake as he tells her, and her power flares again to calm him.

"Thank you for telling me that, Tommy," she says gently. "I'll get up and visit her. Then I'll join everyone for breakfast. Does that sound good?" She drops her hand away from his head and sits up.

"Yes, thank you." He backs away from the bed and just barely catches himself before bowing to her. Straightening his spine, he lifts his chin and meets her gaze. "I'll see you downstairs." She gives him a brilliant smile, trying to tell him without words how pleased she is with his progress. He smiles back and hurries from the room.

Sitting up with a yawn, she swings her legs off the bed and catches her reflection in a nearby mirror. Violet mage eyes stare out from her face. Even after months, the sight still startles her. She still half expects to wake up and find her eyes changed back to gray, but so far it appears the color is permanent.

It turns out that her eyes aren't the only permanent change. Her soul cipher gift is far more powerful now, to the point where she's afraid to push too hard for fear of doing more harm than good. Despite Kade's confidence, she still worries. Especially because she now knows, if pushed, she can rip someone's power right out of them. Oh, and she can tear someone's soul out and end their life.

She's not just a soul cipher now; she's a soul eater too.

That new title fills her with so much disquiet that she refuses to talk about it. The thought of doing that to someone by accident makes her break out in a cold sweat.

Eventually, she'll need to learn to deal with this aspect of herself, but later.

Much, much later.

To her immense relief, since the deadly confrontation with Matheus, the soul eater gift has been silent. She can feel it if she concentrates, but she's mildly comforted by the fact that it would take great effort to actively use it.

Distressingly, the news has gotten out that she's a soul eater, and many from her old pack refuse to talk with her, let alone see her. It turns out being a soul eater is even worse than having a mage for an alpha. Losing those friends hurts, but she has plenty of new people in her life to make up for it. Not only is she busy helping those they rescued, but she's also learning about her new powers.

Thankfully, the gifts she stole from Matheus don't overwhelm her. On top of being able to teleport, she can levitate small objects and throw power as a weapon, just like a proper mage.

She's not very good at levitation or throwing power, but it appears she's got a knack for teleportation. Victor has turned out to be an excellent teleportation instructor, and she no longer finds herself on a roof or any other unfortunate place when she tries to teleport.

At least most times. Occasionally she'll still end up someplace she didn't intend.

She still shudders at the memory of teleporting them all home the day she killed Matheus. She was working on instinct and could have easily dropped them in the ocean, miles from the coast, instead of just dumping Victor in the pool. They got lucky that first time, and Emma's determined she'll never endanger someone with her gifts again.

Despite her trepidation regarding teleporting, Kade pushes her to practice. He's looking forward to the day they can pop off to another country for a long weekend, now that she can teleport herself. She has to admit, she likes this avenue of travel almost as much as plane rides.

Kade is handling her acquisition of power without a second glance. Technically, she's more powerful than him now, but it doesn't seem to bother him in the least. When she asked him about it once, he just shrugged and pointed out she could have ripped open his neck the first night he brought her home. He fell asleep and allowed her free range of the house. He trusted her then, and he trusts her now.

"No one's invincible," he explained to her. "Didn't you already prove that with Matheus? If I'm going to be vulnerable to someone, I want it to be you." The entire house felt her rush of love for him after that.

Voices float up from downstairs, reminding her to get moving. The house is large, but with all of Matheus's victims living with them, it can get a little crowded. Kade had a smaller house built on the property in record time, so everyone could have their own room if they wanted. But no one's moved out there yet. Five of them share a room because they're too scared to sleep alone.

Starting the first time Emma teleported them all here, Franco hasn't made a face or voiced a single protest. Efficient and decisive, he just started ordering everyone around. He took it upon himself to organize the refugees, even ordering clothing, extra towels, food, and toiletries from the local shops. Over the months his unflappable care has done almost as much to help as Emma's soul cipher gift.

Kade didn't act happy about letting all Matheus's former "toys" stay as they recovered, but she knows that's a front. He's been as careful and solicitous of them as she or Franco. He might act disgruntled, but he told Franco to spend as much money as he needed so everyone could be comfortable. He also built the other entire house. He let them all gather to watch as he built not one, but three extra layers of wards around the property on top of the existing one.

Kade meets with each one of them when they're ready to set up accounts and start getting their financial lives back in order so they'll have resources when they decide they want to leave. He won't let them pay for anything while they live with him. Thanks to him, each of them has enough money to live comfortably for many years without needing to find a job.

She doesn't say anything, but she whispers, "Good alpha," to him every once in a while. He might not have set out to have a pack when he first claimed Emma, but that's exactly what he's done now. And like any good alpha, he's making sure everyone in his pack is taken care of.

Kade hasn't left the property much since her rescue. When he isn't busy holding and touching her, he devotes his time to creating mobile wards out of jewelry. Each piece he creates he gives to one of the victims, explaining how powerful the magic is and how to use it.

The first one he gave away was a ring with sapphires. He slid it onto Emma's left ring finger with promises to never make her wear anything around her throat again. Franco off-handedly explained to her that the level of magic Kade imbued the jewelry with would cost at least a quarter of a million dollars to buy on top of the jewelry's intrinsic value.

She loved him for the gifts—not because they were expensive but because he did it as a show of affection, love, and devotion. Her mage is aloof no longer.

Dressing quickly, she pads barefoot to Lauren's room. Knocking gently, she calls out to the fae. "Can I come in?"

"You can, but no one else," Lauren responds, and Emma pushes open the door to find the room dark and Lauren lying in bed. The woman's hair is a mess, and Emma's nose tells her that Lauren hasn't bathed in at least a week.

Striding over, Emma sits on the bed next to her. Listless eyes stare up at her before dropping to focus on the bed, an act Matheus would've approved of.

"I heard you're not eating," Emma states gently, bringing Lauren's eyes back up. Resting her hand on the depressed girl's shoulder, Emma searches out the most pressing traumatic wound and starts healing it.

"Here's what we're going to do today," Emma tells her. "You don't even need to get out of your sweats. Just follow me down to the kitchen and eat breakfast with us. Then you can come back up here and go back to bed. Can you do that for me?" For Lauren, it seems to help to give her one small goal a day. Getting her out of bed and eating is going to be today's goal.

It takes several long minutes before Lauren finally nods. "I can do that. But only that."

"That makes me happy," Emma tells her with a smile. To her delight, Lauren returns the smile. Emma uses that moment of happiness to help heal one of the woman's many wounds.

Standing up, she helps Lauren to her feet and guides her downstairs. No one comments about her appearance. With kind voices, they all welcome her to the table and encourage her to eat. Each of them is fighting their own demons. None of them is going to judge another's battle.

She stinks. Can you make her shower? Kade asks, his voice plaintive in her mind.

Hush, Emma responds. *She'll bathe when she's ready. Matheus tortured her with water, so she battles panic every time she tries to shower. Give her time.*

Fine, Kade grumbles. *I'm working on her ward next. Maybe that will help with the fear of water. I can imbue it with some water repellent magic she can activate at will.*

That might help. That's very thoughtful of you, my love. Through their mate bond, she feels his pleasure and embarrassment at the praise and endearment.

Kade still struggles with their love and the vulnerability that goes with it, but if anything, it makes him pull her closer rather than pushing her or the others away. Matheus taught him a valuable lesson about loss, pain, and sacrifice. After dealing with that twisted mage, Kade's priorities changed dramatically. Hence, his mostly willing concession of having so many in his house and his patience with their healing.

Tommy sits down next to her with a plate full of waffles and a small grin. Franco sets another plate down in front of her and one in front of Lauren.

"Where's mine?" Kade asks, eyeing Emma's plate.

"Next," Franco answers briskly as he hurries away to grab more food and bring it out. Kade makes a disgruntled sound, but when Lauren jerks and drops her fork, he looks over and smiles at her.

"It's nice to see you," he tells her, his voice light and pleasant. "It's a beautiful day out, and the wildflowers are blooming. You should have Emma take you for a walk to see them."

Lauren doesn't meet his eyes, but she nods and picks her fork back up instead of jumping up and running away. That's amazing progress for a girl who shrieked with terror the first few times she saw Kade. Emma gives Kade a thankful smile and leans over to kiss him.

"Where's mine?" Tommy asks playfully, fluttering his eyes at Kade. Smirking, Kade sits back and crosses his arms. Tommy's expression turns fearful as Kade's violet eyes regard him unblinkingly. Then Kade leans his massive body over the table and gives Tommy a smacking kiss on the cheek.

Sputtering from surprise, Tommy's face turns beet red, his expression a combination of shocked and appalled. After a moment of startled silence, Lauren snickers, and that breaks the dam. By the time Franco is walking in with more plates of food, everyone at the table is laughing, including Kade.

"Many wouldn't recognize you," Emma whispers to him as the laughter dies down and people talk about their plans for the day. "You're so happy and open. Very un-Kade like. Un-mage like as well."

"That's probably a good thing," Kade murmurs to her. She can't argue with him.

EPILOGUE
TWO YEARS LATER

Leaning back to better see the results of her efforts, Emma balances easily on top of the tall ladder. She inspects the string of lights she just finished hanging. She has three more boxes of lights. Should she hang them? Are the dozens of boxes she's already strung enough?

Tomorrow is the winter solstice, and she's looking forward to the party. Her parents are due to arrive later that day, as well as her brother and Avery. Most of the survivors rescued from Matheus have long since healed and left, but many of them plan to visit for the party. Only Tommy and Lauren still live with them, and both of them are eager to celebrate and see old friends.

"That's a lot of lights," Kade says as he grabs her around the waist and lifts her off the ladder. Giggling, she wraps herself around him and nuzzles his neck.

"You can never have enough lights for a winter solstice party," she counters.

"I believe this is even more than last year. Are you trying to show off, my little wolf?"

"Absolutely not," Emma counters with a grin. "Well, not with the lights, anyway."

Kade looks mildly concerned. "If you're not trying to show off with the lights, that must mean my kitchen is overrun with food. Is there a deer in there?"

Biting her lip, Emma tries hard not to laugh. "Maybe?"

With a mock sigh of aggravation, Kade throws her over his shoulder and strides to the kitchen. "There better not be a deer in there!" he warns her. He comes up short just inside the kitchen to find not one, but two deer carcasses piled on the large work island, dripping blood all over Franco's pristine floor.

"He's going to leave me," Kade sighs, making Emma laugh even harder. "He's going to leave, and we're going to die of starvation."

"No, he's not," she assures him between fits of laughter. "He was really sweet about the deer I brought in last year."

"Perhaps he was civil to you, my sweet wolf, but I got an earful when you were out running with Jason." Swinging her off his shoulder, he sets her down on her feet in front of him, hugging her tightly to him. "But I don't care. You love me. That's all that matters. If Franco leaves, we can starve together."

"That might be romantic if it didn't sound like you were trying to convince yourself instead of declaring your undying affection for me," Emma points out wryly.

The pantry door opens, and Franco emerges, looking flushed. Puzzled, Emma is about to ask him if he's feeling okay when a blushing Lauren emerges right behind him. Cackling with delight, Emma pulls away from Kade to hold up her palm for Franco to reluctantly slap.

"Hell, yes! Getting the party started early!" Emma crows, making Lauren's pink face turn red. "It's about time. You two have been circling each other for ages."

"No… I… we weren't…" She fumbles for words and then finally just shrugs and leaves the room at a speed just short of running. Franco moves to follow her, but Kade stops the smaller man with a shake of his head.

"Perhaps give her a moment to compose herself. Lauren will value that," Kade suggests gently.

"You're probably correct," Franco murmurs and then looks over at Emma. "I hardly think a few months of gentle wooing is ages."

"You don't think I saw those looks you started giving her the moment we brought her here? You can't fool me, Franco." Tapping her chest right over her heart, Emma gives him a knowing look. "This is my realm right here, so don't try to tell me you didn't fall in love the moment you set eyes on that fae."

"She's so wounded," Franco whispers, almost to himself. "He hurt her so badly."

"Yes, but not irrevocably. She's healing, especially in the last six months." When Franco's expression doesn't change, she adds, "If it makes you feel any better, she's close to realizing she loves you too."

Joy blooms on his face. "Truly?"

"Yup. Who's the soul cipher around here, huh?" Then to distract all of them, Emma slaps a hand down on the rump of one of the deer. "Can I help you butcher these guys?"

That's when Franco notices the large animal carcasses befouling his kitchen. His shrieks of outrage fill the downstairs.

"I guess it all worked out," Jason says absently as he watches Avery and Kade talk. Both mages are focused intensely on whatever they're discussing. Emma's torn on whether she wants to know what they're talking about or not. "Who would have thought we would have both ended up mated to mages?"

"I read a few gossip columns. They're trying to figure out if it's because we're both wolves or siblings," Emma comments.

Confused, Jason just stares at her. "Huh?"

"Everyone's speculating that either we have some kind of familial DNA that draws mages to us or that mages are drawn to wolf shifters."

"That sounds dumb," Jason says with a small, aggravated sigh. "I hate that we have paparazzi now. It's weird and annoying. They can't get a picture of her, but my face is constantly showing up. I got accosted by this lady when I just wanted to get coffee the other day. She demanded I take her to see Avery. She wanted to be made young and beautiful again. So dumb."

Wincing, Emma gives Jason a sympathetic look. "Yeah, there's a lot of false information out there about mages. Someone asked me if I was real or if Kade conjured me with a spell. And there's a YouTube channel out there dedicated to revealing all the people whose souls I've eaten. Thankfully, everyone seems more interested in the whole soul cipher thing than soul eater part." She gives him an unrepentant grin and taps a finger next to her right eye. "And guess what, mages are fucking terrified of me now!"

That makes Jason bark out a laugh. "You're kidding!"

"I wish I was. I was stitching a meeting for Kade and a mage named Thomas, but the instant he saw me, Thomas left. Poof, gone, right out of the dreamscape. I thought I'd booted him by accident, but when Kade called him later, he said he didn't want to be anywhere near me. He also commented that he couldn't understand how Kade had the courage to keep me around. Turns out, for all their power, mages are a bit cowardly."

"They're used to being the biggest bad-ass in the room, and now there's this wolf who can do magic." Jason waves his hands around dramatically like a magician. "It's not just scary; it's humiliating. You could at least be aristocratic, like a jinn. But no, you're just a lowly wolf!" His words make both of them burst out laughing.

When they finally sober, she becomes thoughtful. "But at least the paparazzi aren't a problem for me anymore." Holding up her finger, Emma taps the ring Kade gave her. "One of the wards he put on this makes it impossible for them to take pictures of me. I'll ask him to make you one."

"Can he use steel? A plain steel cuff for my wrist would be great," Jason asks, running his hand over the scars on his left wrist. It's been several years, but he still won't tell her what happened in those first few tumultuous months with Avery as she healed from years of substance abuse. She tried to use her soul cipher gift on him once, but he gently pushed her away and told her he was fine, no healing needed. Eventually she knows he'll be ready to tell her. Until then, she'll wait patiently. He's family, and that's what you do for family.

Suddenly Kade is there, dragging Avery behind him. Jason stiffens at seeing Kade's hand on Avery's arm. Meeting Jason's flashing golden eyes, Kade lets go of Avery, but his grim expression remains. He's very upset about something.

"Talk to her, Emma," Kade demands. His voice is even, but she hears tension in his words. Worry and fear are coming through their mate bond loud and clear.

"What going on, guys?" Emma asks as Avery pushes herself into Jason's arms.

"Did you tell him?" Jason asks her. "Did he agree to help?"

"I asked, but he refused." She buries her face against Jason's chest. Although she's now sober and healthy again, Avery still struggles occasionally with emotional stability. As she clings to Jason, Emma knows she's using the mating bond to steady herself.

"Easy," Jason rumbles, folding his big body around Avery. He looks up at Kade, his expression both annoyed and exasperated. "We're just asking for a simple masking ward, man. We'll even pay."

"No," Kade bites out. "It's too dangerous. To make the kind of ward you're asking for is very heavy magic." Jason turns unhappy eyes down to Avery.

"You told me it was safe," Jason accuses Avery.

"It would be safe if she wasn't pregnant," Kade says, running his hand through his hair, mussing the careful effort he put into it earlier.

Over the last few years, the cold, aloof mage facade Kade shows the world has gone by the wayside, revealing a warm and loving man who's willing to open his home to strangers and his heart to Emma and her family. This harsh attitude is a jarring throwback to the former Kade. For a moment, anxiety rises in her; then his words sink in.

Pregnant?

With wide, excited eyes, she steps close and invades Avery's personal space to put her nose right against Avery's neck. The pregnancy is early yet, but from the smell of her, a healthy baby is resting and growing in her belly.

"Pregnant!" Emma whisper-screams and grabs Avery up in a hug, careful to be gentle despite her excitement. She sinks her soul cipher gift into Avery and finds the developing fetus, warm and content in her mother's belly. "It's going to be a girl."

A little sob comes out of Avery, and she clings to Emma. "I'm so scared," she gasps as terror for her unborn child radiates off her.

"Which is why you need to move in here for the duration of your pregnancy," Kade demands, his face softening as a single tear rolls down Avery's face. The two women separate, and Jason draws Avery back into his arms. "And you should stay after the baby's born. Between two and a half mages, we can keep the child in check."

"Hey!" Emma protests. "Stop calling me half a mage. Both my eyes are violet. That means I'm a full mage!"

"Is that right? He offered to let us stay here?" Jason asks Avery, ignoring the teasing byplay between Emma and Kade. "Because putting a ward on you to mask the baby would be dangerous?"

"Magic babies are problematic to begin with," Kade informs them, giving Avery a meaningful look as he talks. "Putting that much magic on Avery would upset the baby and potentially cause Avery harm. The reason Avery's going to be vulnerable is because she can't risk using much magic right now. Usually, female mages don't have children with anyone but another mage who can keep them safe while they're defenseless. But she chose you, a powerless wolf shifter. That means—"

"Remember what we talked about?" Emma interrupts him, grabbing his hand and pricking his palm with her claws. "We don't talk to people like that anymore, especially not family."

"I'm not insulting your brother," Kade argues, looking flustered but not pulling away from her potentially painful embrace. "I'm stating a fact. They both need to move in here for Avery's safety."

"I didn't want Jason to feel like he had to do anything," Avery mumbles. "I forced so many things on him. I didn't want to make him live with you on top of dealing with me."

"Hey, I live here too," Emma points out with a smile. "And I'm everything charming and fun."

"He's pack," Jason argues. "Of course, I'm okay with moving in with Kade. It's his job to help protect other pack members when they need it."

Kade jolts at Jason's words, but then relaxes. A warm sensation comes through the bond, telling Emma that Kade likes being included as part of Jason's "pack." When she gently pushes her soul cipher power into him, all she finds is excited anticipation at the idea of Avery and Jason coming to live with them.

She didn't notice before, but now she realizes he's withdrawn a little since so many of the people they rescued have left to live their own lives. A house full of voices, laughter, and care became the norm for almost two years and she understands that Kade yearns to have that again.

This once cold and distant man wants to keep his house full of people.

"Mage on the outside," Emma whispers in his ear. "Wolf on the inside."

"I've never held a baby before," Kade declares to the small group in a quiet voice. Avery and Jason fall silent as they regard the tall mage. "I find I wish to know what it feels like to hold one."

Eyes soft, Jason reaches out to pull Kade into a hug, squishing Emma between them. "You're going to be an uncle," he tells Kade. "So, there's going to be a lot of baby holding in your future."

Love, affection, and contentment flood their mate bond even as Kade pulls away from Jason and tries to sneer. "I don't see why I need to touch you. I was referring to your child."

That makes them chuckle a little, and Kade's shoulders relax.

"Thank you, Kade," Avery says, wrapping one of Jason's arms around her shoulder. "It would be an honor to stay here."

"For as long as you need," Kade insists firmly.

"For as long as we need," Avery dutifully repeats, a relieved smile lighting up her face.

"Did I hear you're pregnant?" Emma's mother asks loudly enough for the entire room to hear. Soon Emma and Kade are pushed to the fringes of the room as everyone crowds around Jason and Avery.

"Thank you," Kade says, a slight frown on his face as Emma snuggles into his embrace.

"You won't be thanking me when you get diaper duty," Emma teases, but Kade's expression doesn't change.

"Thank you for loving me. For showing me…" He gestures around the room at their family and friends, laughing and celebrating. "For showing me all of this. I was only living a half-life before you, unaware of the riches I was missing out on."

"That's what loves does," Emma says. "It makes us whole."

"And joyful," Kade adds.

"And horny," Emma whispers, rising on her toes and nipping at his neck. Chuckling, Kade lifts her and gives her a long, soul-searing kiss.

"Having the pack here is all nice and grand," Emma tells him. "But maybe we should go check on our room to make sure no one got lost up there or something."

Amused, Kade looks around the room for a gap in the crowd. "You want to leave your party?"

"Just for a little while," she demurs. "They won't even notice we're gone."

No one saw them again until breakfast the next morning. When the teasing started, all Kade would say is, "One does not rush the important things in life."

Dear Readers,

Thank you for reading *Alpha Mage*. If you want more to learn about what happened with Jason and Avery you can read their book, *His Alpha Mage* (Alpha Series, Book 1.5) for free by signing up for my newsletter! The second book in the series, *Alpha King*, is also available on Kindle and KindleUnlimited.

Links for the free books, social media, and other good stuff is on my website:

www.RK-Munin

I hope you enjoyed *Alpha Mage* enough to leave a review! As an indie writer without the support of a publishing company, I need all the help I can get. Your good reviews keep me writing.

Cheers,
Rye

Other books by RK Munin

-Science Fiction-

Hissa Warrior Series
Rescuing Halin (Mian and Halin)
Buying Tiran (Mara and Tiran)
Tempting Selon (Lara and Selon)
Defying Kilan (Deena and Kilan)
Healing Mavito (Raleen and Mavito)
Claiming Yopin (Mouse and Yopin)
Teasing Woken (Safena and Woken)
Defending Revin (Kamaril and Revin)
Trusting Warik – Coming soon

Human Pets of Talin Series
Loving Captivity (Sora and Searin)
Escaping Captivity (Lakin and Dalt)
Negotiating Captivity (Nalia and Derani)
Fighting Captivity (Zia and Palforma)
Tender Captivity (Jinna and Holian - This is a novella you can
get for free by signing up for my newsletter)
Craving Captivity (Lasha and Tamerin)
The Twelve Nights of Halloheen: A holiday mashup novella
(Isla and Tisuran)
Stealing Captivity (Kasi and Ignatias)
Redeeming Captivity – Coming soon

Origins (A Human Pets of Talin Series)
Creating Captivity (Ari and Bazium)
Gossamer Chains (Rain and Hesarium)
Golden Cages – Coming soon
Purring, Presents, and Parties – Coming soon

-Paranormal /Urban Fantasy-

Ours Evermore Series
Two Wolves for Soren (Soren, Kalli, and Quinn)
A Hacker, Vampire, and Chimera Walk into a Bar… (Tobias,
Briar, and Memphis)
When Darkness Meets Dawn (Imani, Lex, and Mac)
Tag, You're It (Novella)
Kidnapping Their Third (Cora, Pike, and Kimble)
Pastries on a Plate and Blood in a Mug – Coming soon

Alpha Series
Alpha Mage (Emma and Kade)
His Alpha Mage (Avery and Jason – Novella)
Alpha King (Cathleen and Lazlo)

New Clan Series
Stray Wolf (Steph and Eli)
Lost Lion (Maeve and Cyrus)
Reluctant Cervid (Tavi and Donovan)
Broken Thorn (Sabina and Theodosius)